*. . . but the heart
never lies for long.*

"You are *not* my husband!"

"My husband is dead, do you hear? Stop tormenting me."

He circled from behind the desk to stand over her. "Oh, you have no idea what true torment is, Madeleine."

Madeleine's hands were shaking now. He was too close. Too large. Too supremely *male*. "We made a mistake, Merrick," she whispered. "We did something rash and foolish, and then we regretted it. Please, let it stay in the past. I have a family—a child—to think of now."

His handsome mouth curled into a sneer. "You were ashamed of me, Madeleine?" he asked. "Is that it?"

"By God, how dare you?" Madeleine did not even realize she had swung at him with her open hand until he seized hold of her wrist.

He pulled her hard, almost fully against him. She could smell the heat of his skin. "Oh, I dare, madam," he gritted, his mouth just inches from hers. "I dare because it is my right! I bought and paid for it with the blood you wrung out of my heart."

No True Gentleman

"One of the year's best historical romances."
—*Publishers Weekly* (starred review)

"Carlyle neatly balances passion and danger in this sizzling, sensual historical that should tempt fans of Amanda Quick and Mary Balogh."
—*Booklist*

A Woman of Virtue

"A beautifully written book. . . . I was mesmerized from the first page to the last."
—*The Old Book Barn Gazette*

"I can't recommend this author's books highly enough; they are among my all-time favorites."
—Romance Reviews Today

A Woman Scorned

"Fabulous! Regency-based novels could not be in better hands . . . ."
—*Affaire de Coeur*

My False Heart

"*My False Heart* is a treat!"
—Linda Howard, *New York Times* bestselling author

Three Little Secrets

LIZ CARLYLE

POCKET **STAR** BOOKS

New York   London   Toronto   Sydney

An *Original* Publication of POCKET BOOKS

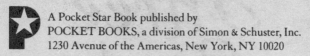 A Pocket Star Book published by
POCKET BOOKS, a division of Simon & Schuster, Inc.
1230 Avenue of the Americas, New York, NY 10020

This book is a work of fiction. Names, characters, places and incidents are products of the author's imagination or are used fictitiously. Any resemblance to actual events or locales or persons, living or dead, is entirely coincidental.

ISBN-13: 978-0-7434-9612-4
ISBN-10:   0-7434-9612-4

This Pocket Star Books paperback edition April 2006

10 9 8 7 6 5 4 3 2 1

POCKET STAR BOOKS and colophon are registered trademarks of Simon & Schuster, Inc.

Cover art by Alan Ayers; lettering by Ron Zinn

For information regarding special discounts for bulk purchases, please contact Simon & Schuster Special Sales at 1-800-456-6798 or business@simonandschuster.com.

Manufactured in the United States of America

To my beleaguered crtitique partner,
Deborah Bess,
who has read everything I've ever written—
over and over and over . . .

Prologue

❦

The devil n'er sent a wind oot
o' hell but what he sailed w'it.

They found him alone in the stable yard. It was early; well before cockcrow, with the damp of an evening rain yet clinging to the grass, and the scent of hay and horses heavy in the stillness. The brace of pale gray coaches with their crests blacked and their curtains drawn came snaking down the hill through the morning's mist like so much malevolent quicksilver.

He had thought to save himself a shilling and hitch up his horses himself. He had thought like a fool. His was not a trusting soul, but his guard was down, and his mind was still abed. Abed with the young bride who had kept him awake into the wee hours and beyond, until night neared dawn and there were no more secrets left to tell. No more pleas to be carried on breathless, urgent whispers. No more laughter to be muted in the folds of the innkeeper's musty old counterpane.

She slept at last, one fist curled into the pillow, one long, coltish leg thrown across his side of the bed in a gesture which was at once delightfully new, and comfortingly familiar. He did not sleep. Perhaps he knew, even then, that every moment was precious.

He rose and watched her for a time. The delicate pink shell of her ear. The long, creamy turn of her neck. The rise and fall of breasts so small and so perfect, he wondered God had meant man to see them at all. And then he hitched up his trousers with grave reluctance, and went about the business of saving that shilling, for God knew they hadn't one to spare.

In the stables, no lamp yet burned. He saw one, lit it, and found his horses. Methodically, he fed them and brushed them, then fetched water from the trough in the yard. These were simple tasks; comforting routines for a man still finding his footing in the world. And when the tasks were done, he took the first harness down from its wrought-iron hook.

The hand, when it touched him, was heavy and cold as death.

They say when the Old Scratch comes for a man, his life passes before his eyes. He saw not his life, but his wedding day, flickering through his mind like some fairy-tale cottage glimpsed through the trees from a fast-moving phaeton.

He dropped the leather traces he'd been inspecting and turned around on his bootheel. Ah. He had seen that black-and-silver livery before. He had even seen a few men larger than the one who stood behind him, already sweating in the morning's warmth. But not many.

The hand dragged him from the shadows of the stable. "Someone wants a word wiv you." The voice matched the hand. Cold as death.

The men who awaited him did not look predisposed to chitchat. He gave it his best, of course. But they were four, and he was one. He was a big man himself, and inured to hard, physical labor, but it did not take them long to strip him to the waist and beat him nigh senseless. He half drowned one in the water trough, though, and sent another headfirst into one of the glossy gray coaches. He broke the nose of the third and took great satisfaction in watching blood spurt down the lapel of his fine, flawless livery.

He had known, of course, that his luck would not last. He knew, too, that they meant to kill him. And eventually, they brought him down like a stag run to ground by a pack of slavering dogs. And when he lay in the stable yard spitting up blood and muck and God only knew what else, they jerked him up and started again.

He did not remember throwing them off. Did not remember the pitchfork, nor how it came to be in his hand. He remembered only the feel of it sinking into the other man's flesh, and the girl in the shadows of the stable screaming. And screaming. And screaming.

Then the glossy gray carriage door opened, and a well-shod foot stepped out.

The voice which followed was calm. Almost civil, really. But the black horsewhip wrapped around Jessup's hand looked anything but.

Of course, he fought like the devil. But three of Jessup's men held him fast; held him whilst his new father-in-law explained, clearly and succinctly, his daughter's recent change of heart. In between lashes, of course.

And when he finally collapsed, only then did Jessup find the guts to step near. "Perhaps now you are persuaded that my daughter has changed her mind about this Gretna Green business," he said.

He was not persuaded. He would *never* be persuaded. Somehow, he managed to lift his head from the dirt, and turn to the girl who still cowered in the shadows. "He *lies*." He had choked out the words. "Tell me . . . that Jessup . . . *lies.*"

The girl—his wife's maid—stepped at last from the gloom and drew a deep, hitching breath. "Alas, no, monsieur," she answered, clasping her hands before her. "My lady, she has change her mind. She says that she is—is *très désolé. Oui,* so sorry. She—she is sick for the home, monsieur. And *très jeune*—too young, *oui*? She wishes now her papa, and to return to Sheffield."

It came back to him then on a sickening rush. Her urgent questions. Her little worries. Her niggling doubts about rent, and servants, and society's disdain . . .

Had she? Good God, had she changed her mind?

Jessup was rewrapping the whip around his hand. With a calm, quiet smile, he climbed back into his quicksilver carriage. The footmen walked away, leaving their handiwork torn and bloody in the stable yard, lying ignominiously in the filth. The maid returned to the shadows and began quietly to cry.

No. He did not believe it. He would never, ever believe it.

The bastard. Jessup would not get away with this. Dazed and enraged, he somehow summoned the strength to stagger to his feet and make one last dash for Jessup's carriage as it passed. Instead of slowing, the driver sprung the beasts and plowed him down without a moment's hesitation.

He felt an instant of pain; felt his body go tumbling across the gravel, pitched about like some insignificant clump of mud beneath the axles. And then the horrid, crushing agony. The snap of bone and the wrenching of flesh. The sensation of his skull cracking against the gatepost. And then there was naught but the blackness. The blessed oblivion of death—or something comfortingly near it.

Chapter One

Money's like the muck midden;
it does nae good 'til it be spread.

The Scots say that a tale never loses in the telling, and the tale of Merrick MacLachlan had been told a thousand times. In the drawing rooms and club rooms and back rooms of London, MacLachlan had been growing richer and darker and more malevolent by the season, until, in the summer of his life, the man was thought a veritable Shylock, ever searching for his pound of flesh.

Those who did business with the Black MacLachlan did so honestly, and with a measure of trepidation. Some became rich in return, for the color of money often rubs off. Others fared less well, and their tales were told, more often than not, in the insolvent debtors' court. Miss Kitty Coates had scarcely fared at all and couldn't even spell *insolvent*. The sort of business she did with MacLachlan meant that she was always giving her bawd an ample cut.

At the moment, however, Kitty had better things to think about than her ill luck at arithmetic and spelling, for the afternoon sun was slanting low through the windows of MacLachlan's makeshift bedchamber, casting a keen blade of light across the gentleman's bare shoulders. And across the scars, too—hideous white welts that criss-crossed the hard flesh of his biceps and even down his back. Kitty had long since grown accustomed to them. She spread her fingers wide in the soft, dark hair which dusted his chest, and held on tight as she rode him.

Just then, a clock in the outer office struck five. With three or four hard thrusts upward, MacLachlan finished his business, then rolled Kitty onto her back and dragged a well-muscled arm over his eyes. The message was clear.

"We don't have to quit just yet, Mr. MacLachlan, do we?" Kitty rolled back up again and traced one finger lightly down the scar which curled like a scimitar's blade up his cheek. "Why, I could stay on a little longer—say, two quid for the whole night?" The warm finger drew back up again. "Aye, we'd have us a fine old time, you and me."

MacLachlan threw back the sheets, pushed her away, and rolled out of the narrow bed. "Put your clothes on, Kitty." His voice was emotionless. "Leave by the back stairs today. The office staff is still at work."

Her expression tightened, but she said nothing. MacLachlan stood, gritting his teeth against the pain in his lower leg. He did not move until he was confident he could do so without limping, then he went into the dressing room and meticulously washed himself.

By the time he returned to his pile of carefully folded clothing, Kitty was wriggling back into her rumpled red dress, her eyebrows snapped tautly together, her expression dark. " 'Ow long, Mr. MacLachlan, 'ave I been coming round 'ere?"

MacLachlan suppressed a sigh of exasperation. "I have no notion, Kitty."

"Well, I knows exactly 'ow long," she said peevishly. "Four months and a fortnight, to the very day."

"I did not take you for the sentimental type." MacLachlan was busy pulling on his drawers.

"Every Monday and Thursday since the first o' February," Kitty went on. "And in all that time, you've scarce said a dozen words ter me."

"I did not realize that you came all the way from Soho for the erudite conversation," he answered, unfolding his trousers. "I thought you were here for the money."

"Aye, go on, then!" She snatched up her stockings from the pile on his floor. "Use your fine, big words ter poke fun and push me round. *Lie down, Kitty! Bend over, Kitty! Get out, Kitty! I have an appointment, Kitty!* Ooh, you are a hard, hateful man, MacLachlan!"

"I collect that I have fallen in your esteem," he remarked. "Tell Mrs. Farnham to send someone else on Thursday, if you prefer." *Someone who doesn't talk so damned much,* he silently added, stabbing in his shirttails.

"Well, I can ask, but I'm the only redhead Farnie's got," warned Kitty, tugging the first stocking up her leg with short, sharp jerks. "And I get hired a lot on account o' this hair, let me tell you."

"Any color will do for me," he answered, watching her arse as she bent to put on her last stocking. "I really could not care less."

Something inside Kitty seemed to snap. She jerked upright, spun around, and hurled the stocking in his face. "Well, why don't you just go fuck a knothole in a rotten fence, you ungrateful, blackhearted Scot!"

For a moment, he glowered at her. "Aye, 'tis an option—and a cheaper one, at that." He was beginning to consider it, too. After all, he was a businessman. And fences did not talk, wheedle, or whine.

Ruthlessly, Kitty shoved her bare foot into one of her shoes. "Well, I've had enough o' your grunting and heaving and rolling off me wiv ne'er so much afterward as a fare-thee-well! I might be a Haymarket whore, MacLachlan, but I'm damned if I'll—"

The ten-pound note he shoved into her clenched fist silenced her. For a long moment, she stared at it, blinking back tears.

Somehow, MacLachlan dredged up the kindness to give her hand a little squeeze. "You've held up admirably, Kitty," he murmured. "And I am not an ungrateful man. But I do not care to strike up a friendship. Have Mrs. Farnham send someone else on Thursday. We need a change, you and I."

With a disdainful sniff, Kitty tucked the banknote into her ample cleavage—clearly Mrs. Farnham wouldn't be getting a cut of *that*. She let her gaze run down him, all the way to his crotch, then she heaved a theatrical sigh. " 'Fraid it ain't my heart that'll be aching, MacLachlan," she remarked. "Much as I hate to credit you. But however gifted you might be, *you just ain't worth it.*"

MacLachlan was rewrapping his stock around his throat. "Aye, doubtless you are right."

Kitty made a harrumphing noise. "Fine, then. I'll send over Bess Bromley on Thursday, and let 'er put up wiv you for a spell. Monstrous mean, that cat-eyed bitch. You two'll get on like a house afire." And on that parting remark, Kitty swished through the makeshift bedchamber and jerked open the door to his private office, where she promptly melted into the gloom.

For a long moment, MacLachlan simply stood there, staring into the shadows of his office. He knew that a better man would feel regret, perhaps even a measure of guilt. But he did not. Oh, Kitty had served him well enough, he reminded himself as he finished dressing. She'd been clean and polite and punctual. Certainly her broad, round arse would be forever fixed in his memory.

But that was about all he would likely remember. Indeed, it had been the first of April before he'd troubled himself to learn her name. Before that, he'd simply told the girl to strip and lie down on the bed. On especially busy days, he had not even bothered to undress, he recalled as he returned to his desk. He would simply drop the front of his trousers, bend the girl over the sofa in his office, and get on with the business of satisfying an otherwise annoying itch.

No, he did not care. Not then, and not now. Because there was one thing MacLachlan craved more than the sight of a fine, wide arse—and that was raw, unadulterated power. And Kitty's complaints, however heartfelt, would never alter the two most immutable laws of capitalism. Time was money. And money was power. He had very little of the first nowadays, and he would never have enough of the last.

MacLachlan rolled out the next set of elevation drawings and impatiently yanked the bell for his clerk. It was time to fetch his solicitors down from Threadneedle Street. There was work which wanted doing. Within the week, MacLachlan meant to break ground for three new properties, sell another six, bankrupt an uncooperative brick merchant, and plow down a neighboring village— all in preparation for the next terrace of elegant, faux-

Georgian houses which were destined to help him part the profligate English from yet another cartload of their pence and their pounds. And *that* he would truly enjoy.

The house in Mortimer Street did not look precisely like that of a wealthy and powerful peer. It was not in Mayfair, but merely near it. It was not a wide, double-fronted mansion, but just a single town house with two windows and a door down, and four unremarkable floors above. From its simple brick facade, one might suppose the place housed a banker or a barrister or some moderately prosperous coal merchant.

It did not. It housed instead the powerful Earl of Treyhern, a solid, sober-minded citizen if ever there was one. A simple man who, it was said, brooked no foolishness, and hated deceit above all things. Worse still, the Countess of Bessett, who stood trembling on his doorstep, had not even come to see the earl. She had come instead to see his governess—or more precisely, to *steal* his governess, were it to prove even remotely possible.

Money was no object. Her nerves were another thing altogether. But the countess was desperate, so she patted the little bulge in her reticule, swallowed hard, and went up the steps to ring the bell. She prayed the woman still worked here. Only when the door had flown open did it occur to her that perhaps it was not perfectly proper to ask for a servant at the front door.

Alas, too late. A tall, wide-shouldered footman was staring her straight in the face. Lady Bessett handed him her card with an unsteady hand. "The Countess of Bessett to see Mademoiselle de Severs, if she is available?"

The footman's eyebrows lifted a little oddly, but he escorted the countess up the stairs and bade her be seated in a small, sunny parlor.

The room was fitted with fine French antiques, buttery jacquard wall covering, and yellow shantung draperies which brushed the lush Aubusson carpet. Despite her state of anxiety, Lady Bessett found the room pleasant and made a mental note of the colors. Tomorrow, if she survived this meeting, she was to buy a house. Her very first house—not her husband's house or her father's house or her stepson's house. *Hers.* And then she, too, would have a yellow parlor. It was to be her choice, was it not? She would tell the builder so tomorrow.

A few moments later, a tall, dark-haired woman came into the room. She looked decidedly French, but she was dressed perhaps a little more elegantly than one might expect of a governess. Her bearing was not especially servile, and her expression was one of good-humored curiosity. Before she could think better of it, Lady Bessett leapt from the sofa and hastened across the room.

"You are Mademoiselle de Severs?" she whispered, seizing the woman's hand.

The woman's mouth twitched. "Well, yes, but—"

"I wish to employ you," Lady Bessett interjected. "At once. You must but name your price."

Mademoiselle de Severs drew back. "Oh, I am afraid you mistake—"

"No, I am desperate." Lady Bessett tightened her grip on the woman's hand. "I have a letter of introduction. From the Gräfin von Hodenberg in Passau. She has told me everything. About your work. Your training in Vienna. My son . . . I fear he is quite ill. I must hire you, Mademoiselle de Severs. I must. I cannot think where else to turn."

The woman gave her hand a reassuring squeeze. "I am so sorry," she said in her faint French accent. "The gräfin is misinformed. Indeed, I have not spoken to her in a decade or better."

"She said as much," agreed Lady Bessett.

"How, pray, do you know her?"

Lady Bessett dropped her gaze to the floor. "I lived much of my marriage abroad," she explained. "Our husbands shared an interest in ancient history. We met first in Athens, I think."

"How kind of her to remember me."

Lady Bessett smiled faintly. "She knew only that you had gone to London to work for a family called Rutledge, who had a poor little girl who was dreadfully ill. It was quite difficult to track the family down. And London—well, it is such a large place, is it not? I have visited here but once in the whole of my life."

Miss de Severs motioned toward a pair of armchairs by the hearth, which was unlit on such a late-spring afternoon. "Please, Lady Bessett, do sit down," she invited. "I shall endeavor to explain my situation here."

Hope wilted in Lady Bessett's heart. "You . . . you cannot help us?"

"I cannot yet say," the governess replied. "Certainly I shall try. Now, the child—what is his age, please, and the nature of his illness?"

Lady Bessett choked back a sob. "Geoffrey is twelve," she answered. "And he—he has—well, he *imagines* things, mademoiselle. Odd, frightening things. And he blurts out things which make no sense, and he cannot explain why. Sometimes he suffers from melancholia. He is a deeply troubled child."

Miss de Severs was nodding slowly. "These imaginings take the form of what? Dreams? Hallucinations? Does the child hear voices?"

"Dreams, I think," she whispered. "But dreams whilst he is awake, if that makes any sense? I—I am not perfectly sure, you see. Geoffrey will no longer discuss them with me. Indeed, he has become quite secretive."

"Does he still suffer them?" asked the governess. "Children often outgrow such things, you know."

Lady Bessett shook her head. "They are getting worse," she insisted. "I can tell that he is worried. I have consulted both a physician and a phrenologist in Harley Street. They say—oh, God!—they say he might have a mental disorder. That eventually, he might lose touch with reality altogether, and need to be restrained. Or—or *confined*."

"Oh, what balderdash!" said the governess, rolling her eyes. "Why, I should like to restrain and confine some of the physicians in Harley Street—and never mind what I would do to the phrenologists."

"You—you do not believe them?"

"Oh, almost never!" said the woman breezily. "And in this case, certainly not. A child of twelve is not sufficiently developed, mentally or physically, for such dire pronouncements. And if he has odd bumps on his head, it is likely from a game of conkers gone awry. Perhaps your son is merely sensitive and artistic?"

Lady Bessett shook her head. "It is not that," she said certainly. "Though he is quite a fine artist. He has a great head for mathematics, too, and all things scientific. That is why these—these *spells* seem so out of character."

"He is not a fanciful child, then?"

"By no means."

"He otherwise functions well in the world? He learns? He comprehends?"

"Geoff's tutor says he is brilliant."

"Has there been any childhood trauma?"

For an instant, Lady Bessett hesitated. "No, not . . . not trauma."

The governess lifted her eyebrows again, and opened her mouth as if to speak. But just then, a lovely girl with blond hair came twirling through the doorway in what could only be described as a fashionable dinner gown.

"Mamma, it is finished!" she cried, craning her head over her shoulder to look at her heels. "What do you think? Is the hem right? Does it make my derriere look too—"

"My dear, we have a guest," chided the governess— who was, it now appeared, *not* the governess after all. "This is Lady Bessett. Lady Bessett, my stepdaughter, Lady Ariane Rutledge."

The girl was already flushing deeply. "Oh! I do beg your pardon, ma'am!" She curtsied, and excused herself at once.

"I say!" murmured Lady Bessett, feeling her cheeks grow warm. "Who was—I mean—was that . . . ?"

"Lord Treyhern's poor little girl who was so dreadfully ill," said her hostess. "Yes, that is what I have been trying to tell you, Lady Bessett. We were married, he and I. And Ariane, as you see, is quite a normal young lady now. We have three other children as well, so my work nowadays consists of little more than giving the odd bit of advice to a friend or relation."

"Oh." Lady Bessett's shoulders fell. "Oh, dear. You are Lady Treyhern now! And I—well, I do not know what I shall do."

Her hostess leaned across the distance, and set her hand on Lady Bessett's. "My dear, you are very young," she said. "Younger, I think, even than I?"

"I am thirty," she whispered. "And I feel as though I am twice that." Then, to her undying embarrassment, a tear rolled down Lady Bessett's cheek.

Lady Treyhern handed her a freshly starched handkerchief. "Thirty is still rather young," she went on. "You must trust me when I say that children *do* outgrow such things."

"Do you think so?" Lady Bessett sniffled. "I just wish I could be sure. Geoffrey is my life. We have only one another now."

"I see," said Lady Treyhern. "And how long are you in London, my dear?"

Lady Bessett lifted her sorrowful gaze. "Forever," she replied. "I am the dowager countess and my stepson is newly wed. Tomorrow I am contracting to purchase a house nearby."

"Are you?" Lady Treyhern smiled. "How very exciting."

Lady Bessett shrugged. "Our village doctor thought it best for Geoff that we be close to London. He said he had no notion what to do for the boy."

Lady Treyhern patted her hand comfortingly. "You must take your time and settle in, my dear," she advised. "And when you have done so, you must bring young Geoff to tea. We will begin to get acquainted."

"You . . . you will help us, then?"

"I shall try," said Lady Treyhern. "His symptoms are indeed mysterious—but I am not at all convinced it is a disorder."

"Are you not? Thank God."

"Even if it were, my dear, there are a few physicians in London who have been attending to the events unfolding in Vienna and Paris," said her hostess. "Forays *are* being made into the field of mental diseases—psychology, they call it. They are not all uninformed nitwits, Lady Bessett."

"Mental diseases!" Lady Bessett shuddered. "I cannot bear even to think of it!"

"I rather doubt you shall have to," said Lady Treyhern. "Now I shall ring for coffee, and you must tell me all about this new house of yours. Where is it, pray?"

"Near Chelsea," said Lady Bessett quietly. "In a village called Walham Green. I have taken a cottage there until the house is complete, but that will be some weeks yet."

"Well, then, you are but a short drive from town," said Lady Treyhern as she rose and rang the bell. "I confess, I do not know a great many people in London myself. Nonetheless, you must allow me to help you with introductions."

Again, Lady Bessett felt her face heat. "I fear I have been very little in society," she admitted. "I know almost no one."

"Well, my dear, now you know me," said her hostess. "So, what of this new house? I daresay it has all the modern conveniences. And of course you will be buying a great many new furnishings, I am sure. How very exciting that will be!"

Chapter Two

Better half-hanged than ill-married.

The bell-ringers at St. George's Hanover Square were already milling about on the portico when MacLachlan's carriage arrived in the early-morning haze. With a curt bark, he ordered his driver to wait for him in Three Kings Yard, then stepped down onto the pavement. In another hour, the corner would be choked with traffic, and he'd no wish to become ensnared in it.

On the church portico, one of the ringers shot him a faintly curious look. A second was rubbing at a callus on his hand as if contemplating the task before him, whilst another complained none too quietly about the late-spring damp. Just then, an arm draped in flowing vestments pushed one of the doors open. One by one, the bell-ringers vanished into the church. Soon he could hear them treading one after the other up the twisting steps into to the bell tower.

MacLachlan was grateful. He saw no point in striking up idle chitchat with people he did not know. Certainly he had no wish to go inside the church until it was unavoidable. With restless energy, he paced up and down the street, admiring St. George's fine Flemish glass and classical columns, but in a vague, almost clinical sort of way. He was never comfortable anywhere near this bastion of the English upper crust. Certainly he had never thought to come here for a wedding—well, not in more years than he could count, at any rate.

But today was to be his elder brother's wedding day. Today, MacLachlan had no choice. He turned and paced the length of the pavement again. Phipps had tied his cravat too tight, blast it. MacLachlan ran his finger around his collar and forced it to loosen.

Traffic along St. George Street was picking up now. Damn. He had no wish to keep pacing back and forth like some caged creature. But neither could he bring himself to actually go inside the place. Abruptly, he turned and paced down the shadowy little passageway adjacent to the old edifice. It was not the first time he had slipped away into the shadows of St. George's. Here, the air was thick with the smell of mossy stone and damp earth. The smell of crypts and catacombs and cold, dead things. The sepulchre, perhaps, of a man's hopes and dreams.

It had been a mistake to come here. To this church. To this passageway. He looked up to see the sun dappling through some greenery beyond, the movement somehow disorienting. He shut his eyes. The clamor and rattle of street traffic quieted, then faded away.

"Kiss me, Maddie." His voice was rough in the gloom.

"Merrick, my aunt!" She flashed a coy look, and set the heel of one hand against his shoulder. *"She'll scold if we linger behind the others."*

He set a finger to her lips. "Shush, Maddie," *he returned.* "They've not even noticed we're gone." *He bent his head, and lightly brushed his lips over hers. But as it always did, the kiss burst at once into flames. He took her deeply, his tongue surging inside her mouth, their hands roaming urgently over one another.*

His head swam with the scent of her. He could feel the silk of her dress beneath his fingers, the swell of her buttock, firm and promising against his palm. Maddie's breathing ratcheted up until it came in sweet, delightful pants. She had the good sense to push him away.

"Merrick, this is a church!"

He smiled down at her. "Aye, lass, so it is," he agreed. "But there's naught sinful about my feelings for you. They are good and pure in the eyes of God."

She lowered her lashes, and looked away, her face flushing petal pink. He wanted to kiss her again. He wanted to touch her the way a man ought when a woman was to be his. But he dared not risk it here. Instead, he set his temple to hers, and felt her shoulders relax against the cold stone church wall.

"Maddie." He whispered her name into her hair, and gathered her against him with both arms.

"What?"

"Is this where you Mayfair folk are wed?"

"I'm not Mayfair folk," she whispered back. "Not really. But yes, it is."

"Then I'm going to marry you here, Maddie," he vowed, his voice tight with emotion. "At the end of the season, before all these fine people, I swear to God, I am."

"Will . . . will they let us, Merrick?"

He forgot sometimes how young she was. "They cannot stop us," he rasped. "No one, Maddie, can stop true love."

But her aunt's tread was heavy on the pavement beyond . . .

"Good God, there you are!" The footsteps stopped.

Merrick turned on the narrow pathway, blinking his eyes against the morning light.

"It is half past the hour." Sir Alasdair MacLachlan's voice was a near growl. "Are you coming inside or not?"

"Aye, presently."

"No, *now,*" said the groom-to-be. "You agreed to this, Merrick. And it cannot be as bad as all that. You've only to stand up with me, not get a tooth extracted."

Merrick collected his wits as he walked slowly back along the side of the church. He hoped his agitation did not show. "You are right, of course," he said, stepping from the shadows into the sun. "I beg your pardon. My mind was elsewhere."

"Your mind was where it always is, I'd wager," snapped his brother. "On your blasted account books." As he spoke, an open landau passed along the church's columned portico, then jerked suddenly left and drew to the curb. A portly man leapt out and came stalking up the pavement toward the MacLachlan brothers, one hand balled into a tight fist.

"Who the devil?" said Alasdair under his breath.

Coolly, Merrick lifted his hat. "Good morning, Chutley."

The man looked apoplectic, and reeked of spirits. "You may well say so!" he answered accusingly. "'Tis pure providence, my running into you, is it not?"

"I could not say," Merrick responded. "May I introduce my brother, Sir Alas—"

"Don't trouble yourself," the portly man snarled. "I had a visit last night, MacLachlan, from one of your Threadneedle thugs."

Merrick lifted one eyebrow. "One of my solicitors from the City, do you mean?"

"Call them what you will," snapped the man. "Do I understand this aright, MacLachlan? You mean to call in my note? After all that we agreed to?"

Alasdair cleared his throat sharply, but Merrick carried on. "You agreed to pay back the loan in quarterly installments, Chutley."

"Good God, man! This is still May!"

"Aye, barely, but the loan was made on February 2," Merrick countered. "Payment was due ninety days hence."

"Gentlemen, must we have this discussion now?" Alasdair hissed. "We are standing in front of a church, for pity's sake."

The two men spared him not a glance. "But everyone knows that quarterly means June 24!" Chutley protested. "*That* is the next quarter day!"

Merrick lifted both eyebrows. "Is it indeed?" he murmured. "By that reckoning, then, I should have had the first payment on Lady Day. I begin to think, Chutley, that you did not read the fine print. Rest assured, the payment was due weeks ago."

Chutley faltered. "But—but I haven't got it, MacLachlan!" he said, his voice low. "You'll put my brickworks under, damn you! Is that what you want? *Is* it?"

"Then at least I shall have some bricks for my trouble," Merrick retorted. "If I must own the bloody brickyard to get the job done, so be it."

Alasdair touched him lightly on the shoulder. "Really, Merrick, this is beyond bourgeois."

His brother's head whipped around for an instant. "Aye, 'tis *business*," he returned. "Chutley, my superintendent tells me you've run us a fortnight late on our last three ventures. I cannot build without bricks, man, and I did not make you that loan out of the kindness of my heart—"

"No, for you haven't any!" interjected the man.

"Aye, and you'd do well to remember it," Merrick advised. "The loan was made so that Chutley Brickworks might upgrade their equipment and get me my bloody building materials on time. Now, I need bricks, Chutley, and you've got a yard full of them. I know, for I saw them yesterday."

Chutley's color deepened. "But that inventory is promised to Fortnoy!"

"Then unpromise it, damn you!" said Merrick. "Did Fortnoy loan you ten thousand pounds? No, I thought not. Good day to you, Chutley. I shall expect a dozen cartloads of bricks in Walham Green before nightfall, and the rest before the week is out."

The man was shaking with rage, and looking very much as if he might fall dead on the pavement. Without another word, he turned on one heel and returned to his waiting landau.

"Oh, thank you, Merrick," said his brother coldly. "Thank you for making this day so very special for me."

Merrick turned, and looked at Alasdair blankly. Abruptly, his mind cleared, and he recalled where he was. By now, a small crowd of wedding guests were lingering at the opposite end of the portico, averting their eyes, and speaking in hushed tones. He realized at once that they must have overheard at least the tenor of the quarrel, if not the words.

He felt his own face flush with heat. The groom's brother grinding some small-minded merchant beneath his bootheel on the portico of St. George's—yes, that was just what Merrick's reputation wanted. Ordinarily, he would not give a damn. But his brother had waited almost thirty-seven long years before going to the altar, and he was very happy now to be doing so. Alasdair had met the woman of his dreams. And unlike Merrick's, Alasdair's dreams appeared destined to come true. He was not apt, thank God, to trip over their rotting remains in some moldering old churchyard one day when he least expected it.

Somehow, he found the presence of mind to put an arm around his brother's shoulders. He had often envied Alasdair's blithe charm and golden beauty, but never had he wished him ill. "I am sorry, Alasdair," he said quietly. "This *is* a special day. Come, let us go in, and get down to the business of making Esmée a part of this family."

As with most duties one thoroughly dreads, this one did not amount to much. The ceremony itself was soon over, and Merrick's obligation finished—or so he thought. The crowd spilt out of St. George's to the resounding peals of the bell-ringers at their most jubilant.

With the clamor echoing off the high brick walls of Mayfair, the wedding party began to trickle toward nearby Grosvenor Square, where the wedding breakfast was to be held at the home of Lady Tatton, one of society's most upright matrons—and now Alasdair's aunt by marriage.

At the corner of the church, Esmée caught up with him. She looked radiant today. "May I have your arm, Merrick?" she asked. "You are my brother now, you know."

He offered it, of course. Alasdair was accepting the congratulations of some of his more disreputable friends. He stood beside Esmée, shaking their hands in turn, and wearing that vaguely stunned expression so common to men newly wed.

"You will remain a while at Aunt's house, I hope?" Esmée enquired.

Merrick hesitated. "I had not thought to stay," he confessed. "You will forgive me?"

"No, I shan't," she answered flatly. "Where is your carriage? Why must you go?"

"At the Three Kings," he said. "And I have an architectural meeting this afternoon. My staff will be waiting."

"The afternoon is some time away," said Esmée. "And if you mean to go to the Three Kings, you may as well go but a few yards farther, Merrick, and drink us a toast, at the very least?"

It seemed such a small thing to ask. "You are Alasdair's only relation in London," she chided. "Society will expect you to attend."

Merrick did not much give a damn what society expected. Society had done nothing for him, and precious little for his brother. A moderately endowed Scottish baronet did not carry much weight this far south, and his younger brother, even less—especially when he dared actually *work* for a living. Alasdair had met and fallen in love with Esmée by a pure twist of fate, and much to her aunt's disapprobation.

No one, Maddie, can stop true love.

Well. At least Merrick had been proven right on this occasion. Alasdair and Esmée loved one another unreservedly. No one had been able to talk them out of this marriage. It was a union which would last forever, Merrick had become increasingly certain. Now, for his new sister's sake, he forced a tight smile.

"Society expects it, eh?" he said. "Well, God knows I shouldn't wish to disappoint them."

Esmée's green eyes danced with laughter. Merrick searched for something affable to say. "You are looking forward to your wedding trip, I hope? Alasdair's estate will be beautiful this time of year."

Esmée's expression softened. "Oh, it will be like going home again!" she said wistfully. "I have longed for Scotland ever since leaving it. I only hope that . . ."

"Hope what?" Merrick pressed.

"I only hope that your grandmother will not feel uncomfortable," she said. "I know that Castle Kerr is her domain, and that Alasdair has left her to run it as she sees fit. I hope that I can convince her nothing need change."

"Then you must simply say so," Merrick advised. "Granny MacGregor speaks her mind, and expects others to do the same."

"Well, *that* seems to be a family trait." Esmée teased him with her eyes. "Look, Merrick, why do you not come with us? It is, after all, your childhood home, too."

He looked at her incredulously. "Come along on your wedding trip?" he answered. "No, Alasdair would not thank me for that."

"Merrick, Alasdair loves you," she said quietly. "Sometimes, yes, he even envies you. As I think you envy him, perhaps? But you are his brother, and you mean the world to him."

"Our brotherly competition is in the past, Esmée," he answered. "We are very different people, and we have accepted that. But to go north with you? No, I think not."

"Then join us later," she persisted. "We mean to stay through the autumn, if not the year. Come at any time. Your grandmother would be so pleased. *I* would be so pleased."

She sounded as if she meant it. Merrick didn't know why. He had not been especially kind to Esmée early on. She had every reason to dislike him.

"We shall see how things go on," he lied, sketching her a neat bow. "I thank you, Lady MacLachlan, for the invitation."

Esmée smiled, but just then, the Marquess of Devellyn passed by, seizing Esmée's face in both his big paws and kissing her, quite shamelessly and loudly, on each cheek. "My dear child!" he said, elbowing Alasdair in the ribs. "Saddled with this dreadful old roué! How old are you? Seventeen? And this one is what? Five-and-forty if he's a day! I swear, fate has done you an appalling injustice."

Esmée's cheeks flamed with pink. Though she hardly looked it, the chit was almost three-and-twenty, and Devellyn surely knew it. Beside the marquess, his wife began to scold him and to cluck at Esmée sympathetically.

Merrick took the opportunity to slip away and vanish into the crowd. At least, that was the plan. But by the time he arrived at Lady Tatton's town house, one of Merrick's few friends amongst the *ton,* the Earl of Wynwood, caught up with him.

"Where is your lovely wife?" Merrick asked Wynwood as the crowd swarmed around them.

Lord Wynwood grinned and jerked his head toward the stairway. "Vivie's stuck in the midst of that mob," he said, "receiving the accolades of her many admirers."

Merrick twisted his mouth wryly. "I am not at all sure I should wish to be married to a famous Italian soprano."

Wynwood shook his head. "I spent too many years, my friend, *not* being married to Vivie," he returned. "Better her fame than my misery. Besides, *you* do not wish to be married to anyone at all, famous or otherw—" Then, as if realizing what he'd just said, his face fell. "Ah, sorry about that, old chap!" He set a warm hand between Merrick's shoulder blades. "Look, might we talk business for a moment? Vivie and I need your help."

"What sort of help?"

"We want a new house," said Wynwood. "We are in quite desperate straits, truth to tell."

Merrick was surprised. "You wish to leave Mayfair?"

"Oh, you know Vivie! She doesn't give a fig for Mayfair. It is space we need, and to get it, we'll have to move out of town just a bit. I thought Walham Green might be perfect." He flashed Merrick a shameless grin. "You do mean to level the whole village, do you not? Be so obliging as to save a couple of hectares for us."

Merrick smiled tightly. "Contrary to the darkening rumors, I will be plowing down only what the good citizens of Walham wish to lease or sell."

"Yes, but your money's awfully green, isn't it?" said Wynwood. "And there's a vast deal of it, too."

Merrick shrugged. "I pay a fair price."

Wynwood laughed so loud he drew stares. "Oh, a Scot never paid a fair price for anything!" he answered. "But will you do it, Merrick? Will you design something for us? And have it built somewhere near Chelsea?"

"Why me, Quin?" Merrick's voice was soft. "I have a dozen fine young architects on my staff. Indeed, I've scarce taken up my drawing pencil these last ten years."

"We need something special," said Wynwood. "And you are said to be not just a financial genius, but an architectural genius as well."

"Aye?" Merrick made a snorting sound. "By whom?"

Wynwood shifted a little uncomfortably. "Well, those fancy plaques and awards you have covering three walls of your study say so," he responded. "And those—those academic things from St. Andrews and such which are hanging between the windows."

"Things?" said Merrick archly.

"Look, I did not go to university," grumbled Wynwood. "I scarcely know what they are, but I know what I hear. Now, I need a house—a bloody big one—and I want top quality."

"What of Cubitt? His group still has one or two houses for sale in Belgrave Square."

Wynwood shook his head. "I've looked Belgravia up and down, and it just doesn't suit me. Everything is beautiful, but it all looks alike—which just goes to show that he is a fine builder, yet not an architect. You were acclaimed as a genius before you'd built so much as a watchman's box."

"All a decade and a half past," said Merrick. "In the world of architectural design, Wynwood, one must be a starving artist to win such acclaim. Once you are rich, that is thought to be reward enough."

"Ah!" Wynwood's tone was disconcertingly insightful. "And is it?"

Merrick hesitated but a heartbeat. "Aye, you're damned right it is."

"I see," said Lord Wynwood. "Then you will have luncheon with me tomorrow at the Walham Arms, and give me a tour of the village?"

"If that is your wish," said Merrick, casually lifting one shoulder. "Meet me there shortly after one. And Wynwood, if you are serious—"

"I am."

"Aye, then bring a bank draft. I am, as you say, a Scot."

Wynwood laughed again and melted into the mob which still surrounded his beautiful new wife.

Chapter Three

If ye canna see the bottom,
dinna wade in.

After residing in Walham Green all of a sen'night, Lady Bessett found that late morning in the pretty village had already become her favorite time of day. Shortly after daylight, the busy market garden traffic—the vegetable-laden carts rumbling into the city, the tumbrels heaped with hay, the crates of flapping, squawking poultry—all of it vanished into the fringes of London, leaving the little village on its outskirts blissfully serene.

On this particular morning, the countess sat in the tiny rear garden of her cottage nibbling at tea and toast. She closed her eyes, and listened to the birdsong as she sipped the last of her cup. The scents of spring were redolent in the air—the smell of fresh-turned earth, and the fragrance of the season's flowers. Yes, she could almost imagine she was back in Yorkshire again.

She really did miss it dreadfully. She opened her eyes, and took in the tiny walled garden with its rosebushes, its neat little path, and the ancient swath of wisteria which rambled up and over the kitchen window. Since coming to this charming place, she had not allowed herself to think about Yorkshire—not until she had been required to explain her circumstances to Lady Treyhern.

The truth was, however, the Yorkshire dales had been her home for just four short years. But in that time, she had come to love the vast, rich, rolling emptiness of the place. And she had come to love the freedom which widowhood had brought her. A newfound sense of self-esteem had slowly settled over her as Loughton Manor came back to life after long years of her husband's absence and neglect.

Perhaps more importantly, she had come to love Loughton and its people. They would miss her, she thought. Mrs. Pendleton had cried quite shamelessly as she and Geoff had climbed into the carriage for the long trip down to London. Even Simms, the old butler, had twice been compelled to blow his nose. Yes, they would miss her—and they were not pleased to be gaining a new mistress.

The Earl of Bessett, her stepson Alvin, had chosen a wife immediately upon his majority. Unfortunately, he had chosen one of whom the staff was not fond. Miss Edsell was the daughter of a neighboring squire, and had often been a guest at Loughton. She had set her cap at poor Alvin early, and openly. She had made it plain, too, that things would change at Loughton when she became its mistress.

For his part, Alvin wished only for a placid existence of farming and shooting. He was not unkind, but he was a little dull. So far removed was Alvin from the fervent, single-minded scholar his father had been, that people often marveled they were kin at all.

Perhaps a childhood spent roaming through Italy and Campania had made Alvin long to put down roots. He wanted neither adventure nor travel in his life now. "And after all,

Cousin Madeleine," Alvin had said, "why go down to London for a season when a local girl will suit me well enough?"

So he married Miss Edsell. Madeleine had helped Mrs. Pendleton supervise the washing-up after the wedding breakfast. Then she went upstairs to pack.

Oh, Alvin had not asked her to leave. Indeed, he was fond of her—they were first cousins once-removed, and she had been his stepmother since he was eight. Alvin was very fond of Geoff, too. He had never resented the boy, so far as Madeleine could tell.

But Miss Edsell resented them both. Madeleine had seen the look in her eyes often enough to know which way the wind would soon be was blowing. Besides, Geoff needed to be near London. The village doctor had been most insistent. And she—well, she needed a change. A diversion. An adventure or an avocation. *Something*. Something that might jerk her from the clutches of those tenacious little blue-devils which had plagued her these many years.

So London was their home now, for good or ill. And Madeleine felt a little better after having met with Lady Treyhern. She was said to be very knowledgeable about troubled children. Indeed, she had once been thought something of a miracle worker on the Continent.

Just then, Geoff wandered out of the house, stretching as he came, as if his bones had grown an inch during the night and now wanted to be popped loose. Certainly he was eating enough to grow at such a rate.

"Good morning, Mamma," he said before kissing her on the cheek. "You slept well?"

"Quite well, my dear," she said. "You look as though you did, too."

And he did look rather well rested. Madeleine felt a

wave of relief as he plopped down on the adjacent garden bench. As a young boy, he had begun to suffer dreadfully from insomnia. She suspected he still did, though at the tender age of twelve, he had learned to hide it from her.

Clara, the new housemaid, bustled out with a breakfast tray, and Geoff set upon it with relish. Madeleine let her eyes drift over him. Dear God, he was going to be handsome. Already, he was but a head shorter than she—and she was quite tall for a woman. But Geoff did not have her pale blond looks. Madeleine looked away and poured him a cup of tea.

"I told Eliza to set out my walking shoes this morning," she said. "Do you still wish to go out?"

His eyes lit. "Oh, yes, I wish to go see the Chelsea hospital," he said, his voice cracking with adolescent excitement. "And I want to walk along the Thames as far as possible, and look at all the merchant ships."

Madeleine laughed at his enthusiasm. "I believe the Thames goes all the way to the sea, my dear," she said. "And most of the merchant ships will be too far downriver. London is a large city. But we can take the carriage, I daresay?"

Geoff shook his head. "Just the hospital today, then," he said. "I wish to walk all around it. Mr. Frost says it was built by Sir Christopher Wren—just like St. Paul's."

They had visited St. Paul's Cathedral their first week in Walham Green. Geoff had been awestruck by the soaring roofs and the sheer magnificence of the place. His tutor, Mr. Frost, had filled the boy's head with all the wonders of London. Consequently, Geoff was obsessed with drinking in all the history, commerce, and architecture which surrounded them.

Madeleine finished her tea and rose. "In fifteen minutes, then," she said as she headed toward the door. "Will you be ready?"

Their walking tour of Chelsea presented little challenge to a pair accustomed to hiking the dales. They spent a good two hours enjoying the landscaped grounds of the hospital, and the feel of the sun's warmth on their faces. Afterward, they strolled back along Cheyne Walk, admiring the views of the Thames, and lovely houses which lined it.

"Look, Mamma," said Geoff, when they reached the foot of Oakley Street. "Look at this wrought-iron gate. Mr. Frost says the houses of Chelsea are famous for their magnificent ironwork. I know! Perhaps we could buy a house here? I should like to see the river every day."

Madeleine laughed. "We have already bought a house, Geoff," she replied. "Or promised to do so, which is quite the same thing. And you shall have a view of the river from upstairs."

"Shall I?"

"I can show you this afternoon," she suggested. "I am going by to have a look around, and dream about paint and draperies."

His nose wrinkled. "No, thank you, Mamma!"

Madeleine smiled indulgently. "Very well, then," she said. "As punishment, I shall paint your room puce. Or purple. Or pumpkin, perhaps? Now, it is almost time for luncheon. How shall we walk home? Look, up ahead is Beaufort Street. I believe it will take us up to the King's Highway. That might be pleasant."

"That way, then," Geoff agreed good-naturedly. "But hurry, Mamma. Now that I think on it, I *am* getting hungry again."

They set off arm in arm, pausing once or twice to look into shop windows or admire a house which caught Geoff's eye. They were but halfway up the street, however, when

Madeleine sensed the child's mood begin to shift. His arm slipped from hers. His boyish chatter ceased, and his pace began to flag. Suddenly, he stopped on the pavement, his expression stark yet stubborn. Madeleine turned to look at him.

"Geoff, what is wrong?"

"I want—I want to go back, Mamma."

Madeleine knew the signs. Dear God, not now. "Geoff, we need to go home," she cajoled. "Come along, now. We are blocking the pavement."

"But I don't wish to go!" cried the boy. "I want to go back."

Exasperation told in her voice. "Go back where?"

A man in a brown greatcoat pushed past them, scowling over his shoulder. "Bloody tourists!" he muttered beneath his breath.

Geoff stared right through him. Madeleine could feel the strange terror taking the boy into its grip. "Back— back to Cheyne Walk," he rasped. "Back to the river."

"Geoff, darling, that makes no sense."

"Whatever you wish, then." His jaw hardened, and his face began to darken. "I just do not wish to go any farther."

"On Beaufort Street, do you mean?" Madeleine exhaled sharply. "Then which way do you wish to go, pray?"

"How should I know?" he choked. "Not this way. But I do not know another way. *Please*, Mamma, just *do it*." The boy was staring at his feet and visibly trembling. His hands were fisted, his knuckles white.

Madeleine knew that if she challenged him, his anxiety would only worsen. Once, during their last year in Campania, he had refused to board a ferry bound for Palermo. He had been but seven years old, and yet he had clung to the gangway railing and screamed incoherently for all of ten minutes, tears streaming down his little face. Madeleine had not possessed the heart to tear him away, and force him onto the boat.

It was not the first time she had given in to his "temper tantrums," as Bessett had called them. Looking back, perhaps that had been a mistake. Her husband had certainly thought so. Nonetheless, after the ferry departed without them and they had frog-marched Geoff back to the carriage, the child had covered his ears with his hands, and curled himself into a ball on the carriage floor, where he quietly sobbed the entire journey home.

Bessett, of course, had been furious. This time, he had insisted she take the boy upstairs and thrash him—or he would do it for her. She had done it herself, with a green switch to the backs of his legs. It had been one of the most sickening experiences of her life. And it had done not one whit of good. The strange moods and fits had only worsened.

"Which way, then?" she said gently. "Back the way we came?"

Mutely, he nodded, still refusing to look at her. Madeleine took his hand and set off back down the street. Their walk to Chelsea had been warm and companionable. Now she was practically dragging the boy behind her. She was angry, and she was worried. She did not like to see Geoff so frightened, or behaving so irrationally.

She gave his hand an encouraging squeeze, but Geoff did not respond. Madeleine bit her lip to keep from crying, then quickened her pace.

The Walham Arms was a fine old public house built of stone the color of a rainy afternoon, and perched right on the edge of the Thames. In its glory days, when the river was London's main thoroughfare, the Arms had been an upriver watermen's haunt—and the haunt of a few less reputable fellows, too. Nowadays, it was just a village tavern frequented by merchants and farmers rather than dashing smugglers and highwaymen.

Merrick MacLachlan used it often as a place to meet prospective stonemasons, carpenters, and the like, as the nature of his business required. Such men were not always comfortable in a gentleman's office, and when it came to his pet projects like Walham Hill, Merrick refused to employ so much as a ditchdigger without eyeing him across a pint of porter or a tot of whisky first.

Merrick was notorious for his insistence on controlling every step of the building process, from the first spade of earth that was turned to the last bit of slate on the roof. Indeed, he did not care to let out any work at all if he could avoid it—even the brick manufacturing, it now seemed, would fall under his purview.

On top of all these more mundane details, Merrick negotiated all the leases and purchases of the land he would build upon. He wined and dined bankers and investors from three continents. And, when it was absolutely unavoidable, he rubbed an elbow or two at a society affair. Those were few and far between, thank God, since most of London's upper-crust hostesses seemed to fear that Merrick MacLachlan might carry mud in on his boots— or might, God help him, smell of an honest day's work.

Inside the cool, shadowy interior of the Arms' taproom, Merrick wasn't sweating at all. Instead, he was leaned back in his chair, impatiently drumming his fingers on the ancient trestle table. Already he had waved off the serving girl twice. Where the devil was Wynwood, anyway? Merrick hated irresponsibility in any form, and believed tardiness to be its worst incarnation. Then abruptly, he checked himself. He was being unreasonable again. It was not like Wynwood to be late.

Just then, Merrick heard the sounds of a small conveyance pulling up in the Arms' yard. He got up and peered through a window to see Wynwood leap down from his curricle, toss a coin to the ostler, then start toward the door.

"You are late," said Merrick, when his friend sat down. "Did no one ever tell you that time is money?"

"Terribly sorry." The earl was looking, Merrick realized, just a little unwell. "Be a good fellow and send for a bottle of brandy, won't you?"

"It's dashed early for that." But Merrick waved down the serving girl and did so anyway. "Are you perfectly all right?"

He watched as Wynwood's throat moved up and down. "Well enough, I suppose," he said. "I came upon an accident near Drayton Gardens. A young girl, plowed down by some lunatic in a phaeton. I think—I think she was trying to cross the road."

"Dear God! What did you do?"

Lord Wynwood looked into the depths of the public house. "I leapt down, and tried to help," he said quietly. "But there was no helping her. Her pale blue dress—the blood—it was ghastly. The King's Road is straight as a stick, Merrick! How could anyone be so careless?"

"I can guess." Merrick gritted out the words. "Another of our fine Mayfair whips headed out on a lark."

Wynwood leaned intently across the table. "Do you understand now, Merrick, why I worry about the children? London has grown too dangerous."

"Aye, it has that." The brandy came, and Merrick

poured then pushed one in Wynwood's direction. "Drink it. It will settle your nerves."

Wynwood was silent for a long moment. "I want you to build us a big house, Merrick," he finally said. "Quickly. A house where the children can still see the trees, and aren't apt to get mown down by a mail coach. A place where Vivie can have a little peace."

"Your wife is feeling the strain of her career?" asked Merrick.

Wynwood smiled wryly. "No, to be honest, my wife is feeling the strain of being with child," he confessed. "But yes, the opera is wearing her thin, too."

Merrick's eyes widened. "Congratulations, old chap!"

"We are thrilled, of course," Wynwood went on. "Her morning sickness has almost passed. But everything else is going wrong. Her lead soprano quit in a temper last week and went back to Milan. Unfortunately, the understudy sounds like a choirboy fending off puberty. Now Vivie's half-afraid she's going to have to sing the lead herself—which is what Signor Bergonzi wanted all along anyway."

"Ah, Bergonzi!" said Merrick. "I rather like your new father-in-law, Wynwood. He is so politely ruthless."

"I like him, too," said Wynwood. "But he is a part of the problem."

"Aye? In what way?"

"He needs space," said Wynwood. "Music rooms! Parlors! Pianofortes! Merrick, the man has stuffed my smoking parlor full of cellos and violas, and there is an old harpsichord standing on end in the butler's pantry. Worse, the children have nearly burst the seams of the schoolroom—"

"Schoolroom?" Merrick interjected. "I did not know you had one."

"Well, it was my billiards room," Wynwood admitted glumly. "And I should like to have it back *someday*."

"Forget it, old chap. That same misfortune once befell Alasdair."

Wynwood did not look consoled. "Now Mamma, Henry, and my sister Alice have come down for the season with her three children. Alice is as big as a house herself, and they say she's likely having twins this time. Merrick, I'm desperate, and in a dreadful rush. Can you not simply knock out a wall between a couple of those terraced houses near the river? I'll just buy two of the bloody things."

"That is not a bad notion," said Merrick. "Why do we not go have a look? You seem to have lost your appetite."

"What of you?"

"I never had one," Merrick admitted. "I never eat during the day."

Wynwood grinned. "Alasdair claims you never eat at all unless you can do so in *his* dining room," he said. "But that will be hard to do, old boy, with the bride and groom gone back to Scotland."

"I finally built myself a house," Merrick reminded him. "I do have servants."

"You built a house and stuffed all your employees into it," Wynwood corrected. "It is not at all the same thing. Alasdair, you do not even *have* a dining room, last I saw."

"My draughtsmen have need of it," Merrick complained. "I can eat off a tray at my desk. Now, do you mean to come along and look at these bloody houses or not?"

Wynwood shut his mouth, and they set off.

The walk along the river was not a long one, and the breeze blowing in off the Thames helped clear Merrick's head. The sun was unseasonably warm, and both gentle-men were compelled to loosen their neckcloths. Soon they reached an area of excavation where six sweat-stained men were assiduously digging out a cellar. Adjacent, three masons were mortaring the stone foundation of a second house, and beyond that, carpenters were framing up the skeleton of yet a third. Running up the street beyond them were another ten terraced houses, the next nearer com-pletion than the one before it.

"Good Lord," said Wynwood, surveying the scene. "This is like a mill without walls—except that you are churning out houses instead of stockings."

"Just so," said Merrick. "And therein lies a part of the cost savings—or perhaps I should say profit. Now, do you wish a corner house?"

"I should prefer it, yes."

"Well, the topmost house has been spoken for," said Merrick. "Rosenberg sent the papers last week. You will have to wait on these two at the bottom of the hill."

Wynwood's face fell. "Blast!" he said. "That house above is perfect."

"It will take the wind coming off the river," Merrick warned. "So will be more expensive to heat. Besides, a widow from Yorkshire has already contracted for it."

Wynwood winked. "Contracted—but not yet taken title, eh?" he said. "Come, Merrick, we are old friends. The heat-ing means nothing to me."

"Aye, spoken like an Englishman!"

"Besides, you do not even know this woman. What if I paid the costs associated with breaking the contract?"

"My word is my bond," said Merrick coldly. "Choose another, my friend. Or go back to Belgravia and buy one of those white monstrosities from Tom Cubitt. It is neither here nor there to me."

"Yes, yes, you are right, of course," Wynwood had the grace to look embarrassed. "I am just desperate to please my wife. These lower houses are lovely. But they are not even. One will sit a little higher up the hill, will it not?"

"Yes, and I shall use it to good advantage," said Merrick. "If they are connected by short flights of stairs in the public rooms, it will have the feel of two houses, but there will be a measure of privacy on the upper floors. I can design it such that musical rooms and Bergonzi's parlor are on one side, and the schoolroom and nursery needs are confined to the other. Two dining rooms, even, if you wish."

"That sounds perfect." Wynwood scrubbed a hand thoughtfully along his jaw. "Now, what will the interior look like? I must give Vivie a full report."

"I can show you the house at the top of the hill." Merrick extracted a ring of keys from his coat pocket. "Your interior, of course, will be designed to meet your family's needs. But the millwork, the joinery, the floors and ceilings, all that will be similar unless you wish otherwise."

There were no workmen near the top of the hill, and the din of construction faded into the distance as they walked. Still, Merrick could hear a muffled banging noise from within the topmost house as they went up the steps. How very odd.

Wynwood turned to Merrick with a quizzical look. "Someone is inside."

"They damned well oughtn't be," said Merrick. "The first coat of paint went on yesterday and has scarce had time to dry."

The banging did not relent. Merrick twisted the key and went in. Sun glared through the large, undraped windows, leaving the air stifling hot and rendering the smell of paint almost intolerable. At once, he and Wynwood started toward the racket—a side parlor which opened halfway along the central corridor. A tall, slender woman with cornsilk-colored hair stood with her back to them, banging at one of the window frames with the heels of her hands.

Merrick looked at Wynwood. "Excuse me," he said tightly. "The buyer, I presume."

"I shall just wander upstairs," said Wynwood, starting up the staircase. "I wish to size up the bedchambers."

"Oh, bloody damned hell!" said the woman in the parlor.

Merrick strode into the room. "Good God, stop banging on the windows!"

The woman shrieked, and clapped a hand to her chest. "Oh, my!" she said, glancing over her shoulder. "You nearly gave me heart failure!"

"It would be a less painful end than bleeding to death, I daresay."

"I beg your pardon?" she said, turning from the window. She was looking not at him, but at the empty paint containers. She gave one a dismissive nudge with the toe of her slipper. But he could see her face now, and inexplicably, his breath hitched.

No. No, he was mistaken.

"The paint sticks the windows shut," he managed to continue. "They must be razored open, ma'am. And if you persist in pounding at the sash, you're apt to get a gashed wrist for your trouble."

"Indeed?" Her eyebrows went up a little haughtily as she tossed him another dismissing glance. For a moment, he could not get his lungs to work. Dear God in heaven.

No. No, it could not be.

Merrick's thoughts went skittering like marbles. There must be some mistake. That damned wedding yesterday—that trip to the church—it had disordered his mind.

"Well, I shall keep your brilliant advice in mind," she finally went on. "Now, this room was to be hung with yellow silk, not painted." She waved her arm about expansively. "Dare I hope that you are someone who can get that fixed?"

"Perhaps." Merrick stepped from the shadows and into the room. "I am the owner of this house."

"Oh, I think not," she said, her voice low and certain. "I contracted for its purchase on Wednesday last."

"Yes, from my solicitors, perhaps," said Merrick. *Good God, surely . . . surely he was wrong.* For the first time in a decade, he felt truly unnerved. "I—er, I employ Mr. Rosenberg's firm to handle such transactions," he managed to continue. "Pray look closely at your contract. You will see that the seller is MacGregor & Company."

At last, she turned to fully look at him. Suddenly, her expression of haughty disdain melted into one of grave misgiving. There was a long, uncomfortable silence. "And . . . and so you would be Mr. MacGregor, then?" she asked breathlessly.

There was more than a question in her words. There was a pleading; a wish to avoid the unavoidable. Her clear green eyes slid down the scar which curved the length of his face. *She was not sure.* But oh God, he was.

"You look . . . familiar," she went on, but her voice was no longer steady. "I am Lady Bessett. Tell me, have—have we met?"

Dear God! Had they met? A sort of nausea was roiling in his stomach now. He could feel the perspiration breaking on his brow. He opened his mouth with no notion of what he was to say. Just then, Wynwood came thundering down the stairs.

"Eight bedchambers, old chap!" The earl's shouting echoed through the empty house. "So a double would have sixteen, am I right?" He strode into the room, then stopped abruptly. "Oh, I do beg your pardon," he said, his eyes running over the woman. "My new neighbor, I collect? Pray introduce me."

Merrick felt as if all his limbs had gone numb. "Yes. Yes, of course." He lifted one hand by way of introduction. "May I present to you, ma'am, the Earl of Wynwood. Wynwood, this is . . . this is . . ." The hand fell in resignation. "This is Madeleine, Quin. This is . . . my wife."

The woman's face had drained of all color. She made a strange little choking sound, and in a blind, desperate gesture, her hand lashed out as if to steady herself. She grasped at nothing but air. Then her knees gave, and she crumpled to the floor in a pool of dark green silk.

"Christ Jesus!" said Wynwood. He knelt, and began to pat at her cheek. "Ma'am, are you all right? Ma'am?"

"No, she is not all right," said Merrick tightly. "She can't get her breath. This air—the paint—it must be stifling her. Quick, get back. We must get her air."

As if she were weightless, Merrick slid an arm under Madeleine's knees, then scooped her into his arms. A few short strides, and they were outside in the dazzling daylight.

"Put her in the grass," Wynwood advised. "Good God, Merrick! Your *wife*? I thought—thought she was dead! Or—or gone off to India! Or some damned thing!"

"Rome, I believe," said Merrick. "Apparently, she has come back."

Gently, he settled Madeleine in the small patch of newly sprouted grass. She was coming around now. His heart was in his throat, his mind racing with questions. Wynwood held one of her hands and was patting at it vigorously. On his knees in the grass, Merrick set one hand on his thigh and dropped his head as if to pray.

But there was little to pray for now.

He had prayed never to see Madeleine again. God had obviously denied him that one small mercy. He pinched his nose between two fingers, as if the pain might force away the memories.

Madeleine had managed to struggle up onto her elbows.

"I say, ma'am." Wynwood was babbling now. "So sorry. Didn't mean to frighten you. Are you perfectly all right? Haven't seen old Merrick in a while, I collect? A shock, I'm sure. Yes, yes, a shock."

"Shut up, Quin," said Merrick.

"Yes, yes, of course," he agreed. "I shan't say a word. Daresay you two have lots to catch up on. I—I should go, perhaps? Or stay? Or—no, I have it! Perhaps Mrs. MacLachlan would like me to fetch some brandy?"

On this, the lady gave a withering cry, and pressed the back of her hand to her forehead.

"Do *shut up*, Quin," said Merrick again.

His eyes widened. "Yes, yes, I meant to do."

Madeleine was struggling to her feet now. Her heavy blond hair was tumbling from its arrangement. "Let me up," she insisted. "Stand aside, for God's sake!"

"Oh, I shouldn't get up," Wynwood warned. "Your head is apt to be swimming still."

But Madeleine had eyes only for Merrick—and they were blazing with hot green rage. "I do not know," she hissed, "what manner of ill-thought joke this is, sir. But you—you are *not* my husband."

"Now is hardly the time to discuss it, Madeleine," Merrick growled. "Let me summon my carriage and see you safely to your lodgings."

But Madeleine was already backing away, her face a mask of horror. "No," she choked. "Absolutely not. You—you are quite mad. And cruel, too. Very cruel. You always were. I came to see it, you know. I *did*. Now stay away from me! Stay away! Do you hear?"

It was the closest she came to acknowledging she even knew him. And then she turned and hastened up the hill on legs which were obviously unsteady.

A gentleman would have followed her at a distance, just to be sure she really was capable of walking. Merrick no longer felt like a gentleman. He felt . . . eviscerated. Gutted like a fish and left to rot in the heat of his wife's hatred.

Lord Wynwood watched her go, his hand shielding his eyes as they squinted into the sun. "You know, I don't think she much cares for you, old chap," he said, when Madeleine's skirts had swished around the corner and out of sight.

"Aye, that would explain her thirteen-year absence, would it not?" said Merrick sourly.

"More or less," his friend agreed. "I hope you were not looking forward to a reconciliation."

"Just shut up, Quin," said Merrick again.

Wynwood seemed to take no offense, but nor did he listen. "Tell me, Merrick," he said. "Have you any of that fine Finlaggan whisky in your desk?"

"Damned right I do. A full bottle."

Wynwood let his hand fall. "Well, it's a start," he said, turning and heading down the hill. "Now come along, old fellow. I very much fear we are going to need it before this night's out."

Chapter Four

Ne'er marry for money;
ye can borrow it cheaper.

Madeleine rushed through the village in a blind panic. *Home.* She had to get home. This was insane. This was not possible. On the next corner, she pushed past a gentleman leaving the tobacconist, forcing him to step off the pavement. Farther along the street, Mrs. Beck called out a cheery hello from the post office. Madeleine looked at the woman blankly and hurried on by.

Home. She had to get home. Her eyes searched wildly for her street and, seeing it, she turned. The tidy stone cottage sat at the end of the lane, solid and reassuring. She hastened toward it, looking, she later realized, a bit like a madwoman. She flung herself against the door, threw up the latch, and darted in, slamming the door behind her and sending the rest of her hair tumbling down.

Mrs. Drexel, her new housekeeper, was passing through the sitting room with a tray in her hands. "Good afternoon, my lady!" she said in mild surprise. "Is . . . is something amiss?"

"Eliza," said Madeleine, gasping for breath. "I need Eliza. Where is she?"

The woman bobbed. "In the kitchen with Clara. I'll send her straight up."

Madeleine went up to her room and threw back the draperies which overlooked the little lane below. Her eyes ran the length of it, seeing nothing. But how foolish she was to even look! Did she really imagine he had *followed* her? If he hadn't bothered to do so thirteen years ago, why would he trouble himself now?

Perhaps she really was going insane. Perhaps Merrick— or the thought of him—had finally succeeded in driving her stark staring mad.

Her maid came in, crossed the room, and touched her lightly on the shoulder. "My lady, what is it? What is wrong?"

"Oh, Eliza!" Madeleine let the draperies fall, and turned, her fingertips pressed to her lips. "Oh, dear God! It is *him.*"

"Who, my lady?" Eliza's hand was warm and reassuring. "It cannot be as bad as all that."

"It can." The words came out low and desperate. "He—he has come back. After all these years, he has come back."

Eliza stiffened abruptly. "Mr. MacLachlan?" she whispered. "Is that who you'd be meaning?"

Mutely, Madeleine nodded.

"Mary, Jesus, and Joseph," she whispered. Then, as if thinking better of her words, she gave Madeleine's shoulder a reassuring squeeze. "Perhaps, my lady, you imagined it? Perhaps you saw . . . a relation? Someone who resembled him? There was a brother, you once said."

"Sir Alasdair." Madeleine shook her head. "But they look nothing alike."

She went to the bed and sat down on it, tired and beaten. In flat, emotionless words, she relayed the entire story to her maid. "And so he is the man, it seems, who has built all these grand houses," she finished. "Or he owns the company that built them. Or *something* like that. It seems he did not go back to Scotland after all."

"Dear Lord!" said Eliza. "And his *wife*, he claimed? Why, of all the nerve!"

"Why would he say that, Eliza?" She looked up pleadingly at her maid. "Why, after all these years would he say such a thing?"

"Why, I cannot think!" said the maid. "Perhaps that's how he sees it?"

"How could he?" Madeleine cried. "He—he *wanted* to be free of me! Or he wanted Papa's money, at any rate. No, he never wanted me. Not really. Oh, Eliza, it is too cruel! I thought with Bessett dead, I might live out my life in peace. Is that too much to ask, Eliza? *Is* it?"

Eliza took her hand, and gave it a reassuring squeeze. "It is cruel, ma'am, and that's the truth," she said. "But perhaps this will be the last of it. Perhaps you'll never see him again."

"Oh, I pray I shall not!" Madeleine's shoulders fell. "He looks—oh, Eliza, he looks . . . so different. So dark. Almost demonic. His hands are so long, his eyes so cold! And there is this scar—a horrid, horrid scar—oh, I cannot quite explain it. He looked himself, and yet entirely different. Does that make any sense at all?"

"I think I understand," said Eliza, beginning to fluff the bed pillows. "The wicked never age well, or so they say."

Madeleine flashed her a skeptical look. "I never heard that."

Eliza gave a lame smile, and changed the subject. "Your new friend Lady Treyhern called whilst you were out."

"Did she? Why, I did not expect . . ."

"She wishes you to come to tea on Saturday. And she wishes you to bring Mr. Geoffrey."

"Oh, my!" Madeleine set her fingertips to her temple. "Geoff. Where is he?"

"He went out about two o'clock, my lady," said Eliza. "He seemed his happy, regular self again. You—you do not mind, do you?"

Somehow, Madeleine found the energy to shake her head. "The exercise does him good," she said quietly. "Dr. Fellows said it was not good for his—his *moods* to sit around with his nose stuck in a book."

"Aye, he's twelve now, and a grown-up twelve at that," said Eliza. "There's no harm that'll come to him in the village."

"No, I doubt it," Madeleine agreed. "Oh, Eliza! This village! That *house*. How can I live in it now, knowing he is here?"

Eliza patted her hand again. "Oh, I doubt he means to make trouble, ma'am," she said. "If he'd meant to, he'd have done it a long time ago. And you'll not need to see him. *Will* you, ma'am?"

"I—I do not know," Madeleine admitted. "This is such a small village. If he means to go about telling people that I am his *wife*—well, I simply cannot have it. He really must be made to stop. Oh, perhaps I should go to Mr. Rosenberg tomorrow and just ask him to tear up the contract? Perhaps we shall live in Town after all? Would you mind terribly, Eliza?"

"I think *you* would mind, my lady," said Eliza soothingly. "And I think you would be angry with yourself for giving up yet another thing that you had your heart set on."

A wry smile tugged at Madeleine's mouth. "You know me too well, Eliza."

"I know you well enough," agreed the maid. "Now, why don't you lie down and have a rest? Your head hurts, that's something else I know. I'm going to fetch a cool cloth for your brow and draw the draperies. You'll think what to do soon enough—and woe betide Mr. MacLachlan then."

Madeleine did stretch out across the bed, but she did not surrender to the tears which had threatened earlier. "No, I shan't let him best me, Eliza," she vowed. "I am down, but far from done for."

"That's more like you, ma'am," Eliza encouraged as she yanked the draperies closed. "You're in the right, and he's in the wrong. That, and you're missing Loughton, and you had a bad morning with Mr. Geoffrey. It takes a toll, my lady."

"But I shall recover, shan't I?" said Madeleine grimly. "If he means to cause trouble for me, he won't find the meek little girl he left behind. I have learnt to survive—and I'll be damned if Merrick MacLachlan will get the best of me again. Not in the long run."

Eliza had her hand on the doorknob. "Are you sure, then, that you wish to see Mr. Rosenberg, ma'am?" she asked, tossing a glance over her shoulder.

For a moment, Madeleine considered it. "Perhaps not, Eliza," she answered. "Or perhaps Mr. Rosenberg can shed some light on this situation. There are some serious questions I should like an answer to."

By the time the maid returned with a cool cloth and a cup of tea, Madeleine had kicked off her shoes, and was staring blindly at the ceiling as she replayed this afternoon's disaster in her mind. But this time, she did not swoon. Instead, she cracked Merrick soundly across the face with the flat of her hand and told him just how much she had hated him all these years.

The tea was blessedly hot, but she soon realized it was laced with one of Eliza's soothing concoctions. Madeleine did not ask what it was, and instead simply drank it down. After today's horrible events, she was content to simply give herself over into Eliza's capable hands. And by the time the maid rechecked the curtains to ensure that not a sliver of light penetrated the room, Madeleine was beginning to drift away.

She was thinking, oddly, of Merrick—not as he was, but as she had once seen him through young and guileless eyes. She had loved him with a depth and breadth she had not known was possible. He had seemed invincible and passionate. Brilliant. Gentle. And worldly—or so she had believed. But in the end, he had proven as naïve and stupid as had she.

No. No, that was not right. Madeleine curled her hand into her pillow, and struggled to think straight. To remember. Merrick had played upon her naïveté. He had pretended to be passionate and gentle. Was that not the truth? Was that not what Papa had said? But as the fog of sleep began to thicken, Madeleine found she was no longer sure. No longer certain where the veil of sweet memories ended, and the harsh, horrid truth began.

"*Look, Maddie!*" *Cousin Becky's lips were warm against her ear.* "*That man—the architect—he's staring at you again.*"

Madeleine drew herself fully up on the picnic blanket and looked across the expanse of grass. There he was. The very tall, very dark young man from last night. And from several nights before that, too. He regarded her as boldly as ever, his ice-blue eyes burning with an intensity she was just beginning to understand. Her pulse leapt wildly. Madeleine steadied herself with one hand, digging her fingers into the spring grass as if it might hold her heart earthbound.

"*He is a nobody, Madeleine!*" *hissed Cousin Imogene.* "*The younger son of some Scottish baronet no one ever heard of—and his brother is a frightful rake. Do not return his gaze, I beg you. Mamma says he is presumptuous, and ought never have been invited here.*"

Becky laughed at her sister. "*You are just jealous, Imogene, because he did not dance with you last night. But he danced with me—and twice with Maddie!*"

Imogene lifted her nose in the air. "*Maddie is just out of the schoolroom,*" *she said.* "*She knows no better. But you do—and I tell you that Mr. MacLachlan is no gentleman. Why, Mamma overheard him offer to design a seaside villa for Lord Morton—and for money!*"

"*Yes, and Lord Morton jumped at the chance, did he not?*" *said Becky in a low, almost seductive voice.* "*As for me, I should jump at the chance to dance with him again. He is a true artist, they say.*"

"*He is a true pauper,*" *said her sister with a sniff.*

"*Well, he is quite the handsomest pauper I have ever seen,*"

Becky returned. "I think I should like to live with a starving artist. It would be divinely romantic, would it not?"

"You would starve, too." Imogene snapped her fingers for emphasis. "Papa would cut you off like that."

"All the more for you, then, Imogene." Becky turned back to her young cousin so fast her ringlets bounced. "Maddie, you could have him! After all, you are an heiress."

"I—I do not know." Madeleine could not tear her eyes away from the dark young man's. "I am afraid Papa will refuse."

"Of course he will!" said Imogene huffily. "You are to marry Lord Henry Winters, and everyone knows it."

"I do not know it," said Madeleine quietly.

Imogene looked impatient. "Oh, Maddie, don't be a goose!" she said. "How is Uncle Howard to become Prime Minister if you do not?"

"I can't see what one has to do with the other," she answered.

"That is how politics works, you gudgeon," said Imogene. "You marry Henry, then Henry's father and his conservative coalition will ally with Uncle Howard's friends, and then Uncle will have a majority in the—"

"Hush, Imogene!" Becky reached out and pinched her sister's arm. "You are just wrong. Uncle would never use Maddie in such a way."

"That is how the world works," Imogene chided. "Honestly, Becky, one would think you are as green from the country as Madeleine."

But Madeleine was barely listening now. The dark young man—Mr. Merrick MacLachlan—was moving toward her, pacing inexorably across the grass, and bringing his burning blue eyes with him. Her heart leapt wildly, and her stomach turned upside down. She hoped—oh, yes, she hoped he would try to kiss her again.

He bent low over their blanket and offered an arm which looked strong and supple. A gold ring glittered on his little finger. "Lady Madeleine," he said in his faint Scots accent, "would you care tae stroll wi' me up the riverbank?"

Madeleine could not get her breath. "Why—I—I don't—" She stopped, and swallowed hard. She was a little bit afraid of him. And even more afraid of herself. "Yes, Mr. MacLachlan. Very much."

Madeleine did not look about for Aunt Emma, though she knew she should have done. She was almost certain Mr. MacLachlan was the sort of man her aunt had warned her about.

He spoke not another word but instead escorted her straight up the river until the picnic was but flickers of sound and color amongst the trees. Until the rhododendron became a thicket. Until the murmur of the gathering and the murmur of the water was one. Then he stopped and set her back against a slender tree. For a timeless moment, his heavy, ice-blue eyes roamed over her face, then his lashes dropped shut, and he lowered his mouth to hers.

Madeleine felt her knees go weak, and felt something delightfully wicked go twisting through her belly, just as it had last night. And then he was kissing her in a different way, opening his mouth over hers, and thrusting his tongue into her mouth with silken, languid motions. The sensation twisted lower, sending raw desire through her body. She began to tremble, and somehow got the heels of her hands against his shoulders. She pushed him halfheartedly away.

He lifted his mouth, and drew back.

"We might be caught," she whispered.

His feverish gaze consumed her. "Aye, but I do nae care," he rasped. "Do you?"

"I—I have no wish to make my father angry," she answered. "And this kind of kissing—it is wrong, is it not?"

"Not if we care for one another," he whispered.

"But you scarcely know me."

There was a stubborn glint in his eye. "I know you well enough," he said. "Well enough to know you're the woman for me. And well enough to know you want me."

"Has anyone ever mentioned that you are a little presumptuous, Mr. MacLachlan?"

The hint of a grin tugged at his mouth. "Do you deny it, lass? Say it plain, and I'll walk awa' "

She licked her lips uncertainly. "No. No, I cannot say it."

The black, sinfully long lashes dropped shut once more, and somehow, they were kissing again. Deeper. More intently. His skillful hands roamed over her body, honing her need to a sharp, keening ache. Her skin was afire, and she yearned for . . . oh, for something!

When he stopped, she could scarcely get her breath. "Mr. MacLachlan!" she managed to say. "You are taking liberties which you oughtn't."

He looked at her with deadly seriousness. "Aye, but I mean to mend that soon enough," he vowed. "I mean to marry you."

Madeleine tried to look at him chidingly. "You are a shockingly arrogant man."

"Och, no," he said. "Just a determined one."

She lifted her chin. "And if I've no wish to marry you?"

"Aye, perhaps you willna'," he acknowledged softly. "For I've no beautiful words tae charm you. And I've little tae give, save the strength of my back and the talent in my hands—but enough of both tae keep a roof o'er your head."

His earnestness impressed her. "And that's all, is it?"

He held her gaze steadily. "Aye, that's all," he said, his grip *on her shoulders tightening.* "*Is it enough, lass, to win you?*"

She looked up at him coyly. "*I am not perfectly sure, Mr. MacLachlan,*" *she teased.* "*Perhaps you ought to kiss me again, and help me decide?*"

His eyes warmed. "*A kiss bedamned,*" *he said, grinning.* "*I want you in my bed.*"

"*Another of your strengths, I take it?*" *she murmured.* "*Or would that be a talent?*"

"*Tormenting wench!*" *he said, dragging her against his chest.* "*Just take me tae bed and judge for yourself.*"

"*I—I dare not,*" *she whispered.*

Something in his eyes commanded her. "*Tonight,*" *he said.* "*Dare. I'll come tae your window.*"

"*Oh, God!*" *Madeleine squeezed her eyes shut.* "*My father will kill you if he finds out.*"

"*Then I'll die a happy man,*" *he said solemnly.* "*I need to see you. We can just talk, Maddie, if that's all you want.*"

Dear God, it was not all she wanted. "*But we won't just talk,*" *she rasped.* "*It—it isn't like that with us, is it? Even I know it.*"

He hugged her tightly to him. "*I shall throw a pebble against the glass. Will you let me in, lass?*"

Madeleine swallowed hard, and almost against her will, nodded. And then his mouth came crushing down again, leaving her weak-kneed and feverish . . .

"Just who is she, Merrick, anyway?" Wynwood asked, some two hours later. His booted feet were propped on Merrick's desk, and he cradled a glass of dark, rich whisky in his hands. "Or rather, who *was* she? I never did hear, you know."

Merrick rose from his desk and went to the sideboard.

Amongst his family and close friends, the rash marriage of his youth was not precisely a secret. But as if by some unspoken agreement, it was never mentioned.

Merrick did not especially wish to speak of it now, but Wynwood had been put in a dashed awkward position. And Wynwood was some years younger than he. It was as well he did not know who Madeleine was, for his ignorance suggested there had been little gossip over the years. Idle talk was a treacherous thing. It could affect a man's business in ways which were unpredictable.

"Are you evading my question, old friend?" Wynwood's voice recalled him to the present. "Feel free to tell me to go to the devil. My feelings are not easily wounded."

Merrick yanked the stopper from the crystal decanter. "Lady Madeleine Howard," he replied, his voice flat as he refilled his glass. "She is the daughter of the Earl of Jessup—or was."

Wynwood's brow furrowed, then cleared. "What, that old ramrod-stiff conservative?" he asked. "Called him 'the Sword of Sheffield,' didn't they?"

"Aye, because he cut his enemies off at the knees," Merrick answered.

"Can't say as I ever followed political intrigue," Wynwood admitted. "And yet the name is known, even to me. A nasty piece of work, I always heard. Dead now, isn't he?"

"He died in his sleep some years past."

And it was a far better death than the bastard had deserved, too. Merrick returned to his chair and sipped slowly at his whisky. Very slowly. Neither Lady Madeleine Howard nor her pompous prick of a father was worth rushing a fine bottle of Finlaggan. Indeed, *she* was not even worth the rage and lust which had been churning in his stomach just two hours past. And so he had cut it off, as one might cut off the head of a snake: quickly and cleanly, lest it bite.

He felt nothing now but the slow burn of the whisky, and his usual impatience to be on with something—his next meeting, his next project, anything that might take him out of himself, and into the world of the practical and the rational. But he could scarcely throw his friend out, particularly when he had, in fact, come to do business.

Wynwood continued to probe, but tentatively. "Your marriage to the chit was not commonly known, I take it?"

Merrick shook his head, and stared into the depths of his office. "We eloped," he answered. "Near the end of her first season. Did Alasdair never tell you that tale?"

"No. Should he have done?"

Merrick gave a bark of bitter laughter. "It was pathetic, really," he said. "I pinched Alasdair's gig, and we bolted for Gretna Green with all of thirty pounds in our pockets."

"The deuce!" Wynwood's bootheels hit the floor. "I never knew anyone who actually pulled that off. How in God's name did you do it?"

Desperately. Passionately. And with the devil's breath on his heels.

"Oh, the usual way." Merrick gave a hard, muted smile. "Fervent messages from maid to footman. A pair of portmanteaus and a ladder to the window. Then a midnight getaway, of course. No elopement would be complete were one to leave at a reasonable hour, would it?"

Wynwood grinned. "And the old man did not catch you?"

"Not soon enough."

"And then?"

Merrick lifted one brow. This had gone far enough, even between friends. "And then what, Quinten?" he murmured. "Old gossip does not line my pockets, you know. Do you not have a house to buy?"

Wynwood regarded him strangely. "Well, if you mean to be—"

His words were interrupted by a sharp knock at the door. Phipps, Merrick's butler-cum-valet came in. "A Miss Bromley is here for a four o'clock appointment."

A woman stood in the shadows beyond Phipps's shoulder. She was dressed head to toe in black silk, wearing a beaded black veil which obscured her eyes and teased at her wide, thin mouth. A small bandbox swung from one wrist, and a vast amount of creamy white cleavage swelled from the neckline of her gown. Miss Bromley definitely had not come to discuss real estate.

Wynwood lifted both eyebrows this time and shot Merrick an appraising look as he came to his feet. "I shall return tomorrow," he said quietly, "and leave you to your—er, your *appointment*, old chap."

Merrick casually lifted one shoulder, and polished off his whisky. "Stay on if you wish," he murmured. "I am feeling generous today."

Wynwood's eyes flared with alarm. "Afraid I gave that up, old fellow." His glass hit the desk with an abrupt *clunk*. "I'd best be off. I shall speak to the wife, and call tomorrow, all right?"

Phipps had already vanished. Miss Bromley observed Wynwood's departure with obvious amusement, her mouth turned up in an odd half smile.

"Your friend is newly wed, is he not?" Her voice was soft, yet somehow raspy.

Merrick did not answer. "You are from Mrs. Farnham's?"

"I'm Bess," she said, lifting back the veil to reveal a pair of cold, dark eyes. *Perfect*, he thought. He was not in the mood for warmth. He was very glad indeed he'd got rid of Kitty and her good-humored, almost childlike, smile.

He locked the office door and crossed the room. The woman followed him into the parlor which he had converted to a bedchamber so that he might remain as close to his office as was possible.

He stood by the window and regarded her for a moment, his arms crossed thoughtfully over his chest. He had quite forgotten that this was Thursday. She was beautiful, if a man liked his women dark, bold, and voluptuous. He did, sometimes. But today, he was half-tempted to send the woman away. He was not in the mood.

Or was he?

He thought again of Madeleine, of what a blow to the gut it had been to see her again after so many empty years. But what had he expected? In thirteen years, there had been not so much as a hint of regret from the woman. Inexplicably, the black, burning rage began to threaten again, licking like a nascent flame at the edges of his mind.

Bess Bromley seemed to feel his wrath. Her eyes flicked up at him, dark and knowing.

She was a full six inches shorter than Madeleine, with hair as dark as a crow's wing, and a mouth which was thin and wide, in sharp contrast to his wife's pale blond hair and full, almost plump, lower lip. Indeed, the two could hardly have been more dissimilar. Good. That was very good indeed. He had given up bedding beautiful, long-legged blondes after the first two or three years had passed.

Bess Bromley tossed her hat and veil onto a chair, and

dropped her bandbox in the middle of the narrow, roughly dressed cot which served as his bed. The box landed on its side with a bounce. The lid fell off, and a thin leather whip unfurled onto the bed. There were other things in the box, too. His quick gaze took them in. He was no fool; he knew the tools of her sort of trade.

As if to dare him, Bess closed the distance between them. She encircled his neck with one arm, drawing her breasts to his chest and gently cradling the back of his head in her palm. Her gaze ran down the scar on his face, then her lashes dropped half-shut. "Poor little Kitty!" she said in her dusky whisper. "She did not know quite how to handle a man like you."

Merrick looked down at her. "Kitty managed well enough."

Delicate as a butterfly, Bess Bromley stroked the tip of her tongue down the scar's length. "Kitty thinks you might like it rough, MacLachlan," she said suggestively. "Tell me, is she right?"

"Sometimes," he admitted.

Without warning, Bess set her hot, open mouth against his throat, and sank her teeth hard into his flesh. His breath seized at the pain, but he did not flinch. "And what of you, my dear?" he whispered, he asked, filling his hand with her arse and pulling her body to his. "Do *you* like it rough?"

She made him no answer, but shuddered in his embrace.

As if it moved of its own volition, Merrick's hand went to her shoulder, dragging the fabric down as stitches popped and silk tore. And why not? He was in a strange, black mood, the mood to tear something asunder, and if one thing was out of his reach, might not another do as well?

Beneath Bess's gown, she wore no chemise—and likely no drawers, either. Instead, one round, bare breast poured from her black corset, which was cut in a fashion long out of style and laced tightly enough to impair her breathing.

Bess did not seem troubled by its restraint. Beneath his gaze, her nipple peaked, and hardened. The areola was large and dark. Merrick looked away. He wished that her breasts were not so lush. He wished that they were smaller, paler, and that he could trace the fine, blue veins beneath her flesh with his fingertip. Indeed, he wished she was someone else altogether. The thought served only to make him angrier.

He set her away a little abruptly. "Take off your clothes," he gritted. "And lie down on the bed."

"But what if I don't wish to?" she whispered, a challenge lighting her eye. "What if you have to force me?"

A sneering smile curved his lips. "Aye, with that black leather whip of yours?" he suggested. "Is that what you want, my dear?"

Bess picked up the whip in one hand and drew the lash across the opposite palm almost erotically, as if she enjoyed every bump and twist of the braid. "Kitty says you've scars." The words were but a raspy whisper. "Lots of them. Deep, wicked ones."

"Kitty talks too damned much."

Bess drew her tongue across her lower lip. "Take off your clothes," she said, her eyes quick and greedy. "I like a man who's marked. Let me see, MacLachlan, just how much you can take."

More than you could dole out in a thousand years, he

thought. More than was humanly possible. But he was damned if he meant to discuss it with her. "I think you forget, my dear, just who is being paid to perform a service here."

She took a step toward him, and made a moue with her brightly painted lips. "Poor Mr. MacLachlan," she cooed. "You've been bedding that bland, boring Kitty for far too long. I know you. I know your type. I *know what you need.* I can smell the rage on your skin."

He caught her wrist and jerked her hard against him, then crushed her mouth beneath his. Still holding the whip, she thrust her tongue deep into his mouth, then drew out again and viciously bit his lip.

Rage exploding in his head. He jerked back. "Why, you little bitch!"

Her eyes glittered dangerously. "That was very cruel of me, was it not?" she returned. "You are angry."

MacLachlan touched the back of his hand gingerly to his bleeding lip and stepped back. "You're goddamned right, I'm angry."

Bess chuckled quietly. "You were angry the moment I walked into the room," she returned. "I have merely given you a place to spend it."

"Hush up, damn you." Merrick kicked the bandbox into the floor. She was closer to the truth than he wished to admit. "Just be quiet and take off your clothes. I want a quick, hard fuck. Then I want you out of here."

Bess Bromley slowly drew down the other sleeve of her tawdry black gown, revealing her shoulder, and then her breast, pushed high and held fast by the harsh restraints of the corset. The thing was laced up the back with leather cording, he realized when she turned to toss the gown onto a chair. And beneath it, she wore nothing but black stockings, rolled high and tight on slender, milk white thighs. The contrast was startling. Erotic.

She turned back around, and smiled seductively. "I have been very cruel," she said again. She set one knee to the mattress, then slowly crawled onto the bed on all fours, her arse as bare as the day she was born. "I have made you angry," she went on, lying down on her stomach.

"I begin to think you might be mad," he remarked.

"Perhaps I am." Her eyes drifted to the whip, which lay curled upon the carpet like a serpent. The tongue darted out again, moistening her lips. "But come, MacLachlan, and play Bess's little game. Come give me just what I deserve," she suggested. "You will enjoy it."

"Will I?"

One of her hands slipped under her belly, and slid lower. "Oh, yes," she said, her eyelids dropping shut. "I know you. Come, now. Make me . . . *oh, make me . . .*"

He was already half-persuaded. Perhaps it was what he needed. Perhaps he was as full of demons as he sometimes felt. But the whip, no. Never that.

The woman was writhing on his bed now. Against his will, his hands went to the buttons of his trousers, tearing them free. Damn his wife to hell, the faithless bitch. In an instant, he was crawling onto the bed, crawling over Bess, and forcing her legs wide with his knee. He entered her on one hard stroke, holding her buttocks firmly between his hands, stilling her to the invasion.

Bess's eyes opened wide, and she cried out from the shock.

He did not stop. Instead, he let the demons drive him, drive him toward the only expiation the black devils had ever yielded to. For long moments, he let the anger take him, until Bess's fingernails were clutching at his woolen counterpane, digging deep as she began to pant and grunt beneath him. Dimly, he heard her cry out, heard her pleading for more.

Merrick obliged her. Beneath him, her whole body seemed to seize. She shuddered once, twice, and collapsed onto the bed. He felt it coming on him then. The utter numbness. The physical collapse and the black, mindless void. The few insensate moments his sated body could buy him. He thrust once more, and felt himself fall.

Chapter Five

*Do na' suppose ye know a man 'til
ye come tae divide a spoil wi' him.*

The carriage ride through greater London and into the city was almost a two-hour trek through hellish traffic. Madeleine crossed her gloved hands neatly in her lap and tried to be patient. But the truth was, she might well have walked it more quickly, or taken one of the smaller, more nimble conveyances which one saw for hire throughout the capital. Her late father, however, had always impressed upon her the importance of looking the part of a wealthy, well-bred lady when paying a call of any sort.

She had been surprised when Mr. Rosenberg's summons arrived this morning. She had spent the last three days trying to decide whether to revisit his office, and if so, just how far she might press without arousing his suspicions. There was a nagging suspicion in the back of her mind. But Rosenberg had taken the matter out of her hands. His missive had come by a uniformed messenger during breakfast. The request had been exceedingly polite, almost fawning—and it had left her burning with curiosity.

From time to time, Madeleine craned her head, as if doing so might part the carts and coaches which choked the street they traveled. Her eyes went to a corner sign-post. *Fleet Street,* it was called. Madeleine had never heard of it, for she had traveled into east London but once in her life, to contract for the purchase of her new house. Indeed, save for the three months she'd spent in Mayfair as a girl, she knew almost nothing of this great, teeming city.

During her first visit to London, she had scarcely been permitted to venture beyond the exclusive shops of Bond Street. While the crooked, narrow, less elegant lanes had held an odd fascination for her, Madeleine's father, and Aunt Emma, who was to bring her out, had warned her early and often about the unseemliness of a young debutante's being seen in any place less refined than Astley's, or any place farther east than Hatchard's.

At the solicitor's office in Threadneedle Street, Madeleine was greeted by an obsequious young clerk, who bade her be seated, and went scurrying up the stairs in search of his master. Mr. Rosenberg greeted her warmly, and sent at once for coffee.

Madeleine made a pretense of asking a number of questions about the house, which he answered almost too cheerfully. "My clerks have prepared this for you," he said, when she paused for breath. He passed a sheaf of thick, cream-colored paper across the desk. "I wished you to have it at once. As you can see, the seller has countersigned here. We need only your signature just there, to the right of his."

He pointed to the bottom of the last page, but the name was not one which Madeleine recognized. "And who is this Mr. . . . . Mr. Evans, is it?"

Mr. Rosenberg waved one hand. "Oh, that is just a formality," he said. "Evans oversees the day-to-day operations of the business. He has signing authority on all deeds and contracts."

Madeleine's brows drew into a knot. "Rather like a clerk, do you mean?"

Rosenberg laughed. "Well, a very high-level clerk, in this case," he answered. "We are talking about an exceedingly large, remarkably successful enterprise which has diverse business interests all over London."

"But this company which built my new house—it is wholly owned by a Mr. MacLachlan, is it not?" Madeleine batted her eyes innocently. "I believe someone once said as much to me."

Rosenberg looked vaguely confused. "Well, yes. Of course."

Madeleine did not see any "of course" about it, but she smiled her most pleasant polite-society smile. "I wonder, Mr. Rosenberg, if you might answer one last question for me?"

"I shall try."

Madeleine decided to be blunt and ask the one thing she burned to know. "I admit to a rather prying curiosity," she said. "Just how did Mr. MacLachlan begin this exceedingly large business of his?"

Rosenberg frowned. "I am not sure I perfectly understand your question, Lady Bessett."

"Well, some men inherit a family business," she went on. "And some build their businesses over two or three decades. Mr. MacLachlan's rise, I gather, has been meteoric. I cannot but wonder how one so young became so successful so quickly."

Mr. Rosenberg nodded affably. "Yes, he is a very young man, is he not?" he answered. "And his—shall we say, *ambition*—is without question. But I think I see what you are asking, Lady Bessett. Mr. MacLachlan's business was begun in the same humble manner as are most. He had a loan from a family member."

"A—a loan?" she echoed disbelievingly. "Is that what he called it?"

Again, the cheerful nod. "And he would not mind my saying so, either," the solicitor went on. "His maternal grandmother financed his first few ventures. Hence the name."

"The name?"

"MacGregor," said the solicitor. "MacGregor & Company."

"He named it for his *grandmother*?"

But Mr. Rosenberg was studying her oddly. "You look skeptical, Lady Bessett," he remarked. "Had you some reason to believe otherwise?"

Swiftly, Madeleine shook her head. "No." She snatched her papers from the edge of the desk. "No, I was merely curious."

Mr. Rosenberg slid back his chair and laid his hands across his rather ample belly. "Well, it has been a pleasure meeting you again, Lady Bessett," he said. "If our paths do not cross again, I trust you will enjoy your new home."

Madeleine did not understand. "I'm sure I shall," she agreed, coming gracefully to her feet. "Kindly send word as soon as it is completed, and I shall bring a bank draft at once."

"A bank draft?" He seemed surprised.

Madeleine looked down at the papers she held. "This is my copy of the purchase contract, is it not? And now I am to bring a bank draft a fortnight hence, and take title to the property?"

Rosenberg slowly shook his head. "No," he said quietly. "No, Lady Bessett. What you hold there *is* the title to the property."

"But—but I have not paid you anything beyond the initial ten percent," she protested.

"A sum which has been remitted to your bank," said Rosenberg. "Mr. MacLachlan has deeded you the property, freehold."

Madeleine sat back down. Her head was swimming now. "He . . . he has *what?*"

Rosenberg looked more confused than she, if such a thing were possible. "Mr. MacLachlan said he was not comfortable being paid for the property under the circumstances," the solicitor tried to explain. "He said . . . he said that you would understand—that you were some sort of relation, or something to that effect."

A slow burn was coming over Madeleine. "He said *what?*" she asked. "Why, he must be mad!"

Rosenberg drew back an inch. "Are you not related, then?"

Madeleine felt her temper burst into full flame. "We are nothing of the sort!" she exclaimed, returning the title to his desk with a firm *thwack!* "I—why, I scarcely know the man! He cannot imagine that—why, he cannot possibly believe—oh, God! What can he be thinking?"

Rosenberg's hands went up in surrender. "I could not possibly say, ma'am," he assured her. "I know nothing of this business. I work for him, no more. You must take up your quarrel—if indeed you have one—with the gentleman himself."

"Yes, indeed!" said Madeleine with asperity. On second thought, she snatched back the deed. "Yes, I certainly shall!"

The dark-haired boy was back. This time, he sat perched on the stone lip of an old, abandoned well in a patch of weeds some fifty paces distant. Merrick had demolished an old cottage and cow byre on the site some months past, in order to make way for his next row of houses. But the well they had kept intact, so that the masons might draw water for mixing mortar.

Merrick had first noticed the lad perhaps a sen'night past. He had been shuffling down the lane which led through the village to the river, kicking stones as he came, his hands shoved deep into his coat pockets. Something in the excavation work at the foot of the hill had attracted his attention, and he had come perilously close to the edge.

Merrick had sent one of the carpenters, a grizzled old goat named Horton, to sternly warn him off. A building site was a dangerous thing. And children, especially bored young lads, were ever a hazard to themselves.

But the boy had not stayed away. Not completely. A little aggravated, Merrick stood in the warm sun now, his coat tossed aside, his shirtsleeves rolled up, and considered what ought to be done. Since the warning, the boy had kept his distance. And in truth, there was little risk to him where he sat. But he was here, quietly watching, almost as often as Merrick himself.

Perhaps he ought to run the boy off himself this time and do the job properly. Suddenly, the boy lifted something to his eyes and tilted back his head just an inch. The sun glinted brightly off whatever he held.

Intrigued, Merrick stepped from the dust and dirt of the construction, and into the road. Curiosity tugged at him, pulling him across the lane and into the patch of weeds. By the time he had reached the abandoned well, Merrick realized the boy had a pair of ladies' opera glasses in his hands and had an almost rapt expression upon his face. So engrossed was the lad in watching the roofing operations, he seemed not to hear Merrick's approach.

"That tall contraption is called a crane," said Merrick quietly.

At once, the lad jerked the glasses from his eyes. "Hullo," he said, scrambling down from the well's ledge. "I was just watching. Honest. I'm not getting in the way."

"I can see that," said Merrick.

He had quite forgotten that he had intended to send the boy away. Instead, he held his hands clasped behind his back and studied the child. He was tall and slender, but a certain sweetness in his face belied his height. He could not have been more than twelve, possibly less. Merrick knew next to nothing of children. Esmée, of course, had a two-year-old sister, but he avoided that little hellion at all costs.

This boy, however—well, he did not look quite so fearsome as a two-year-old in a full-blown fit of temper. He looked . . . almost interesting. There was a premature wisdom in the lad's dark green eyes, and an air of solemnity about him which reminded Merrick of himself at just such an age.

"A crane is a system of pulleys," Merrick explained, pointing at the contraption. "And there is the swiveling mechanism—see, just there?—which enables us to lift the slate up to the roof more efficiently. Have you ever seen one up close?"

The boy shook his head. "Just sketches," he said. "But the Greek temples were built with cranes. My father said that they were used to lift the columns onto the porticoes. He said that the columns were very heavy, and that there was no other way it could have been done."

"Your father is quite right," said Merrick.

It was then that he noticed the small sketchbook perched on the stone rim of the old well. "What have you there? Some sketches, eh? I hope you are not stealing my trade secrets."

The boy's eyes flared with alarm. "N-No, sir," he said. "I did draw some things, but I didn't mean to steal."

"I was merely teasing," said Merrick. "But I suspect, my boy, that you pinched that pair of opera glasses from someone."

The lad's color deepened, and he dropped his head.

"To whom do they belong?" asked Merrick quietly.

"To . . . to my mother." The boy was mumbling in the direction of his dusty shoes. "But I didn't pinch them. I—I just borrowed them."

Ah, well. His mother's wrath was none of Merrick's concern. To change the subject, he picked up the lad's sketchbook. "Do you mind if I have a look?"

The boy's head jerked up. "N-No, sir," he said. "I suppose not. But it's nothing, really. Just scribbles."

Merrick smiled, and opened the book. Slowly, and with mild amazement, he turned the pages. The drawings were by no means the child's play which he had expected to see. Instead, they were quite detailed—and relatively accurate, too. Some were elevation drawings; he'd seen worse from a couple of the more junior architects he'd taken on. But others were true art. There was a close sketch of Ridley, his chief bricklayer, deftly mortaring a brick to be set. One could see the turn of Ridley's knobby fingers, the rough edge of the brick where the frame had been pried away, and even the dollop of mortar which was about to drip from his trowel.

Another sketch was of himself, balancing high on a truss, his legs spread for stability. He well remembered the day, perhaps three or four past, when he had climbed up onto the roughly framed roof, simply because he wished the framers to know he was capable of doing so—capable, at least, when the weather was dry and his hip was rested. But the men knew nothing of his impairment. He wanted them to feel that not even the smallest error would evade his detection—not even seventy feet off the ground.

In the boy's sketch, Merrick was gesturing at one of the carpenters, having taken exception to a sloppy mortise joint. His face was in profile, and his gaze was cold and hard. He had not realized a child was watching. He hoped to God the boy had not overheard the thorough and rather colorful tongue-lashing he'd given his men.

The last page in the boy's sketchbook was a small elevation drawing of the entire terrace as it rose up the hill. But the terrace had become separate houses, and the roofs were not quite the same. The boy had varied them a bit; a hipp roof on one, odd fanciful gables on another, and a French mansard on yet third.

"You do not care for my rooflines, I collect," he said, smiling inwardly.

The boy lifted one shoulder. "That's just how I would do it if they were my houses," he replied. "I shouldn't wish them to look so very much alike."

"But in that very likeness is a cost savings," Merrick explained. "It enables us to terrace the houses to save precious land, and to purchase materials in bulk. Price matters greatly, even to the wealthy people who will buy these houses."

"Does it?" The lad seemed surprised.

"Yes, and if you mean to be an architect, I beg you to remember it," he said. "There are enough impractical people coming out of university as it is."

The boy laughed, and for an instant, the veil of solemnity was lifted.

"What is your name?" he asked the boy.

"Geoff," he answered. "Geoffrey Archard."

Merrick offered his hand. "And I am Mr. MacLachlan."

Geoffrey looked up at him earnestly. "Do you make anything besides houses, Mr. MacLachlan?"

Merrick lifted both eyebrows. "Well, I own a civil engineering concern which makes roads and lays pavements," he said. "And a business which makes copper piping. A large ironmongers. And I recently came into possession of a brickyard. I could go on, but that isn't quite what you meant, is it?"

The lad was shaking his head. "No, I mean do you *build* other things? Like churches, or banks, or—or palaces, perhaps?"

Merrick grinned. "Never a palace, no," he confessed. "But when I was a young man, I designed some fine public buildings like guildhalls, and a great many country houses. Some of them were as big as palaces."

But the boy's face had gone suddenly pale. His lively green eyes had taken on a flat, vacant look, as if he were no longer listening. For an instant, Merrick feared an epileptic fit. "Geoffrey?" He touched the child lightly on the shoulder. "Geoffrey, what is it?"

The boy swallowed hard, and looked up. A sudden emotion sketched across his face. Fear? Guilt? "The crane, sir," he rasped. "The crane. One of the pulleys—it is giving way."

"What?" Merrick squatted down to look him in the eyes. "Geoffrey, what do you mean?"

The boy pushed past him, and ran to the edge of the weeds, staring fixedly at the construction. "It is coming loose!" he repeated. "The men—t-tell them—tell them to *get away now*!"

Merrick was on his heels. He grabbed the boy's shoulder and spun him around to see a look of stark panic. "Geoffrey, what are you saying? How do you know?"

For an instant, the boy's eyebrows knotted. "I . . . I saw it in the opera glasses!" he cried. "I forgot. I forgot to say. Please! Please! Make them move!"

Merrick did not consider it further. He bolted across the road at a run, shouting at Kelly, his site foreman. "Out of the way!" he called. "Kelly, clear! Clear the ground! Run!"

Kelly was looking at Merrick as if he'd lost his mind, but he was trained to be blindly obedient. He pushed the man nearest him away, and shouted for the others to follow. Suddenly, all hell broke loose. The screech of chain and metal rent the air, and a long, hollow groan followed. The container of slate tiles, swinging some fifty feet above, jerked once, twice, and then came crashing down. It clipped the edge of the roof, sending chips of slate and copper flashing flying. Ropes, chains, and chunks of fascia and soffit followed, all of it falling in on the rubble as if the earth beneath had collapsed.

His heart in his throat, Merrick reached Kelly's side. "Mither o' God!" whispered the foreman, swiftly crossing himself.

Merrick seized his shoulder. "Everyone accounted for?"

Kelly's eyes flicked over the handful of men. "Aye, 'tis everyone." Relief was plain in his voice. "Mither o' God! What happened?"

"Something in the mechanism gave way," said Merrick. He jerked his head toward the vacant lot. "The boy there saw it through a pair of opera glasses."

Kelly looked at him blankly. "Go on!"

Suddenly, Horton clapped a hand on Merrick's shoulder. "Aye, the boy, was it?" he rasped. "And ter think, Mr. MacLachlan, that yer meant ter send 'im packin'!" This was followed by either a wheezy laugh or a consumptive cough; Merrick was never sure which.

Above, the roofers had crawled to the splintered edge of the eave, and were peering down, their faces white. Below, the men charged with operating the crane and loading the slate had removed their caps and were staring at the rubble heap as if one of their own lay buried beneath it. But no one did. And for that, they had the boy to thank.

Merrick turned around, and started back toward the old well, but the lad was gone.

One of the men digging the adjacent cellar popped up his head. " 'E left, sir," said the worker. "White as a sheet, he were, and headin' towards the village at a right sharp clip."

"Ah." Merrick stood at the edge of the road now. "I see. Thank you."

He went to the well anyway. For a few moments, he simply stood there, staring down into its stone depths and pinching the bridge of his nose in thought. He was grateful to the lad, yes. But why had the boy not told him sooner? His panic had been obvious, so he must have comprehended the magnitude of what he had seen.

On a sigh, Merrick turned to go, but the toe of his shoe struck something hard. He looked down to see the opera glasses lying in a patch of sheep's sorrel. On impulse, Merrick bent down and picked them up. They were expensive, he realized, balancing their weight in his hand. Experimentally, he held them to his eyes, and turned to face the construction site. He scanned the crowd, able to easily recognize all of his men. But to see the tackle on the crane at this distance . . .

Well. Merrick lowered the glasses. The lad had bloody fine eyesight, that much was certain. As for his part, Merrick reluctantly accepted the truth. At the tender age of just five-and-thirty, it was time he embraced the dreaded scourge of middle age, and bought himself a pair of spectacles.

He returned to the scene of the accident, and instructed Walters to bring down the crane and begin a thorough inspection. If someone had failed to do his job properly, Merrick meant to know who. Walters agreed with relish. Three of the men were already picking through the slate to see how much of it could be salvaged. Above, the broken fascia board was already being pried away. The men would have it replaced by dark, most likely.

There was nothing more to be done here. It had been a bloody close call, but now it was time to move on. He and Evans had a meeting with a land speculator from Greenwich. Time and tide—not to mention business—waited for no man.

Chapter Six

*There never was ebb
without flood following.*

Madeleine's new coachman was twice obliged to stop and ask directions to Merrick MacLachlan's office. Eventually, they drew up before a wide, imposing town house which looked like a larger version of her own, but was situated on the opposite end of the village.

Inside, the ground floor swarmed with clerks and copyists scurrying from room to room, and up and down the broad staircase. The place smelled of fresh ink and, strangely, of newly sawn lumber. No one seemed to know quite what to do with Madeleine. Mr. MacLachlan, it seemed, was not in the habit of dealing directly with his buyers. That was left to Rosenberg.

In the end, a man who looked like a butler decided that Madeleine should be shown upstairs to Mr. MacLachlan's office. She followed him up two flights of stairs. Men were at work in every nook and cranny, as best Madeleine could see. Some appeared to be draughtsmen, for they were perched on tall stools at drawing tables. Others sat at what looked like a dining table, with stacks of ledgers everywhere. In one of the corridors lay a pile of unpainted dentil molding, and beside it, a bushel basket held an assortment of delicately carved corbels. It seemed so very odd, for Madeleine had never actually seen the *pieces* of houses before.

She was left to wait in a large, wood-paneled office which was fitted with fine mahogany furnishings, including a desk which seemed to stretch into infinity. An inlaid longcase clock stood against one wall, ratcheting up Madeleine's nerves with every doleful *tick-tock* of its mechanism.

After a while, she grew intolerably restless and leapt from her chair to roam about the room, picking through the bookcases and peering at the paintings. Most of the latter were very old, and very fine. Dutch and Italian, she thought. On the sideboard, a heavy silver tray held an exquisitely cut decanter encircled by a half dozen matching glasses—Murano crystal, unmistakably. Madeleine's mouth curled with bitterness. Merrick had always had an eye for the very best, and the most beautiful. And at last, it seemed, he could afford it.

There was a narrow door to the left of the desk. On impulse, Madeleine opened it and peered inside. The room was warm, the air yet redolent with the scents of masculinity. Madeleine closed her eyes, drew her breath deep, and let the memories assail her. The scents of soap, chestnut, and a sharp spicy tang teased her nostrils. And underneath it all, Merrick's unique scent, almost undetectable. But she knew it. Yes, she knew it, now and always. Oh, the cruelty of one's memory, keen as the tip of a dagger.

For an instant, she was tempted to go to the narrow, rather ordinary bed and throw back the covers so that she might draw in the fragrance of his bed linen. That, too, was a well-remembered scent. At the memory, heat flooded her face. Angry with herself, she slammed the door shut, and leaned back against it, pressing both hands to the warm wood surface.

He chose that ill-timed moment to enter unannounced, taking her breath away. For a moment, he did not see her. He approached the desk and tossed down a black portfolio stuffed to bursting with untidy papers. As if he were undecided about something momentous, he stared down at the folio, and dragged one of his elegant, long-fingered hands through his hair, his ever-present signet ring catching the sun which sliced through the window.

Madeleine cleared her throat, and at once, his head swiveled around. The expression on his face when he saw her was incomprehensible. Relief? Pleasure? Whatever it was, it was short-lived, and followed just as swiftly by a black glower.

"Madeleine," he said quietly. "What in God's name?"

She went to the desk, and quietly laid down the deed of conveyance which Rosenberg had given her. "What, indeed?" she murmured. "Your Mr. Rosenberg gave me this today."

Merrick lifted one of his slashing black eyebrows. "Yes, he is nothing if not reliable."

In the face of his cool disdain, Madeleine began to tremble with rage again. "How dare you, Mr. MacLachlan?" she demanded, her voice low and tremulous. "How dare you interfere in my personal affairs? Take that back. I won't have it, do you hear?"

He had the audacity to smile, but his eyes were hard. "Mr. MacLachlan, is it?" he said. "Come now, Madeleine! We are alone. You may put away your little artifice."

"You are nothing to me now," she said. "You have no right to go round telling people that you are."

"I am your husband," he retorted. "Though I did not mention that little fact to Rosenberg. And so long as we are wed, the law requires me to provide for you, whether I wish it or not."

"You are *not* my husband!" she cried. "My husband is dead, do you hear? Stop tormenting me."

He circled from behind the desk to stand over her. "Oh, you have no idea what true torment is, Madeleine." His voice was dangerously quiet. "And whatever Lord Bessett may have been to you, he assuredly was not your husband."

Madeleine's hands were shaking now. He was too close. Too large. Too supremely *male*. "We made a mistake, Merrick," she whispered. "We did something rash and foolish, and then we regretted it. Please, let it stay in the past. I have a family—a child—to think of now."

His handsome mouth curled into a sneer. "You were ashamed of me, Madeleine?" he asked. "Is that it? You grew older and wiser in rather a hurry, did you not? It took you all of what—ten days?—to regret throwing in your lot with a penurious Scotsman."

"By God, how dare you?" Madeleine did not even realize she had swung at him with her open hand until he seized hold of her wrist.

He pulled her hard, almost fully against him. She could smell the heat of his skin. "Oh, I dare, madam," he gritted, his mouth just inches from hers. "I dare because it is my right! I bought and paid for it with the blood you wrung out of my heart."

"What heart?" she cried. "You have none!"

He dragged her to him, chest to chest, banding the

arm about her even tighter. "Aye, so I keep hearing," he answered, one hand fisting in her skirts as if he might draw them up. "But I do have a wife. Account yourself fortunate, my dear, that I don't drag you bodily into that bedchamber this very moment, and vent thirteen years of frustration between those long, beautiful legs of yours."

"Just try it!" she hissed. "I shall scream, and everyone in this house will hear me."

"Aye, and they'll do not a damned thing about it, for they know better."

She looked at him and swallowed hard. Dear Lord, he meant it. His hot blue gaze was running over her face, his nostrils wide, his breathing unaccountably rough. A faint beard already shadowed his lean cheeks and the hard bones of his face. And there was something else; that firm, unmistakable sign of masculine arousal, pressed against her belly, growing harder with his every breath. Her eyes must have widened.

"Oh, aye, Madeleine, I lust for you," he admitted. "Does it please you? Are you happy I still suffer? What do you say, my dear? The bed or no? You used to beg me for it. D'ye not remember?"

She squeezed her eyes shut. Dear God, she *did* remember. With every fiber of her traitorous body, she remembered. As if to further tempt her, his free hand slid up to gently massage her hip, slowly and inexorably searing her skin. Beneath the taut fabric of his trousers, she felt his erection throb; felt the strength in his arms and the hunger in his touch, and for a moment—for one wild, heated, insane moment, she actually considered it.

No. No, she could not possibly be that foolish. "Take

your hands off me, Merrick," she whispered. "I am no longer yours to touch."

His sneer deepened, and he shoved her away. "No, I wouldn't have you if you were the last woman on earth," he said. "I wouldna' give you the pleasure, you backstabbing vixen."

She backed away, and wondered if she had lost her mind. "I do *not* want you," she said as if to convince herself. "I do *not*. You are not my husband."

He half turned and casually lifted one shoulder. "Aye, well, if you wish to maintain your facade for society, so be it," he said. "I've never gainsaid your lies, and I never will. But know this, Madeleine—you are my wife. In the eyes of God, and in the eyes of the law, you are my wife, and you ever shall be."

Her eyes were still fixed on his beautiful, sneering mouth. "Oh, you have ever been one to use the law when it was to your benefit!" she returned. "And you were quick enough to cast me aside when there was a profit to be made."

He slowly turned to face her, his visage suddenly stark. "I never cast you aside, Madeleine," he rasped. "Never. What are you talking about?"

Madeleine blinked uncertainly. "The—the annulment," she said. "And the money. My dowry."

Slowly, almost warily, he shook his head. "There is no annulment," he said. "I know nothing of any money."

"Lies!" Madeleine's heart was pounding again.

He stepped back another inch. "Lies, yes," he said. "I've no doubt of it. But they are your father's lies, I'll wager, Madeleine. Not mine."

If he was a liar, he was a good one. Madeleine felt unsteady, as if the ground had just shifted beneath her feet. "Then you are telling me—" She sucked in a deep breath. "You are claiming that you did not annul our marriage?"

Merrick stared at her. "How in God's name could I?" he asked. "Madeleine, we spoke our vows. We sealed them with our bodies. Faith, woman, you weren't even a virgin before the wedding! We certainly had no grounds for annulment after. One of us would have to be insane—or worse."

"I begin to wonder if you aren't." Desperately, she shook her head. "I do not believe you."

"And I do not believe *you*!" he snapped. "What kind of crackbrained gudgeon would believe such a thing possible? An annulment, after all we had done together? Do you think me ten times a fool?"

Dear Lord, he was almost convincing. Madeleine felt the blood drain from her face. There was a leather settee by the hearth. She grasped the back with one hand, and made her way gingerly around it. She felt his hand, steady and strong, come out to grasp her arm as she slid onto the seat.

What kind of crackbrained gudgeon indeed?

God. Oh, holy God. This could not be happening. The room was going dark around the edges. Merrick knelt before her, and began to chafe one of her hands in his with a touch that was not unkind. She could sense something inside him had shifted, dispelling the anger, and turning it to an altogether different emotion.

"Madeleine, what did he tell you?" He seemed to choke out the words. "Jessup—what did he say against me?"

She stared blindly at the wall. "No, I saw them," she said hollowly. "I—I saw the papers. Your signature."

"What papers?" He clasped her face between his long,

elegant fingers and forced her to look at him. "What papers, Madeleine?"

"The—the annulment," she said. "Two or three pages, with a seal. Rolled up and tied with ribbon. And you had signed it, Merrick. Papa showed me."

He narrowed his eyes, and shook his head. "Madeleine, what does my signature look like?"

"I—I cannot remember."

"You cannot remember, because you saw it but once," he answered. "You saw me sign the marriage register at Gretna Green. Did you watch me? Did you remember it?"

She swallowed hard. "I—I was so nervous," she admitted. "No, I don't remember. Did we sign something? I daresay we must have done. But Papa had it undone. He said it was what you wanted."

He still held both her hands, and gave them a hard squeeze. "Madeleine, was it what you wanted?"

Mutely, she nodded, tears pooling in her eyes. "I made a mistake, Merrick," she whispered. "I was so young, barely seventeen. I did not understand quite how the world worked."

Merrick felt the fight go out of him. He felt eviscerated again. Empty. Oh, he was not surprised by Jessup's perfidy. That, he knew intimately. No, what had always surprised him was Madeleine's utter lack of resolve. He had never believed life—or Madeleine's father—would go easy on them. Had she believed it? Apparently, she had. Apparently she had been ill prepared to stand with him and fight the good fight.

"We are still married, Madeleine." He spoke the words with resignation in his heart. "We will be so until the day we die. There is no undoing it. Not then, and not now."

Madeleine jerked her hands from his, a look of horror twisting her beautiful face. "Don't say that!" she cried. "No, I can't bear it! I gave up . . . *everything*, Merrick. My life . . . all those years . . . and for what?"

He tried to take her hands again, but she shoved at him. "No!" she said. "I—I have a child, Merrick. He is all that I have lived for. He is everything to me. I cannot believe—no, I won't believe—that I am a—a what? An *adulteress*? Is that what you are claiming?"

"Madeleine, calm down."

"No. I shan't. This is an outrage. You are saying that my father—that he lied to me. About everything. I do not believe you. I am not your wife. I should sooner die."

"It does not matter, Madeleine, whether you believe me or not," he said sadly. "It changes nothing."

"It changes *everything*." There was an edge of madness in her voice now, and a feverish desperation in her face. "He paid you, he said. He paid you to go away. The equivalent of my dowry, he said. Thirty thousand pounds—the price you asked to give me up. You wished to be in business for yourself, Merrick, and you saw a way to do it."

Madeleine was beyond coherence now. He stood, and began to pace the room. There was no point in arguing with her, or in denying her father's lies. Merrick felt nothing now; not even that which he deserved to feel. Wrath. Pain. Righteous indignation. There was just that cold, numb sensation in his chest where his heart should have been. It was better, he supposed, that the jolt of raw lust he had felt upon seeing her in his office.

But beyond all the lies and the lust and the grief, one thing was profoundly clear. Whether or not she had ever loved him, he horrified her now. "I am sorry, Madeleine," he said hollowly. "I would that we had never laid eyes on one another. Life would have been much less empty. And I wish you had not come back to London. But there was no annulment, Madeleine. There was no money. When you can bring yourself to think on it, you will know the truth."

"Oh, God!" Madeleine squeezed her eyes closed. "Geoffrey!"

"Geoffrey?"

"My son," she whispered.

Dear Lord. The boy by the well?

"Please, Merrick," she begged. "Please say no more of this business. I could not bear it if people called him—"

"They won't dare!" he interjected sharply. "People will call him *nothing*, Madeleine. Good God, do you think I mean to hang our laundry in Mayfair? Do you think I stood idly by for all those years whilst you lived with another man and called him your husband, just so I might stir up a scandal now? Do you think I am proud of what my marriage has come to?"

"You—you are rich now," she whispered. "You could have divorced me—if what you say is true."

"Not this side of hell, my dear," he returned. "You'll go to your grave wishing for that."

"I—I don't wish it!" she cried.

"No, you do not," he agreed. "It is a vile, very public process, and your son would surely be ruined then."

"All I wish is to be left alone," she said. "To live out my life in peace."

"In that, madam, I can oblige you," he said. "I have no interest in cutting up your peace, or even of laying eyes on your again, if possible. You are dead to me, Madeleine. As dead as you were the day you climbed into your father's carriage, and abandoned me to my fate."

She winced at his words, but did not back down. "Very well, then," she said. "Kindly take back your house."

"No. I shan't."

It was irrational, he knew. He had told himself that a man should put a roof over his wife's head, that it was his duty, no matter who she was or what she had done. But did he somehow imagine that if he forced it on her, she would be any more his? The legalities of the matter aside, she was not his and never would be.

"I am not a poor woman, Merrick," she whispered. "But I have lived almost all my life under the thumb of one man or another. Until four years ago, I had never chosen anything—*anything*—for myself, save for the occasional bolt of dress fabric. I have always had what everyone else thought I needed. Have you any idea what that is like?"

The truth was, he did not. And what did it really matter now? She loathed him, and he loathed her. Whatever she had done, it was what she had *not* done which haunted him.

Roughly, he cleared his throat. "Seven thousand pounds, then."

"I beg your pardon?"

"The price of the house," he said. "If you still want it. And Madeleine?"

"Yes?"

He did not look directly at her, nor did he approach her again. He knew better. "Pray do not come here again. Deal with Rosenberg."

"Very well." The words were a soft whisper, followed by the even softer click of the door as she opened it. But on the threshold, she hesitated, her sharp intake of breath un-mistakable.

With a strange sense of dread, Merrick turned in his chair. Bess Bromley stood in the corridor, the thrusting swell of her milk-pale breasts unmistakable, even in the shadows. Phipps was with her, his face flooding bright crimson. Clearly he had forgotten having shown Madeleine upstairs.

Her expression bleak, Madeleine pushed past both of them without another word and vanished. Across the distance, Bess's bold gaze burned into Merrick, already hot and greedy. Merrick's stomach twisted, sending bile surging into his throat.

"My apologies, Mr. MacLachlan." Phipps choked out the words. "It has been a busy day. Miss Bromley is here to see you."

Merrick had already jerked open his top drawer, and withdrawn a sheet of letter paper. "Miss Bromley's services are not required today, Phipps," he managed. "I shall send for her when she is needed. Now kindly show her out."

Madeleine waited until she was situated deep in the shadows of her carriage before she burst into tears. Oh, she was so angry! So angry and so hurt. So humiliated by her own damnable emotions. She did not need more pain; no, not at this point in her life. She had believed herself finally on the verge of contentment, if not happiness. She was not even ready to think about Merrick's wild allegations, claims so outlandish, one could hardly countenance them, let alone comprehend them.

Right now, she had to deal with the shock of simply seeing him again after thirteen years. Their accidental meeting last week almost did not count, the moment had been so surreal. And that woman waiting by his office! Dear God. Her eyes had sent a chill down Madeleine's spine. So flat. So void of feeling. Her purpose, too, had been quite clear.

The carriage was rolling away, the harnesses jingling loudly. For just an instant, Madeleine allowed herself the luxury of giving in completely to the grief. She buried her face in her handkerchief and let her shoulders begin to shake. The sobs came heavily then, the great, heaving gulps of her girlhood. She had not cried thus in better than a dozen years. No, not since she had lost him—or lost the man she had loved, was perhaps a better way of putting it.

The morning after her wedding, Papa had arrived in Gretna Green to tell her that Merrick was not the man she thought him. And he had shown her proof. Now, she was not sure where the facade ended, and the real Merrick began. He was a stranger to her. And yet he seemed the very same: a tall, dark implacable pillar of certainty. A man who knew his own abilities. His own mind. Yes, his confidence—that was what had made her fall in love with him, for at seventeen, she had possessed little of that quality herself.

In the beginning, she had not even believed herself ready for her come-out. She had begged Papa to leave her in Sheffield just one more year. Aunt Emma had pressed him, too. Madeleine had never been out of the country a day in her life, her aunt had warned. She had not had the benefit of a mother to bring her along and initiate her into the ways of the *haut monde*. Indeed, she had turned seventeen only days before. But Papa had not wished to listen. He had patted Madeleine on the head, as if she were one of his prized spaniels, and told her he had the utmost confidence that she would do him proud.

But his confidence had been misplaced. Less than halfway through her very first London season, Lady Madeleine Howard had fallen head over heels in love with a nobody. She had been but six weeks out of the school-room when first she'd set eyes on him. Aunt Emma had taken her to a ball given by the Duke and Duchess of Forne, and if it had not been love at first sight upon seeing Merrick MacLachlan, it certainly had been utter fascination. The duke, a patron of classical architecture, had just engaged Merrick to draw the plans for a magnificent new country house, after interviewing some two dozen older, more prominent architects.

Merrick's name had been on everyone's tongue—and on the duchess's guest list. He had stood in one corner, dispassionately eyeing the crowd over the rim of his champagne glass, looking utterly bored, thoroughly unimpressed, and breathtakingly handsome. He had been with his brother and some of Sir Alasdair's rakish friends. And yet no one would have mistaken Merrick for a rake, or even a fribble, which was what most of the other young men in attendance had appeared to be. No, Merrick had stood apart from everyone, and everyone had noticed.

He and Madeleine had exchanged long glances—several of them—but no words. He had not even bothered to hide his interest in her, and Madeleine had found it flattering. For days afterward, she had been able to think of nothing but the tall, dark, young man with the heavy black hair and haunting, ice-blue eyes. Eyes which were the color, she had imagined, of a glacier, though she had certainly never seen one. Indeed, she had seen almost nothing of the world beyond her papa's vast estate.

After that night, Merrick began to be seen at a great many society affairs, though he never looked as though he enjoyed them. But his brother's title, along with the duke's patronage, gave him entrée, and made him marginally acceptable. Aunt Emma and Papa had been unimpressed. Sir Alasdair's wealth, whilst vast, was not old money, they warned. It came instead from gaming, and in some very low places, too. The younger brother, of course, was worse. He practically *worked* for a living, Aunt Emma had stressed.

Madeleine had been undeterred. Within days, she had begun slipping away to meet Merrick at every opportunity, and looking back, she was not sure where the courage had come from. All the while, Papa had kept pressing the suit of Lord Henry Winters, a pleasant, pimpled boy who still trod on her toes when they danced.

By the end of the season, with Papa holding fast to his vehement disapproval, Merrick had persuaded her that there was but one alternative left to them. And then, somehow, she had simply been overcome by events. She had loved Merrick, loved him simply and deeply. From the very first, her body and her soul had come alive to his touch. It was a touch she had yearned for; and to her undying dismay, the yearning had never ended.

After it was all over, and Papa had come to Scotland to fetch her back, and to pay Merrick the money he had so desperately wanted, Madeleine had been deposited at the family pile in Sheffield to lick her wounds and dry her tears. Then, just as he always did, Papa had gone straight back to Town—this time to see how much damage had been done her reputation.

The answer, apparently, was not much. Perhaps because Merrick was such an unknown, no one in London had seemed to realize he was gone. Madeleine had waited alone in Sheffield, still hoping against hope that Merrick would come for her. But weeks passed without so much as a letter. Aunt Emma, of course, had fired off countermeasures at once. Lady Madeleine had the mumps. She had retired to the country for rest. She would return to town for next year's season.

But she had not been able to return after all. Instead, Papa had married her off to Lord Bessett, a noted scholar of antiquities, and her late mother's cousin. Bessett, who was in the process of packing up his bags and his eight-year-old son for a long expedition to the Continent, had readily agreed that a wife might be a handy thing to have, though he was too busy to actually go out and look for one. For Madeleine, the long expedition had turned into eight endless years of slogging about Italy and Campania, whilst forcing herself to be a dutiful wife to a man more than twice her age.

And now Merrick was claiming that they were still married? That her lonely years abroad had been . . . what? A joke? A lie? A wasted sacrifice? It simply was not possible. The very thought made her tears come harder. At that moment, however, the carriage slowed to make the sharp turn at the village post office. Madeleine did her best to gather herself though she had little hope of fooling Eliza.

She knew at once, however, that something was amiss when Eliza met her at the door, and said not a word about her tear-stained face. Instead, the maid was almost wringing her hands.

Madeleine felt a moment of panic. "What is it, Eliza?" she asked, tossing her shawl across a chair. "What is wrong?"

"It's Geoffrey, my lady," said the maid.

"Oh, God!" She dropped the deed and her reticule, spilling coins and keys across the floor. "What has happened? Is he hurt?"

Swiftly, Eliza shook her head. "No, ma'am," she answered. "But he came home from one of his rambles this afternoon in a state. Went straight up to his room and locked the door. I've left him be, my lady, but . . ."

Without another word, Madeleine rushed up the narrow steps to Geoffrey's door. Her knock went unheeded. "Geoff, it is Mamma," she said. "I wish you to open the door. Now, please."

There was nothing but silence.

"Geoffrey!" Madeleine's voice went up a notch. "You are scaring me. Open the door."

Eliza touched her lightly on the shoulder. "Could he be ill, ma'am?"

Madeleine's hand was shaking now. "Fetch Mrs. Drexel's keys," she rasped. "Quickly, Eliza."

The maid was gone but a minute, returning with a jangling brass ring, one of its skeleton keys between her fingers. Swiftly, she fitted it into the lock and turned it. At the sound of the door, Geoffrey lifted his head from his pillow and regarded his mother with a look of dread. His pallor was shocking. His eyes swam with unshed tears.

Dear God! Was this what life had come to? Both of them in tears, when she had wished only to ensure their happiness and contentment? She went at once to the bed, and sat down beside him. "Geoffrey, what is it?" she asked, stroking a hand down his heavy dark hair. "You have been crying. What has happened?"

At that, he buried his face in his pillow on a horrible sob. "Go away, Mamma!" he said. "Just leave me alone."

"No, I shan't," she said firmly. "Not this time."

"Go away!" He sounded at once like an angry young man and a terrified child. "Just go away! Do you hear me?"

"Oh, Geoffrey, my love!" she whispered. "Why can you not tell me what is wrong? It pains me so terribly to see you this distraught."

"I don't mean to pain you, Mamma." He began sobbing in earnest now. "I *don't*. I'm—I'm sorry. P-Please don't be mad. Please, Mamma, don't hate me."

"Geoffrey, I could never hate you!" She bent forward and kissed his wet cheek. "Oh, my darling, you are the world to me. There is nothing you could do that would ever make me hate you."

"You don't know that, Mamma!" he cried. "You *don't*! There are things—bad things I—I just . . ."

His words withered away. Again, she stroked his hair, just as she had done when he was a small child. Always it had soothed him, but today, it seemed to bring him no comfort.

"What is it, Geoffrey, that I don't know?" she asked quietly. "What kinds of things are you talking about? Did something happen this afternoon?"

He shook his head, his dark hair scrubbing against the pillow. "I—I'm just a freak. That's what happened! J-Just leave me alone!"

"Geoffrey!" she gently chided. "I have asked you not to say that. You are not a freak. You are . . . you are brilliant, and very talented."

His sobs were subsiding now, and he was growing still. Madeleine knew of nothing to do but wait. And so she did, with one hand clenched in her lap, the other rhythmically stroking him, and her heart wrenched with grief.

"Mamma," he finally whispered. "Do you think bad things happen for a reason?"

"Well, I cannot say," she answered. "That question covers a lot of ground. What sort of bad things?"

"I don't know." He snuffled quietly for a moment. "But do you think . . . well, do you think we can make bad things happen? Or . . . or does God make them happen?"

"I suppose we can make bad things happen, my love, if we make bad decisions," said Madeleine. Somehow, she knew that was not quite the right thing to say. She wished desperately that she knew what he was getting at.

Geoffrey rolled over ever so slightly, and looked up at the ceiling. "I mean, Mamma, that if we *thought* a bad thing—even by accident—and then someone . . . someone got hurt because of it, would it be our fault? Would we go to hell?"

"Geoffrey, bad thoughts cannot cause someone to get hurt."

He was very quiet for a long moment, his gaze growing distant and unfocused. "But you do not know that, Mamma," he finally said. "Not really. We can none of us know for sure all the things that are possible on this earth. Can we?"

Madeleine took his hand in hers, and squeezed it very hard. "Geoff, I *do* know," she said resolutely. "Your bad thoughts cannot make something bad happen. That is just—" She had been about to use the word *silly*, but it would upset him, she knew. "That is God's business," she went on. "Not ours. He makes the decisions, according to his plan for us."

"That's what Mr. Frost says," Geoff answered.

Madeleine set the backs of her fingers to his feverish cheek. "Your tutor is a man of good sense and of science," she said. "You should listen to him, Geoff, and talk to him, if you cannot do so with to me."

Geoff looked at her with regret in his eyes. "It is not that, Mamma," he answered. "It is just that—well, you *are* my mother. You—you have to love me, do you not?"

Madeleine wondered if that were so. Had her parents loved her? She had never known her mother, who had died before Madeleine's second birthday. And her father— well, he had been a busy and important man. His political aspirations had often kept him from home. Seeing him for a month at Christmas, and being patted on the head like a spaniel had been about all that Madeleine could hope for. Until Geoffrey's birth, she had believed that that was enough. But then she had learnt what an utterly consuming emotion one's love for one's child truly was.

Gently, she leaned over him, and set her cheek to his. "I do not know, Geoffrey, if I have to love you," she finally said. "I know only that I do, with every fiber of my being, and that it will ever be so."

At that, he seemed to exhale, and relax. "I am glad, Mamma," he finally said. "And I am glad that you are my mother, and not someone else."

She gave a nervous little laugh. "How funny you are, Geoff," she responded. "I am the only person who could be your mother, am I not?"

In her embrace, he seemed to shrug. Then he lay still for a long, silent moment. "Mamma?" he finally said.

"Yes, Geoff?"

"Do you think that Mrs. Drexel might have some of that lemon sponge cake left over from dinner last night?"

"I daresay she might," said Madeleine.

And she knew then that the terrible black mood was over, and that persuade and plead as she might, Geoff would say no more. So she sat up, and dashed a hand beneath her eyes, and raced him down to the kitchen.

Chapter Seven

No hold can be got o' water or fire.

*I*t was dark. So dark and so cold, the wind like a knife cutting clean across the dales. But this was the place. He sensed it, though he could see nothing ahead but the muted glow of lamplight. He shouldered his way into the wind, but the journey went on forever.

He went up the steps, gingerly lifting his bad leg behind, rather like an afterthought. The pain was almost a comfort now. The sound of the knocker echoed hollowly. Then came the shaft of light as the massive door was cracked. Eyes. A face, old and withered. A lifted lamp, flickering uncertainly. "Eh?"

Ruthlessly, he shoved his foot into the crack of light. "Go tell your master I've come for my wife," he said. "And I'll not be leaving without her."

"Eh?" The lamp inched higher. "Wot's that?"

"Jessup," he gritted. "Damn you, go tell him I've come."

The door pressed in on his leg. "Gone dahn t' London, t' master has," said the creaking voice. " 'Ouse is shut up, can't ye see?"

"Lady Madeleine, then! Fetch her down here."

"Eh? 'Oo?"

"Madeleine!" he shouted. "I wish to see Madeleine."

"Gone, too," said the creaky voice. "Gone abroad, 'er an' Bessett. The 'ouse is shut up, see. Now tek your foot out t' door, if ye please."

The lamp shifted, throwing eerie, flickering shadows across the doorstep. "Bessett?" he asked. "Who the devil is Bessett?"

"Oh, he'd be the 'usband."

"No! Stop!" The pressure of the heavy door was like a vise. Good God, did they mean to shatter his leg anew? "Damn it, no! We—we were wed in July. I am her husband now."

The wizened head shook. "Dunt ye undastand, mon? Married at Michaelmas, she was. And gone awa'."

"No! No!" He thrashed, trying to twist his leg from the door's relentless grip. "Fetch her down here now, by God! She's my wife! Mine!"

"Well, we'd be knowing nowt o' that," said the voice. "Now, good neet to ye, sir."

"No!" The crack of light was closing now, wrenching his leg from its hip socket again. "No! No! Open the door!"

"Sir? Sir?" The voice was distant, the pain unyielding.

Merrick lashed out, but the enemy—if there had been one—was gone.

"Sir, your bad leg! Do hold still."

He came half-awake, wincing at the pain. Something bound him. Ropes? No. Good God—sheets! They were snarled about his body like a shroud. And his leg—it was wedged between the spindles of the footboard at the ankle, and turned at a precarious angle.

"You fought a good fight, sir," murmured Phipps as he unfurled the linen from his knee. "Your demons must have taken a proper thrashing last night."

"My goddamned leg!" growled Merrick. "Christ, what happened?"

"Just a nightmare," answered Phipps, still bent over the footboard. "There! You may extract the leg, I believe. Carefully, sir! Yes, there we have it."

Using only the strength of his arms, Merrick dragged himself up into a sitting position. Pain flooded through his weak limb as the blood stirred again. For an instant, he closed his eyes, grappling for control, struggling to quiet his breathing, which was still coming short and fast.

On the night table, he could hear the *chink* of china and silver as Phipps prepared his coffee. The man was a master at pretending nothing was amiss, no matter how bad Merrick's night—or his temper. "Mr. Evans wishes to see you first thing, sir," he said, tinkling a teaspoon about in the strong, black brew. "Something about the bank rates. And your clerk of works from the Wapping warehouse project has brought up a set of drawings for revision."

Merrick managed to grin. "Aye, well, idle hands do the devil's work, don't they, Phipps?"

Phipps gave a tight smile and handed him his cup and saucer. "Speaking of the devil, Mr. Chutley has sent another of his raving diatribes," he continued. "I've put it with the others."

"I begin to think him insane," grumbled Merrick. "And that his bloody brickworks is going to be more trouble than it's worth."

"You may be right, sir," said Phipps. "Also, Sir Edgar Rigg and his investors wish you to meet them at Mivart's for luncheon," he went on. "It's about the Hampstead project. Shall I arrange a private parlor?"

Merrick cleared his throat sharply. "Yes," he said. "Yes, thank you, Phipps. For everything."

"Indeed, sir," said Phipps, going to the windows to pull back the draperies. "And you have not forgotten, I hope, your five o'clock appointment with Lord Treyhern?"

"The fellow from Cornwall?" asked Merrick.

"Gloucestershire, I believe," said Phipps, going to the dressing table to lay out Merrick's razor and brushes. "Though the title is Cornish."

"I dislike blue-blooded investors," grumbled Merrick. "Why can't they just stick to the five-percents? I've yet to meet one with the stomach for this business."

"The gentleman has already made a fortune in banking," cautioned Phipps. "I rather doubt speculative real estate will scare him off. And Evans says he's not afraid to roll up his shirtsleeves and do an honest day's work, either."

That got Merrick's interest. "And he has an option on some coastal property, you say?"

"Near Lyme Regis," said Phipps. "But you'd best speak to Evans about the details. He is convinced that there is money to be made."

As he bathed and dressed, Merrick considered it. He did not like partnerships; he preferred to control his own destiny. But in another few months, he would have wrung all the profit to be had out of Walham Green. And if he was unable to obtain the property in Hampstead at a reasonable price . . .

He needed to build, damn it—and he needed to control every facet of the process, too. Well, *need* was perhaps the wrong word. He knew, logically, that he could live the life of a sultan solely on the income from his civil engineering firm and never do another day's work in his life. Or he could fall back on his reputation as a classical architect, certainly a more socially acceptable option, if one gave a damn. He did not. The ability to build large, unassailable things—and the financial power and independence which such successes brought him—was his only burning ambition now.

To build on a grand scale, however, one needed land. Large tracts of it. And the Earl of Treyhern, it seemed, held the option on a prime swath of acreage. Merrick sighed and resigned himself to another day away from his precious construction sites.

For over a week, Madeleine remained undecided about her future. She and Geoff had visited with Lady Treyhern on three separate occasions, and it had become increasingly obvious to Geoff that the countess was more than a little curious about him. On one afternoon, Lady Treyhern made a pretense of wishing to stroll in the garden alone with the boy. Throughout it all, Geoff remained calm and courteous. Madeleine could not have asked for a better behaved—or more normal—child.

Matters regarding the house were even more unsettled. She did not return to Rosenberg's office to pay for the house, or to return the deed. She felt as if her life had again been set on its edge, and that some momentous change might well lie around the next bend. It was not what she wanted. She wanted, rather, to be settled—settled in a life so mundane and predicable as to almost numb the mind. She did not wish to remember the yearning ache of young love. She did not wish to tremble at any man's touch—let alone *that* man's.

The things Merrick had told her were horrifying. Madeleine still wished to reject them out of hand, but something nagged at the back of her mind. She had long ago come to terms with Merrick's betrayal—or perhaps *duplicity* was a better word. *Betrayal* suggested a change in his affections. Her father had claimed there had been none; that Merrick had never really cared for her. Once, she had been certain of Merrick's love, and of hers.

In any event, she could not bear to revisit that part of her life now. She wished she had someone sensible to whom she might turn for advice, but there was no one, save perhaps for Lady Treyhern, who had her hands full with Geoff. Moreover, Merrick's claims were so wild, so thoroughly life-shattering, Madeleine could bring herself to discuss them with no one, not even Eliza.

She considered, of course, calling upon a solicitor or a barrister or someone who understood legal and ecclesiastical matters; such a person might know how to go about disproving Merrick's allegations. But how did one find or trust such men? What if the mere asking of questions stirred up old gossip? The proverbial dirt had already been swept under the rug by her father, and rather thoroughly, too. What would people say if they even suspected Madeleine had lived all those years as wife to a man she mightn't have been legally married to? What would happen to Geoffrey?

As had become her habit, Madeleine awoke on a beautiful late-spring morning with all these worrisome thoughts milling about in her brain. On this particular morning, however, she was resolved to do something, however small, about it. While Eliza bustled about, tidying the small bedchamber, Madeleine took her morning chocolate to her writing desk and drew out a fresh sheet of letter paper.

"I am writing to Cousin Gerald in Sheffield," she said to Eliza. Gerald was her father's heir, and the present Earl of Jessup. "Would you care to include a letter to anyone at home?"

"Thank you, my lady," said Eliza as she tucked up the sheets. "I might jot a line to Aunt Esther, if you're in no hurry?"

Madeleine looked up from her writing and smiled. "I wonder, Eliza, that you do not often get homesick," she mused. "You have been gadding about with me for an age now."

"But I have seen the world, ma'am," said Eliza. "Or parts of it. And I have seen Mr. Geoffrey grow up. A rare pleasure, that has been."

Eliza's family had long served the successive earls of Jessup. Her aunt Esther had begun as Madeleine's nursery maid, and at the age of eleven, Eliza had been taken on as a seamstress. A few years thereafter, Madeleine's father had chosen Eliza to accompany Madeleine abroad in her new role as Lady Bessett. Madeleine's previous lady's maid had been dismissed without a character for her involvement in Madeleine's elopement.

At first, Madeleine had resented the younger girl. She had not wanted a new lady's maid, nor had she wished to marry Bessett, or even to go abroad, come to that. She had been terrified of the future, and, she now realized, despondent almost to the point of mental collapse. But Madeleine's father had been beyond caring what she wished. He had taken down his razor strop, soundly blistered the backs of her legs, then suggested Bessett do the same if she became a willful wife.

She had not been willful. Indeed, she soon realized she was fortunate Bessett had agreed to take her on at all. He had done so, he told her, out of duty to her late mother, his kinswoman. Bessett's expectations of his wife were simple, and threefold: whilst he traveled and studied, she was to ensure that life's petty annoyances were dealt with, she was to keep the children out of his hair, and she was to warm his bed when the notion crossed his mind—which, thank God, it did not often do. Bessett lived in the past; the realities, or even the desires, of the temporal world were not welcome intrusions.

"I have been glad, Eliza, to have you with me all these years," Madeleine continued. "But if ever you wish to return to Sheffield, I would understand. And I know Cousin Gerald would make a place for you."

"And for you, too, ma'am," Eliza insisted. "If you and Mr. Geoffrey aren't happy here, you can always go home, can't you?"

Madeleine's expression turned inward. "No, I think not," she said quietly. Her last weeks at Sheffield had been horrific ones, and thirteen years had not dulled the pain. Even if Gerald was willing to welcome her . . . no, not even to escape Merrick would she return to that place.

Hastily, she finished her letter. "I am asking Gerald to send down some of Papa's things, Eliza," she said when it was done. "He'll likely need to send a cart. Is there anything you wish brought?"

"No, thank you, my lady." She paused in her work, a

careful refolding of Madeleine's stockings. "What sorts of things, ma'am? If you don't mind my asking?"

Distracted, Madeleine looked up. "I'm sorry?"

"What sorts of things would you be wanting, ma'am, that would require a cart to come all the way from Sheffield?"

Madeleine stared blindly out the window. "Oh, Papa's files, and his letters," she answered. "His calendars, and personal papers; things which Gerald will be glad to be rid of, I am sure. I should have taken them years ago."

"Oh," said Eliza.

Madeleine turned to see that the maid was refolding the same pair of stockings. "Eliza, is anything amiss?"

Eliza looked up, her eyes widening. "N-No, my lady," she answered. "But—well, I was just wondering about something."

"About what, Eliza?"

"Do you remember, ma'am, the girl you had before me?" she asked. "The French girl?"

"Florette?" Madeleine had not thought of her in a very long time. Twice in one day was rather more than she wished. She had always felt a sense of guilt for the predicament she'd got Florette into. To be dismissed without a character was the worst fate that could befall a servant.

"She went back to France, didn't she?" asked Eliza. "After we left for Rome, ma'am, Aunt Esther said that she wrote a time or two—or mayhap someone wrote for her."

"Wrote?" asked Madeleine. "Wrote to whom?"

"Why, to the master, my lady," said Eliza, her face a little pink. "Pray do not think Aunt Esther a gossip, but she found it terrible peculiar, those letters coming from so far away."

"But my father turned Florette off," said Madeleine. "Why would a dismissed servant write to him?"

"I cannot say, my lady," Eliza answered. "But you might find an answer in those papers, if they come."

Madeleine looked at her incredulously. "What is your point, Eliza?" she asked. "What is it you are not telling me?"

"I know nothing *to* tell you," said Eliza earnestly. "But sometimes when a body goes poking about, they find things, ma'am. Just be sure . . . just be sure you are ready to find them. That's all."

Madeleine let her gaze fall to the folded letter. "It is not Florette's fate which concerns me now," she said quietly. "I need, Eliza, to find some papers. I am hoping I shall find them in Papa's things."

"Papers, ma'am?" Eliza snapped the wrinkles from Madeleine's nightdress, and hung it in the wardrobe. "What sort of papers?"

Madeleine felt her cheeks grow warm. "A legal document to do with my annulment," she quietly admitted. "The papers which ended my marriage to Mr. MacLachlan."

"Oh," said Eliza quietly. "I see."

She busied herself by rifling through Madeleine's wardrobe. From time to time, she would pull out a gown, study it, and put it back in again, but Madeleine got the feeling Eliza was not really looking at them. "Are you and Mr. Geoffrey still to take tea with Lady Treyhern?" she finally asked.

"Yes, and then we are to walk together in Hyde Park," said Madeleine.

"Which dress will you be wanting, ma'am?"

"The dark blue silk, I daresay," said Madeleine, rising from her desk.

She went to her small dressing table, and began to comb out her hair. Ordinarily, Eliza would have come at once to assist her, but this morning, strangely, she did not. Instead, she was rearranging Madeleine's shoes in the bottom of the wardrobe. Madeleine gave an inward shrug, and went on to twist up her hair, vaguely wondering what had got into Eliza, whose mind was so decidedly elsewhere.

Five o'clock, Lady Treyhern explained, was the fashionable time to see and be seen in Hyde Park. At that anointed, all-important hour, anyone who was anyone in society would drive out in their high-perch phaetons, or stroll languidly about with their finest parasols, whilst looking deeply, desperately bored.

"But Geoff and I do not know anyone in Town," explained Madeleine, as they stepped off the pavement at Oxford Street. "Perhaps you really *shall* be bored?"

Lady Treyhern laughed her light, tinkling laugh, and linked her arm through Madeleine's. "You must remember to call me Helene, my dear," she said. "And we go not to be seen, but to quietly watch young Geoffrey, and to have a pleasant chat, yes?"

Geoff was walking some paces ahead of them with Lady Ariane Rutledge's hand lying lightly on his coat sleeve. Lady Ariane was a slight, almost fairylike creature, and seen thus together, one could almost imagine them a couple—until Geoff turned around, and the boyish innocence of his features belied his height. Nonetheless, the two had fashioned a friendship of sorts. They played at chess and cards together, and sometimes exchanged books. Lady Ariane was bored to tears in Town, Helene explained, and her three half siblings were still very young. A friend of Geoff's age was a welcome distraction.

"She begged to be brought out this year," Helene confided. "She will be seventeen in a few weeks' time. But my husband would not hear of it. Not this year, he says, and quite probably not next year, either. Ariane thinks him utterly draconian."

"No, your husband is very wise," said Madeleine fervently. "You must not let her persuade him."

Helene shot her a sidelong glance. "You think not?"

"Seventeen is much too young," Madeleine answered. "Far better she should enjoy two more years of her family's protection. She will have time to mature, and learn the ways of the world. She will be much less likely to . . . well, to do something foolish."

Madeleine had not meant to speak with such vehemence, but Helene was looking at her rather pointedly. "You sound as if you speak from experience," said her new friend. "But no! Do not tell me! I, too, was quite shockingly foolish at seventeen."

"Not as foolish as I was," said Madeleine quietly.

Again, Helene laughed, but the sound was faintly bittersweet. "Oh, my dear, I should sooner die than tell you what I did," she murmured. "Suffice it to say that I fell in love, inappropriately so."

"As did I," Madeleine admitted.

Helene gave a Gallic shrug. "Ah, well, I was very fortunate in the end," she said. "It all turned out the best for me. What of you, my dear? Did things . . . work out?"

Madeleine blushed, and shook her head. "They did

not," she confessed. "Indeed, they could hardly have ended worse. That is why, I think, that I sometimes . . . well, I sometimes blame myself for Geoffrey's imaginings and melancholia."

"Why, whatever can you mean?"

Madeleine looked away. "The months of my pregnancy were not happy ones for me," she said softly. "I—I was not well. I felt very alone, and quite despondent. I believe that my—my grief must have somehow affected him. They say, you know, that such things can happen."

"Nonsense!" said Helene briskly. "A child cannot be marked in the womb, my dear, by what one sees or feels, and I beg you will not continue to think so. You cannot help Geoffrey if you succumb to tarradiddles and old wives' tales. You must believe only in the practical and the scientific."

"You are so clear-thinking and so certain," said Madeleine. "I wish I could be more so."

Again, the casual shrug. "With age, my dear, comes wisdom," she said. "And, regrettably, a variety of sagging body parts. I sometimes wonder if the trade is worth it."

"You hardly look past thirty," said Madeleine quite honestly.

"Well, let us speak no further of time's ravages," said Helene. "Let us talk instead of young Geoff. How does he go on?"

Madeleine had already told Helene of Geoff's having locked himself in his room. Since that terrible afternoon, however, his disposition had been even and cheerful, and she told Helene so.

On the pavement ahead, Geoff and Lady Ariane had stopped to watch a man with a pet monkey. The monkey wore a red waistcoat, and was doing tricks in exchange for bits of fruit. Geoff was laughing, his expression carefree.

"He certainly gives every impression of being a happy, normal young man," mused Helene. "I must tell you frankly, my dear, that in the time I have observed him, he has seemed a most sensible boy."

"I daresay I should be glad to hear that," said Madeleine.

"Indeed, you should," said Helene.

For a time, they walked quietly beside one another. Madeleine did not know what else to say. She could not honestly disagree with her friend's assessment.

Farther down the street, one could see the Cumberland Gate into Hyde Park. Lady Ariane and Geoff rushed on ahead. Helene, however, did not quicken her pace but slowed it, her brow lightly furrowed.

"I wish that there was something specific I could tell you that might help you deal with your son, Madeleine," she finally went on. "But I do not think that my opinion of young Geoff will change."

"You see nothing wrong with him, then?" Madeleine's voice was hopeful.

"I do not," said Helene. "He is bright, and he obviously has artistic leanings, but that does not make him fanciful. He is polite, and even a little grown-up for his age. Indeed, I do not think that your son suffers from anything remotely like a mental disease."

"Do you not?"

"No," said Helene slowly. "Which leaves only one rather odd possibility."

Madeleine stopped walking altogether. "And that would be . . . ?"

"That his fears are not unfounded," said Helene, lifting

her elegant shoulders. "What is it, my dear, that Hamlet says to Horatio about 'things wondrous strange'?"

Madeleine searched her mind. "Why, he says that . . . that there are stranger things on heaven and earth—"

"—than are dreamt of in your philosophy," Helene finished. "Yes, yes, that is the one. And perhaps, my dear—just *perhaps*—there is something here which we have not yet dreamt of?"

Madeleine looked at her dubiously. "I cannot imagine what."

"Nor can I." Helene's gaze had turned inward now. "No, nor can I. But I am going to think on it, my dear. I am going to think on it very carefully indeed."

Chapter Eight

*Ken yourself, and your neighbor
will ne'er mistake ye.*

Merrick's meeting with Lord Treyhern dragged on for the better part of an hour. He had called upon the gentleman at his Mortimer Street town house promptly at five, but the earl had a great many questions, and a vast deal of information to share. Moreover, he was taking his time, Merrick realized, in assessing his prospective business partner's character.

Treyhern owned a vast amount of property and had options on a great deal more, including twenty building lots near the village of Kensington which he was willing to let on ninety-nine-year ground leases. The earl seemed a meticulous and shrewd businessman. Almost as important was the fact that his home was comfortable but not ostentatious. When it came to the extravagant English aristocracy, Merrick had learned, opulent surroundings usually meant there was a teetering dun heap on some poor bastard's desk.

"There is one other small matter which I should touch on before we get into more confidential matters," said

Treyhern some thirty minutes into their conversation. "I like my business done a certain way."

Merrick frowned. "A certain way?" he echoed. "What way would that be, Treyhern?"

The earl cleared his throat. "Let me be blunt," he said in a steady voice. "I like things done honestly and above-board. I do not believe in riding roughshod over anyone, and I don't bully people with my purse. You have a reputation, Mr. MacLachlan."

"Aye, that I do," answered Merrick. "But not for dishonesty or duplicity."

Treyhern flashed a rueful smile. "You are right," he agreed. "Those are accusations which have yet to be flung in your direction."

"As to any bullying or intimidation, that, like beauty, is often in the eye of the beholder," Merrick continued. "I've found the incompetent to be rather quick with their insults."

Treyhern was toying with a mechanical pen on his desk. "You are a brilliant man, MacLachlan," he said, his voice softer now. "And a cynical one, too, I think. I can't help that—men usually turn cynical for a reason—just be careful you do not let it get the better of you."

Merrick was beginning to wonder what the man was getting at. Surely he was not naive? "Wealth was never built on a charitable nature, Treyhern," he returned. "I am a success because I have separated sentiment from common sense. I run a business, not an almshouse. But if at any time you find my methods do not suit you, speak it plain, and we'll part ways."

"Fair enough," said the earl drawing a leather-bound ledger from his desk. "Let's get down to the numbers then, and see how we get on."

Merrick relaxed into his chair, and accepted the glass of brandy the earl offered. He respected the man for his bluntness, though he bristled at some of his words. But Treyhern, it seemed, had had his say and was ready to move ahead. In short order, his desk was covered with maps, plats, and accounting sheets which the two of them pored over.

They were both surprised when the clock struck six. Treyhern began to shuffle through the pile of papers. "I am afraid I have not been attending the clock," he said a little fretfully. "We have not even discussed these options near the Dorset coast."

Merrick straightened in his chair and set aside his empty brandy glass. "I should like to do so," he answered. "If now is inconvenient, I can return tomorrow."

"Ah, tomorrow I am promised to my wife!" said the earl, his expression sheepish. "It is her dear old nanny's birthday, and we are bound for Hampstead for the day. Look—perhaps we might finish this over a bit of beef? Could you stay, MacLachlan? We needn't change for dinner. It is just my wife, my daughter, and I."

"I have the most delightful idea, Madeleine," said Helene as the four of them made their way back up Mortimer Street. "Why do you and Geoff not stay to dinner? It is just Cam, Ariane, and I."

"Oh, yes, please!" Lady Ariane Rutledge laid a plaintive hand on Madeleine's arm. "We are so frightfully dull here, just the three of us."

Madeleine exchanged glances with Geoff, whose eyes were alight. The gorgeous afternoon had passed, and the air was growing heavy with the evening's damp. "Well, Geoff is but twelve," she began.

Helene frowned. "Surely, my dear, he is not always relegated to the schoolroom?"

Madeleine felt her cheeks warm. "Not at all, lately," she admitted. "Geoff's tutor is in Norfolk spending a few weeks with his family. I am ashamed to say the two of us have been eating in the kitchen since taking our little cottage."

"Excellent, then!" said Helene. "We are agreed. Mrs. Trinkle said Cook was putting on a huge joint this morning, so we shall have plenty. Ariane, be a dear and run up ahead to tell her we'll be five for dinner."

Looking very pleased with herself, Lady Ariane did as her stepmother bade and hastened her steps along. "When is your new house to be ready, Madeleine?" asked Helene, as the girl darted across the street. "It cannot be much longer now, can it?"

"I—I am not perfectly sure," said Madeleine. The truth was, the house was probably ready for occupancy, but she was still undecided about what to do. She did love the house. She had invested a great many hopes and dreams in it. But to be so close to Merrick . . . ah, that she did not think she could survive.

By the time they reached the front steps, the first fat drops of rain were falling. Madeleine saw that a dark, handsome man with a hint of silver in his hair was waiting with the door thrown wide. It was the earl himself. His height and posture made him unmistakable. He greeted his wife with much affection, even going so far as to kiss her cheek once the door was closed.

"Good news, my love," said Helene as they went up the stairs. "Lady Bessett and her son are to dine with us."

Lord Treyhern waved his hand in the direction of the

yellow parlor. "What a pleasant surprise," he said. "I, too, have a dinner guest. Pray let me introduce you."

"Oh, I do hope we have not intruded," said Madeleine.

"Nonsense," Treyhern replied.

Just then, they stepped into the parlor. A tall, lean man stood by the fireplace, one well-shod foot propped almost languidly on the brass fender. He lifted his eyes from his tumbler of brandy and pinned Madeleine with his ice-blue gaze, just as he had that fateful evening in Lady Forne's ballroom.

It was like a physical blow to the stomach. Stunned, Madeleine almost tripped over the opulent Aubusson carpet, catching herself at the very last instant.

Treyhern seemed unaware of her discomfort. "Lady Bessett, may I present Mr. Merrick MacLachlan?"

Merrick set his drink aside, and bowed. "We are quite well acquainted," he said in a low, almost suggestive voice. "Good evening, Madeleine."

Madeleine could not find her voice. His glittering eyes had sucked the very air from her lungs.

Helene was clearly wondering if some sort of faux pas had been committed. "Why, you know one another!" she said with specious cheer. "How lovely."

Only Geoff seemed to have his wits about him. "Mr. MacLachlan's workers are building a house for Mamma," he said. "I'm to have a new drawing table, and I will be able to see the river from my schoolroom."

Their hosts instantly relaxed. "Oh, a house!" said the earl.

"Yes, of course," said Helene. "Madeleine's dream house. What a remarkable coincidence."

"Is it indeed your dream house, Madeleine?" Merrick

softly inquired. "I was not aware. I must endeavor to make it utterly perfect, then."

Madeleine did not like the way his words and his eyes melted over her. And she did not like the sensation which went twisting through her body at the sight of him. Moreover, no one but Geoff had missed his use of her Christian name. "I . . . I like the house very well indeed," she managed, opening her hands rather lamely. "And it is very close to the river."

Merrick was smiling, but the smile did not reach his eyes. He surprised her by turning his attention to her son. "Hello, Geoff," he said. "I have not seen you around in a while."

"I—I have been busy," he said, his gaze dropping to his shoes.

"Busy with your sketching, I daresay?"

A frisson of something like fear ran down Madeleine's spine. Merrick had tilted his head to one side, as if attempting to see the boy's eyes. What on earth was going on?

"Geoffrey," she said, her voice too sharp. "You cannot be acquainted with Mr. MacLachlan. I mean . . . *are* you?"

Merrick stepped nearer. "I have seen him round the village," he remarked. "And Geoff has been by the site to make a sketch or two."

"Geoffrey!" said Madeleine, her heart in her throat. "You—why, you must not do such a thing. Indeed, I must forbid it."

"You *forbid* it?" Merrick's voice dropped an octave. "May I ask your reason?"

Madeleine felt her face heat. "It is not safe," she answered. "And I cannot think you wish to have children round a work site where there are all manner of dangers and . . . and uncertainties."

"Let me assuage your concerns, ma'am," he answered. "Geoff keeps his distance. He is perfectly safe, I do assure you. Building projects tend to attract bright young lads, and if you forbid it, I fear it will be all the more interesting to him."

Lord Treyhern cleared his throat. "A valid point," he interjected. "Forbidden fruit, and all that, of course. Speaking of which, may I offer you a glass of wine, Lady Bessett?"

"Yes, we have madeira and French vermouth on the sideboard," said Helene on a rush. "And Ariane, my love, will you ring for some lemonade?"

"To be sure, Mamma." Lady Ariane darted toward the bellpull. "Mrs. Trinkle usually makes it quite sweet, Geoff. Have you any objection?"

Geoff shrugged both shoulders. "I don't mind."

Madeleine smiled apologetically at Helene. "And I should adore a glass of vermouth."

Helene had gone to the sideboard to pour. Fleetingly, Madeleine debated simply snatching the decanter. Her nerves could have used it.

Merrick MacLachlan was still staring at her, his eyes hard and surprisingly dark now. He looked like a sleek black cat poised to pounce. Then, suddenly, something inside him seemed to relent. He rocked back onto his heels, his body relaxing. "MacGregor & Company will be finished in Walham Green early next year," he remarked, his tone casual. "After that, Geoff, you will have to look elsewhere for your entertainments, I am afraid."

It was on the tip of Madeleine's tongue to rebuke him, but something in Merrick's silvery blue eyes kept confounding her. She had forbidden Geoff the construction area, and she had meant it. Hadn't she? Their quarrel had already distressed Helene and her husband.

She looked at Helene apologetically when her hostess pressed the glass of wine into her hand. "Thank you."

"It is my favorite," said Helene.

Just then, a maid came in with two glasses of lemonade. Ariane took one, and passed the second to Geoff, who was attending the gentlemen's conversation with a rapt expression.

"Lord Treyhern has some property to let near Kensington," Merrick said, turning to the boy. "If we can work out the rents, I was thinking I might build some houses. Not terraced buildings, mind. More like the ones in your elevation drawings."

Treyhern was nodding. "It might be just the thing," he remarked. "Not everyone wishes to live in Town, stacked cheek by jowl to one another. People want a bit of space—and Kensington is still little more than a bucolic village."

Helene laughed. "Oh, not for long, my love!" she warned. "Here, may I refresh your brandies?"

"What sort of roofs, then?" asked the boy, as Helene took the gentlemen's glasses. "I like mansards best."

Helene turned around. "Do you indeed, Geoff?" she asked. "They are French, you know. Like me."

"They are French," her husband solemnly agreed. "And for that reason, they will never sell well in London, or anywhere this side of the Channel."

"*Ma foi,* how foolish!" Helene responded, withdrawing the stopper from the brandy decanter. "The English love French wine. French food. French fashions. Why may they not have our roofs?"

Merrick smiled. "Admittedly, my lady, it makes no

sense," he agreed. "But the stubborn English want their roofs gabled or hipped. They do not take such matters lightly."

"You are Scotch, are you not?" said Helene, returning with Merrick's glass.

"Through and through, ma'am."

Helene gave a mischievous smile. "I think you poke a little fun at the English, no?"

He smiled back, and this time, it reached his eyes. "A little, perhaps."

But Geoff asked another question of Merrick, something about foundations, and the gentlemen's attention returned to the subject of building things. Ariane looked a bit put out. She had lost her playmate to dull, masculine pursuits. Helene shot Madeleine an apologetic look and struck up a conversation about a dress Ariane had admired in the park.

"I do think that shade of green would look lovely with your hair, my dear," she said. "Perhaps the three of us might go shopping tomorrow?"

"I should love to," said Madeleine, though she was barely attending the conversation.

She was still watching Geoff from the corner of one eye. She was surprised by his eager, almost confident manner tonight. His face had again taken on that enthralled look, and it greatly worried Madeleine. She had never approved of his passion for drawing things—well, technical things. His sketches of birds and plants were excellent, too, and she had encouraged him to confine his attentions to those more edifying subjects.

Soon they were summoned to dinner, which turned out to be a delicious but simple meal. The gentlemen continued to talk about land speculation and construction, and Geoff continued to watch, his eyes wide.

Merrick was clearly in his element. His eyes kept crinkling at the corners with laughter, and one could see he'd spent a great deal of time in the sun. She wondered when he had come to look so lean and so hardened. She wondered, too, how he'd got such a horrific scar—not the neat, straight slash of a rapier's blade, but more like a hacking blow from a dockside brawl.

The scar did not, however, detract from his dark good looks, more was the pity. The boyish eagerness had long ago left his face, and in its place was a hard, blasé sort of worldliness. He was telling some sort of story now, the hand which held his empty wineglass gesticulating energetically. He seemed wholly unaware of her presence, or unconcerned by it, at the very least.

How Madeleine wished she felt the same. How she wished the mere sight of him did not make her heart ache from the flood of old, sweet memories. She wondered if he had any regrets at all about what had happened between them so long ago. Had he ever meant to be her husband? Or had Papa's unexpected arrival in Gretna Green given him a way out and a way to have what he really wanted, all at the same time? That was the one question she would like to ask him. Perhaps she would. Perhaps she would just screw up her courage and ask.

She could still remember the smells and sounds of the old inn at Gretna Green, even the creak of the ancient floorboards seemed forever fixed in her memory. And she could still see the letter Papa had tossed down on her narrow, rickety bed with a disdainful flick of his wrist. He thought Madeleine a fool, and he told her so. She had fallen, he told her, for the oldest trick in the book. The only hope of a penniless young man was to marry for money.

"Where d-did you get this?" Madeleine had asked her father, sniffing back tears as she read it.

"I paid for it," he had snapped. "And damned generously, too."

The letter had been addressed to one of London's most prominent architects, a gentleman named Wilkerson who was opening a new firm to design and construct magnificent buildings all over London. And Merrick, apparently, had been invited to join. But opening such a business was a costly venture. Each partner would be required to front a large sum of money. Merrick's letter had promised he would be able to produce a bank draft by the first week of August.

Madeleine had been married on the twenty-second of July. Merrick had timed his seduction well. No wonder he had rushed off first thing that morning to ready the horses. But the frightening thing was, Madeleine almost did not care. It had hurt, yes, and more than a little. But even the realization that Merrick had married her for her money had not lessened her desire to be with him.

"It's not too late, Madeleine," he father had insisted. Against her protests, his servants had already begun packing her things. "I've hushed this business up, though it's cost me a bloody fortune. And I've agreed to give MacLachlan his goddamned thirty thousand, much as it grieves me. In return, he's agreed to an annulment."

"An-an *annulment*—?" Madeleine had been crying in earnest by then. "What is that?"

"Just leave it to me, girl," he father had snapped. "Now

for pity's sake, stop sniveling, and dress. I'll take you back to Sheffield. Lord Henry Winters will be back in Town by the spring. Thank God it is not too late to salvage this mess."

But Madeleine had refused, thinking that Merrick would return; that he would burst indignantly into the room and declare it all a lie. But he never came back. No doubt his shame at having been bought off had kept him away. And in the end, Madeleine's father had ordered his footmen to carry Madeleine bodily from the room, the room in which she had last gazed upon her husband's face. Until that awful Thursday two weeks past.

And now she was living within half a mile of him. Of her husband. Dear God, could it be true?

But what did it matter? The awful truth was, in her heart, he always had been her husband. In her heart, she had never moved beyond that one sweet day in Gretna Green, when life had held such joy and promise. A part of her—the foolish part—had never stopped loving him, never stopped yearning for the rush of desire she had so fleetingly known in his embrace. Even now, in merely looking at him, she could feel her breath catch and her stomach bottom out. But beneath it all was that simmering rage, that awful sense of betrayal, which she had tried to numb by turning her energy to the raising of her child and the simple tasks of living an everyday life.

From across the table, his gaze caught hers, dark and demanding. For an instant, she could not get her breath. For an instant, they were alone in the room, and time had spun away. It was as if her innermost confessions had just flung open a door; some sort of portal to the past which she had kept carefully shut all these long and lonely years. Now, suddenly, it had burst open. Dear God.

She did not realize she was still staring at him until Helene recalled her to the present. "Will you have a little sliver of Stilton, Madeleine?" she asked, thrusting an assortment of cheeses in her direction. "It is quite excellent."

But Madeleine's hands were trembling. She dared not take up so much as her wineglass. "No, thank you."

Helene set the platter away. "Well, shall we retire to the yellow parlor, and leave the gentlemen to their port?"

"I think that would be wise," she managed to say.

Forcing away her memories, Madeleine rose, and motioned for Geoff to follow. His lower lip came out a fraction, but he did as she had bid. Lady Ariane, too, flounced from the room, looking perhaps a little less put out.

"Mamma," she said, when they had settled down with a tray of coffee, "I wish to show Geoff the *tarocchi*. May I?"

Helene looked less than pleased. "I think not, Ariane," she said as she poured Madeleine's coffee. "Why do you not play at backgammon or chess?"

"Oh, poo!" said the girl. "We are so tired of those games. Why may I not show Geoff the *tarocchi*? Aunt Catherine gave it to me so that I might practice."

Helene looked at Madeleine almost apologetically. "It is a set of fortune-telling cards," she said. "My husband's sister bought them back from Tuscany."

"I once met a woman in Campania who had quite a way with those things," said Madeleine. "It was just a tad unsettling. But they are harmless amusements, I am sure."

Lips still pursed, Helene gave a tight nod in Lady Ariane's direction. "Very well," she said. "But remember, it is nothing but a game."

Looking very pleased, the girl went to a burnished wooden box on the bookcase and returned with a pack of cards. "First I shall tell Geoff's fortune," she said, pulling a small game table to the center of the room. "Nonna Sofia taught me how to lay out the cards."

"Sofia is Catherine's mother-in-law," Helene explained to Madeleine as Geoff helped unfold the tabletop. "And something of a mischievous old crone, too. My husband thinks her quite mad."

Madeleine was intrigued. "And what does Catherine think?"

Helene shifted her gaze. "Catherine believes the old woman has some sort of unnatural ability," she admitted. "I confess, she can frighten you with—well, let us call them her insights."

As Helene began to speak idly of the shops they might visit the following day, Lady Ariane asked Geoff to cut the cards. Madeleine watched from the corner of her eye as the girl began to lay them out in a horizontal row. Soon the game table was covered. The girl began to turn them up in no particular order Madeleine could discern. The cards were vividly colored, and captioned in a foreign language.

"This card means that you have recently moved from a faraway place," said the girl authoritatively.

"But you already knew that!" Geoff protested, causing Helene to suppress a mischievous smile.

"Shh!" Lady Ariane furrowed her brow. "I believe you will soon be going away again—"

"But I just got here," Geoff interrupted.

"—and you will have a great adventure and learn many wondrous things," she finished. "Ah, yes! I believe—I believe that you shall be going away to university."

Geoff smiled. "Well, of course I shall *someday*," he answered. "What else would I do?"

Lady Ariane shrugged, and continued to weave her story as she slowly turned the cards. Geoff's destiny was in her hands, and with her veracity challenged, the girl began to embellish her tale. "Now, this very stern gentleman on the horse," she went on, "is *il Cavaliere di Anfore,* the Knight of Chalices. This must be is your brother, Lord Bessett. He is very worried about you, and he stands ready to give you material and spiritual guidance."

Geoff looked at her mischievously. "But Alvin has red hair," he returned. "Bright, burning thatches of it. That chap is dark. Besides, Alvin never worried about anything a day in his life."

"Pray do not be silly, Geoff." Ariane waved her hand vaguely. "It is all meant to be symbolic."

The more Geoff teased the girl, the wilder her tale grew. Soon there were great riches, travel to lands afar, and even a kidnapping by mysterious pirates or bandits or perhaps it might even be highwaymen. Lady Ariane was still pondering it when Madeleine turned back to her hostess.

"Your daughter seems enthralled," she whispered. "It is quite charming."

Helene lifted one shoulder in her usual French gesture. "She has been watching Nonna Sofia," she said quietly. "But she does not really know what the cards mean. I am glad, though, that they are enjoying it."

"Now I shall read my own fortune," the girl announced.

"Are you permitted to do that?" Geoff chided. "Aren't there some sort of fortune-telling rules that say you mustn't?"

Ariane shook her head, and after shuffling and cutting the cards to the left, she began to lay them out again. Helene returned to the topic of shopping. She seemed quite persuaded that Ariane should have the new green dress. Madeleine tried to respond politely at each turn of their conversation, but something in Geoff's posture began to draw her eyes.

He was looking decidedly pale now, and the teasing had stopped. He was no longer watching the cards. Instead, he was watching Lady Ariane's face as if transfixed. Madeleine began to have a very ill feeling in the pit of her stomach.

"In any case, the dinner party is to be next week." Helene's voice barely cut into Madeleine's consciousness. "You will just *adore* my sister-in-law Frederica. Do you think I ought to invite Mr. MacLachlan to even up our numbers? I think him dreadfully handsome, if one does not mind the dark, dangerous type."

Geoff's gaze had gone soft and distant. Suddenly, he caught Ariane's hand. The girl looked at him strangely, and tried to draw away. Madeleine had to suppress the urge to fly across the room to them.

"Madeleine?" Helene's voice was arch. "My dear, do you think him handsome or not?"

Madeleine's head jerked around. "I—I beg your pardon, Helene. Who is handsome?"

Helene laughed lightly. "Mr. MacLachlan, silly girl! Now, do not pretend you did not hear what I said. After all, the man has scarcely taken his eyes off you all evening—and you've been little better."

A sudden flash of motion caused them both to turn toward the game table. "But that is my Papa!" said Ariane sharply. "He *is*. That card is *il Re di Mazze*. The King of Wands. My authority figure. It can be no one else."

Geoff dropped the girl's hand as if it had burst into flames. "But your father—" He seemed unable to get his breath. "Your father . . . that cannot be. He is—he is dead."

"Dead?" the girl shrieked, leaping up such that she knocked the table sideways. "Geoffrey Archard, what a horrid thing to say!"

Geoff was blinking rapidly and looking rather dazed. "I—I am sorry!" he said. "I—what did I—Ariane, do sit down. I didn't mean—or what I meant was—"

"Well, I know what you said!" The girl set her hands on her hips. "And you cannot take such a thing back, Geoffrey! Oh, you are the horridest, vilest boy I ever did meet in all my life!"

Madeleine had leapt from the sofa, and gone to the game table. "I am so sorry, Lady Ariane," she said, kneeling to pick the cards from the floor. "Geoff did not mean—well, whatever he said, he did not mean it. His—his mind was elsewhere. Was it not, my love?"

"My mind was elsewhere," Geoff repeated mechanically. "Oh, Ariane, please do not be angry. I forgot where—what—what we were doing. I—I touched your hand. I'm sorry. It just—it just mixes me up sometimes."

Madeleine restored the cards to the table, and looked to Helene for support. But Helene had gone deathly white. She was staring at Geoffrey as if he had just sprouted horns and spewed hellfire out his nose. Lady Ariane had slammed her cards back into the wooden box.

"Oh, Helene, do forgive us!" said Madeleine, returning to the sofa. "Geoff is young. He—he was just teasing, and did it badly."

Helene seemed to snap from her trance. "I—yes, of

course, my dear," she said, forcing a smile. "He is just a child. What can children know? Ariane, kindly get out the backgammon. I do not like those cards."

Ariane eyed Geoff nastily. "There is nothing wrong with the cards," she said, her tone petulant.

Helene lifted both brows. "I said *kindly get out the backgammon*," she repeated in a no-nonsense tone. "Those cards—they have upset Geoffrey. And me. Now be a good hostess."

Ariane hung her head. "I am sorry, Geoff," she said. "I—I know you were just teasing."

"But I did it badly," he muttered. "It was not funny, I know. I cannot think what came over me."

Ariane looked mollified and went to the shelf for the backgammon set. Madeleine still stood between them, trying not to wring her hands.

"I think perhaps we ought to go, Helene," she said. "We have had such a lovely afternoon and evening with you. But I think we are all very tired. I know that Geoffrey is."

Geoff was looking at her with utter remorse. "Mamma is right," he said quietly. "I am a little tired."

Helene smiled and rose gracefully from the sofa. "I completely understand," she said, floating across the floor to kiss Madeleine's cheek. "I will make your good-byes to my husband, and to Mr. MacLachlan. I cannot think what they are doing still in the dining room."

"Hiding from us, most likely." Madeleine flashed a rueful smile. With her eyes, she again asked Helene's forgiveness, and was rewarded with a sincere hug.

Just then, the dining room door flew open. "How unforgivably rude we have been," said the earl, opening his hands expansively. "We fell into a conversation about business, and time quite escaped us. Lady Bessett, please do not say you are leaving. The night is young, is it not?"

Madeleine was trying to look at the earl, and not at Merrick. Merrick, however, had no such compunction, and was staring at her quite overtly. "I am afraid Geoffrey needs his rest, my lord," Madeleine managed to say. "And we have intruded upon your hospitality quite long enough."

Merrick stepped farther into the room. "I am afraid, Treyhern, that I must be going, too."

After a little polite protestation, the earl ceded to their wishes and called for both their carriages. They stood chatting almost awkwardly, until a footman bowed himself into the room to inform them the two conveyances awaited.

Helene waved good-bye as Madeleine started down the steps. At the front door, Merrick offered his arm, but she pretended not to notice. To her disconcertion, he instead set a warm, heavy hand to the small of her back, and went down the rain-slick steps beside her. Lord Treyhern already stood on the pavement, motioning to the coachmen.

There was a break in the drizzle, but the cobbles still glistened with damp. It would be good to get home, where she could perhaps begin to relax. She needed to put away these maudlin thoughts of what once had been and think only of the here and now. She must focus on Geoffrey and try to figure out what could be done for him. His outburst tonight had been beyond the pale.

Suddenly, Geoff tugged at her sleeve, the gesture almost childlike. She looked down to see that his eyes were round, his face again bloodless.

Oh, dear God. Not again.

"Mamma," he said, "I think Mr. MacLachlan should ride back to Walham with us."

Merrick leaned forward on his gold-knobbed stick, caught her eyes, and lifted one eyebrow almost insolently.

Madeleine cut her gaze away. "Do not be silly, Geoff," she said coolly. "Mr. MacLachlan has a carriage."

"But—but I think the three of us should go together!" he said stridently. "I—I wish to speak with him. I wish to—to ask him something. About building things."

"About building things?" Madeleine echoed.

"Your son has a naturally inquisitive mind, my lady," said Lord Treyhern.

"Yes, I do," said the boy a little desperately. "And I wish—I wish to build something."

"What?" she asked flatly.

Geoff licked his lips. "Well, a—a windmill. You know. Like the one we saw in Scarborough? Mr. MacLachlan, have you ever seen a windmill? Are they not quite amazing?"

"I have seen a few in East Anglia, but they are less common in Scotland," said Merrick. "And yes, they are quite amazing."

"May he, Mamma?" whined the boy. "May he not come up with us in our carriage?"

Suddenly, Madeleine saw the way of things. Geoff was afraid he was going to be scolded for his outburst with Lady Ariane—and he was. But he was hoping to forestall it with a guest in the carriage.

This time, Merrick leaned so near, his shoulder touched her. The arrogant devil was enjoying her discomfort. "I should be happy to accompany you, Lady Bessett," he said, his lips far too near her ear. "I should in no way wish to disappoint a child."

Madeleine stiffened. Merrick's scent teased at her nostrils, just as it had that day she had so foolishly peeked into his bedchamber. Suddenly, the vision of their bodies pressed together in his office returned, and with it came the heat and the carnal awareness of his very large, very male body.

Beside her, Lord Treyhern shifted his weight uncomfortably. "Shall I send Mr. MacLachlan's coachman on ahead, then, ma'am?"

Madeleine forced a tight smile. "Yes, my lord," she managed. "I thank you."

"Grimes may go home without me," said Merrick. "I shall walk from Lady Bessett's house."

The earl went to the horses' heads, and spoke a few words up at the driver, who tossed a strange look at Merrick, then clicked to his horses and set off in a clatter of hooves and a jingling of harness. Madeleine was stuck with him now.

With an artful flourish, Merrick threw open her carriage door, and presented an elegantly gloved hand. "After you, my lady?"

Chapter Nine

The devil's boots do na' creak.

Merrick watched in barely veiled amusement as Madeleine shot him one last contemptuous glance, then reluctantly took his hand to climb into the carriage. He despised her, of course, but did not mind tormenting her. Indeed, he had agreed to the boy's outrageous scheme in part to infuriate her. So it was more than a little humbling when the sight of her blue silk skirts slithering provocatively over her arse made his mouth go dry. A just punishment, that.

But blister it, she was *his wife*. The wife he had never forgotten. The wife he could not touch. It was damnable, and it had blighted his life. Was he to be left hanging in purgatory until one of them died?

She had not waited, had she? She had taken another man to her bed, and her stuttered excuses about an annulment were naught but guilt-ridden blither. Suddenly, Merrick's situation seemed more intolerable than ever.

Behind him, Treyhern cleared his throat. Merrick realized that they were waiting on him.

He followed the boy into the carriage, a sleek, well-appointed barouche, took the empty rear-facing seat, and laid his walking stick across his legs. He and Madeleine were so close their knees brushed. Merrick made no effort to move. The carriage gave a sharp jerk and rattled away from the curb.

The silence in the carriage was deafening. Oddly, the boy was fidgeting almost nervously and staring out the window, barely aware of their presence. Merrick looked again at Madeleine, and deliberately caught her gaze. He wondered what she was thinking. Unfortunately, he knew what *he* was thinking.

"I find it very odd," he said in a low, quiet voice, "how one moment in time can suddenly throw one back to another time and another place, often when one least expects it."

She shrugged. "I daresay."

He gave a muted smile. "There is something about a summer's rain that is almost romantic, is there not?" he murmured. "Indeed, I remember another such carriage ride like this. In the early evening, following an afternoon rain, when the roads had just such a sheen."

"I have had a hundred such carriage rides," she said coolly. "This is England. We get rain."

"Ah, and so I would have said myself," he answered. "But this, Lady Bessett, was a ride to remember. The atmosphere, you see, was just as it is now. And the scent in the air—tell me, my lady, what is that lovely perfume you are wearing? A sort of jasmine, is it not? Yes, the air was filled with just such a fragrance."

She was glowering at him now, but she was none the less lovely for it.

He smiled, and made a stab at her jugular. "Tell me, Lady Bessett, have you ever driven north beyond Penrith through the Vale of Eden?"

At that, Madeleine went utterly pale.

Most certainly she had made that drive—with him, during their impetuous, impassioned flight to Gretna Green. Fleetingly, he closed his eyes, and remembered. Good God, they had been wild for one another then. Just a touch, just a sidelong glance, and desire would spring forth as if it had been weeks instead of days or mere hours.

"The Vale of Eden," he echoed pensively. "It makes one think of—well, of sin, and of temptation, does it not?"

It was an apt description of their visit. They had been within a day's drive of the border, and he had been growing increasingly desperate to wed her with every passing mile. And so he had pushed the horses hard, driving well into the early hours of the evening. The maid had slumped against the hood and begun to snore, as had become her frequent—and quite convenient—habit. At some point, Madeleine had set her small, warm hand on his thigh a little anxiously.

He could no longer recall what had troubled her; the deepening gloom, or a perilous bend in the road, perhaps? He remembered only that he had returned the caress, settling his hand reassuringly over hers. And then he had kissed her, a swift but gentle meeting of their lips which had somehow lingered longer than simple reassurance required. By then, Madeleine had proven herself a sweetly insatiable lover. Her hand had inched higher, her nails had dug deeper.

In response, he had slid one arm around her, pulling her against him. And somehow, as it so often did with them, matters got out of hand. Whatever discomfiture she had suffered had turned to something very different. They had exchanged knowing, heated glances. Madeleine's small, clever fingers had slid farther up his thigh, then a little farther still, to lightly stroke the growing evidence of his arousal. In an instant, he had pulled the carriage off the road and lifted her down.

Just then, Madeleine recalled him to the present, twitching at her skirts to neaten the folds.

He cleared his throat sharply. "I believe, Lady Bessett, that stretch of road is my most fondly remembered in all of England," he said quietly. "There are many scenic spots at which one may pull over and admire the—oh, what would one call them?—yes, the beauties of nature."

"Are there indeed?" she said coolly. "I cannot recall."

Ah, but she did. Merrick could see it in her eyes, which were simmering with heat now. They had simmered with heat on that earlier night, too, albeit from an entirely different sort. Together he and Madeleine had strolled deep into the gloom of some farmer's empty pasture, far enough to ensure at least a measure of privacy. Still, it had been a rash, passionate thing to do, and the risk of being caught, of making love like wild things beneath the open, moonlit skies, had been like an aphrodisiac—not that either of them had needed it.

With hands which shook, Merrick had undressed Madeleine then and there, with naught but the stars above, and an old woolen blanket spread beneath their fevered bodies to cover the lush Cumbrian grass.

"Cumbria, I believe, has a lot of soft grass," he remarked.

"Yes," she said tightly. "I believe they, too, get rain from time to time."

But on that night, his mind had not been concerned with the weather. Because the ground was hard and the grass damp, he had taken the bottom, and set his hands around her slender waist. She had laughed and caught her balance when he lifted her on top of him, her eyes widening with delight. She had enjoyed her newfound power, quickly learning how to ride him. How to torment him. How to pull her muscles taut about his throbbing cock and rise up slowly, drawing out his desire like a fine, twisting ribbon of fire. Even now, after all the bitter years, he could still see the faint sheen of moonlight on her small, round breasts. The delicate pink nipples, so firm and proud. Her lovely face, a mask of near ecstasy.

Her breasts were much fuller now, he thought, staring at the cut of her bodice. He wondered, a little less dispassionately than he might have wished, just what they looked like. Would those nipples still be just as deliciously delicate and pink? How would they weigh in a man's broad palms? Would they fill his mouth and drive him insane? God, perhaps they already had.

"Did you know, Lady Bessett, that it can get quite hot in Cumbria?" he asked. "Indeed, I get a little overheated just remembering that particular evening."

She was now too indignant to speak. He was not perfectly sure why he was bent on tormenting her—or himself. But on that long-ago night, it had been she who was bent on torment.

Over and over, Madeleine had risen up on her finely muscled, milk white thighs, milking him, driving him right to the edge, then leaving him there, until at last her own release edged near. She had cried out, and tossed her head back in the faint moonlight, her hands flowing over her body, caressing her belly and her breasts, stroking herself and stoking her own passion as she lost herself in a release which had left him feeling wild with desire and almost wickedly voyeuristic. And he had known then, as he pumped himself into her with all his joyous, youthful fervor, that he was the luckiest man on God's earth.

He leaned across the carriage, closing the distance between their bodies. "I can tell you quite certainly, Lady Bessett, that I have rarely been better satisfied with a good, hard ride," he murmured. "Those rich, rolling hills and perfect, swelling mounds. The hidden treasures. The sheer fertility of the landscape. It makes one wish to simply reach out and . . . well, *touch* it."

She jerked back so sharply she almost bumped her head.

He grinned at her across the carriage.

"I am sorry," she said. "I fear I have the headache. Would you mind awfully?"

"Mind what?" he asked solicitously. "Being quiet? Why, not at all, my dear. I shall simply sit here and just envision it in my mind, laying bare every little detail. In my imagination. Quietly."

"How merciful of you," she snapped.

Her face had flooded with lovely color. As if suddenly realizing it, Madeleine turned away, her haughty profile cast into shape and shadow by the flickering carriage lamp. Perfect beauty. Perfect cruelty. He sometimes thought Madeleine the epitome of both. And even knowing what she was, goddamn it, he still burned for her.

He let his eyes run down her simple, but well-cut gown. He had bought enough female finery to know that such elegance came dear. Her jewelry, too, was expensive.

The late Lord Bessett, it seemed, had left his widow well provided for.

But perhaps it was not her husband's money which sustained Madeleine in such style, he thought as the carriage turned the first corner. Perhaps it was that bastard Jessup's. Or perhaps it was the vast wealth which had passed to her through her deceased mother. As it happened, Madeleine had been quite an heiress—a fact he'd learned only after falling head over heels in love with the girl.

But what difference would it have made? He had not chosen to love her—indeed, it had been damned inconvenient. He had been too young and too poor to take a wife, and she—well, she had simply been too young. Like many girls of her class and age, Madeleine, he had come to realize, had simply been in love with the *notion* of love. After living the life of a bored little rich girl in the country, she had come to Town ready for a bit drama. She had wished to be swept off her feet. And he, foolishly, had wielded the broom.

He was almost grateful when the boy spoke, his voice tentative as he looked up at Madeleine. "Mamma, are you angry with me?"

Merrick watched Madeleine's hands fist in her lap. "Geoffrey, I am not angry," she said. "I am *not*. But you really mustn't say such hurtful things. And where on earth did you get such a silly notion anyway?"

Merrick wondered what the devil they were talking about, but it was none of his concern. Madeleine seemed to have forgotten his presence, and the boy was literally squirming now. "I don't *know*!" he cried. "It just—it just popped into my head, that's all. One minute I was watching the cards, and then her—her hand, it . . . it was just *there*, in mine. And then the words burst out."

Madeleine's exasperation showed. "My dear, you simply must stop spouting off such nonsense when it 'pops into your head,'" she scolded. "Have I not cautioned you time and again about that habit?"

"It is not a habit," said the boy.

"Well, what would you call it?"

"I do not know," he whispered. "I hate it. I hate myself. I wish to God it would stop."

"I believe that is quite enough self-loathing one night, Geoffrey," Merrick interjected. "I do not know what it is you stand accused of—"

"No, you do not!" said Madeleine with asperity.

"—but since I am now obliged to listen to its aftermath," Merrick continued, "I feel duty bound to tell you, Geoff, that a man does not wallow in self-pity. If he has erred, or committed some social faux pas, then he writes a letter of apology to his hostess on the morrow."

Madeleine's eyes sparked with angry fire, but the boy looked pensive. "I—I could do that, I daresay," he answered, his voice a little hopeful. "Do you think that it would help?"

"I cannot say," answered Merrick. "But it scarcely matters. A man does his duty, regardless."

"Does he indeed, Mr. MacLachlan?" Madeleine's tone was subtly acerbic. "I have known a few men, regrettably, who failed in that regard. How *kind* of you to explain how things are supposed to work."

"Bitterness does not become you, my dear," he said in a low undertone.

But the truth was, it did. Even by the sputtering light of the carriage lamp, Madeleine's eyes still blazed. Her posture was haughtily erect, and her shoulders were set stubbornly back. *There was the girl he remembered,* the thought. There was his Madeleine. The old Madeleine, not the new, ice-cold, heartless version.

God, there was no denying her beauty. There never had been—not then, and certainly not now. Madeleine had always turned heads. But sometime in the last decade or so, her wide-eyed innocence and long-legged, coltish beauty had become a woman's splendor. She was utterly breathtaking, with her warm blond hair and vivid green eyes. The nose was thin, and a little blunted at the end, whilst her mouth was full, especially her lower lip. Her skin was still the shade of milk heavy with cream, and so flawless she bore not so much as a freckle. A Nordic princess, he had once thought her. It was still quite an apt description.

But as always, Madeleine behaved as if she were unaware of her beauty. He wondered why that was. Perhaps she was just especially clever. She looked across the carriage at him as they made the turn below Hyde Park, and he could see the rage still simmering in her eyes. Why on earth had he goaded her so tonight? He could easily have pretended a mere passing acquaintance with the woman. Instead, he had claimed to know her well and claimed perhaps a good deal more with his eyes.

The fact that his claims, both spoken and unspoken, were perfectly true did not excuse him. He had once known Madeleine as well as he had known himself—or so he had believed. Certainly he had known her body, every warm, creamy inch of it. Even now, the thought of her long, naked thighs was making his groin tighten and his stomach bottom out—and that, in turn, disgusted him.

Why was he even bothering to imagine it? Innocence

no longer held any sexual attraction for him. The more hardened and practiced his women were, the better satisfied he was. What he needed to do was take a mistress. Someone older. More experienced. Someone not quite so depraved as Bess Bromley, perhaps, but similarly skilled. A dark-haired woman who was full-figured, and licentious enough to satisfy a man's baser appetites without asking any questions. Mrs. Farnham knew his tastes; he would ask her to engage someone.

He wished the boy would say something, damn it. But Geoff seemed to have forgotten Merrick was in the carriage. In the dimly lit compartment, the boy's gaze was distant. He sat slumped against the side, his face looking suddenly ageless and weary. He was tired, Merrick supposed. Children were often so, he gathered.

He looked again at Madeleine. The anger had left her eyes, and instead, she was looking down at the boy almost protectively. She stroked one hand down his hair in an act which was purely maternal. She loved the child. In that way, at least, she could truly love. It was better than nothing, he supposed.

Still, he wished that he could bed her just one more time.

The thought came to him again, unbidden and horrifying. Dear God. Madeleine was cold as ice now. At best, she was a spoilt and pampered rich girl. At worst, a manipulative bitch. But as he watched her hand slick over the boy's hair again, he realized that he would have cut off his left ballock just to get her under him one last time. Just to bury himself in that fine, creamy flesh and ride her until the damned demons left him.

The vividness of his fantasies was disturbing. Dear God in heaven, hadn't he already done that once too often? Or more like fifteen or twenty times too often. Yes, well before it had been his right, he had taken Madeleine to his bed and claimed her in the most irreversible of ways.

Then, however, his intentions had been somewhat honorable. He had known from the moment he'd first set eyes on the girl that he meant to marry her—or ruin himself trying. In his desperation to have her, he had done the unspeakable, thinking, foolishly, that once it was done, there would be no turning back. That Madeleine would be his, and no one would be able to stop them. That same wild logic had led him to elope with her, too.

Well, Jessup had shown him the error in his reckoning, and more starkly than he'd ever imagined. A broken heart was one thing. A broken leg, a dislocated hip, and a fractured skull—well, those were something else altogether. No, those things did not hurt at all—not unless one was unfortunate enough to live through them and actually regain consciousness.

He must have stared too long. Madeleine looked at him with an almost mocking regret.

"I fear your grand sacrifice has been for naught, Mr. MacLachlan," she said in her quiet, throaty voice. "It seems my son has fallen asleep."

The boy was not asleep—he was staring down at the floor of the barouche almost dazedly, but Merrick did not trouble himself to correct her. He knew almost nothing about windmills, and couldn't have cared less to discuss them just now. Oh, he liked the boy well enough—well, quite a lot, actually. But Merrick's swollen cock was throbbing like a hammered thumb, and the vile taste of his own self-loathing was bitter in his mouth.

He tore his gaze from hers and did not look at her again. Instead, he stared out the window, watching as the last of Belgravia rolled by. *A man does not wallow in self-pity.* The rain had started up again, glistening like oil and diamonds beneath the gaslights. Here and there, well-dressed people dashed along the pavements beneath broad black umbrellas, some in laughing pairs, others alone and somber. And thus was divided the world, he thought. He knew into which category he fell.

Soon they were nearing the village. There was an almost empty stretch of road ahead, fenced with stone on either side; that last little transition from Chelsea into what was still an almost rural landscape. Rain ran in rivulets down Madeleine's carriage windows, obscuring the world beyond and creating a false sense of intimacy inside the compartment. As if it made her ill at ease, Madeleine cleared her throat.

Just then, something which sounded like a shot rang out. The carriage pulled sharply left.

"Dear God!" Madeleine jerked upright on the banquette. "Highwaymen?"

"Nonsense," said Merrick. "Not in Walham Green."

But the carriage was slowing, and Madeleine's coachman was calling out to the horses to steady. Merrick twisted on his seat to see that up ahead, his own carriage had come to a stop, and beside it, an open landau was pulled to the side at an awkward angle, halfway blocking the lane.

"There has been an accident before us, I believe," he said. "And some damned fool has been driving an open landau in the rain."

But he could not see an overturned carriage, or even a

lame horse. Madeleine's carriage had rolled to a stop. Impatiently, he slapped on his hat and pushed open the door.

"No!" cried Geoffrey sharply. "You mustn't! Shut the door!"

The terror the boy's voice was real. Merrick did as he asked. The coachmen were shouting back and forth now, their voices vaguely alarmed. Madeleine was rummaging below the seat. "Here," she said, extracting something long and bulky.

"Good God!" said Merrick, pushing the pistol away. "Is that thing loaded?"

"A woman alone must look to herself for protection."

Merrick had no time to argue the point. Madeleine's coachman was clambering off the box, his boots thumping awkwardly. "Now, now, sir!" he shouted. "No call for that! None a'tall! Put it down, I say!"

"What the devil?" Merrick's hand went again to the door, but Geoffrey's fingers shot out, covering his wrist and squeezing with amazing strength. "Stay with us," he whispered. "Please, sir! *You must.*"

Above the fray, a wretched voice rang out in the night, the words slurred. "Come out, MacLachlan!" someone shouted. "Get out of that fine, fancy carriage, and prepare to meet your maker, you thieving Scotch bastard!"

Suddenly, it registered. "Good God!" Merrick said. "Chutley?"

Madeleine leaned nearer. "Who?"

Merrick grimaced. "A man who does not wish me well."

"Well, fancy that," said Madeleine.

The man was still bellowing. "Come on out, I say!" he repeated. "I'll teach you, you goddamned cheating cattle reiver! One of us shan't walk away this time!"

"The carriage is empty, sir!" shouted Grimes from atop his box. "Kindly give way so we may pass."

"Give way!" roared Chutley. "I'll show you the way! The way to hell!"

"Grimes!" cried Merrick. That drunken lunatic was *not* going to kill his coachman. This time Merrick snatched Madeleine's pistol and leapt from the carriage, keeping carefully to his good leg. "Grimes, get down! Run!"

But Grimes was no fool. The box was already empty. Heavy footfalls pounded toward the hedgerow. Merrick's carriage door was open, swinging wildly on its hinges. He had almost reached it when the shot rang out. Geoffrey's bloodcurdling scream rent the air. At once, chaos erupted. Madeleine's horses squealed wildly and shied toward the ditch, sending the carriage lurching. Merrick heard the mad clatter of hooves, and the snap of wood. He dared not turn back. Chutley was a madman. He meant to kill someone. Merrick caught his carriage door, lifted the gun, and pushed the door fully open.

He had killed someone.

Chutley himself lay slumped against the banquette, the pistol still clutched in his hand. A bright flower of red was flooding through his coat, and spreading into his snow-white linen. His eyes were still open, and there was a horrid gurgling noise in the back of his throat. Then the weapon clattered to the carriage floor, bounced, and skidded out onto the rain-slick cobbles.

Merrick set two fingers to the man's jugular vein and turned to shout to Madeleine. Only then did he realize her carriage had been pitched halfway onto its side, the weight caught by the tall stone fence. The tongue was twisted awkwardly. Grimes and the other coachman were doing their best to quiet the horses.

He returned at a run. Madeleine's door hung at an awkward angle, swinging on its hinges. She was on her knees in the now-slanted carriage floor, holding Geoffrey in her arms. His forehead was cut, and his eyes were closed.

"Good God!" Merrick gathered the boy in his arms, and gingerly lifted him out. He knelt to lay him on the cobbles and swiftly began to examine him.

"Geoff," Madeleine cried, crawling out after them. "Geoff, say something!"

Geoff had been knocked unconscious. "His pulse is strong," said Merrick as he rapidly loosened the boy's clothing. "He just needs air."

In seconds, the boy gave a faint moan. But Madeleine was on her knees now, rain and tears streaming down her face. "This is your fault!" she cried, balling her hands into fists as if she might strike him. "Your fault, Merrick! Yours! Do you hear me!"

"Aye, it is," he solemnly agreed. "Geoff! Geoff? Can you hear me, laddie?"

Grimes returned, bending one knee to the cobbles. "Poor mite!" he said. "Took it on the head, did 'e?"

"Aye, a hard one, by the look of it," said Merrick. "He's out cold, but his color is returning."

"What of t'other chap?" Grimes jerked his head in the direction of Merrick's carriage.

"His color won't be returning," said Merrick grimly. "Not in this life. But you'd best fetch a doctor, Grimes, and the village constable, if you can find him. The name is Chutley. Jim Chutley of Camden Town. He—he has a family there."

"Yes, sir." Grimes left.

Merrick touched the backs of his fingers to the boy's cheek. He had been out for less than a minute, but it felt like an eternity. Just then, Geoff gave a quiet whimper and fluttered his eyelashes. Merrick felt a surge of relief.

"Mamma?" Geoff's voice was almost drowned out by the intensifying rain. "Mamma, what . . . ?"

Madeleine all but threw herself on top of the child. "I am here, Geoffrey!" she cried. "Mamma is here! Oh, God! Oh, thank you!"

Merrick moved as if to lift the child. "Lean back, Madeleine," he said, coming to his feet and lifting Geoff with him.

Madeleine leapt up after him. "What are you doing?" she cried. "Where are you taking him?"

"Home," said Merrick. "He might need this wound tended. But what he does not need is a case of pneumonia from lying in the rain. Let the coachmen sort out the rest of it."

Madeleine was on his heels, her voice quivering with barely suppressed rage. "You could have got us killed!" she said. "If Geoffrey is seriously hurt, Merrick, I shall never forgive you! Never!"

"You have never forgiven me for anything else, Madeleine," he gritted, stepping up his pace. "I should hate to see a leopard change its spots."

"You—why, you insufferable ass!" she said. "You and that—that madman! Who was he? How dare you let this happen to Geoff!"

Merrick forbore to point out that it was Geoffrey who had insisted they travel together, though that fact certainly was not lost on him. Indeed, were he not already guilt-ridden at the thought of Chutley's widow, Geoff's odd behavior in Mortimer Street would have been at the forefront of his mind.

"Where do I turn?" he demanded. They were already striding down the main thoroughfare. The damp had got into his hip socket now, making it ache like the very devil.

"Farther along," said Madeleine, pointing. "Just past the post office, then to the end of the lane."

"I think I can walk, sir," said Geoff, his voice muffled against Merrick's coat. "Please, put me down."

"No!" said his mother firmly. "Geoffrey, you are hurt. Indeed, we are lucky you weren't killed."

"Do not overdramatize the situation, Madeleine," said Merrick. "The boy is imaginative enough as it is. If you wish to fret over someone, fret over Jim Chutley's children."

Madeleine was rushing to keep up with him. "Yes, he's probably got a dozen, poor mad creature!" she answered. "What did you do, Merrick, to make a man like that wish you dead?"

"He was not the first," gritted Merrick. "And he was significantly less successful than some who came before him."

"Yes, you are limping now," she said, as if it were a complaint.

"Trust me, Madeleine, I am well aware of it," he returned. "Is that your cottage at the end of the lane? If it is, kindly go open the door."

"Why on earth are you angry with me?" she muttered, fumbling about in her now-sodden reticule. "It was that Mr. Chutley who wished to shoot you, not I."

"Are you quite certain of that, my dear?" he returned.

"Yes, quite." Madeleine finally extracted her key. "Had

I wished to shoot you, Merrick, I would never have missed."

He started to say that he did not believe her; that he did not think she had it in her to kill anyone. But in her present mood, he was not at all sure.

She was very different tonight. It was as if the old Madeleine was coming back to life—not even as the youthful, starry-eyed girl he had married, but Madeleine as he had expected her to one day become. Full of grit and gumption and plain, old-fashioned sass.

The MacGregor and MacLachlan lines had long been rife with strong women; females who were the sustenance and the backbone of their families. Women who could rock the cradle, run the household, and see the fields tilled, too—and all without a whimper. Merrick knew well the value of such a wife, and he had seen the makings of it in Madeleine. He had never expected his life to be easy, and he had been relieved to find a woman who could shoulder through it with him—which made her faint-hearted surrender all the more bitter to bear.

They had reached the cottage entrance. Madeleine thrust her key into the lock, but the door flew open before she could turn it. A servant carrying a lamp stood in the shadows, and behind her, a neatly dressed young man.

Madeleine rushed in. "Oh, Eliza!" she said. "And Mr. Frost! Thank God you're back. Geoffrey has had an accident."

Merrick could sense Geoff's embarrassment. Gingerly, he set the boy on his feet, keeping one hand firmly beneath the lad's elbow. "Our carriage almost turned over," said the boy. "I hit my head. But I'm all right now."

The young man had come forward to assess the damage. "Well, that's a whacking great knot, my boy!" he said, almost admiringly. "Looks like you took a cricket bat to the head."

"Hullo, Mr. Frost." The boy looked sad, and strangely, a little guilt-ridden. "I didn't even feel it."

"Because it knocked you cold," said his mother. Then she pursed her lips, and stepped a little away from the child to remove her damp cloak. She was trying, Merrick realized, not to hover. But it was a struggle.

The young man straightened up and offered his hand. "Jacob Frost," he said. "I am Geoff's tutor."

"MacLachlan," he returned. "Merrick MacLachlan."

He did not miss the servant's sharp intake of breath. He realized the woman was staring at him with something akin to hatred in her eyes.

Madeleine pretended not to notice. "We must go into the parlor and light all the lamps, Eliza," she said, her voice perfectly calm. "I wish to have a better look at Geoff's head."

"Aww, Mamma!" he said. "May I not go upstairs now? I—I am so tired."

Madeleine shot him a quelling look. "Be so good as to ask Clara to send up a pot of coffee before she goes to bed, Eliza. And if you will, take Mr. MacLachlan's damp coat to dry."

Merrick shucked the miserable garment willingly, and with a parting glower, the servant vanished into the depths of the small house. Madeleine led them into a parlor, and the young man began to light the lamps.

"Thank you, Mr. Frost." Madeleine settled herself into a huge, old-fashioned armchair. "I trust you found your family well?"

"Quite so, my lady," he answered, setting down his candle. "Now, how does that bump look?"

Madeleine pulled Geoff nearer to her knees. "Hideous," said, gingerly drawing back his hair. "For a few days, at any rate. But at least it shan't need stitching."

Mr. Frost squatted down by Madeleine's chair. "I brought some of Mother's taffy back from Norfolk, Geoff," he said. "We'll have a go at it when you're feeling better."

"I *am* feeing better," the boy protested. But his face still bore the strange, stricken expression.

Madeleine clasped both her hands in his. "But surely you must be chilled? Perhaps you ought to have a warm bath."

Geoff shook his head. "I am too tired, Mamma. I just want my wet things off."

Just then, there was a faint sound at the parlor's entrance. A stout little housemaid came in bearing a tray laden with a coffee service. She set it down, and bobbed. "Will there be anything else, my lady?"

Madeleine exhaled, and let her shoulders roll inward, as if she were suddenly exhausted. "No, Clara, thank you," she said. "Just go to bed. And take Eliza with you. It is late."

The girl looked relieved, and left at once.

Mr. Frost stood up again. "Why don't I take Geoff upstairs, too, ma'am?" he suggested. "I have a few sketches to show him from my travels. Then, when he drifts off, I can sleep the night on the cot."

Madeleine looked up with a grateful smile. "You are very kind, Mr. Frost. I think that is just the thing to do."

But on the threshold, Geoff hesitated and turned toward Merrick. "Thank you for carrying me, sir," he said quietly. "I am so sorry the other man died. Very sorry indeed."

Merrick felt something tighten in his throat. "I am sorry, too, Geoff," he admitted. "I wish—I wish it could have been otherwise."

And he did. He could not get the thought of Chutley's family out of his mind. Merrick had been well within his rights in seizing the man's brickyard—he had even kept all the men on—but never once had he thought of Chutley's family. Not until the man lay breathing his last before him. Well, little good did it do any of them now. Remorse would not put food on their table or keep a roof over their heads.

Forgetting quite where he was, Merrick bent his head and pinched his nose between his thumb and forefinger until it hurt. Tomorrow he would send Rosenberg up to Camden Town to arrange an annuity for the widow. He did not regret dispossessing the man of his brickworks. No, not exactly. Business had to go on, and Chutley's taste for the bottle had rendered him incompetent. But perhaps he could have done something for the family. Perhaps, had he given it a moment's thought, he could have kept the suicide from happening.

He did not even realize Madeleine was standing before him until he smelled the brandy under his nose. His head jerked up. She held two glasses and was urging one at him. "I decided I needed something stronger than coffee," she said. "I wish to know, Merrick, about that man. How did you come to know him?"

Merrick accepted the brandy, and took a slow, pensive sip. "I loaned him some money to shore up his brickyard," he answered. "He couldn't repay me, nor could he deliver my bricks. So I called in the loan."

"You seized his brickyard?"

"I had sites in Wapping, Southwark, and Walham about to shut down for want of bricks," he said tightly. "It was business, Madeleine."

"Oh, it is not I to whom you must explain yourself." She was drifting around the room, cradling her glass in her hand. "It is the Widow Chutley."

He set his brandy aside with a clatter. "Damn it, Madeleine, do you think I don't know that? Do you think I enjoyed what I had to do?"

She looked at him, her eyes narrow in the lamplight. "I think it entirely possible, yes."

He drew a deep breath, but to say what, he hardly knew. He was saved by a sudden, hard knock at the door. Madeleine's eyes flared wide.

Merrick was already halfway to the corridor. "I shall get it."

Madeleine set her brandy down. "You certainly shan't," she said. "I think you forget whose house this is."

He stopped on the parlor threshold and stalked back toward her. "And I think you forget English common law, my dear," he said. "Technically, we could say this is *my* house."

"I beg your pardon?"

"You are my wife, Madeleine," he gritted. "The law endows me with just about everything you own, or lease, or create—until death us do part. And as you have seen tonight, I'm a hard bastard to kill."

"Good God, you are mad!" she said. "You are nothing to me."

"Unfortunately for us both, I am your husband, Madeleine," he returned. "And I can prove it. Did you think me fool enough to throw away our marriage lines?"

"You—you still have them?" she whispered. "And now you are threatening me with them? Oh, you are despicable!"

The knock came again, harder still.

Merrick exhaled wearily. "Oh, sit down, Madeleine, for God's sake!" he said. "I can promise you that this is just the village constable come to call. Now, do you really wish to be further involved in this sordid business? If so, have at it, my girl. I'll go fetch my coat."

Madeleine recoiled. Clearly, she did not wish to relive tonight's horrors in the presence of a police constable. With one last warning look, she returned to her chair.

Chapter Ten

Pride's an ill horse tae ride.

Merrick recognized the young man who stood bracketed in the doorway. His name was Wade, and his father was the village butcher.

"Good evening, Mr. MacLachlan." Wade paused to tug politely at the brim of his hat. "Mr. Grimes says that the lady and the young man involved in the accident reside here?"

"Yes, Lady Bessett and her son," said Merrick calmly. "But the boy has been put to bed, and her ladyship is indisposed, as I am sure you can understand. Why do you not call upon me at my office tomorrow? I shall tell you everything."

The constable lifted one shoulder. "Well, they are witnesses," he said reluctantly. "Though the matter seems clear enough. The Chutley chap was drunk and tried to kill you, did he not?"

"Oh, Lord no!" said Merrick.

The constable lifted his eyebrows. "Your servants were misinformed, then?"

"I did not have time to explain the matter," said Merrick smoothly. "Mr. Chutley was a business associate. He recognized my carriage and merely wished to speak with me."

"I see," said the constable. "So he simply waylaid your carriage in order to exchange a few words of greeting in the night?"

"Just so," said Merrick. "He did not realize, of course, that I was not *in* my carriage. I believe he must have slipped whilst climbing in."

"And he just happened to be carrying a cocked and loaded pistol?"

"Foolish of him, was it not?" said Merrick. "Alas, poor Chutley had an irrational fear of highwaymen. He often carried it at night."

"Highwaymen?" echoed the constable. "In Walham Green? Not in this century, sir. And your servants are of the impression that the fellow killed himself in drunken despair upon finding his intended victim missing."

Merrick feigned surprise. "Are they indeed?"

"Yes." The constable looked implacable. "Indeed."

Well, there was nothing else for it, then. Merrick set a hand on the young man's shoulders. "Mr. Wade, it is like this," he said quietly. "The poor devil *is* dead, is he not? And he leaves to mourn a widow and a family. Now, whom are we really punishing if we pursue this distasteful business? And which version of events do you imagine his family will find most comforting?"

Wade hesitated for a minute, the whole ugly scenario clearly running through his mind. The shame of a suicide—and a wild, drunken suicide, at that. The ignominious burial beyond the churchyard. The paperwork. The gossip. The poverty which might well result.

Wade lifted his hat, and scratched his head. "Aye, perhaps you've the right of it after all," he finally said. "Perhaps you ought to speak with the servants, though, and remind them of how things stand?"

This time, Merrick patted him on the shoulder. "At my earliest convenience, Wade," he assured him. "They'll not speak another word. Bring all your papers round tomorrow, and I shall sign anything you please."

Constable Wade bowed himself back out and into the night. Merrick returned to the parlor to see Madeleine pacing the room, her brandy still in her hand. She had finished fully half of it. How very surprising. He had never figured her to have the stomach for spirits.

Over one shoulder, she tossed him a strange look. "What an accomplished liar you are, Merrick," she said coolly. "One would almost imagine you'd had a wealth of experience."

He flashed her a tight smile. "You are rather well schooled in deception yourself, my dear," he said. "Now, do you understand what it is you are to tell your coachman?"

"I think I can manage it, yes," she returned. For a long, silent moment, she eyed him across the rim of her glass. "You have changed, Merrick. Or perhaps not. I never really knew you, did I?"

He stalked fully into the room. "Well, you certainly do not know me now, Madeleine," he replied. "And do not you dare get on your moral high horse with me, my dear. Not after what you've been doing all these years."

"Do not start that nonsense again," she warned. "I have had quite enough of it, thank you."

"Good God, I did not come here to squabble with you, Madeleine," he said. "Frankly, I wish to hell you'd stayed in Athens or Borneo or Switzerland or wherever the hell it was you'd been keeping yourself all this time."

Madeleine turned away and went to her chair, almost collapsing into it. "Naples," she said quietly. "We last lived in Naples, my husband and I. But I have been back in England, Merrick, for over four years now. I wonder you didn't come up to Yorkshire, if you were so determined to make my life a living hell."

"As you could have sought me out, Madeleine," he said in a low undertone. "Did you never spare me a thought? Did you never once wonder if I had survived?"

At that, she laughed, but it was not a mirthful sound. "Oh, you are the ultimate survivor, Merrick," she said. "You are strong. Self-confident. Arrogant, really. And once upon a time, I was fool enough to find that seductive."

Merrick smiled, but it was bitter. He had meant the question quite literally. He very nearly had not survived the beating her father's henchmen had given him all those years ago. Indeed, Jessup had promised him a slow and painful death—not because Merrick had seduced his beloved daughter, a sentiment with which Merrick might have sympathized. No, he had done it because Merrick had dared to ruin his political ambitions.

Merrick had lain five weeks in the inn, unconscious, with no one knowing whence he'd come, nor how to find his family. And when he finally awoke, the pain had made him wish to God he had not.

But perhaps Madeleine knew nothing of that. In the desperate letters he had written her afterward, he had said only that he was hurt; that he would come for her as soon as he was able. Or perhaps she had known and had not cared?

No. No, not that. Madeleine might have been spoilt and faithless, but never had she been deliberately cruel. More likely she had never laid eyes on the letters and had no inkling of her father's true nature. Well. It was not his job to disabuse the woman of her fantasies.

Madeleine's voice drew him back to the present. "You are fortunate, Merrick," she said quietly. "Fortunate that that pathetic bedlamite did not succeed in killing you."

Until she spoke, his most recent brush with death had not quite struck him. In the aftermath, his mind had been obsessed with Geoff's wound and Chutley's family. But Madeleine was quite right on one score. Had Geoff not begged him to join them, Merrick would have been alone in his own carriage. A carriage Chutley had seen a dozen times or more. The poor sod had obviously been lying in wait for him along the road to Walham.

"Chutley did not kill me, Madeleine, for the same reason he could not run his brickworks or pay his bills," said Merrick coldly. "Because he was an incompetent inebriate."

Her visage darkened. "You feel not one whit of remorse, do you?" she said. "And Chutley was not the first, if what they say of your business dealings is true. You are heartless, Merrick. And this is what comes of it."

"Aye, spoken like one who knows what heartless is, my dear." Merrick tossed off the last of his brandy and all but slammed the glass down. "You love none but yourself— and that boy, I pray. God knows you never loved me. Not enough to stick it out, at any rate."

"Oh, so this is all my fault!" she cried, leaping from her chair. "You've been steeping in your rage and your bitterness all these years—and it is *my* fault?"

"Oh, hush, Madeleine!" he shouted. "Just hush, for God's

sake. Yes, I'm sorry the man is dead. Yes, I would do things differently, could I do them over again. And yes, I am heartless. Because someone ripped it out years ago. But I take full responsibility for my failings, madam, and I would to God you'd do the same."

"Dear Lord!" Madeleine sat back down abruptly and let her face fall forward into her hands. "Perhaps you are right. Perhaps we are still married. Heaven knows we sound like it."

Merrick stared at her incredulously. "Is that what marriage is to you, Madeleine?" he asked. "A constant quarrel? A ceaseless attempt to wound one another? What was he like, this Lord Bessett, anyway? I should really like to know what the attraction was."

Madeleine looked at Merrick and wondered if she had lost her mind. She wanted to answer his question. She really truly did. And that would have been madness. *The attraction?* How dare he!

The attraction was that Bessett had been the only man willing to have her. The attraction was that a seventeen-year-old girl with a babe in her belly needed a husband's name. The attraction was that if she just said *yes* at the altar, she'd soon be a thousand miles away from her memories, her father, and his razor strop.

Yes, she wanted to scream the truth at Merrick. Instead, she leapt up and went to the brandy decanter. She put down her glass, shocked to realize she was blinking back tears. She felt all her shame and all her failings spring forth anew. She did not even realize Merrick stood by her side until he touched her elbow lightly.

Madeleine turned to face him and wished at once she had not. His eyes were still dark with unfettered emotion, but it was not rage. And it was not sympathy. Indeed, she was still pondering it, and wondering why her knees were weakening, when he set his hands on her arms and lowered his mouth to take hers.

Madeleine meant to shove him away. She truly did. She planted her hands firmly against his chest to do so, but her traitorous fingers had other ideas. Instead, they curled into the soft, fine wool of his coat as Merrick's mouth molded over hers. She ached with grief and loneliness, and when his arm slid down to draw her body firmly against his, she welcomed it. His other hand slid up to settle, strong and warm, between her shoulder blades, then slid higher still, plunging his fingers into her hair.

She felt the silk of her gown crush against him, felt the heat of his breath on her cheek. He held her to him almost desperately, and in a foolish response, she let her body come fully against the strong, solid wall of his chest. Somehow, her hands had found their way beneath his coat and were set at the slender turn of his waist. Merrick made a soft sound, and, without further encouragement, Madeleine opened her mouth beneath his.

She knew it was madness; knew full well she would regret it. But in that instant, the memory of a hundred such kisses came rushing back to her as he slid his tongue languidly inside her mouth. Her head swam with the scent of angry, aroused male. Like the gudgeon she was, Madeleine kissed him back, hotly and openmouthed, without a hint of hesitation or doubt. She entwined her tongue with his, and came onto her tiptoes. He tasted of wine and of smoke and of himself, something unique and yet sweetly familiar. Something eternally unforgettable.

Suddenly, the sound of tinkling glass cut into her consciousness. They had backed against the sideboard, almost upsetting the arrangement of glassware. As if stirred from a dream, Merrick lifted his lips from hers. "Good God," he whispered. "Maddie."

Madeleine held his gaze and pushed him away. He did not resist. Instead, he turned at once and strode to the windows, leaving an awful chill to settle where, but an instant earlier, his body had warmed hers. She felt empty. Cheated. And angry at herself.

"I never could bear to see you sad, Maddie," he said quietly. His back was still turned to her, his hands clasped tightly behind him, as if he were restraining himself.

She lifted her fingers to touch her lips, which felt swollen, and a little bruised. "Is . . . is that what it was?" she asked. "Just pity?"

He shook his head. "No, it was . . . stupidity, too," he admitted. "I cannot help it. I think of you sometimes, Maddie, of what we once had together, and I . . . I just . . ."

His words fell away for a long, quiet moment. Madeleine did not stir, did not move. Dared not even breathe, though she hardly knew why.

He broke the silence by clearing his throat sharply. "I am sorry, Madeleine," he managed. "That was not wise— for either of us."

She gave a sharp, bitter laugh. "Restraint was never our strong suit," she agreed. "Especially not when we were . . . oh, God, never mind that now!"

"We were speaking of Lord Bessett," he said quietly. Again, he cleared his throat. "Madeleine, was he cruel to you? I have never wished that, you know."

So this time, they were to pretend that nothing had happened. Perhaps that was best.

"He was not cruel," she said, turning to refill her brandy, which she desperately needed now. "Bessett cared for me, in his own way."

"And what way was that?" Merrick's voice had turned raspy.

She shrugged. "Like—like a fond relation," she answered uncertainly. "Which, of course, I was."

"He believed you were his wife."

She set the decanter down carelessly. "I *was* his wife," she said wearily. "But we—we were cousins, too. Did you not know?"

"No." He turned slowly from the window to face her. "No I did not."

She dashed her hand discreetly beneath her eye, and it came away damp. "He and my mother were very close," she said. "Bessett did not like Papa, I always suspected. I think he wished to . . . to take me away, perhaps? And he had a son—Alvin, my stepson—who needed a mother. He was a good boy. I loved him very much."

"Oh, Madeleine," he said almost chidingly. "It sounds like a miserable existence."

She looked at him with hurt in her eyes. "It was not miserable," she insisted. "It was safe. And yes, a little dull. But I do not regret it."

"You turned your back on me, Madeleine, so that you could have *safe* and *dull*?" His voice was softly incredulous. "I never thought you such a fainthearted creature!"

"I turned my back on no one," she said honestly. "You took Papa's money, and annulled our marriage."

"Madeleine!" The chiding tone was back. "Did you even know what an annulment was?"

Madeleine dropped her chin. "N-No, not then."

Not then—and not now. Not really. She had spent much of her marriage cut off from the world in a series of foreign outposts. After her return to Bessett's estate in rural Yorkshire, she had thought about consulting a solicitor to ask how such a thing worked. But she had been too embarrassed. And what purpose would it have served? Merrick was gone. Geoff had Bessett's name. He was an Archard, as her mother had been, an old and noble name the Normans had carried to England generations before.

"An annulment is a difficult thing to obtain," said Merrick. "The grounds are few, and relatively inflexible."

"I do not know how he obtained it, but he showed me the papers," she insisted. Good God, why were they even discussing this again? "And I had heard nothing from you in weeks and weeks, Merrick. So I married Bessett. I wished to go away. I—I thought it would be adventureous to travel across Europe."

"You had heard nothing from me," he echoed, beginning to slowly pace the room. "And knowing, as you did, just how much your father disapproved of our relationship, it never occurred to you, Madeleine, that there might have been a reason for my silence?"

Madeleine bit her lip and said nothing. She had not enjoyed the luxury of second-guessing her father, or his motivations. By then, she had had her own motivation. She and her father both knew she carried a child. His grand plan to return her to London's marriage mart had been hopelessly dashed, and she was of no further use to him. Indeed, he had sought the most expedient means of ridding himself of her, of getting her as far from England and as far from his precious career as was humanly possible.

Merrick seemed lost to her, and she could think only of

his child, of keeping it safe at all cost. And the cost had been her marriage.

She'd grieved for her losses then as she grieved for them now. Time had altered Merrick, but regrettably, it had not altered her body's reaction to him. His scent. His touch. The sensuous sound of his voice, with its faint Scots accent, and low rasp. It was a cruelty which had to be endured. She wished she were a stronger woman.

Madeleine moved away from the sideboard and went to the window. "It scarcely matters now," she said, pulling back the curtain and staring out into night's utter blackness. "I believed what Papa said."

She felt the heat of him hovering behind her, and looked up to see his reflection, impossibly broad and tall, just behind her. "You were awfully easy to convince, it would seem," he countered. "You had doubts about us, Madeleine. Do not deny it."

"I *do* deny it," she said fiercely.

He laughed. "Well before we reached Scotland, Madeleine, you were taking on a case of nerves," he said. "You were asking questions with every breath. Where would we live? How would we pay our bills? Could we afford servants? Would our friends still receive us?"

"Of course I asked questions!" she cried. "But questions are not the same as doubts. I was *seventeen*, Merrick. I was out of my depth."

"You chose a fine time to start asking," he gritted. "Halfway between York and Darlington, when it was too bloody late to turn back."

Madeleine turned around, only to find him standing far too close. "Oh, Merrick, it was already too late to turn back!" she whispered, holding his angry gaze. "I had given my body to you weeks before. Even had I wished to turn back, I could not have done so."

She saw a flash of raw emotion, the tightening of his face as if he were in pain. "I cannot think what stopped you," he said, gripping her upper arms with both hands. "You were willing to leave England with another man just two months later."

Madeleine hung her head and did not answer. She did not dare tell Merrick the truth. God only knew what he might say or do. He was half-mad, she was beginning to fear, but beautiful in his madness. The passion which he brought to his drawing table spilt over into ever facet of his life, that she had long ago learned. But tonight, his passion was ill timed.

She remembered, suddenly, the woman she had seen in his office that day. In her distress, she had pushed hastily past her, but there had been no mistaking the woman's profession. "And what of you, Merrick?" she asked quietly. "You have scarcely lived the life of a monk, have you? I saw her, you know. That—that harlot who was waiting by your office."

"I have not lived the life of a monk, no," he admitted. "I have needs, Madeleine."

"Yes," she said. "I remember." And she did. It was not possible to forget.

His grip on her arms tightened. "And if I have slaked my needs from time to time with women who knew what they were about, am I to be damned for it?"

Madeleine held his ice-blue eyes steadily. "It is not for me to judge you," she said, and she meant it. "Our lives have taken different paths. We are nothing to one another now. But that woman . . . she looked . . . she looked dangerous. Depraved."

He jerked his gaze away. "Perhaps she is both," he rasped. "Perhaps she has crossed that fine line between—oh, I hardly know what. I ought not even speak to you of such things, Madeleine."

"Does she . . . do things that you enjoy?" Madeleine whispered. "Things that please you? Are you happy with her?" She touched him lightly on the face, and turned his eyes back to hers. *Tell me something,* she silently begged. *Tell me something that will make me not want you.*

He closed his eyes entirely. The apple of his throat went up and down. "I—I do not know," he said in a voice of quiet confession. "It is not a matter of happiness. I have known a score of women like her. And I am not sure I know what pleasure is."

"Nor do I," she whispered.

Suddenly, and a little sadly, Madeleine realized that she felt more alone than ever, even though Merrick's wide, strong hand still gripped her arms. She felt as if she belonged nowhere, and to no one. Whatever Merrick had once been to her, he was that no longer. He had changed into a man she no longer knew. And yet there was enough of the man she had once loved to tempt her. To make her angry. To give her a foolish, foolish hope. To remain near him threatened everything.

She had come so far in the years since Bessett's death. She had remade herself in the mold of a strong, confident woman. For the first time since those few passionate weeks of Merrick's courtship, she had been . . . almost content. No, more than that. Only her fear for Geoffrey had kept her from unalloyed happiness. She could not go back. She *would* not. She would never again be the door-mat daughter her father had dragged back to Sheffield and packed off to the continent.

She had moved to this place with a warm spot of hope in her heart, but seeing Merrick again had ruined everything. The yearning was like a knife in her heart. His eyes. His touch. God could only ask so much of her. And Geoffrey—well, there was no help for him here. Of that, she was increasingly certain.

The heat from Merrick's body still warmed her, though he touched only her arms. Madeleine stepped a little away. He let her go, watching her almost warily.

"I think you should leave now," she said quietly. "It is very late."

He gave a twisted smile. "Yes, I must be up early," he answered. "I have villages to pillage and businesses to rape."

She tore her gaze from his, and to warm herself, set her own hands where his had been. "Do not make a joke of it, Merrick," she whispered. "Please, not with me. Let me remember the young man I once adored."

"I am that man, Madeleine," he said. "I have not altered."

"Have you not?" she said quietly. "Then perhaps I have had a fortunate escape."

"Perhaps you have, after all."

She left him standing by the parlor windows and went to the kitchen to get his coat. When she returned, he was by the front door, his fingers already curled around the handle.

She draped the coat over his arm. "I have been meaning to tell you," she said awkwardly. "I have decided—" She paused to swallow hard, and to consider one last time. "I have decided against the house. Indeed, I have decided I made a mistake in coming to London altogether."

He held her gaze, his blue eyes ice-hard and glittering. "Is that right?"

She nodded, and clasped her hands together, then, realizing the childishness of the gesture, let them go again. "I have found I do not care for Town after all," she said, going to the desk in the corner of the room. "And Geoff is to go up to university before long. I—we—we have decided to move to Cambridge so that I can be near him. Indeed, we ought to have done so from the start."

She finished shuffling through the desk until she found what she sought. She returned to the door, and handed it to him. "Those are Mr. Rosenberg's papers," she said. "Will you be so good as to return them? Or—or simply burn them? I never signed them, nor did I take him the money. You—you will not hold me to my contract, will you?"

He shook his head. The fire had gone from his eyes. "Only the heart can bind a person, Maddie," he said. "To a home. Or to anything else that truly matters. A piece of paper with a signature is otherwise meaningless."

She dropped her gaze to the floor. "Yes, perhaps," she said. "So . . . so we are finished, then, are we not?"

Merrick nodded. "Yes, Madeleine," he responded. "We are finished."

He put the papers in his coat pocket and took his hat from the hook by the door. She held the door wide for him, and he limped out into the night without another word. She watched until he was halfway down the lane, until the wind and rain had soaked her hems. Until her face was wet with tears.

Merrick MacLachlan never looked back.

Chapter Eleven

Every man can guide an ill wife weel,
save him that has her.

"It seems, old friend, that you are in luck," said Merrick to Lord Wynwood over a pint of ale the following week. "If you still wish to have the pair of houses atop Walham Hill, I am now in a position to oblige you."

The earl looked at him incredulously. "I thought that sort of treachery was beneath you, old fellow," he said. "Surely you would not renege on your contract with your—your—well, you know whom I mean."

"Yes." Merrick gave a bitter, inward smile, and pushed his empty glass away with the back of his hand. "But she who shall remain nameless has changed her mind. And I have assured her I would not enforce the contract."

"Good God, the Black MacLachlan is going to leave money on the table *and* show mercy?" The earl shoved his chair from the trestle table and stared at the flagstone floor. "Let me make sure the earth is not going to crack open and swallow us whole."

"You look in vain, for I am not leaving money on anyone's table," said Merrick. "I am going to sell the house—

and the one adjoining it—to you, Quin. And at a premium, too, by the time my joiners and carpenters have finished all the renovations which your bursting brood requires."

Wynwood grinned. "This calls for two more," he said, motioning for the serving girl. "Vivie will be thrilled. With a little luck, we can move in before the child is born, do you not imagine?"

"I daresay you might," agreed Merrick in an even tone. "Let's see—you were wed mid-January, so that would be what? Late October, or thereabouts?"

The earl's eyes flashed with chagrin. "You wretch!" he said. "You are worse than the old tabbies back in Buckinghamshire."

"Ah!" said Merrick knowingly. "The child plans to arrive a little early, does it? When, then, old fellow? I merely wish to know what force of nature my carpenters are up against."

"More like late September, I collect." There was just a hint of a blush settling over Wynwood's cheeks. "Whenever it is, it won't be soon enough to suit me, and the old tabbies bedamned. Still, a man in my position cannot be too careful."

"September I can manage," said Merrick as the serving girl set down two frothing tankards and swept the others away. "Though the haste and inconvenience might drive up the price a tad."

Wynwood's mouth twisted into a dry smile. "I feared as much," he said. "A chap is always paying for his pleasures, isn't he?"

Merrick tried to laugh. "That has been my experience, yes."

Suddenly, Wynwood's expression shifted to one of seriousness. "What happened, Merrick?" he asked quietly. "With Madeleine, I mean?"

Merrick cleared his throat a little roughly. "It seems the lady has had a change of heart ab—"

"Yes, that has happened before, hasn't it?" Wynwood interjected sourly. "I admit, she does not look quite the fickle creature I had imagined her, but still, one oughtn't be surprised."

"Perhaps not," said Merrick vaguely.

Wynwood seemed to be indignant on his friend's behalf. "What did she imagine, anyway?" he asked, pushing a little away from the table as if disgusted. "Did she think she could just trot back to London when it suited her and never be called to account for her actions?"

"It was a safe assumption," Merrick countered. "I do not plan to call her to account. Indeed, what would one do if one wished to?"

Wynwood's eyes flared with outrage. "Why, sue her for restitution of conjugal rights!" he said. "Females do it all the time."

"Yes, if they have been abandoned and left to starve, what course is left to them?" he said.

"You are in a precarious legal situation, Merrick," said his friend. "Her debts are your debts. Her contracts are your contracts. Indeed, it could legally be held that her child is yours. You have no private separation deed. Think of the financial liability. What if she realizes how wealthy you have become and decides that perhaps you are her husband after all?"

"I would not have her."

"No, but you would have her debts," warned his

friend. "You might have to furnish her a home. Indeed, you are lucky you are not now in the position of enforcing your own contract of sale and paying yourself for your own bloody house."

"Quin, have you any notion how idiotic that sounds?" asked Merrick. "You don't even seem to know whether you wish me to separate from the woman or force her to reside beneath my roof. Now be so good as to drop this conversation. I do not want the woman, and she does not want me. And there will be no debts or contracts to trouble me."

"Then you are more trusting than I."

"I trust no one," he said grimly. "Madeleine thinks our marriage was annulled."

"*What—?*"

"She claims her father showed her some papers which dissolved our marriage," he said. "She thinks she has an annulment."

"But—but—that is just not possible. Is it?"

"I cannot see how," Merrick agreed. "It is more of Jessup's treachery, most likely. But be that as it may, she does not perceive herself as a bigamist, and since I do not give a damn, where, Quinten, is the harm?"

Lord Wynwood eyed him skeptically for a long moment. "About that 'I do not give a damn' part, old chap," he said, "why do I sometimes get the feeling that you give a much bigger damn than you might like me to believe?"

"I once loved unwisely, Quin," he said quietly. "And I paid a price for it. Beyond that, I really have no wish to discuss it."

"The trouble is," said the earl, "you can go neither forward nor backward with your life. She has trapped you in a sort of purgatory. Otherwise, you might have a wife—a real wife—and a family by now."

Merrick snorted. "Spoken like a newly married man," he said. "Talk to me of purgatory in another ten years, my friend!"

Wynwood took no offense. "In ten or twenty years or fifty years, nothing will have changed for me," he said. "With some people, you just know that that is so."

How strange it seemed to hear such words from another. Merrick had once said something very similar to Alasdair, when his brother was in the process of attempting to talk him out of pursuing Madeleine. Like Wynwood, he had simply *known*. Madeleine was the only one for him. And she had been. She still was—or rather, having had her, he now knew that no other would ever do.

He was not fool enough, as Quin had once been, to convince himself that another wife might do as well—or at least do well enough. There was a hole in his heart where his love for Madeleine had been, and to alter his existence now would be like trying to fit a round peg into the proverbial square hole. The hole was Madeleine's. He no longer loved her, but he could love no other. He knew it instinctively, as he had always known it. Her leaving him had stripped away the larger part of his character. The best part, perhaps. He really did not know.

In one of his raving missives, Chutley had once called him a soulless bastard. The insult had not greatly wounded Merrick. He felt soulless. And he had found that to seek out the sort of women who were much like himself was the only way to survive. Women who were apathetic inside. Women who did not cast back the reflection of a dark and gaping chasm where one's better nature should have been. That was in part why he had been so glad to get rid of Kitty Coates. She had been kind, and innocent in a way he could not explain.

Wynwood had taken out his silver vesta box, and was flipping it open and shut almost nervously. "I have been thinking of something again, Merrick," he said a little oddly. "Something—something from our past."

"The past?" Merrick gave a grunt of disgust. "God help us."

"I mean the recent past," Wynwood clarified. "Do you remember that day last September when we all went to that boxing match down in Surrey, and the gypsy told our fortunes?"

"She told us no such thing," said Merrick. "She took our money and rattled off a lot of balderdash."

"Yes, that's what I thought, too," said Wynwood musingly. "But remember how she told me that I had ruined my life by acting rashly? And how she claimed . . . well, she claimed that there was a wrong I had done because of it and that I had to make amends for the wrong before I could be happy. I think, Merrick, that she was talking about how I had treated Vivie."

"Hardly a surprise, old fellow," said Merrick. "After all, what man has not acted rashly where women are concerned?"

Quin muttered an oath beneath his breath. "No, honestly, Merrick," he pressed. "I treated her shabbily all those years ago. And I *did* commit a wrong against her. A grievous wrong. I shan't go into the details, but—"

"Aye, spare me!" Merrick interjected. "And make your point, man."

"Well, do you remember how she said we were all

wasting our lives?" asked Quin. "I mean, I *knew* Alasdair and I were wasting our lives. We were doing it quite intentionally, and enjoying ourselves pretty damned thoroughly, too. But you—well, I never thought of *you* in that light."

"In what light?" Merrick was growing impatient.

Quin's brow furrowed. "The wasteful light," he said. "I mean, it seems as if you are doing great things, but what if, after all is said and done, you are wasting it? She said that you were a great artist, but that excessive pride and a bitter heart had hardened you."

"Oh, thank you, Reverend Wynwood!" snapped Merrick. "My day wanted but this—a tidy little lecture about wasting my life." He pushed back his chair and stood. "Now, if you will pardon me, I must go piss away a bit more of it down at Wapping, where I am about to complete another twelve thousand square feet of dockside warehousing. Or perhaps that, too, is just another figment of my imagination?"

"There are many ways a man can waste his life, Merrick." Quin looked a little wounded. "Just sit back down, for pity's sake."

For the sake of peace, Merrick obliged him. "Quin, I do not even remember what that woman told me," he admitted, his tone more conciliatory. "Whatever it was, it cannot possibly have any bearing on reality."

Quin leaned urgently across the table. "Do you believe, Merrick, only in what you can see and hear?" he asked. "Can you not accept that there might—there just *might* be things we cannot yet understand? That perhaps there are some people who—who know things the rest of us do not?"

Merrick hesitated. The question left him oddly uncomfortable. It was the curse, he thought, of a Scottish upbringing. He had grown up having the dour Scottish doctrines of hard work, pragmatism, and thrift drilled indelibly into his young mind, and yet all around them had been the strange lore of the Highlands, which was anything but pragmatic. His grandmother MacGregor was a perfect example of that bizarre dichotomy. But he was not about to discuss his grandmother with Quin.

"I do not know, Quin," he said. "Those considerations are for greater minds than mine. I am a simple man. I build things. I believe only in brick and iron and strong, straight lumber. Those are the things of which my world is built."

Quin looked resigned and pushed back his chair. "Well, all the same, Merrick, you ought to think about that pride issue," he warned, as they rose from the table. "You ought to at least ask yourself if you have let your pride get the better of you, and consider if perhaps you have let it stand between you and something which your—well, which your *soul* might need. I can't think what—I cannot pretend to know what is inside you—but . . . well, you ought to just think about it."

To placate him, Merrick nodded and set a hand on his friend's shoulder. "That is good advice, I daresay, for any man," he agreed. "Yes, Quin. I shall try do as you ask. I shall try to give a little thought to such serious matters. Thank you."

Quin gave a skeptical grunt, and tossed a few coins onto the table. "I collect I am being humored," he grumbled. "Well, come on then. Walk with me up to Walham Hill, and let us speak of more exciting things—like wall covering and draperies."

*   *   *

Madeleine was in the garden attempting to persuade a particularly recalcitrant rose to go up its trellis in a more orderly fashion when she heard the door knocker drop. In her rush, she pricked her finger and gave a little yelp. Wrapping one corner of her smock about the fingertip, she hastened through the house. Mrs. Drexel had needed to make a last-minute dash to the butcher's, and this was Clara's half day.

She was surprised to see Lady Treyhern standing on her doorstep in a red riding habit. Behind her, a groom held the reins of two dashing gray horses.

"Helene!" she said, sliding out of the dusty smock. "What an unexpected pleasure."

Actually, it was as much a relief as a pleasure. In the week since their unfortunate dinner party in Mortimer Street, Madeleine had heard nothing at all from her new friend.

The countess was blushing faintly. "I thought if I called round fourish, you and Geoff might be persuaded to give me a spot of tea."

"I am so sorry," she said. "Geoff is not here."

Lady Treyhern was already removing her hat. "Perfect. Then we may gossip with impunity."

Madeleine laughed and gave instructions to the groom, who led the horses away. "Now, just let me find Eliza, and ask her to fix tea."

When Madeleine returned, Helene was in the parlor, drifting aimlessly amidst the teetering stacks of books and papers. "This looks just like my brother-in-law Bentley's study," she remarked in her teasing voice. "Did someone's desk explode in here?"

Madeleine blushed. "These are some of my father's personal papers," she said. "I had a cartload sent down from Sheffield a few days ago. I thought that it was time I began going through them."

Helene smiled sympathetically. "Oh, that is *such* a chore, is it not? My mother's things are still stuffed in a trunk at Hampstead. How long has your father been gone?"

"Several years," Madeleine answered. Strangely, she felt little grief. "He died whilst I was away, and my husband just after our return."

Helene's expression of sympathy deepened. "How very sad for you, my dear."

Madeleine shrugged. "I had lived my adult life abroad. Geoff never even met him." Hastily, she moved the pile of papers she had been sorting that morning from a nearby chair. "Do sit down," she said, shifting the load to the desk. "This is quite the most comfortable chair."

Helene took the seat with a grateful smile. "What a cozy little cottage," she said, stripping off her riding gloves. "Did you let the place furnished?"

"Mostly, yes," Madeleine admitted. "It is a little shabby round the edges, but comfortable."

"You have a vast deal of shopping to do for the new house, then, do you not?" Helene said. "And furniture makers take forever."

Madeleine returned to her chair and sat down. "I have had a change of heart, Helene," she said quietly. "I think I shan't take the house after all. Indeed, I do not think we shall stay much longer here in London."

"But Madeleine, why?" Helene looked surprised. "I thought you were quite set on the place."

Madeleine lifted one shoulder and looked away. "I can

see no point now," she said. "After all, as you have said, there is little to be done for Geoff here, and that was my only reason in coming."

"Will you make your home with your stepson, then? Or your cousin Lord Jessup, perhaps?" Helene paused to frown. "I believe, my dear, you would be unhappy with either of those alternatives. You are so very young."

"I think I shall go to Cambridge," said Madeleine vaguely. "Or—or perhaps I shall buy a house by the sea. I have always wished to live by the sea."

"Well, I should hate to lose such a lovely new friend so soon," said Helene sadly. "But the truth is, my husband hates London, and we are here but a few weeks a year ourselves. I know! Lyme Regis!"

"Lyme Regis?" said Madeleine. "I have heard that it is very beautiful."

"My husband and Mr. MacLachlan are going to begin building some new houses near there," she said. "Perhaps by the end of the year. I am sure Mr. MacLachlan would build you just what you wish."

Madeleine felt her face flame. "No," she said firmly. "No, I do not think so."

Helene grimaced. "Oh, dear."

"What?" asked Madeleine.

Helene gave a little shrug. "My husband was afraid that perhaps Mr. MacLachlan had been forward toward you at our house last Friday," she confessed. "And he was under the impression that the gentleman might have inveigled his way into your carriage."

"No, not at all," said Madeleine smoothly, not at all sure why she wished to defend him. "Geoff invited him."

"I see," said Helene. "My husband will be reassured.

Mr. MacLachlan, for all his dark good looks, does not have a pristine reputation."

"Does he not?" Madeleine feigned surprise. "Is he thought to be a womanizer?"

Helene gave a sharp laugh. "Oh, not where women of quality are concerned," she said. "And much to their dismay, I do not doubt."

"Indeed?" said Madeleine. "I was given to understand that society was ambivalent toward him."

"Certainly they once were," she admitted. "Perhaps the high sticklers still are. But women do love a dark, dangerous-looking man, and sometimes, the blacker his name, the better—so long as he has money. MacLachlan is rich as Croesus now, and there is no better balm to society's heart than a tub of newly minted money."

"You seem to know a vast deal about him."

Helene eyed her across the narrow room. "My husband makes it his business to know such things before he will do business with a man," she admitted. "Mr. MacLachlan keeps company with the sort of women we do not talk about in polite society. I am sure you know the sort I mean?"

"I know that such women exist," Madeleine confessed. "But we are not precisely awash in them up in Yorkshire."

Helene burst into laughter. "Oh, Madeleine! You are so refreshingly honest."

"I wish sometimes that I were not," she admitted. "As to Mr. MacLachlan, what is the truth about his business dealings? Is he thought to be dishonest?"

"Not that, no." Helene shook her head. "He seems to be equally hated and admired. He is said to drive a hard bargain and count every farthing. He has been known to crush his competitors. And I know he controls a vast deal of real estate here in Town, and has business interests throughout the city."

"Does he indeed?" This Madeleine had not heard. "Of what sort?"

Helene blinked uncertainly. "My husband says he builds roads and pavements and bridges," she answered. "And warehouses, some of which he owns. And last year, he bought an interest in a concern which is to begin building railroads. My brother-in-law Bentley tells me that railroads are the future and anyone who invests in them will soon be rich."

"But Mr. MacLachlan is already rich."

Helene looked at her oddly. "Yes, but he obviously does not mean to rest on his laurels," she answered. "Well, enough of him. Tell me, my dear, how does Geoffrey go on?"

Madeleine dropped her chin. "He is not himself," she admitted. "Though his tutor has returned, and that has helped a little. Still, the melancholia has struck him again, and very hard this time. He looks as though he is not sleeping."

"Oh, dear!" said Helene. "I do hope he is not still fretting over that silly quarrel with Ariane?"

"A bit, yes," Madeleine admitted. "Which, were he otherwise well, would not be bad thing."

Helene smiled weakly. "Well, do not be too hard on the boy," she said. "But I do wonder, Madeleine—what do you think that was about? What put the notion into his mind? I really should like to know why he would say such a thing."

Madeleine shrugged. "I really have no idea," she answered. "And I don't think he does. I am so sorry. Unfortunately, that is not the first bizarre thing he has blurted out. Sometimes he—he just *thinks* them. I can tell, you see, that some wild notion has struck him by the look on his face. But as it happens more frequently, he becomes more and more secretive. Still, I know it was a horrible thing to say to Lady Ariane."

Helene seemed to have relaxed into her chair. "Well, it does not signify," she said. "But if not Ariane, what do you think is troubling him?"

"I think it is more the death of that poor Mr. Chutley," Madeleine admitted. "He has taken it unusually hard."

"That sounds dreadful!" Helene set a hand to her chest. "But who, pray, is Mr. Chutley?"

Madeleine looked at her in mild surprise. But then again, how could Helene know of Chutley's suicide? Merrick had cleverly turned a scandalous bit of gossip into a mere accident. Tragic, yes, but it likely had not even warranted space in the newspapers. She explained the situation much as Merrick had explained it to Constable Wade, glossing over Chutley's true intent.

Helene had lost a little of her color. "Well!" she said a little breathlessly. "How dreadfully sad. I hope poor Geoffrey did not actually *see* anything?"

Madeleine shook her head. "No, our horses started at the gunshot," she said. "Poor Geoff took a bump on the head and was knocked senseless."

"How frightful!" said Helene. "What did you do?"

"Mr. MacLachlan was kind enough to carry him home."

Helene smiled faintly. "Did he indeed? How very good of him."

"I daresay."

Just then, Eliza came in with the tea tray and a small

platter of biscuits. Madeleine was glad for the distraction. They busied themselves for a few moments with the intricacies of preparing their cups, but as soon as the room fell quiet again, Helene's mouth curled into the faintly mischievous smile which Madeleine had come to recognize.

"I hope, my dear, that you will not forget our little dinner party on Tuesday?" she said, plucking a pair of biscuits from the platter. "Ooh, almond! My favorite."

"I beg your pardon?" said Madeleine quietly. "A dinner party?"

Helene's eyes flashed with mischief. "Yes, for Ariane's birthday," she said. "The one I mentioned Friday evening?"

"Oh. Oh, yes."

"Of course it is a few weeks early," Helene went on. "But she really did beg to have something whilst we were still here in Town. I know she is not yet out, but as I assured her father, it will be nothing very grand. Just family and a few close friends. Dinner, and perhaps some country dances afterward. Now please do not say you have changed your mind?"

Madeleine did not recall hearing, let alone accepting the invitation. But she had been so absorbed in Geoffrey's distress at the card table, there was no knowing what she might have agreed to do. "No, of course I shall come," she said.

"It will do you good," said Helene. "Even though you mean to leave London, my dear, you really should get out a bit. Indeed, I know you will think me quite forward, but at your age, you really ought to think of marrying again."

"No." Madeleine felt a moment of panic.

"Oh, never say never, my dear!"

"No," she repeated. "I—I am quite sure you mean to be kind. But I cannot remarry."

"Cannot?" Helene looked at her chidingly. "Come now, Madeleine. That is rather harsh. One never knows when the perfect husband might turn up. Now, let me think who I might know that is sensible and unattached."

"No. No, I beg you will not." Madeleine set her cup down awkwardly, splashing hot tea across her wrist.

Helene leapt from her chair, and snatched up a tea towel. "Oh, Madeleine!" she said, dabbing at her cuff and wrist. "Oh, you poor dear. I did not mean to distress you."

"I—I am fine," said Madeleine. "I just—the cup just—lost its balance."

"And look at this!" said Helene, turning her hand over. "You have been bleeding."

"I pricked myself," Madeleine admitted. "On the rosebush earlier. It is nothing."

Helene folded her fingers gently inward, and patted her closed fist. "You have had a hard day," she said, her tone lightly teasing. "First your rosebush turns on you, and then your friend. I did not mean, my dear, to prod into your business. I shan't do so again."

"I—I was not distressed," she said. But to her mortification, tears had begun to trickle down her face.

Helene went down on one knee. "Oh, *ma foi!*" she said. "I wish myself to the devil just now!"

"It—it is nothing," said Madeleine, trying to stifle her sobs. "I—I just . . . well, it has been a hard week, actually. There is much on my mind. It was not you, Helene."

Helene had extracted a handkerchief and pressed it into Madeleine's hand. "I cannot help matters when I pry into your business," she said. "I am so sorry, my dear. I hate to see you so distraught. Please, can you not tell me what is wrong?"

Somehow, Madeleine found a way to laugh. "You just swore, Helene, to stay out of my business."

"Yes, quite right." Helene snagged her lower lip between her teeth and returned to her chair. "I shall endeavor to do so. Perhaps I ought simply to go, and get out of your hair?"

"No, please do not." Madeleine blew her nose and tucked the handkerchief away. "Let us talk of more pleasant things. What sort of gown shall I wear to Lady Ariane's dinner party? I have a deep green silk which I had made up for Alvin's betrothal. It sits just a little off the shoulders. Would that do?"

"Perfect!" said Helene. "You must look lovely in dark green."

Madeleine forced herself to relax as the conversation turned again toward more mundane matters. Helene was excited about treating her stepdaughter, and Madeleine's mortification was slowly receding. Indeed, she was not at all sure of what had just happened. She had never been much of a watering pot—well, not since losing Merrick. After that, there had been very little worth crying over. So why now?

It had been Helene's pointed question about remarriage. It had frightened her in a way she had not expected. But she had answered the question quite truthfully. She could not marry again. She never would. Papa's papers had been spread about the parlor for all of two days, and Madeleine had been pawing through them like a madwoman. What she sought was not there.

Cousin Gerald had sent eight crates of files, calendars,

and correspondence. Three appeared to be personal, the other five, the larger ones, were clearly related to his work in the government. Madeleine had pried open the small ones first. But inside, there was no mention of her marriage—either of them—nor of her dowry nor of her annulment. Nothing. Indeed, there was not even so much as a mention of her name in her father's papers.

It had been a horrible, stark reminder—not just a reminder of her failed marriage, though that was bad enough. It also left her acutely aware of the truth which she had fought to avoid for the whole of her conscious life: that to her father, Madeleine had barely existed at all.

Helene cleared her throat sharply, snapping Madeleine back to the present. "So, as I was saying, I shall wear dark purple, since you are to wear the dark green," she said. "We shall make a striking pair, shall we not, you with your pale blond hair, and me with my inky black locks?"

Madeleine managed to smile. "We shall indeed," she answered, picking up the platter of biscuits. "I look greatly forward to it. Here, Helene. May I offer you another?"

Chapter Twelve

Kindle not a fire which
ye canna put out.

Phipps gave one last neatening tug on his employer's lapels. "There!" he said in some satisfaction. "You look quite splendid, sir."

Merrick lifted his gaze to the pier glass and studied himself in its reflection. He saw nothing but the scar. Especially vivid against his evening blacks, the thing curled like a thin, pale snake along his jaw and down his neck, then slithered away beneath his starched white collar.

"What kind of fool am I, Phipps, to have agreed to this?" he asked.

"The kind of fool who will die a very rich man," murmured Phipps, reaching up to neaten the knot of his cravat.

"But a birthday party," he grumbled. "And for some chit not yet out of the schoolroom."

"A chore, to be sure," said Phipps pragmatically. "But given who her father is, at least a few of the City's bankers will likely turn up. Besides, it is not precisely a high society affair."

"Damn me if I have any use for such things, high or

low." Merrick stuck a finger in his collar and gave it a little tug. "But when a man looks you in the eyes, and asks you outright, it's dashed hard to think of an excuse."

Phipps had bent down to run a bit of flannel over Merrick's evening slippers. "But they are a pleasant enough family, sir, are they not?"

"Bloody cheerful," Merrick agreed. "Sweetness and light all around. You'd think Lord and Lady Treyhern never exchange an ill word."

Phipps stood, and admired his handiwork. "Perhaps they do not," he suggested. "In an ideal world, all marriages should be so. Otherwise, why bother being married at all?"

Merrick gave one of his sarcastic grunts. "Your naïveté shocks me, old fellow," he said. "These people marry for dynastic concerns."

"Some do, yes." Phipps snapped open his silver cheroot case, and persuaded that all was in order, slipped it into Merrick's coat pocket. "But Lord Treyhern, as I hear it, did not."

Merrick's eyes widened in surprise. Treyhern struck him as just the sort of man who would marry for practicality, at the very least. "A love match, eh?"

"Oh, very much so."

Merrick was skeptical. "How the devil do you know?"

Phipps smiled faintly. "Servants' gossip, sir," he said. "The most reliable source on earth. Treyhern's housekeeper, Mrs. Trinkle, is a stepsister to Agnes's mother, Mrs. Barney, over in Stepney."

"Agnes?"

"Agnes Barney who works in the kitchen, sir."

"Ah, yes, the thin, quick one," he recalled.

"Yes, she is quite a hard worker," Phipps agreed. "And

Agnes reports that her aunt Trinkle claims that Lord and Lady Treyhern once had something of a scandalous past."

Merrick grinned. "A *past*, eh?"

"Childhood sweethearts," he clarified. "But the girl was poor, French, and considered far beneath him, so the family split them apart and sent the girl to Switzerland to become a governess. The earl married money, but it was a troubled union. The wife was thought to be . . . " Here, Phipps paused to clear his throat sharply, "—well, of questionable constancy, sir, if you know what I mean?"

"Aye, I've a fair notion."

Phipps smiled tightly. "In any case, she died, and Treyhern married her ladyship after all."

"Ah!" said Merrick. "But let's go back to that part about his marrying money, Phipps."

Phipps lifted one eyebrow. "Such a cynic, sir!"

"Fine talk of love and romance is all very well, Phipps," he said, giving the collar another tug. "But someone must pay the bloody butcher's bill. And women, you see, know this. Perhaps Lady Treyhern was wise enough to bide her time."

Phipps sighed as if deeply put upon. "Perhaps so, sir," he said, handing Merrick his purse and pocket watch. "Shall I call for your carriage now?"

"Well, that is one way to win an argument." Merrick grinned. "Pack me off to that hell they call society."

That hell they call society was packed eight carriages deep down Mortimer Street when Merrick arrived at Treyhern's town house. Friends and family indeed! It had the look of a minor crush. With a growing sense of frustration, Merrick craned his head toward the window, wondering if there was any last minute excuse which might be seized upon. Regrettably, no lightning strike or earthquake obliged him. Of course, he could always simply snatch up his carriage pistol and just shoot himself out of frustration, as poor old Chutley had done.

Just then, the angle of the moving carriages shifted, and the next in line rolled up to the door. *Well, hell and damnation.* A perfectly turned ankle peeped out, and then a swath of dark green skirt slithered down to cover it. Perhaps it was time for that pistol after all.

It was the carriage which his subconscious mind had recognized. Or perhaps, God help him, it really was the ankle. Even at a distance, it seemed so little changed. Lady Bessett had taken the hand of one of Treyhern's footmen and was alighting with a grace which would have become an operatic diva. Her pale blond hair was twisted up into an elegant but unfashionably loose arrangement which shone like liquid fire in the last slanting rays of daylight.

As if she moved in slow motion, Madeleine looked up at the footman and smiled. Her matching cashmere shawl slipped off one shoulder, and a dainty little reticule swung from her wrist. Up and down the steps and the street, heads were turning. He did not wonder why. Madeleine was ageless elegance and even at thirty, pure physical perfection. And fleetingly, she had been his. She had given him twelve glorious weeks of euphoria at a time when he had not believed euphoria existed. He still did not. It had been, in retrospect, a surreal interlude in his life.

Lord Treyhern hastened down the steps to greet her personally. He set her hand on his arm, and they went up the stairs to vanish into the depths of the house. Merrick fell back against the banquette. He felt not admiration, but anger. Not righteous indignation, but resentment. Damn it, he should have guessed the woman would attend. Perhaps his subconscious mind had suspected *that*, too.

No. No, that simply was not true. Besides, he had the power and the will to control his own reactions. He was here purely as a matter of business. If that business dictated he be polite to the woman, so be it. For the right amount of money, Merrick MacLachlan could sup with the devil if he had to.

On the other hand, he could also afford to walk away. He did not need Treyhern's money or his real estate. Life was short. He rapped harshly on the roof of his carriage. His liveried footman leapt down, and opened the door. "Yes, sir?"

Merrick opened his mouth, then closed it again. For an instant, he vacillated. Then his manners got a chokehold on his misanthropy, and wrestled it to the ground. "Nothing," he snapped. "Never mind. No—stop. Just let me out here. Turn round and go down to the Blue Posts."

"Yes, sir."

Merrick climbed down and fished through his pocket for a few coins. "You and Grimes get a pint and a bit of supper," he said. "I'll meet you there as soon as I may."

The footman pocketed the coins cheerfully. He did not look surprised. He was well aware of his employer's penchant for making quick escapes. Merrick snatched his stick from the carriage, and stalked off down the pavement toward Treyhern's town house.

He was greeted very graciously by the earl and his wife. The daughter—Arabelle or Marianne or Maribelle or some other bright, tinkling sort of name—curtsied very prettily. He bowed low over her hand and wished her a happy seventeenth birthday, a remark which set the girl to blushing and stammering and left him feeling like Methuselah's great-uncle.

He moved swiftly away, wondering at the sensibilities of today's youth. Then he recalled with some discomfort that seventeen—and barely that—was the age at which Madeleine had agreed to marry him. He turned around, and looked at the chit again. Good God, she was a *child*. And damned if there wasn't a distinct resemblance to Madeleine. Treyhern's girl was a fetching little thing—tall and slender, with hair the color of summer cornsilk. Her features were pretty and delicately formed, with that full lower lip which looked at once sensual and innocent.

Lord, what a bit of parson's bait that was! But surely she was too young to wed? She could not possibly understand the full depth of commitment and duty which a marriage would bring. At seventeen, she could not grasp the gravity of life, or comprehend the obligations and challenges which adulthood forced on a person.

Which left him to wonder—how had he expected Madeleine to comprehend?

But it was too late to start making excuses for Madeleine's faithlessness. She *had* married him. And she had given him up with scarcely a thought.

Just then, Maribelle-Arabelle caught him staring at her. The delicately formed features flushed three shades of pink, then the chit waggled her fingers at him, and burst into giggles. *Giggles.* Good God. It was time for him to slink off into some conspiratorial corner with the other unattached males.

At least the crowd was much smaller than one would

have guessed, given the number of carriages, and no one seemed to be standing on any ceremony. Treyhern was wise, Merrick thought, to bring the chit into society in this gradual way, rather than to thrust her into the limelight at once, with a costly debutante ball or some other such nonsense.

Treyhern's servants drifted through the withdrawing room with ease, balancing glasses of sherry and orgeat on wide silver trays. Merrick recognized most everyone present and knew a few of them well.

"MacLachlan!" Someone slapped him heartily on the shoulder. "I trust I find you hale and hearty?"

Merrick turned to see one of the directors from the Bank beaming up at him.

This was, he reminded himself, one of his reasons for being here. "Quite well, sir. Yourself?"

And thus began a series of those meaningless little conversations which one is required to sustain during society affairs. In the process of making his way around the room, Merrick was required to expound twice upon the age and health of Queen Adelaide—who was definitely *not* enceinte—thrice upon the issue of whether the Lords were dragging their feet over reform—they definitely were—and five times upon the weather, which was generally allowed to be fine. Or dampish. Or too warm. Or verging on rain. Depending upon whom one asked.

By means of his willingness to rattle on about such inanities, and to make a few geographically strategic maneuverings, Merrick was able to keep Madeleine on the opposite side of the room. Until they were called to dinner, when he discovered that Lady Treyhern had seated them together.

Madeleine looked a little stricken. He bowed to her politely and pulled out her chair. "Lady Bessett," he said. "Good evening."

"Mr. MacLachlan," she murmured. "What a surprise." There was a flash of fire in her eyes.

"Don't look daggers at me, my dear," he said in an undertone. "I did not choose the guest list. Did you?"

She said nothing, and slid into her chair, holding her body a little away from his as she did so. Her scent settled over him like a cloud. It was the light fragrance of soap and jasmine and something else he could not name. Something faint, and achingly familiar.

The dark green silk, he noticed, matched her fiery eyes, and looked magnificent against her pale skin. The gown was unadventurous by Town standards, but cut low enough to reveal the turn of her shoulders and the delicate span of her collarbones.

Merrick forced his attention to the others being seated. In keeping with the occasion, the meal was not especially formal, nor the food particularly elaborate. At first, there was much laughter, and good-natured ribbing of the chit, whose name he finally remembered was Ariane, not Arabelle. The worst of the teasing came from a handsome young man introduced as the girl's uncle, Treyhern's brother, who had a look of pure devilment in his eye and whom the girl seemed to adore.

Merrick and Madeleine were seated nearer Lady Treyhern's end of the table, and the lady seemed determined to see everyone comfortable, and conversed all around her with ease. Treyhern himself was more taciturn, but he managed well enough. He was, however, throwing the occasional glance down the table at Merrick, as if he were troubled by something. Well, society bedamned. Between his host and his dining companion, Merrick was beginning to feel just a tad unwanted.

Madeleine had turned to speak to the gentleman on her right. Her soft, buttery-colored hair was curling in tiny tendrils at the back, and the perfect turn of her neck was unadorned by so much as a strand of pearls. Indeed, it hardly needed ornamentation. For a moment, he was unable to tear his eyes away. There was a spot—yes, just below her pulse point—which had once fascinated him for the whole of one evening. Her skin was warm there, and exceptionally soft. It was the sort of spot, he well knew, where a man might set his lips and be rewarded with little shivers of delight.

He had always imagined that if ever he saw her again, she would be greatly altered—that the sun of Italy would have aged her, and that the years of marriage would have left something—a furrow in her forehead or a sag beneath her chin. But there was nothing. Nothing save for a few tiny lines about her eyes and a sort of weary skepticism in her gaze. She was the same, and, to his undying disappointment, he still found her lovely.

She must have felt the heat of his gaze. Her eyes, when they turned on him, were hostile for an instant. He felt suddenly like a raw lad again and looked away. Then he turned back. This simply would not do. Good manners, the bane of his existence tonight, obliged him to talk to her. Up and down the length of the table, everyone was chattering like old friends. Surely he and Madeleine could manage it?

"How is your son, Lady Bessett?" he asked, as the footmen began move unobtrusively around the table, laying the next course. "I trust he has recovered?"

"How kind of you to ask." Her voice was so cool they

might have been strangers. "He goes on reasonably well."

" 'Reasonably well' sounds a bit paltry for a bright, vigorous boy like Geoff," Merrick replied.

"I did not know you had an interest in children, Mr. MacLachlan."

"I have an interest in Geoff," he returned, forcing a civil tone. "He is quite a remarkable boy."

She turned fully to face him, her eyes widening. "Remarkable?" she echoed. "What do you mean, pray?"

"He has a curious mind," said Merrick. "And he is quite a gifted artist. He seems quite bright, too, for a lad of his age. By the way, I have been meaning to ask, how old is Geoff? I don't think he ever said."

For a long moment, Madeleine seemed to stare straight through him, almost quivering with indignation. "Would you kindly—" She halted, blinked rapidly, and began again. "Would you kindly move your chair leg, Mr. MacLachlan? I believe it is sitting on my hems."

"Lord, is it?" Instinctively, he lifted the chair a fraction, and gave it a little scoot away from her.

She turned away at once, and resumed her discussion with the gentleman on her right. Merrick was left to stare at the turn of her bare neck yet again.

But he knew better, and so he struck up a conversation with the lady on his left, a dark-haired, dark-eyed beauty named Frederica Rutledge, the wife of Treyhern's brother. She was from a family of painters, some of them famous, and was extraordinarily well versed in the world of art. They chatted amiably about the most recent exhibit at the Royal Academy, and about the parallels between art and architecture. He was surprised to find himself actually enjoying the conversation.

Farther down the table, Lady Treyhern was congratulating one of the more elderly guests on his son's upcoming nuptials. The younger ladies were atwitter with excitement. A society wedding in the works, no doubt.

"And will your son's marriage require a new house, Mr. Wagstaff?" Lady Treyhern's almost musical voice drifted down the table. "If so, you must speak with Mr. MacLachlan, and beg for one of his. I am told he has some splendid mansions in Walham."

Merrick smiled politely. "You are too kind, ma'am. They are very fine town houses, but not quite mansions."

"Fortunately, my new daughter brings a house with her dowry," said the gentleman, a portly, prosperous underwriter whom Merrick knew vaguely. "But MacLachlan's work is known to us all. One could hardly do better."

Merrick smiled faintly. "I hope not, Mr. Wagstaff. My business depends upon it."

"A good attitude!" said the portly man, then he turned his attention to Madeleine. "By the way, Lady Bessett, you look dashed familiar. Have we met before?"

"I do not think so, Mr. Wagstaff."

The red crease on the gentleman's forehead deepened prodigiously. "Who are your people, my dear? I am struggling mightily to place you."

Madeleine seemed to falter. "My father was Jessup of Sheffield," she finally answered. "And my mother was an Archard of West Yorkshire."

"Oh, yes, yes, yes!" said Wagstaff, stabbing his fish fork in Madeleine's direction. "I remember your mother from her come-out in '97. What a pretty thing she was! And I remember *yours*, too, my dear, because you looked just like her."

"Thank you, sir," said Madeleine quietly. "I hold that to be high praise indeed."

Wagstaff's face was taking on a puckish expression. Outwardly, Madeleine appeared composed, but Merrick could sense her ratcheting anxiety. He could feel his own, too. He did not like the look of this, and Wagstaff was—well, an old wag.

"Yes, Miss Archard was a lovely girl," the gentleman continued. "Now, I also remember—" His fork pointed at Merrick, then back again to Madeleine, the mischievous look deepening. "Yes, do I not remember . . . that the two of you . . . ?"

Merrick wanted it over and done with. "That the two of us what, Wagstaff?"

A wide smile followed. "Yes, I can see that I am right, MacLachlan!" said Wagstaff in a teasing tone. "You and this pretty little lady here were quite an item of gossip for a few weeks, as I recall. And there was a little bit of money laid in the betting books round town."

With an innocent expression, Treyhern's daughter leaned forward. "What were they betting on, Mr. Wagstaff?"

"Ariane!" said Lady Treyhern sharply.

To his shock, Madeleine's hand crept into his lap, and her nails dug into his thigh. Wagstaff was still beaming like a jackass.

"Why, they were betting, Lady Ariane, as to whether Lady Madeleine here was going to marry this upstart Scot"—the fork turned on Merrick—"or whether she was holding out for Lord Norting's boy, Henry."

Merrick covered Madeleine's hand with his own, and gave it a reassuring squeeze. "Whom did you bet on, Wagstaff?" he asked, his voice cold.

The gentleman likely would have blushed, had his complexion permitted it. "I—well, I—put my money on Norting's lad," he admitted. "I did not think you'd go the distance, MacLachlan."

"Then we all three lost, did we not?" Merrick's voice was arctic now. "The lady was wise enough to quit London and marry at home, where people are doubtless more sensible."

The fingernails in his thigh relaxed. Madeleine's hand slid away, leaving nothing but its warmth behind.

"Well, what fun it is to talk about old times!" Lady Treyhern interjected. "Now, would anyone care for crème brulée?"

"*Burnt* cream, Mamma," interjected Lady Ariane.

"Yes, quite right!" Lady Treyhern began to rattle on. "We have the loveliest assortment. Cook baked them in a water bath, and burnt them with a hot salamander. There is an orange, and a lemon, and an almond—my favorite—and even a sort of cinnamonish thing with a little pumpkin in it."

"Pumpkin," said Madeleine swiftly. "I should like pumpkin."

And I should like a drink, thought Merrick. *A big one.*

In deference to the chit's birthday, the gentlemen did not linger long over their port. They returned to the withdrawing room to see that the small ballroom opposite had been opened, and Mrs. Rutledge had taken a seat at the piano. The young people collected about her, rifling through the sheets of music and calling out suggestions.

Soon the dancing was well under way, and the French windows were flung open. Seeing an opportunity, Merrick slipped out into the cool darkness. A narrow terrace ran the length of the house. No lanterns had been lit, and there was only the ambient light of the ballroom to guide him. Just a few feet along was a column surrounded by a collection of tall, potted palms. Merrick situated himself just to the other side of it and withdrew a cheroot from his case. The match flared to life on the first strike.

Through the door adjacent, he could hear the gay laughter and the tinkling of the piano. The footmen were back, this time with trays of champagne. Merrick was not a champagne drinker. Indeed, he would have given a great deal for a glass of good Scotch whisky just then. He could still feel the pressure of Madeleine's hand on his thigh. Could still feel the heat of her palm, warming his skin through his trousers.

He closed his eyes, and remembered it. He wished she had not turned to him in her moment of distress. And he wished he had not welcomed it. Still, he had done what any proper gentleman would have done under the circumstances. He had cut Wagstaff off sharply and sent him the clear message that his intimations were not wanted.

But the damage was done, and Madeleine would have to answer to the curiosity of others now—or at least to Lady Treyhern. Merrick had not missed her little intake of breath nor the way her eyes had widened.

His musing was ended when a woman's sharp voice sounded near the ballroom windows. "Bentley, *ma foi!*" she said. "You are hurting my arm."

Lady Treyhern herself appeared on the terrace, propelled forth by her husband's brother, who had seized her upper arm in a determined grip. "Helene," said Rutledge quietly. "I must see you alone."

"About what, pray? Bentley, I have guests."

They paused on the other side of the column, beyond the thatch of ornamental trees. Still caught in his own ruminations, Merrick did not make his presence known as he should have done.

"I hear there's been talk, Helene." His whispered words were grim. "Talk about Thomas Lowe. Good God. After all these years?"

"Your brother overreacted." Lady Treyhern's voice was reassuring. "I ought never have mentioned anything. It was just the Archard boy, teasing Ariane. He meant nothing by it. He knows nothing at all of Lowe."

"Well, goddamn it, I heard what was said," replied Treyhern's brother. "He did not dream it up, Helene. Now, someone has been engaged in idle gossip—very *dangerous* gossip—and we must put a stop to it. One of the servants, I daresay. Who has come with you from Gloucestershire?"

"No one," said Lady Treyhern, her voice tart. "No one save the governess, and she has been with us but six months. And kindly mind your language!"

"Your pardon," said Treyhern's brother tightly. "But I think my distress is understandable, don't you? Now, this boy, where is he from? What is his age?"

"He is from Yorkshire, and came to Town only last month," she retorted. "He is but twelve years old—hardly a malicious age—and has lived most of his life abroad. Trust me, it was just a child's foolishness. The boy is known to have—well, strange notions. And if you insist upon stirring this scandalbroth, you will do naught but make matters worse."

"Good God!" Rutledge said again, pounding his fist on the brickwork. "Poor Ariane. A slow death is what that bastard Lowe deserved. And if I could but shoot him again, I'd aim a good deal lower to ensure it."

Merrick had heard enough. Indeed, he had not wished to hear what little he had. He had no notion what they were talking about, but he knew the nature of man well enough to know that Treyhern's brother was in a black rage.

But it *was* Geoff they were discussing. Bloody hell. It had to be. Merrick did not like to think of the boy's being in trouble. Then again, it was none of his damned business, was it? After one last draw on his cheroot, Merrick paced stealthily down the terrace as far as he could go, cleared his throat sharply, and tossed the stub onto the lawn. Then he paced back up the terrace, whistling "God Save the King," and making as much noise as was humanly possible without actually falling over the edge and into the shrubbery.

When he reached Lady Treyhern, he feigned surprise, and shook the hand of her brother-in-law as if he'd never before laid eyes on the gentleman.

"Mr. Rutledge," said Merrick smoothly. "What a pleasure."

Lady Treyhern smiled, and made a few aimless remarks regarding the weather. They seemed unconcerned by his presence. After a moment, Merrick bowed to the countess and moved on. Beneath the brilliant chandeliers, a half dozen couples were breaking ranks from a lively country dance, some of them breathing hard, others gaily laughing.

He found Madeleine alone and drifting toward the piano. He caught her lightly by the arm. She turned around, and her expression faltered. Mrs. Rutledge had struck up a waltz.

"Dance with me," he said.

Fleetingly, she hesitated.

"It is too late, Madeleine," he said grimly, taking her hand in his. "Our cat is out of the bag now."

"Yes, and whose fault is that?" she asked, as he hauled her onto the dance floor.

"Not mine, by God," he gritted. "You are the one who chose to return to Town after all these years."

"I see," she said tightly. "And this is your idea of being finished? Of never laying eyes on me again?"

"Madeleine, acting the bitch does not become you," he answered, pulling her to him. "This is one dinner party. One dance. Had I known you were to be here, I would have stayed away. But I did not, and now we will cause more talk by walking circles round one another than we would if we simply behaved with common civility."

He sensed it the moment she surrendered. She allowed him to draw her to him, and they waltzed in silence for a time, the silk of her gown brushing his clothing each time they swept into a turn. It had been a long time, Merrick thought, since he had danced with a woman. He remembered none of them save Madeleine. Her hand was small and warm in his, and her scent of soap and jasmine teased at his nostrils as her skin warmed from the exertion.

He wanted, inexplicably, to continue their conversation of the previous week. He wanted to ask her *why* she had given up on them so easily. And as he looked down at her, there was a deep and sudden yearning in his belly, a sort of weakness and an aching sense of loss. He wanted to pull her closer, to set his hand between her shoulder blades, instead of leaving it oh-so-properly at the turn of her waist. He wanted to melt his body to hers. And though it sounded physical, it was not. It was more than that. It was his heart and his body's remembrance of that sweet, brief time when they had been one.

Thirteen long years. And only to himself could he admit that he had missed her. Even now, knowing that she was not the woman he had once loved, he missed her still. He missed the girl she had been, not the stiff, querulous woman she had become. He missed the hope of a happy life to come and a steadfast partner with whom to share it. And even for that small weakness, he despised himself. Good God, he had to find a way past this, to shut it out, or the pain would eat him alive again.

He forced it away, and returned to his original concern. "I need to talk to you, Madeleine," he said, his lips near her ear. "It is about Geoffrey."

She stiffened in his embrace. Only his hand, firm at her waist, kept her from pulling away. "I do not care, Merrick, to discuss my son with you," she said. "Kindly leave us alone."

He ignored her. "What did Geoff say, Madeleine, to Treyhern's daughter?"

Something in her seemed to shift. She cut an apprehensive glance up at him as he whirled her into the next turn. "What are you talking about?"

"I hardly know," he admitted. "But I hate to think of Geoff in trouble."

"In . . . in trouble?" Her grip on his hand tightened, and he felt rather than saw her falter. Her toe caught something. He took her weight against his body, and righted her seamlessly.

"I am sorry," Merrick said when she was steady again. "I overstate the matter. I chanced to hear a snippet of a conversation between Lady Treyhern and her husband's brother, that is all. But he did seem distressed about something Geoff had said to the girl. Damned if I know what—or why he should even care. But . . . but he did. And I just wondered what had been said."

Madeleine was quiet for a moment.

"Maddie, I don't mean the boy any harm," he finally said. "Look, you are quite right. It is none of my concern. Just . . . just take what I've said and do what you think best. If he has been tormenting the girl, make him stop."

"It—it is not that," Madeleine blurted. "Geoff would never torment anyone. Indeed, he is quite sensitive."

"I know that, Madeleine," he answered.

He watched her lick her lips uncertainly. "The trouble is," she said. "Geoffrey is not . . . not quite well."

"What?" The boy looked healthy as a horse to him. "Madeleine, there is nothing wrong with Geoff."

"But there is," she countered. "It—it is just not the sort of thing one can easily see."

"Madeleine, do not put notions in the boy's head."

She pursed her lips for a moment, and her eyes filled with pain. "Oh, you cannot begin to understand!"

"Give me the benefit of the doubt, Madeleine, before you decide that."

"I am a *good* mother, Merrick," she answered indignantly. "And you have not given me the benefit of the doubt. I *know* my son. I have devoted the whole of my life to him. And I know that something is wrong, and getting worse."

"I am sorry," he said. "You are right. I barely know the boy. Tell me what it is you think is wrong, and I shall listen."

Suddenly, her look of stubborn resolve faded to uncertainty. "It is just that Geoff imagines things, and has strange notions." Madeleine had lost much of her color. "And he suffers from melancholia, often severe. That is why, you see, we came to London. I did not come back, Merrick, so that we might quarrel. I never dreamt we would even see one another again. I—I just needed desperately to find help for my son, but . . . but in that regard, I have failed."

There could not have been a less opportune time for his hip joint to seize up. But the sidesteps which the waltz required were exacting a price. The pain was sudden, and severe. Madeleine could not have missed the hitch in his gait.

"Merrick?" Her voice was sharp. "What is wrong?"

"I have to stop," he gritted, a statement which was superfluous, since he already had.

He led her by the hand from the dance floor. "I need to speak with you in private," he said. "Someplace besides this ballroom."

It was, perhaps, a measure of her desperation that she agreed. "The yellow parlor?"

He closed his eyes against the pain, and shook his head. "No stairs. Not . . . for a bit."

She nodded and left the room. Merrick followed her out into the corridor, struggling not to limp. There was a door opposite the stairs, not a grand door signifying a formal room, but a small, ordinary one. Madeleine pulled it open. The room was rather like a large butler's pantry, with two walls of cupboards, and beyond them, a plain worktable with four stout chairs. There were no windows, but a sconce burned by the table, and along the counters, one could see the evening's dinner service laid out in neat stacks, already washed, dried, and ready to be locked away.

Madeleine went in, and pulled out two chairs. "I think you should sit," she said.

Merrick did not argue. He braced his hand flat on the worktable and eased down. The relief was immediate. She went to the door, and turned the key in the lock, then joined him. They sat facing one another, their knees inches apart in the narrow room.

"My leg is rarely this bad," he said apologetically. "But sometimes it just seizes up. I apologize."

"You do not dance often." It was not a question.

"It shows, does it?" He smiled ruefully. "No, almost never. My sort of life does not require it."

She regarded him solemnly for a moment. "What sort of life is that, Merrick? I—I cannot help but be curious, you see."

He said nothing for a moment. "It is the sort of life I always expected to have," he said. "More or less. It is a life of work and duty, not a life of social obligation—or rarely, at any rate."

"I see." She paused, as if hoping he would continue. He did not.

She looked about nervously and clasped her hands in her lap. "Perhaps we oughtn't be in here."

"We are hardly a pair of young innocents now, Maddie," he said. "Besides, what would they do if they caught us? Make us get married?"

She gave a sharp bark of laughter, but there was little humor in it. A heavy silence fell over the little room.

"You wished to ask about Geoff," she finally said. "I am sorry I was sharp, but I have told you all I know. I think perhaps the sooner we leave London, the better it shall be for him. I think he was more settled in the quiet of the countryside."

"But what did you mean, Madeleine, when you said

melancholia?" he gently probed. "Is he just unhappy sometimes? Boys often become moody at a certain age, you know."

She held his gaze, her eyes wide and candid. "I know that, Merrick," she said. "But this is a sadness which goes beyond that. And it is so hard to explain. He seems to think that he is—well, at *fault*. For everything, it sometimes seems."

Merrick drummed his fingers on the tabletop for a time. "Give me an example," he said.

Madeleine cut her gaze away. "Well—that poor Mr. Chutley," she said. "He seems to have taken it into his head that he was somehow to blame for his death."

"Good God!" said Merrick. "Nothing could be further from the truth. If anything, he saved me from taking a bullet to the head."

"Just as I tried to tell him," she agreed. "Mind you, he has not come right out and *said* he feels responsible. It is just that I know how his mind works. I have seen it over and over. And—well, he *cries*. Often—though he tries to hide it. Do you know, Merrick, how humiliating it is for a twelve-year-old boy to cry? It is a weakness which mortifies him."

Merrick said nothing. He well knew what it was like for a twenty-two-year-old man to cry. He would not be too quick to shame poor Geoff. The boy would learn soon enough that his tears would bring him no comfort.

"Does he . . . does he pine for someone?" he asked. "His father, perhaps?"

Madeleine hesitated, then shook her head. A tendril of warm blond hair had slipped from its loose arrangement to tease at her bare shoulder. "They were not terribly close," she said, still clutching her hands in her lap. "My late husband was very busy with his research. Geoff and his half brother are fond of one another, but Geoff was like this even in Yorkshire with Alvin. Indeed, he showed the signs of it in Italy as a small boy. I have always known that Geoff was . . . different. I thought, though, that he would outgrow it. He has not. Instead, it has worsened."

Merrick was flummoxed. He believed her. Oh, Madeleine might be coddling the boy a bit, but coddling did not account for the things she described. "He just does not look to me to be an overly emotional boy," he remarked.

But what the hell did he know? He had known but one child in the whole of his thirty-five years.

"What did he say to the girl, anyway?" he asked. "If you will tell me."

Madeleine lifted one shoulder weakly. "It was nothing, really," she said. "I suppose he meant to—to tease her, perhaps? They were playing cards, and he blurted out something about her father being . . . well, *dead*. He meant it, I am sure, as a joke, but it didn't come out that way. He has been upset with himself ever since."

"Children do have strange notions," said Merrick. "Alasdair and I took many a sound thrashing for saying things we thought funny, when our mother did not find them nearly so entertaining."

The pain in his leg was gone now, but there was still a strange ache in his heart. He felt sorry for Madeleine. Despite what the years had wrought, despite how she had abandoned him, it seemed he no longer had the heart to wish her ill. Certainly he did not wish the boy ill. He quite liked Geoff. They shared so many of the same interests. He had never before thought of children as appealing.

He took her hands in his, and leaned forward. "Maddie, I am so sorry," he said, lightly chafing her hands in his. "I would never wish you unhappy. There was a time, perhaps, when I thought I did. Yet now that I see you so, I take no pleasure in it. But I cannot think of a damned thing I could do to help the boy. If—if you think of something—anything—you have only to let me know."

"There is nothing," she said sorrowfully. "And Geoff is not your responsibility."

He gave a muted smile. "Well, all the same, you have only to ask."

She tightened her lips, as if trying not to cry. It damned near broke his heart. It was time to get out of this narrow little room before he did something incredibly foolish. If Geoff was not his responsibility, God knew Madeleine was not. He rose, still holding her hands, and drew her lightly to her feet.

"I think, Merrick, that I shall go home now," she said. "I shall find Helene and make my apologies."

"I shan't be far behind you," he said. "I cannot think what I was doing here to begin with."

He gave her hands another reassuring squeeze and let them go. She turned to step past him, and into the narrow passageway between the cupboards, and unthinkingly, he caught her shoulder.

Her gaze snapped to his. For an instant, they were frozen in time, and the years were stripped away. Somehow, he found his voice. "Maddie, I—" He shook his head, and tried again. "Good God, Maddie. I wish you had never come back."

She was still staring up at him, looking terribly alone, her porcelain skin soft in the lamplight. "And I wish you had been not so kind to me tonight," she answered. "Somehow . . . somehow, Merrick, it is easier to hate you from afar."

"Bloody hell," he said, suddenly wishing the world to splinters.

Her innocent gaze was still holding his. "God, what a mess we have made, Merrick. Of—oh, of everything, it seems."

Like a fool, he stepped nearer. They were but inches apart in the little room. Her eyes were wide, tinged with pain and regret and some other emotion he could not name. He realized in some shock that he wanted to kiss her again, and he sensed, strangely, that she would not resist.

Dear God, it would be so wrong, so cruel to take advantage of her grief. But Merrick had never been known for his humanity. He lifted his hand, and slid it around her face in a smooth, hungry caress. Her lashes fell shut, feathering softly over her cheeks. On a breathless sound, she turned her face into his palm.

"Oh, *don't,*" she whispered, her lips brushing feather light over his thumb. "Oh, Merrick. Please."

Please what? Oh, God, he was going to regret this. But he yearned to know what it would feel like to touch her again. Already the hurt and need and outright lust were twisting in his belly like a living thing. Driven by them, Merrick blocked out all else, and bent his head to hers, gently taking her mouth.

It was like an oil lamp hurled into a hearth of cinders. Heat and flame exploded, then roared to life, consuming them. Her lips seemed to swell and soften beneath his as he tasted her, his hands and his mouth greedy and urgent.

She made a hungry, desperate sound in the back of her throat.

He was afraid to speak. Afraid to stop kissing her, for fear one of them might come to their senses. Instead, he let the kiss take them deeper as he gently probed the seam of her lips. On a soft groan, she opened for him, tilting her head back in surrender. Hotly, harshly, plunged his tongue deep, giving her no quarter. Giving her fair warning of his intent. But Madeleine did not back away. Thirteen empty years went up in flames.

He surged deep inside again on a shiver. Against him, Madeleine trembled with unmistakable hunger as he slid his tongue sinuously along hers, tasting and plumbing the depths he remembered so well. She pressed herself against him without hesitation, God help them both.

In his dreams, when he kissed her, it was a kiss of almost violent emotion; a carnal onslaught, as if he might release the demons of a dozen years by taking her harshly. This kiss was fierce and wild, tinged with regret, sensuous even in its sadness. He cupped her face in both his hands and kissed her again, turning his face to slant his mouth over hers as he remembered the hot rush of young love.

Madeleine's eyes were still closed, but she was returning his kisses with an escalating hunger. She was starved for this; he sensed it, and urged it on. She pressed her breasts against him and let her other hand come up to slide beneath his coat, and then beneath his waistcoat, too, until he could feel the heat of her hand through the thin fabric of his shirt.

"Maddie," he whispered, his mouth dotting kisses beneath her eye.

Her other hand fisted in his lapel. "Don't talk," she whispered. "Just . . . oh, God. Don't stop."

Merrick cupped her breast in his hand and listened with satisfaction to her little gasp of pleasure. Lightly, he brushed his thumb across the sensitive tip. She tempted fate when she urged herself against his palm. Somehow, he eased the fabric of her dress down her shoulder to reveal the swell of her breast, so plump and perfect he felt his knees go weak. The sweet, dark peak, however, was still hidden from his view. He tugged at the gown from beneath, and was rewarded.

She gave a sharp cry of pleasure when his mouth covered her. "Oh, God," she whispered.

At her words, blood rushed to his head and to his groin. Her nipple hardened like a precious pearl between his lips. Over and over he suckled her, drawing the sweet creamy flesh of her breast into the warmth of his mouth. She had set her shoulders to the wall now, exposing herself fully to him. It was a position of total surrender.

He was going to give her what she begged for—here and now, in this narrow little room, and damn the consequences. Merrick's hand eased down, cupping the swell of her buttock through the slippery silk of her gown. She made a sound of insistence as he circled and caressed her. In response, he lifted her a little against him, and let her feel his body's urgency.

Her head fell back, her mouth open, her breathing fast and shallow. "Oh," she whispered. "Oh, God, Merrick, *please* . . ."

Merrick felt her body go limp as she yielded to his hands and his body. She shuddered with desire now, so complete was her capitulation to her own needs. Madeleine—dignified, perfect little Madeleine—made not even a pretense of backing away. It had ever been so;

Madeleine had always desired him, physically, at least, and she had never possessed the artifice to pretend otherwise.

Dimly, he tried to consider the principles of the thing. She was widowed. She must be lonely. She might never forgive him.

And if he did not have her now, he would never forgive himself.

His impatience, his utter lack of self-control with Maddie was what had landed them in Gretna Green in the first place. It was not a quick, hard fuck he wanted from her. But just now, it was what his body craved. It would have to do.

Her hand had somehow burrowed beneath his shirt, and her nails were digging into the muscles of his back, begging for it. Good sense failed him, and he began to inch her skirts slowly upward. With rough, urgent motions, he pushed her drawers down.

Madeleine shuddered in his embrace when his hand slid around to cup her bare buttock. Her eyes opened, afire with lust, but filled with questions. The heels of her hands came against his shoulders, but it was a halfhearted gesture. "Oh, God," she whispered. "What are we doing?"

"What we were meant to do, I'm afraid," he murmured, setting his mouth to the turn of her throat.

Madeleine knew she should refuse him, but she could no longer remember why. For so long, her body had ached for this. She wanted to surrender to the yearning. Wanted that slow, sweet ache to pool in her belly. His hands were hot and urgent, his body strong. She let her head fall against the solid weight of his shoulder, and set her mouth to the turn of his neck.

The scent of warm male and woodsy cologne drifted

about in a tantalizing cloud. Her drawers were some-where around her ankles now, all but forgotten. She heard fabric tear, and vaguely, she wondered what sort of mind-less idiot took such a risk. But it was that very risk which seemed to exhilarate her. The risk of scandal. The risk of being caught. Perhaps the risk of losing her heart again.

She kissed the turn of his throat and worked her way along his jaw. Merrick's breathing was rough in the gloom as his hand eased between them. His warm, nimble fin-gers slid down her belly and lower still, leaving her gasp-ing. Two fingers teased at the joining of her thighs, sliding deeper into the heat with each gentle stroke. His breath was warm against her throat. *Good God, she had to have him.*

Wantonly, Madeleine rode down on his hand. As if to draw out her pleasure, he lightened his strokes, and let his mouth return to her breast.

"Ohh," she whispered. It was a plea. It was her surren-der.

His mouth returned to hers with a new urgency, his hands caressing her body almost desperately as he plunged over and over into her mouth with hungry strokes. His mouth moved down her throat. Lightly, his teeth nipped at her, and Madeleine could hear herself pleading for some-thing; something sweet and long remembered.

Merrick urged her from the wall. The edge of the table touched the backs of her legs. The flickering lamplight seemed to cast the room in a warm golden haze which drew them inescapably deeper. She let her hands slide be-neath his coat again, then skimmed them up the solid slab of muscles which formed his back. The warmth of his body, along with his warm male scent, surrounded her.

You are making a fool of yourself again, she thought dimly. His fingers stroked deep into her flesh now, brushing her most sensitive spot, and leaving her shuddering. *He wants only one thing.* But the thought did deter her, for she wanted that one thing, too.

Merrick's nostrils were wide now, and both her breasts were bared to his touch. He molded them in his hands, lightly thumbing her taut, aching nipples. The light of the wall sconce was enough to reveal the intensity which burned in his eyes. "Madeleine," he rasped. "Dear God, Maddie."

He bent over her and slid a hand beneath her hips again. A little roughly, he pushed her down onto the table, lifting her slightly as he did so. He stood between her legs, one hand beneath her gathered skirts, as his eyes feasted on her face, her throat, her bared breasts. The surface of the table was hard and cool beneath her hips as he tormented her. The warm weight of his hand beneath her skirts, between her legs, caressed her intimately, driving her need to a fevered pitch.

"Oh, Merrick!" Her head went back against the firmness of the table, and her body arched hard against his hand. "Merrick, please. *Please.*"

"Please what, my love?" He choked out the words. "Tell me."

She dragged herself up, and reached for him. Using his stronger leg, he followed her onto the table, mounting her. He took her mouth again, and bracing himself above her, kissed her deeply. "What?" he asked again. "What do you want, Maddie love?"

"You. Inside me." Her hands went to his trousers, greedily caressing the thick bulge of flesh, the promise of earthly pleasures. *"Now."*

He groaned and let his body tremble against hers. Impatiently, she slid her hand down, found a button, and slipped it free. Another and another followed. The powerful weight of his erection jutted from the crumpled linen, and with one hand, she pushed it away until she could grasp the heated flesh in her hand.

He lifted his mouth from hers, and quietly cursed. "You won't regret it?" he rasped. "You won't blame me?"

She shook her head, her hair scrubbing the table. "No," she whispered. "Please. Just this once."

Bracing himself on one hand, Merrick rose up and shoved away his shirttails. She could see the swollen head of his shaft. Good Lord, she had not remembered quite how generously nature had made him. But she set one slipper against the table, curled the other leg around his waist, and pulled him to her.

She felt the hot weight of him probe at her entrance, then ease into the warm slickness of her desire. Greedily, Madeleine's hips arched up to take him. Another heated inch, and he was well inside her. Oh, God. It felt so good to be impaled on his body. To be stretched almost beyond bearing. To refuse to give in to good sense.

Urgently, she pulled him down, pulled him deeper, and joined his body to hers. Merrick's breathing ratcheted up another notch. Still, she ached. There was a cry, a little catch in her voice. Her hands were on him, hot and urgent. "More," she pleaded. "Merrick, let me—"

He lifted his hips, and thrust deep on a triumphant grunt. Madeleine felt her whole body start at the sudden invasion, and then it was not an invasion at all, but a sweet torment. Eagerly, she pressed upward, urgently searching.

"Holy Christ, Maddie," he whispered, bracing both

hands on the table. Slowly, he began to ride her, but his heavy, stretching weight was like a spark to tinder. Oh, she was so close. Another two or three strokes, and she was writhing and whimpering beneath him. Merrick thrust himself inside her, his timing perfect, his angle exquisite as his body pulled at her hungry flesh.

Suddenly, his every muscle seemed to stiffen. His face a mask of strain, he withdrew, then sank himself deep on one last, sweet stroke. His throat worked soundlessly, the sinewy tendons of his neck drawing taut as his warmth flooded deep inside her. And then she splintered and came apart, the dim little room exploding with pleasure and light. He covered her mouth with his, and swallowed her scream of release.

When she returned to her senses, he was still bent over her, holding her tightly to him. He kissed her again, deeply and longingly, as if he could not bear to release her. For a long moment, they clung to one another silently. "Good Lord," he said, when his breathing had calmed.

Dimly, Madeleine understood that when she came to her senses, she was going to regret this. But just now, the risk seemed worth it.

Merrick's gaze was rueful as he finally shifted his weight away. "We are going to have a devil of a time, Maddie, pretending that *this* did not happen."

She did not know what to say. It was slowly dawning on her the terrible risk they had just run. Her hand went to her sleeve and began to tug it back into place. "It was just this once, Merrick," she reminded him. "That was what we said, was it not? I—I shall be gone soon enough, and . . . and then we can forget again. We can forget this ever happened, if that is our wish."

Merrick shifted his weight, and stood. Gently, he helped her from the table and began to right her clothing. "I daresay it will be," he quietly agreed, unwilling to hold her gaze. "I daresay we will both think better of this tomorrow, Maddie."

She felt her face warm. "Will we have been missed, do you think?"

He shrugged. "Most likely," he said. "I suppose . . . I suppose you'd best return to the ballroom. Without me."

Somehow, Madeleine found the presence of mind to nod. She watched him methodically stuffing his shirttails back into his trousers. "Are we mad, Merrick?" she whispered. "Did we learn nothing all those years ago?"

Merrick dropped his hands, and stepped away. "Oh, I learnt a vast deal," he said.

He bent down and picked up her gossamer shawl, which had slid off her elbows. "Here. Put this back on. Go on without me."

Go on without me.

Good God, wasn't that what she had been doing? And it had brought her no joy. But this—this quick, desperate coupling of their bodies and their souls had made her heart soar.

Madeleine slid the shawl back on to her shoulders, surprised to see that her hands were shaking. Merrick looked as if he were angry with himself, and perhaps with her, too. If this had been a mistake, yes, it had been worth it. And from the look on his face, it might have to warm her heart for a very long time to come.

With one last uncertain glance, she turned away, and left the little room.

Chapter Thirteen

Haste and anger hinders guid counsel.

H e waited in the gloom for all of ten minutes. Long enough, he thought, for Madeleine to make her apologies and leave. *Just this once.* Good Lord, his heart could not take much more than that. He prayed he never saw her again. She was going to leave London, she had said. Thank God. It would be wise if he did nothing to deter that leaving.

But just now, he could not bear to think on it. What had just passed between them—dear God, it had been dangerous and foolish and soul-searing, and yet carnal on a level which he had not known with even the most skilled of prostitutes. It had been . . . his dream again. Or a glimpse of it.

Feeling thoroughly enervated, Merrick leaned back against the wall to take the weight from his hip. Absent the blinding desire, he could actually feel that the muscle spasm had returned, albeit milder this time. When he judged himself capable of walking evenly, he left the little room, closing the door tightly behind.

In the ballroom, the music was still going on. Lady Ariane was dancing with her uncle, the angry gentleman he had seen on the terrace earlier.

"*Bon soir,* Mr. MacLachlan," said a soft voice at his elbow. "You are a man of many surprises."

He looked down to see Lady Treyhern staring pointedly up at him. Her expression was candid, but there was a mistrust in her gaze which he did not miss.

"I rather doubt there is anything surprising about me, ma'am," he countered. "I am just what you see before you."

She tapped him lightly on the arm with her fan. "Ah, but your past!" she said quietly. "By the way, dear Madeleine has left, you may wish to know."

"Her going or coming is no business of mine," said Merrick.

"Is it not?" she answered. "Well, in any case, I should very much like to hear the details of this youthful dalliance between the two of you."

Merrick lifted both brows, and shot her his darkest glower. "Then you will have to have them from Lady Bessett, ma'am."

"Ah, a man of discretion." Lady Treyhern snapped her fan shut, and looked at him appraisingly. "One can appreciate that. Come, Mr. MacLachlan, and take a turn about the room with me. There is something I should like to discuss with you."

Merrick started to refuse her. His mind was decidedly elsewhere. But he was the lady's guest, after all, and he was not rude by nature. Merrick reluctantly offered his arm and thanked God the spasm in his hip had subsided.

Lady Treyhern smiled up at him. "By the way," she

murmured. "I have been meaning to ask about your lovely signet ring. The sign of St. Thomas the Apostle, is it not?"

"Yes, the patron saint of builders." The ornate ring winked in the candlelight as he extended his finger. "This one is a family heirloom, passed down by some long-dead Catholic ancestor."

Lady Treyhern smiled. "Are you a papist, Mr. MacLachlan?"

He gave a muted smile. "No, though I would not be ashamed of it if I were."

She looked at him approvingly. "My father was Catholic," she remarked. "A pity he did not wear the symbol of some patron saint. It might have saved his neck from the guillotine."

"My sympathies," he murmured.

She inclined her head. "I trust St. Thomas has guarded you well?"

"Well enough," he answered.

The countess then chattered on amiably until they reached the back of the room by the French windows. Then she turned to him and flashed him that strange, appraising look again.

"You must forgive my brother-in-law, Mr. MacLachlan," she said out of nowhere. "Bentley often lets his temper override his good sense."

Merrick looked down at her. "Mr. Rutledge seems all that is pleasant, ma'am. I have no quarrel with the gentleman."

"But alas, Bentley sometimes talks when she should listen," the lady continued, seemingly apropos of nothing. "Me, I say little and see a good deal more."

He was not in the mood for games. "Precisely what are you getting at, Lady Treyhern?"

She had the good grace to blush, but not deeply. "I realized too late that you were on the balcony tonight," she said. "Bentley took me unawares."

It was Merrick's turn to be embarrassed. A gentleman would have made his presence known at once. He gave a stiff bow of acknowledgment. "My apologies," he said. "I confess, my mind was elsewhere."

"And you hoped we would go away, and leave you to peace, I am sure," she said breezily. "Nonetheless, we did not. And now I find myself in a most awkward position, Mr. MacLachlan."

"And what position would that be?"

She lifted one shoulder, the gesture more nonchalant than her words. "I am beholden to you," she answered. "You are now in possession of certain bits of information. Information which, if repeated, might wound someone very young, and very innocent."

"Your stepdaughter, I collect."

"Yes, my stepdaughter." Lady Treyhern's eyes were pleading now.

"Then you are in luck, madam," said Merrick. "I am not in the habit of wishing children ill."

"You must understand," Lady Treyhern persisted. "She is a good girl. Indeed, I love her as I love my own three—and in some ways, more. Ariane had a tragic childhood. I had hoped that the tragedy was at an end. Now it is up to you."

"Up to me?" Merrick drew back an inch. "That is one hell of a burden."

Lady Treyhern pursed her lips and shook her head.

"No, I mean only that her future happiness depends, to some extent, on your discretion."

Merrick's mouth curled a little bitterly. "Well, I am, as they say, the soul of discretion, ma'am," he answered. "And frankly, I am not much given to gossip. I have enough troubles of my own."

Lady Treyhern smiled faintly. "May I have your word, then, that you will hold what you heard in the utmost confidence?" she asked. "I am sorry. I know I have no right to ask it of you, but—"

"You need say no more," said Merrick. "I beg you will put it from your mind. I certainly have."

The lady's smile warmed a degree, but she was still troubled. It seemed an opportune time to make his exit. With another bow, this time over her hand, he took his leave of her.

The hall clock was striking half past ten when Madeleine arrived home. Clara let her in, and took her things. Madeleine went into the parlor to pour herself a glass of wine and to consider the almost overwhelming emotions which had assailed her in the wake of Merrick's lovemaking. But her solitude was not to be. Mr. Frost sat by the windows with a well-thumbed book in hand. He did not, however, look as though he had been reading it, for his gaze was bleary and a little dejected.

Upon seeing her, he came at once to his feet. "My lady. Good evening."

"Good evening, Mr. Frost," she said. "Pray sit down. Will you take a little wine?"

"Thank you," he answered. "It would be most welcome. You are home early, are you not?"

"Yes, and glad to be so." She took the glass to him and sat down nearby. "Tell me, how was Geoffrey tonight?"

Mr. Frost had laid aside his book. "Not himself," he admitted. "I confess, ma'am, that the lad has me a little worried this time."

Madeleine nodded sadly. "He is truly cast down," she answered. "This is the worst spell ever, I believe."

"I wonder if you aren't right," Frost agreed. "May I ask, my lady, about the man—the chap who shot himself—did Geoffrey know him?"

She lifted one hand impotently. "Not so far as I am aware. How could he?"

"I think he could not have," said Mr. Frost pensively. "And yet—and yet he seems to feel the grief most strongly. He even went so far as to say he felt he should have *done* something. But what could he have done? I cannot think—and when I ask, he will not tell me."

Madeleine sat silently for a time. Mr. Frost's concerns were too similar to her own for comfort. Geoff's worsening despair, along with the events of tonight, made her feel that an escape from London was imperative.

She set her glass down with a sharp *chink*. "I think, Mr. Frost, that my bringing Geoff to Town has hurt rather than helped," she confessed. "There is just too much going on here."

"Too much going on?" He sounded confused.

"I am not explaining myself well, am I?" Madeleine shook her head, as if to clear her thoughts. "It is just that . . . well, sometimes I feel that there are too many people here, too much activity. It is as if . . . as if it all affects Geoff somehow, if that makes any sense?"

"Nothing about Geoff's fears makes much sense," the

young man admitted. "But regarding London, I think you may be right."

"Perhaps a change of scenery is in order," she said quietly. "Will you let us uproot you once more, Mr. Frost? I was thinking we might give up on London and remove to Cambridge instead."

"Cambridge is my favorite place in all the world, ma'am," he said. "I should be pleased to go. I only hope we do not find that Geoff's problems follow us."

With that, the young man laid aside his book, finished his wine, and excused himself for the evening.

Madeleine clutched her glass in both hands, and looked dejectedly around the room at the piles of papers and correspondence. It was going to be a long night. Already, she knew that sleep meant to elude her. Tonight she would spend a few hours going through the next crate of her father's files.

She was more determined than ever to find something—anything—related to the dissolution of her first marriage. She *must*. The doubt was beginning to crush her. Her reactions to Merrick were obviously spiraling out of control. That was yet another reason she had no wish to go to bed tonight. Dreams of him—feverish, restless fantasies—had begun to torment her. In those dreams, she was seventeen again, and full of a wild, heedless passion. And Merrick—oh, God! He came to her lonely bed cloaked in shadow and mystery. Not the Merrick of her past, but the man he was now.

That was the most frightening thing of all. She could tell herself he was no longer the man she had fallen in love with, but she was no longer certain it was true. His touch tonight had inflamed her to madness, just as it always had done. In that narrow, humble room, she had acted the common tart, wanton and rash. She had allowed him intimacies which left her blushing with shame. Even now, her body ached for his rough, hungry touch.

Dear God! If she could just find those papers Papa had shown her! If she could just prove to herself that it was over, that it had, in fact, ended long ago, somehow it would make matters so much clearer to her now.

Regrettably, she was down to her father's work-related materials. All else had been closely examined, and yielded nothing. But all might not be lost. Perhaps her father had considered her ill-thought marriage to be an issue related to his political aspirations, rather than a personal matter? Perhaps that was all she had ever been to him—just a pawn to be married off in order to build a political alliance. Cousin Imogene had once said as much.

With a heavy heart, Madeleine went upstairs to change into her nightgown and wrapper, and to send Eliza on to bed. There was no point in both of them suffering a sleepless night.

Merrick made his escape from Lord Treyhern's house some four hours after his arrival, only to recall he had sent his coach away. With his mind in a turmoil over Madeleine, he had already hiked halfway down to the Blue Posts, praying Grimes and the footman were still sober, before he began to piece together just what it was which Lady Treyhern had been so worried about.

Thomas Lowe. It was not a familiar name. But whoever the poor devil was, he was dead.

"If I could but shoot him again, I'd aim a good deal lower," her brother-in-law had said. Very interesting, that. And

Mr. Rutledge had looked perfectly capable of shooting a man—in the back or otherwise. But what did the death of a man named Lowe have to do with the girl? Something was nagging at the recesses of his mind now, and driving him to distraction.

At the Blue Posts, he waded into the crowd which spilt from the yellow glare of the front door, and saw nothing of Grimes inside. He tossed a coin to a passing potboy, and enquired.

"Round back, gov'," said the lad, tucking the coin away. "Asleep, too, from the sound of 'em."

They were racked up inside the carriage, Merrick discovered, both sawing logs fit to be heard across the inn yard. At his solid thump on the door, they rousted up, climbed down, and shook the sleep off, both looking faintly mortified. At least they were sober.

"Home, Grimes," he said, climbing up.

The trip across west London was uneventful. This time, no one tried to shoot him. Once inside the house, Merrick went upstairs to his office, yanked off his neckcloth, and poured himself a tot of Scotland's crowning glory. Then, deciding it did not look quite glorious enough, he sloshed in another dram and fell into his favorite chair. He loosened his waistcoat, toed off his evening slippers, and propped his feet up on the tea table.

Now, what was that niggling thought in the back of his brain? And what had it to do with the Rutledge chit? Or Geoff? Or Madeleine, come to that? Something, damn it. Something. What was it Geoff had said to the girl to start this row in the first place?

That her father was dead. On its face, it sounded like a macabre thing to say, especially when one blurted it out for no discernible reason. Madeleine had said, too hopefully, that perhaps it was simple teasing. Lady Treyhern had claimed that Geoff was known to have "strange notions." Treyhern's brother had shot a man named Thomas Lowe. Shot him dead, apparently. And now the Rutledge family was very worried about gossip.

Well. It seemed they had had more than a passing acquaintance with that particular trouble. And somewhere in all this mess was a thread of truth which was inexplicably teasing him.

Treyhern's first marriage had been a mess, by all accounts. And his first wife had been, as Phipps had so discreetly put it, *"of questionable constancy."* In other words, she had been unfaithful to her husband. Seen in that ugly light, Lady Treyhern's apprehension began to make sense. It sounded as if the mysterious Mr. Lowe had got himself shot for a bloody good reason. And the simple fact was, Treyhern's daughter might not be . . . well, *his.* Her ladyship knew it, too—as did the earl himself, his brother, and, quite possibly, some of his servants. Lady Ariane, however, apparently did not know it.

Damn. *That* was the sort of gossip that could ruin a young girl's prospects, not to mention break her heart. No wonder they were all trying to hide it. Then poor little Geoff went and blurted out the truth—or a bit of it—in front of the chit.

Now, there was the part that made no sense.

Just then, Phipps came in. "Good evening, sir. Will you wish to undress?"

"No." Merrick sat his glass down awkwardly. "I'm in one of my black moods, old fellow. I believe I shall get rip-roaring drunk and sleep in my clothes."

"Very good, sir," said Phipps, going to the desk. "I'll pencil it in on your calendar. By the way, a package came for you this evening. Mr. Harbury delivered it himself."

"Harbury, eh? That was quick."

Phipps was unwrapping a small leather case. He opened it, and presented it to his employer with a flourish. "Your new spectacles, sir," he announced. "May they be a comfort to you in your old age."

"You are growing increasingly impertinent, Phipps," said Merrick, unfolding the strange bits of wire and glass. Gingerly, he placed them on his nose, and hooked the wires behind his ears. But nothing changed.

"Blister it, man, you look the very same!" he said. "Did I pay good money for these?"

"Indeed, sir."

"Well, what the devil are they supposed to do?"

"Not much, I collect," said Phipps. "The lenses are quite thin. Indeed, Harbury said he saw no need to fit you at all, but that you insisted you could not see."

Merrick glowered up at him. "Give me a book, damn it."

Phipps produced a manual on modern road construction from the corner of Merrick's desk. Merrick turned up the wick, and flipped the book open. The print inside looked just as small and cramped as ever. "Damn!" he said, snapping it violently shut. "What made me think I needed spectacles, anyway?"

"One wonders, sir," the servant said over his shoulder. "Harbury claims you've the vision of a man half your age."

Phipps had gone into the bedroom and was turning down Merrick's bed, and, despite Merrick's threat to sleep in his clothes, the impudent fellow was laying out his nightshirt. Merrick refolded the fragile-looking wires and restored the spectacles to their leather case. Rather than call Phipps back, he rose and went to his desk so that he might tuck them away into a side drawer.

It was then that he saw Geoff's opera glasses. He had meant to return them, but Geoff had stopped coming to the work site, and Merrick had let them slip his mind. He took them out, and studied them for a moment. There was a bit of withered sheep's sorrel stuck beneath the adjustment screw. He pulled it out and weighed the glasses in his hand. How odd it all seemed to him now.

That day by the old well, Geoff had claimed to have seen the crane slip using his mother's opera glasses. Then he claimed to have *forgotten* he'd seen it. That made no more sense now than then. But in all the rush and danger, Merrick had let it go. Later, however, when Merrick found the glasses in the grass, and looked through them at the accident scene . . .

Good God. How very strange.

And yet there were other things, too, things that, when his mind was clear of lust for Geoffrey's mother, he realized made no sense. There was, now that he thought on it, the night of Chutley's suicide. The way the boy had begged him to ride with them, then grasped Merrick's hand when he tried to get out of the carriage. And then there was the aftermath.

"Thank you for carrying me, sir. I am so sorry the other man died."

Those had been Geoff's last words before going up to bed. Again, something about it had piqued his curiosity, but then he and Maddie had blown up at one another, and amidst all the cannon fodder, he had failed to consider it further. Merrick snatched his glass, and polished off the

rest of the whisky in one toss. Damn, why had this not occurred to him before? There was a world of meaning in
that one, simple sentence. *I am so sorry the other man died.*

He dragged his hands through his hair. Yes, there had
been a gunshot. The horses had shied against the stone
fence. But Geoff had been out cold by the time Chutley's
body was found. Merrick had carried the boy home in the
rain, Madeleine dogging his every step. He remembered
every bitter word, too, which they had spoken to one another. *But never once had they mentioned that anyone had
been killed.*

He was utterly certain, now that he thought on it. Indeed, he had been quite careful to dance around the topic.
A child of Geoff's age did not need to be exposed to all the
world's ugly truths at once. But Geoff, he was beginning to
fear, knew more of the world's truths than one might wish.

A cold, horrible fear was beginning to steal over him. A
truth more chilling than he had ever dared contemplate.
No. No, it just *was not* possible. Quin had poisoned his
mind with that gypsy curse balderdash.

But Madeleine claimed tonight that she had always
known Geoff was "different." Now where had he heard
that before?

*"Do you know, Merrick, how humiliating it is for a
twelve-year-old boy to cry?"*

Christ Jesus. He had felt sorry for Madeleine tonight.
Now, however, his sympathy—and his patience—were
coming to a swift and rocky end. Dear God, that poor,
poor boy! Twice he had asked her the child's age. And
twice Madeleine had turned the subject. He had not really
cared; he had been making polite conversation. Now,
however, he was beginning to care a vast deal indeed.

"The Scottish Gift," Granny MacGregor called it. Well, it was no gift. It was a goddamned curse, and it was ruining the boy's life. Damn Madeleine Howard to hell and back! The knowledge left him reeling. Why had he never suspected? All the signs were there. Christ, he had just made love to her again. And afterward, it had taken every ounce of his self-control not to go down onto one knee and pledge his undying—

Dear God! With hands that shook, Merrick slammed the drawer shut, and dropped the opera glasses into his pocket. He had his shoes half on before he realized he was leaving.

Phipps stood in his bedchamber doorway. "You are going out, sir?"

"You're bloody well right, I am," Merrick retorted. "I am going across the village to throttle the last breath of life out of Lady Bessett—and you can pencil *that* into my goddamned calendar."

"Very good, sir."

Merrick yanked the door open, and paused. "No, better yet, Phipps—use ink. *Black* ink."

Chapter Fourteen

No lie lives long.

Madeleine had almost reached the bottom of the first box of files when the faint knock at her door sent her almost leaping from her chair. Good heavens, it was past midnight! Like the country girl she was, however, she went to the door and opened it unquestioningly, despite the fact that her hair was down and she was in her nightclothes. She realized her mistake at once.

Merrick MacLachlan stood her threshold, looking like he'd just ventured up from the bowels of hell. His hair was a mess, and his blue eyes had gone dark with rage. His shirt was open at the throat, the tails half-out, and his waistcoat hung unbuttoned. For an instant, she thought him intoxicated, but his ungloved hand was rock-steady when he smacked it flat against the door. He pushed it wide on silent hinges and came in without invitation.

Madeleine could only stare. "Good Lord, do you know the time?"

He held her gaze with his mad, black eyes. "Aye, it's the witching hour," he said. "That little space between life and death, that sliver of corporeal uncertainty, when the dead walk and the graves give up their secrets."

Madeleine looked at him askance. "You are drunk, Merrick," she said. "Please go home."

He stalked toward her like a predator. He smelled of whisky, but his gaze was sharp. Agitated, she backed up a step, but he caught her hair, and twisted it around his fist, drawing her nigh. He set his cheek against hers, and whispered into her ear. "Tell me, Maddie lass—have *you* been keeping any secrets?"

She was frightened. "I—I don't know what you mean."

He dragged her harder against him. *"Try again,"* he growled, his voice terrifyingly quiet. "Let's have them out, my wee wifey. Confession is good for the soul, aye?"

Just then, a shadow appeared, hovering on the staircase. "Is anything amiss, my lady?" said a servant's voice.

Merrick turned his face but an inch. "Go back upstairs, and mind your goddamned business," he snapped.

"It—it is all right, Eliza," said Madeleine, her voice surprisingly steady. "Go back to bed. I'll come up shortly."

The shadow hesitated, then disappeared. Madeleine set her hand over Merrick's. "Kindly release my hair," she said coldly. "Then sit down and say your piece, for heaven's sake."

"Oh, there'll not be enough years left to us, Maddie, for me to say all that I have to say to you." He gritted the words against her ear. "And none of it, my dear, is going to be pretty." But to her surprise, he let her go.

She stepped away, but the sight of his sneering face was more harrowing than his voice. "Is th-this about what happened tonight?"

His sneer deepened. Oh, she had a very ill feeling about this. She swallowed hard and took yet another step backward.

"When were you going to tell me, Maddie?" For the first time, she could hear the tinge of pain in his words. "No, let me answer. *Never. Ever.* Aye, you meant to let me go to my grave in ignorance, did you not? You wanted me to die never knowing that boy was mine."

Dear God. This was her worst nightmare come true, but there was nothing to do but brazen it out. "You are insane," she said. "What makes you think you can come into my home in the middle of the night and say such vile things to me?"

His mouth curled bitterly as he drew a thin leather pocket case from his coat. "This," he said, extracting a fold of paper, its edges yellow, its corners soft with wear.

He flicked open the top half, just enough that she could see her own name so boldly written on it. She closed her eyes and shook her head. "That is nothing but a piece of paper, Merrick."

"Oh, if you think that, my dear, you are about to get a lesson in English jurisprudence."

He was deadly serious. Fleetingly, she considered snatching it and touching it to one of the candles. She must have twitched.

He jerked the paper away and laughed darkly. "Oh, no, Maddie." He restored the paper to the case, and tucked it away. "I have not held on to that little document for thirteen long years only to have you snatch it from my grasp now."

"It is just a piece of paper," she said again. "For God's sake, Merrick, we were practically handfasted over an anvil! It means nothing."

"Are you willing to bet on that, my dear?" he snarled. "Let's go down to the Court of Common Pleas tomorrow and see what our learned justices think. And whilst we're there, perhaps we can ascertain the penalty for bigamy. It is transportation still, is it not? I hear New South Wales is lovely this time of year."

"You bastard," she whispered. "Go ahead, then. But if there is a God in heaven, Merrick, you will lose."

"I don't think you understand." His voice was lethally soft. "I *have* nothing to lose. I have already lost everything, Madeleine. You took it from me, mercilessly and unilaterally."

She drew her lips into a firm, straight line, and steeled herself. "We had an annulment, Merrick," she said.

"Aye, back to that again, are we?" He waved his hand about the room, which was still untidy with papers. "Have you found it yet, by the way? That elaborate paperwork which your father ginned up? East End forgers are two-a-penny, in case you did not know."

"Just hush, Merrick," she snapped. "Just hush up and get out."

Instead, Merrick had the audacity to go to the small sideboard and fix himself a drink. "Do you know, Maddie, what I wonder?" His hand was steady as he poured. "I wonder what Jessup told Lord Bessett. Did the poor devil know you were still married? And did he know he'd be saddled with another man's get?"

Madeleine dragged both hands through her hair. "You will not be satisfied until you have driven me insane," she whispered. "Yes, Bessett was shown the same papers as I was. And yes, Merrick, he knew I was with child."

Merrick snorted. "And he married you anyway?"

"Yes," she said quietly. "He married me anyway. Because he cared for me, which is more than I can say for you. Where were you, Merrick, when I was sick every morning for three months running? Where were you when the child came, and I lay two days in labor? Or when Geoff fell learning to walk and bit a hole in his lip? Or when his pony threw him, and he needed six stitches?"

"You heartless bitch."

Madeleine ignored him. "No, Bessett was not my dream husband," she hissed. "But by God, he was *there*, and he did the best he could, which is all I ever expected of you."

"You left me, Maddie."

"I was *taken* away, Merrick!" she cried. "There is a difference. What was I to do? My father said you took the money. You never said otherwise. Indeed, you never said so much as fare-thee-well! And yet, I lingered *ten weeks* in Sheffield, praying you would change your mind and come for me. But you never did, Merrick. You never did. And by then, I needed a husband. I was damned lucky Bessett would have me."

His eyes narrowed. "Well, that's a new turn on an old tale," he said. "And I could not come for you, Madeleine. I was hurt. I wrote you as soon as I was able."

"Oh, my heart bleeds!" she said sarcastically. "I got no letters from you. But good God, what difference does it make now, Merrick? We have been thirteen years apart. Indeed, we scarcely knew one another to begin with."

"I knew my heart," he said hollowly. "And I thought I knew yours."

"Well, you did not," she snapped. "Now kindly get out of my house, Merrick. I have a life to lead. I have a child who is not well and who needs me desperately."

He tossed off half his brandy, and set the glass down. "What a coincidence!" he said. "I do, too."

She looked at him, the horror slowly dawning. "No," she whispered. "No, Merrick. You do *not*. You cannot do this to me. I—I shall leave here, do you hear me? I shall go far away where no one can find me."

"A capital notion," he said coolly. "And one which I meant to bring up. You had best get packing, my dear. Geoff and I are leaving tomorrow at ten."

"L-Leaving?" she sputtered. "Good God, you really are mad! You are not taking that boy one step from this house."

"Oh, tut, tut, Madeleine!" he said mockingly. "Did I not earlier explain to you that this is my house?"

"Go to hell, you arrogant ass!"

Merrick shrugged. "If you do not believe me, my dear, consult a good solicitor," he said. "And pray don't forget to mention that annoying little detail about our being husband and wife. If he is worth his salt, he will break you some very bad news indeed. To wit, your debts are mine. Your home is mine. Your child is mine. In short, Madeleine, *you* are mine, much though it may grieve me. And if you are a very, very good girl, my dear, perhaps I shan't remember to ask the courts to prosecute you for bigamy."

She flew at him then, the first cracking blow landing soundly across his cheek. She struck at him blindly, over and over, until Merrick caught her hands and drew her fully against him. "You are still a hellcat, aren't you, Maddie, underneath all that prim perfectionism?" he said, tucking his chin to stare down at her. "Perhaps I won't bother with that bigamy business. Perhaps I shall just hang on to you and insist on my conjugal rights, as the law fully allows me to do."

Still gasping for breath, Madeleine tried to knee him, but he pulled her cleverly away. The arrogant devil merely lifted one eyebrow. "Perhaps you failed to notice, my dear, but your body keeps rubbing mine most provocatively every time you lunge," he murmured. "Now, I shan't be so pressing as to insist you make up a bed for me tonight. Instead, I shall do you the courtesy of leaving—for now. I will be back at ten for the boy. You may go or stay, as you wish."

At last, the tears came in an explosive rush. "Oh, you really are as cruel as they say!" she cried. "Good God, Merrick! Think of Geoff! Think what this will do to him!"

He did not let her go, but instead pulled her near, until they were utterly face-to-face again. "I am thinking of Geoff," he said, enunciating each word. "The boy is a god-damned emotional soss, and he has his mother to thank for it."

"How dare you say it is my fault!" she retorted. "And just where do you think you are taking him?"

"To Scotland," he said succinctly. "Where he can be properly looked after by his family—his *blood* family, Maddie. Do you think you are the first person with a child who possesses the sight?"

She looked at him incredulously. "The . . . the *what*?"

"The sight," he bit out. "The *gift*. The ability to spae what's to come. Call it what you will."

She tried to back away. "Oh, you—you really are quite mad," she whispered. "You cannot possibly believe what you are saying. For God's sake, Merrick, this is the nineteenth century, not the Dark Ages."

"Maddie, the boy is fey, and any fool can see it," he said calmly. "Now, you will be ready at ten o'clock, and the three of us can go away in relative peace, or you can behave badly, and I shall have the justice of the peace on you by eleven. Which will it be?"

She jerked away. "I hope you burn in hell!"

Merrick shrugged and refilled his glass. "Ten it is, then," he said, starting to the door with his brandy in hand. "I shall see you in the morning."

Madeleine could only stand there and blink. "You are a pig," she answered. "And you—you are taking my glass! It was a wedding gift!"

He lifted it in a final, parting toast. "Well, cheers, then, Maddie!" he said blithely. "It's about time I got to use it, don't you think?"

He had been drunk, she decided. Madeleine sat on the edge of her bed as dawn finally lit the sky, turning it a strange mélange of blue and pink. He had been drunk, and this morning when he awoke with a sore head and a churning stomach, he would think better of this nonsense. Indeed, he would doubtless be embarrassed. Perhaps he mightn't even remember it. He could not possibly wish to be saddled with a child.

Go to Scotland indeed! Why, Merrick MacLachlan did not intend to do any such thing. She and Eliza had sat up until—well, more or less until now—discussing the possibility. It had been Eliza who hit on the truth of the matter. A perfectionist like Merrick would no more leave his businesses unattended than fly to the moon. He loved too well the wealth and power they brought him.

And so she had packed nothing. Told Geoff nothing. Done nothing, not even dress. Instead, Madeleine remained rigidly stiff on the edge of her bed, listening to the sounds of the house beginning to stir. She heard the back door squeal as the ashes were taken out and the fresh coal brought in. Draperies were drawn and sashes thrown up. Dustbins clattered and a costermonger passed by, his cart rumbling on the cobbles. Soon she heard the unmistakable sound of Mr. Frost beginning to stir in the room above her. He would wake Geoff, and together they would go down to breakfast.

It was a normal day. *A normal day*. And Merrick MacLachlan would *not* come and ruin her life all over again.

And then she realized she was crying again, and that it was faintly possible the man would do just what he had said he would do. Then there was the embarrassment of what she had done with him last night. Oh, God help her! Why had she not swallowed her pride and consulted a solicitor to begin with? Or would that have given her bad news all the sooner? In her lap, her fingers had turned faintly blue from being clutched too tightly.

Just then, Eliza came in and frowned. "You must get dressed, my lady," she said gently. "If he *does* come— which I daresay he won't—then you will not wish him to see you this way."

Madeleine nodded and began the process of bathing and dressing. After a while, she heard Geoff and Mr. Frost go thundering back up the steps to the makeshift schoolroom in the garret. Breakfast was beyond her, so she sent Clara for coffee, and went back into the parlor to begin her thus-far-fruitless search all over again.

In the morning sunlight, she looked about the room. It looked most unpromising. But she sat back down anyway, and made at least a pretense of looking as she listened to the clock tick off the minutes.

It was a quarter of ten when she heard the loud ring of horses' hooves coming down the lane. *Many* horses. Not just a passing gig. Her heart in her throat, she rose and peeked through the window, already knowing what she would see. Merrick MacLachlan stepped down from the glossy red town coach, a vehicle larger and more elegant than any she had ever seen. He lifted his gold-knobbed stick and rapped soundly on the cottage door.

She answered it herself.

He did not waste words. "Are you ready? You do not look it."

"I cannot believe you are serious," she said. "You—you were drunk, Merrick. Perhaps we both said things we did not mean. But to do this to Geoff—oh, please do not."

He pushed past her and came in. "I know you do not believe it, Madeleine," he said, laying his elegant top hat aside, "and I really do not give a damn, but I am thinking of Geoff."

She followed him into the room. "How?" she whispered. "How can this possibly help him? The boy thinks Bessett his father. He thinks Alvin his brother. Now, on top of all else which troubles him, you mean to tell him his entire life is a lie? Pray tell me, Merrick, how this will help him. And if it will, then yes, I will go, and willingly."

He was stripping off his gloves, and laying them aside. "The boy is mine, Madeleine." There was sorrow in his voice. "He has a right to know that. He has a right to know his true heritage."

"I think this is more about what you want," she said. "And this is about punishing me."

He slapped the second glove down. "Goddamn it,

Maddie, what do you think that boy feels like just now?" he demanded. "What? He feels like some manner of freak, that's what. A bizarre trick of nature, not a normal child."

A freak. Madeleine cringed inside. On more than one occasion, Geoff had used that very word to describe himself. "And what will change in Scotland, Merrick?" she whispered. "What? Tell me one thing."

He had picked up his gloves again, and was studying the stitching rather intently. "In Scotland, he will not be alone," Merrick finally answered. "He will not feel like a freak. He will fit in—at least a *little* bit. And to a boy of his years, that is the most important thing on earth. Why do you think, Maddie, that I am so sure the boy is mine?"

"I—" She stopped, and shook her head. "I do not know."

"It is a curse in my family," he said quietly. "Or a blessing, depending upon your viewpoint. My grandmother. A great-uncle. A second cousin. And a dozen more who lie dead in the kirkyard, on both sides."

"Surely . . . surely you jest?"

"You do not believe it." His voice was flat.

"No, and I cannot believe you do."

He shrugged. "I never really thought about it," he admitted. "God knows it's not a talent I possess. But in parts of Scotland, it is considered . . . well, perhaps not normal, no. But it is generally accepted by more than a few— which is about all one can hope for."

"I cannot see how this will help him," she whispered. "His whole world will be turned upside down."

"No, *your* whole world will be turned upside down," Merrick returned. "It will be dashed inconvenient for you, a husband and a marriage you so expediently forgot about so suddenly turning up. And it will be inconvenient to me, as well. Indeed, it will likely run half my businesses into the ground. But Geoff's world will be right-side-up for perhaps the first time in his life."

She touched her fingertips to her forehead. "Oh, God! I cannot believe this."

"Maddie, *someone* has to help the boy," he said, setting his hands on her upper arms. "Can you? I think we have already seen that you cannot. And Lord knows I can do no better. But someone—my grandmother MacGregor, I am thinking—might be able to."

Madeleine wrung her hands. His words had an awful ring of wisdom to them. Geoff *was* peculiar. She had always known it. And now Geoff knew it, too—and it was killing him. "How can she help him, Merrick?" Madeleine asked softly. "Can she . . . can she make it go away?"

He shook his head. "I do not think so," he admitted. "But I know that someone must teach the boy, Maddie, that 'knowing' things and being responsible for them are not at all the same. Someone has to explain that seeing glimpses of things to come does not mean one can alter them—or even *should* alter them. And someone needs to show him how to control these . . . these random fits in his head. Good God, one can only imagine what the poor child's mind has been bombarded with these last many years."

Madeleine slowly closed her eyes. Dear Lord! What he described . . . it was so close to the truth—or the truth so far as she knew it—that it was blood-chilling. And he was right; she did not know what to do. *The Scottish gift.* She still was not ready to admit that it even existed. But if it did . . . If it did, and did nothing to help him . . .

"How long?" she whispered. "How long will we be gone?"

"I cannot say," he admitted. "Weeks, certainly."

Madeleine dragged a hand through her hair, tearing some of it from its arrangement. "Geoff's studies—he cannot just abandon—"

"Frost must come along," Merrick interjected. "There is nothing else for it."

"You leave me little choice, do you?" she said softly.

"No, none at all," he said grimly. "Because Geoff has no choice. And in this one small way, perhaps I can help him. You have cheated me of my right to help him as any normal parent might."

She lifted her gaze to his and held it firmly. "I will go," she said. "But only because I would do anything to help my son. And will I go only under one condition."

His eyes narrowed. "And what is this condition?"

"Prove to me, Merrick, that this is truly about helping Geoff," she said. "And that it is not about punishing me. Do not tell him the truth about Bessett."

He cut her a dark, sidelong look. "The truth about me, you mean," he corrected. "You do not wish him to know that I am his father."

She nodded. "I am not asking you, Merrick, not to befriend the boy or spend time with him. I am just asking— for now, at any rate—that we not throw his life into such disarray."

His lips thinned as if he were biting back bitter words. No doubt he was. "I cannot promise," he said at last. "It mayn't even be possible. When we reach Argyllshire, there will be questions, Madeleine. Perhaps even talk."

She turned away, and went to the window. The

thought of giving in to him stung her pride. The thought of traveling hundreds of miles in his company was worse. But in truth, what choice had she? Oh, she was beyond worrying about courts or magistrates. She was beyond even the shame of what she had done with him last night. When all was said and done, Merrick was offering her a way—slender reed though it might be—to help Geoff.

Madeleine let her shoulders fall. "I will go," she said quietly. "But I will go not because I am afraid of you, Merrick. I will go because . . . because as outlandish as your idea sounds, I have none better. Indeed, I have none at all."

"Well, at least you are honest, Madeleine," he said brusquely. "Now get packing, please. We have many hard miles of travel ahead of us."

Chapter Fifteen

*A man goes nae faster tae his
guid than tae his ruin.*

The journey north was not a pleasant one. Almost a week of wind and damp left even the paved roads muddy, and tried tempers to the breaking point. Madeleine passed the days by staring out into the rain-swept countryside, and wondering if she had lost her mind. The worst of it was the sight of the quaint little inns in which she and Merrick had once stayed—and made love—during their rash, romantic elopement. Every crossroads, every village brought back some little remembrance of the hope those early days had held.

Across the width of the carriage, she looked at Merrick, studying him just as she had been doing at least a dozen times a day since leaving London. This afternoon, his black hair had fallen forward to shadow his eyes and partially obscure the brutal scar down, his face. The scar, while intriguing, did not trouble her. It was his arrogance, his utter high-handedness, which left her angry and a little shaken. The harsh words he'd flung at her in Walham still rang in her ears. Perhaps she had been fortunate to escape their reckless marriage. Perhaps the thing she had mourned all these years had not been worth her tears.

She hoped he did not continue his threats. He had been in a black rage that night, and surely had not meant all that he had said. Well, save for the threat about Geoff. That he had meant, and she was sure of it.

It really was quite mortifying when she considered the whole of what had happened between them these last weeks. And she was especially appalled when she considered what they had done together in Lord Treyhern's pantry. Even now, the thought of it made her face flush with heat.

But why? Was she embarrassed to have a woman's needs? Was it a sin to be lonely? The awful truth was, what they had done probably wasn't even a sin in the eyes of God, because she very much feared she was still married to the man. Now that she had had a week of near solitude in which to consider it, she had to admit that her father had most likely lied to her about the annulment so that he might persuade her into a marriage which suited his political needs.

It was *insane*. It never would have worked. And why had he bothered to keep up the pretense? Once her father had learned she carried Merrick's child, why had he not simply let her go to him, when she had been willing to swallow her pride and do so? Why force her to leave England when she had been willing to beg Merrick to take her back? She was of no further use to her father's career when she was already with child. Surely his hatred of Merrick could not have run that deep?

But perhaps it had. She had grown up a great deal since then, and had come to face some stark realities. And now that she had faced them, now that she had accepted that what Merrick said might well be true, what did that make her? Not a wife. Not a widow. Probably not even Lady Bessett. Was she an adulteress? A bigamist? And what did that make Geoff? She prayed Merrick would keep their secret, for she had no notion how she would ever explain this awful predicament.

A little part of her wished she had dredged up the courage to tell Merrick the truth about Geoff as soon as she began to suspect her father's lies. Then, he might have forgiven her. Now, he never would. And yet they were married. They would be man and wife until one of them died. Neither of them could go forward with their lives, even had they wished to.

Lady Madeleine MacLachlan.

Dear God. After all these years!

Merrick must have felt the heat of her gaze upon him. He looked up from the folio in which he had been penciling, his eyes dark and wary. He was still angry with her. Very angry, though to his credit, he was trying to keep up appearances in front of Mr. Frost and Geoff. Madeleine bit her lip and turned away. Perhaps she did not deserve even that one small courtesy. She was no longer certain.

They had brought but two carriages on the trip, piling the baggage wherever it would fit. The four of them shared Merrick's huge town coach, whilst Eliza, Merrick's valet, and a groom followed in Madeleine's smaller barouche. Madeleine often considered exchanging seats with Phipps, but she was not certain she should leave Geoff's side.

It was not that Madeleine did not trust Merrick with the boy. Despite his threats, she believed him when he said he had Geoff's best interests at heart. But she was the child's mother. She had been so long accustomed to keeping watch over him and being constantly on guard against any little alteration in his mood, she could not see her way clear to leave him. And in the back of her mind, there lurked a fear that perhaps Merrick was right. Perhaps Geoff's gloomy moods and strange notions were somehow her fault.

During the first few days, Mr. Frost made a valiant effort to keep up with Geoff's studies. They had brought traveling desks and a satchel of books from which Mr. Frost assigned reading. But the constant sway of the coach made matters difficult, and the changing scenery was a persistent distraction to the boy. His questions were endless, and matters were not helped when, just east of the Yorkshire dales, Geoff spotted a familiar sight.

"Look!" he cried, pointing through the window. "Mamma! Mr. Frost! There is the road to Ripon! And to Loughton!"

Mr. Frost slid his spectacles down his nose, and peered out at the signpost. "Why, so it is, Geoff."

"Loughton?" Merrick echoed.

"Loughton is where we used to live," Geoff eagerly responded. "Before we moved to Walham."

Merrick looked at Madeleine.

"Loughton Manor was my late husband's estate," she said quietly. "Now it belongs to Alvin, Geoff's brother."

She watched Merrick stiffen against the banquette. "I see," he answered, his tone hesitant. "Well. I daresay we might stop briefly, if Geoff wishes."

"No," said Madeleine swiftly. "We must press on."

Geoff's face fell. Madeleine understood his disappointment, but she did not know how she might explain Merrick's presence, or the reason for this trip, to Alvin. Certainly she had no wish to explain it to the new Lady Bessett.

Mr. Frost leaned forward to pat the boy's knee. "Loughton is many miles out of our way, sir," he said to Merrick. "I am sure Geoff can visit his brother another time."

Merrick seemed to relax, but Madeleine could feel his heated gaze still burning into her. To distract the child, Mr. Frost drew a history of England from his leather satchel and opened it to the spot they had left marked the previous day.

"What are you studying now?" asked Merrick, glancing at the open book.

"The Jacobite Uprisings," said Frost a little shyly. "It seemed like good timing."

"Hmph," said Merrick. "Now there are two phrases one rarely hears used in the same sentence."

Mr. Frost blinked nervously. "I beg your pardon?"

"'Jacobites' and 'good timing.'" Merrick smiled faintly. "They did not historically go together."

Geoff laughed, but Mr. Frost looked ill at ease. "I daresay you had family who would have been involved in the uprisings, sir."

At that, Geoff leaned forward on the banquette, his eyes wide. "Crikes!" he said. "*Did* you, sir?"

Merrick nodded. "Aye, in the last," he said. "It was my grandfather, the first baronet. There were others, too. Mostly Jacobite Catholics, since we hailed from just north of the Tay—but the family was sharply divided, politically and, to some extent, religiously."

"Indeed," said Frost, pushing his spectacles up his nose

with one finger. "I gather family disharmony was not un-common."

"No, not in Scotland," murmured Merrick.

"What did your grandfather do in the uprising, sir?" asked Geoff eagerly. "Did he get killed by Cumberland at Culloden?"

Merrick had withdrawn his pocket watch and begun to polish it with his handkerchief. "No, no, he lived to a great old age," he answered. "For he fought with Cumberland, not against him."

"Did he indeed?" Mr. Frost seemed to relax. "How fortunate for your family."

"Fortunate for the ones who sided with the King, yes," said Merrick. "But as I said, a great many of them did not, and most all of them died."

"That sounds sad," said Geoff. "Was your grandfather upset?"

"More than you will ever know, Geoff," said Merrick quietly. "For a time, he was a tormented man."

Geoff's face wrinkled with thought. "Why was he tormented, sir?"

At last, Merrick restored the timepiece to his waistcoat, and tucked the handkerchief away. "Well, Geoff, I shall tell you," he said, looking very much like a man who had just made a serious decision. "He knew, you see, what many did not: that the Jacobite cause was lost. He had spent the months preceding the prince's return trying to convince his kin of that fact, but for the most part, he could not. And when the worst came, he felt as if he had failed them."

Geoff's eyes were wide as saucers now, and Mr. Frost was leaning intently forward. "He could not have known for certain, sir," said the tutor. "He should not have blamed himself."

Merrick set his head a little to one side. "But he did know," Merrick averred. "He had the gift, you see. But no one believed him."

"The gift, sir?" Mr. Frost sounded confused.

"Or the curse, if you like." Merrick turned to look at Geoff. "Have you studied yet the mythological tale of Cassandra?"

The boy shook his head.

Frost cast a strange look at Merrick. "Cassandra was the daughter of the King of Troy," the tutor explained. "Apollo fell in love with her and gave her the gift of prophecy. But when she did not return his affections, Apollo doomed her with a curse which ensured that though she saw the future, no one would ever believe her prophecies."

Geoff had gone utterly colorless. "Wh-what happened to Cassandra?"

With a dark look in Merrick's direction, Madeleine slid her arm around the child. "Nothing," she said sharply. "Though I am sure she led a very frustrated life."

"Quite so," said Merrick, his tone almost languid. "Very frustrated indeed."

Geoff's color had not returned. Mr. Frost gave a nervous little laugh. "But surely, sir . . . surely you do not believe . . . ?"

Merrick lifted one of his slashing black eyebrows. "Do I not?" he asked.

Frost was turning pink now. "But to see into the future—"

Merrick shrugged. "It is common enough in Scotland," he said.

"But—but you are a man of science."

"Quite so," Merrick agreed. "And that is why I am certain there is some perfectly reasonable explanation for it. After all, Frost, we used to think the world was flat. And none of us knew anything about gravitation until that illustrious apple hit poor Newton in the head."

"Well, that is true enough." Frost seemed to be pondering it. "Have you a theory, sir?"

Merrick was staring out the window now, his expression pensive. "I think that the sight is something like intuition," he said. "But stronger, and—I do not know—more highly developed, perhaps?"

"Mamma says she has women's intuition," said Geoff hopefully. "Is that what you mean, sir?"

Merrick nodded. "Yes, women are generally more intuitive than men," he agreed. "I think the sight is like that, and no one person who has it is quite the same as the next. Some people see the future in their dreams, and they see it abstractly. Others say they feel things 'in their bones,' or they see bits and pieces in flashes. Others can shut it out altogether, or heighten their awareness of it when they choose to do so."

"You have given this a great deal of thought." Mr. Frost relaxed against the banquette. "Have you ever known anyone, Mr. MacLachlan, who had this gift?"

"My grandmother," said Merrick. "But it is not something she particularly cares to talk about. You will find that is always the case with those who truly possess the skill of prescience. If they are hanging out a shingle and reading tea leaves for a tuppence, then you can safely assume they are charlatans."

Geoff was taking it all in, his mouth practically hanging open. Merrick leaned over and patted him on the knee as Mr. Frost had done. "Well, enough of that for now," he said. "This lad needs to study, does he not?"

Just then, however, the carriage began to slow.

"Ah, I perceive that we have reached Bedale," said Merrick, peering out the window at the sky. "And I believe we are in for more rain. Perhaps we'd best rack up here."

The coaching inn at which they stopped was perfectly serviceable. Merrick arranged for dinner to be served in a private parlor near the taproom. A pink-cheeked serving girl carried in trays of roast mutton, fried whiting, and a tureen of pea soup, but Madeleine had no appetite. Afterward, Geoff expressed a wish to roam around the village. It was market day, and though the event was long over, the town was still bustling.

Merrick rose from his chair. "I daresay a stroll would do us all good," he answered. "Lead on, Geoff."

At the foot of the stairs, Madeleine turned to go up. Geoff hesitated. "You are not coming, Mamma?"

Her hand already on the newel post, she turned to look at them. "I thought not."

Merrick cut an unfathomable look in her direction. "We shan't be long," he said, offering his arm.

With grave reluctance, she laid her hand on his sleeve, and they walked out into the early-evening light. The danger of rain seemed to have passed. Geoff and Mr. Frost set off at a brisk pace, pausing once or twice to peer into shop windows, though they were all closed and unlit now.

Merrick seemed set on a more sedate stroll. It was the first time they had been alone during the whole of the journey. "You did not eat," he murmured, as they walked. "Was the food not to your liking?"

"I was not hungry," she replied.

He cast a sidelong look down her length. "You have lost weight," he remarked. "It does not suit you to be so thin."

She tried to suppress a flash of temper. "Has no one ever mentioned, Merrick, that you are patronizing and meddlesome?" she asked. "I am hardly in danger of blowing away on the wind, much as that might please you."

She was further irritated when he did not take the bait, but instead, placed his hand over hers where it lay upon his coat sleeve. "It does the boy no good to see you distraught," he answered. "He notices when you do not eat, or when you withdraw into yourself."

"Oh, for pity's sake, Merrick," she said wearily. "I am hardly distraught. And children do not notice such things."

"Oh, Geoff does," he said warningly. "Indeed, Madeleine, we have no notion what he may actually *know*. I beg you to have a care."

"I see you are still clinging to that clairvoyant nonsense," she retorted acidly. "I pray you will not tell Geoff any more of that ghastly business about Cassandra."

"It is an important myth," Merrick countered.

"It is a pack of nonsense," said Madeleine. "Good Lord! The poor woman was raped, taken as a sex slave, then murdered. I do not think Geoff will find her story particularly heartening."

"The poor woman?" Merrick had the audacity to grin at her. "Do you believe in Cassandra or not? You certainly seem willing to spring to her defense with all your guns blazing."

He had a point. Madeleine was forced to turn away and restrain a spurt of laughter. "It is a lurid tale, be it true or false," she finally said. "I collect you are trying to comfort him, and I am not ungrateful, but haven't you anything more cheerful in your raconteur's repertoire?"

Merrick appeared to consider it. "I daresay could tell him about my dead uncle who used the second sight to cheat at hazard," he suggested. "He outlived four wives, then died fat, rich, and happy at ninety-two—but so far as I know, he was never a sex slave. Though he mightn't have much minded it."

She did laugh then, her fingers flying to her lips, too late. "Please tell me you are lying," she managed.

"You have become very hard to please in your old age, my dear," he responded. "You seem not to care for any of my stories. Yes, I am lying."

"And I am *not* old," she continued. "I am but thirty."

"Ah, but you will be thirty-one come the sixth of March," said. "You certainly are not young."

"I believe we may have to return to the topic of my weight," she said tartly. "You will be more apt to see thirty-six that way."

But despite her biting rejoinder, Madeleine could scarcely believe the man had remembered her birthday after so many years. They walked in silence for a time. "I never had much in the way of charm, did I, Madeleine?" he said out of nowhere. "I always wondered . . . I always wondered what it was you saw in me."

"You were too impatient for charm," she said. "Nor did you suffer fools. I think I liked that you were so confident."

He looked at her, one dark brow lifted. "Confident? Or arrogant?"

She pursed her lips a moment. "At the time, it seemed like confidence."

"And now?"

Madeleine shivered against the suddenly chill air. "Do not ask me about now, Merrick," she said quietly. "I hardly know myself anymore. I certainly do not know you."

He said no more for several moments. She could sense that his mind was turning, but over what, she could not guess. At least they were able to walk together and speak with relative civility. It was, she supposed, an improvement.

Or was it? They still walked arm in arm, and she could feel the heat which his long, lean body radiated down her side. She cast a sidelong look at him and wondered what she had missed. What would it would have been like to have lived with him these last dozen years, to have watched the beautiful young artist he had once been turn into this stern, striking, and very hardhearted businessman? Could she have softened him? Shaped him? Saved him from himself?

Perhaps it would not have been all bad. Certainly, there would have been side benefits. The picture of herself pinned beneath Merrick's body came suddenly and swiftly to mind. For an instant, she closed her eyes, grateful for the fading light. Dear Lord, what they had done together had been . . . utterly *illicit*. Deliciously wicked. And wildly satisfying. In that narrow little room, Merrick had pleasured her in a way she had not known possible.

As a young man, Merrick had been a sweet and attentive lover. But that night—oh, there had been nothing sweet about it. It had felt as if all their pent-up needs and wrath and overwrought emotions had suddenly exploded in a firestorm of passion.

She must have shivered again.

Merrick stopped, turned to her, and set a warm, solid hand between her shoulder blades. He was so close, his breath stirred her hair. "Are you cold, Maddie?"

Maddie. Oh, she wished he would not call her that. Each time, a little piece of her resolve seemed to melt. "A little chilled," she said with a muted smile. "It is my emaciated condition, no doubt."

He looked at her with a dubious half smile. They had circled the marketplace now and were continuing down a lovely little street. Mr. Frost and Geoff were a few yards ahead, looking up at the village church. Merrick turned, and called out to them.

"Be so good as to escort her ladyship back to the inn, will you, Frost?" he said when they reached the church. "Geoff and I shall walk on a few moments longer. I wish to speak with him."

Madeleine looked back and forth between them uncertainly. She did not wish to leave them alone.

"This is a very important church, from an architectural perspective," said Merrick to the boy. "I thought we might have a look inside, since you are interested in such things?"

Geoff's eyes were alight, but Madeleine hesitated. Still, what choice did she have? And what, truly, was the right thing to do? "Yes, of course," she said, taking Mr. Frost's arm. "You shan't be long, shall you?"

"We shan't be long," said Merrick solemnly.

Madeleine gave Geoff a warm smile. "Knock on my door, then, when you come up, Geoff," she said. "I might need you to tuck me in."

At that, he laughed, and she turned away. It was very hard to allow someone else into Geoff's life, but it had to be done. Not because Merrick had threatened her but because it was slowly coming clear to her that it was the right thing to do. She set off in the direction of the inn with Mr. Frost, and resolved not to look back.

Merrick glanced down at the boy, who was eagerly surveying the church in the approaching dusk. "It is beautiful, Geoff, is it not?" he said. "St. Gregory's is mostly a late-medieval church, but the nave incorporates some significant Saxon remains. If we hurry, perhaps we can see it before it's too dark. I will show you how to identify the Saxon elements."

Inside, the church was dimly lit, and empty. They walked about the nave as Merrick pointed out the oldest parts, including the original features and the ancient arcade. "Now take a good look up at the bell tower," said Merrick when they came back out again. "This is a rare type of tower. Can you see why?"

In the gloom, the boy squinted. "Well, it looks rather more like a sort of castle than a church."

Merrick was oddly pleased. "Quite so, Geoff," he said. "Because this is a bell tower which was fortified for war."

The boy's eyes grew round again. "Really, sir?"

"In the mid-1300s," said Merrick. "Because here, you see, we are very close to those wicked, rowdy Scots. I think the good citizens of Bedale must have feared them, so they fortified themselves against invasion."

The boy laughed.

"Oh, you may well laugh now," said Merrick, as they set off in the direction of the inn. "But we Scots were a bold, brave lot back then. The English rightly feared us."

Geoff cut a glance up at him. "Did the Scots ever take Bedale, sir?"

Merrick shook his head. "Not as I know," he admitted. "Though they came close to this area many times."

They walked in silence for a moment. "What did you think, Geoff, of the story I told this afternoon about my grandfather?" he asked, keeping his tone deliberately light.

"That it was sad, I guess." Geoff paused to kick a little stone from his path. "And that I didn't understand why no one would listen to him."

Merrick set a hand on the boy's shoulder. "It is the way of the world, Geoff," he said quietly. "People have trouble conceiving of or believing in things beyond their realm of knowledge. It is a form of . . . of benign ignorance, I daresay."

The boy looked up at him, his brow furrowed. "But people believe in God," said Geoff. "And he is beyond our . . . our realm. Isn't he?"

Merrick nodded. "Oh, aye, but people have the Bible and the clergy to guide them," he said. "Have you read very much of the Old Testament, Geoff?"

The boy looked a little pained. "Well, some," he said. "Mamma makes me."

"As well she should," he remarked. They turned the corner back into the marketplace. "Are you familiar with the Book of Joel? I ask, you see, because it says some astounding things."

"What sort of astounding things?"

"Well, some people believe that it talks about people like my grandfather."

Silence hung heavy in the air for a long moment. "What does it say, sir?" Geoff finally asked.

Merrick tried to remember the precise words. *"And it*

shall come to pass," he quoted, *"that I will pour out my spirit upon all flesh; and your sons and your daughters shall prophesy, your old men shall dream dreams, your young men shall see visions."*

Geoff stopped in the middle of the marketplace. "Is that truly what it says, sir?"

Merrick nodded. "I have read it many times."

The boy stared at the ground beneath his feet as if pondering something.

Merrick set a hand on the lad's back. "Geoff, if ever there is anything . . . well, anything you should like to know, I hope that you will ask me," he said. "Just remember that, will you? That you can talk to me, and tell me anything, or ask me anything you like? I would never laugh, or dismiss your concerns."

Geoff blinked twice, then nodded. "Thank you, sir," he said. "I shall remember that."

Merrick smiled. "Well, that is enough high talk for one day," he said. "It does not do to fill a boy's head with too much heavy thought, does it?"

"My head does feel a little stuffed," Geoff admitted.

Merrick slapped him cheerfully between the shoulder blades. "On to the inn, then," he ordered. "Tomorrow is another day, and it will be a long one."

Chapter Sixteen

*Nothing comes fairer to licht than
what has been lang hidden.*

They reached the turn to Gretna Green in the middle of a golden Thursday afternoon. Madeleine had been watching the signposts for a good twenty miles beforehand and praying that they would pass on by. Given the glorious weather, there certainly was no need to stop. But as they neared the village, the road did not look quite as she remembered it, as if it had been altered to bypass the little village altogether.

Accounting that a lucky bit of happenstance, she relaxed a little in her seat and continued to stare out the window.

Suddenly, Merrick cleared his throat, and rapped firmly on the carriage roof. His coachman slowed, and the groom leapt down. Merrick opened the door, and leaned out into the brilliant afternoon sunshine. "Go round by Gretna Green," he ordered. "We will put up there for the night."

"Put up for the night?" echoed Madeleine when the door was closed. "It is but half past three. Why do we not continue on until dark?"

"I have some letters to write." Merrick looked resolved. "Business letters, and I should rather pen them whilst sitting still."

With her heart heavy, Madeleine watched through the window as they rolled slowly into the village, and past the old blacksmith's shop. Though she hid it well, the sight of the place where she and Merrick had spoken their hasty vows all those years ago left her unaccountably distraught. Save for a fresh coat of whitewash, the smithy looked little altered. The village, too, was still just as small and tidy as she remembered it, and the choice of lodgings still regrettably limited.

To her dismay, Merrick stopped at the far end of the village, in the yard of the very coaching inn at which they had spent that first fateful night of their marriage. After ordering the coachmen to see to the horses, he strode into the place as if he owned it. When the innkeeper greeted him by name, and enquired into the state of his health and business, Merrick answered graciously. If it troubled him in the least to revisit the shabby little place, one could not discern it from his actions. No doubt he had stopped here many times through the years as he traveled back and forth from his family home to London.

As she had done at all the previous hostelries, Madeleine insisted on registering separately and paying for the accommodations her party would require. As soon as her portmanteau was brought up to the room she and Eliza were to share, Madeleine opened it and snatched out her shawl.

Eliza looked at her from across the bed. "Are you going out, ma'am?"

"Yes, for a walk," she said. "I need some air."

Eliza looked at her skeptically. "Will you wish me to accompany you?"

Madeleine shook her head. She wanted no one, not even Eliza, to know what a silly, sentimental fool she really was. "Thank you," she said. "But I shan't be long. Why do you not finish the unpacking, then have a rest?"

Downstairs, the reception parlor was empty, save for a rotund woman in a gray serge gown and a white cap who was dashing a feather duster rather ineffectually over the lamps and lintels. Madeleine nodded politely as she passed, and slipped out the door. She felt seized with a restless energy and set off for her destination with a strange determination. She really was quite angry at Merrick for requiring them to stop here. Surely they could have simply crossed over the Sark, and gone on to one of the newer, better inns on the main road?

The irony of it all did not escape her. Never once during her first fateful trip to Gretna Green had she questioned the wisdom of Merrick's choices. Nor had she regretted her own impulsive decision to run away, or the hope and the joy that that choice had engendered in her heart. She had told Merrick the truth in that regard. But now she questioned all of it wholeheartedly. They had been so young, and the entire world, it seemed, had been solidly against them. And now, all that hope and joy had been crushed out of her by the inexorable grind of everyday life.

Her father had claimed he had paid Merrick thirty thousand pounds to go away, she recalled as she strode down the narrow lane. Madeleine no longer believed that. Rosenberg had said that Merrick started his business with financial backing from his grandmother, the very woman they were on their way to see. It would be a simple enough matter to ask her if it was true.

The blacksmith's shop had come into view. In the distance, she could already hear the rhythmic *clank! clank! clank!* of a hammer on hot metal. She was not even sure why she was here; perhaps after all the grief, she was ready to revisit just a few moments of that lost joy. Madeleine waited for a passing farm cart to rumble by, then, on a deep breath, dashed across the lane.

In the graveled yard of the smithy, a tumbrel was tipped forward on its tongue, moldering straw poking from its slats, and its axle clearly broken. There was an old iron bench, and beneath it, a sleeping hound, who bestirred himself faintly at her approach. The smell of hot ash and the acrid tang of burnt coal carried on the faint breeze. The main entrance to the shop was clearly marked, and Madeleine hastened in without giving herself time to think about it.

She closed the door behind, turned, and almost fainted dead away.

Merrick was there before her, standing at the rough-hewn counter, his hands clasped tight behind his back in that familiar gesture of rigid restraint. He appeared especially large in the small, sparse room as he turned and lifted one of his hawkish eyebrows.

"Looking for something, Madeleine?"

Still frozen by the door, she opened her mouth, but nothing came out. The roiling heat of the distant forge suddenly seemed almost suffocating. She thought she had perhaps been saved from her folly when a squat, bald man in a leather jerkin emerged through a door behind the counter. Alas, it was not to be.

"Here ye are, sir," said the man, slapping a bound

leather book down on the counter. "This would be everything from 1818. Now, what month did ye say t'was?"

Merrick extended an arm, as if inviting Madeleine to the counter. "It was July, was it not, my dear?" he asked. "The twenty-fourth, perhaps?"

"The twenty-second," she blurted, darting forward.

Merrick's eyes flashed with satisfaction. "Quite so, my love!" he said. "I just wanted to see if you remembered."

Madeleine narrowed her eyes.

Oblivious to the sudden tension, the man smiled. "Aye, and happy's the man who always remembers his anniversary!" he remarked, winking at Madeleine as he flipped the book open.

"Oh, I never forget it," said Merrick dryly. "I celebrate it every year unfailingly with a drink or two—or twenty."

The man flicked him a curious glance, then returned to his book. "July, July, July," he muttered, shuffling through the pages with a beefy fingertip. "Aye, July! Och, a slow month, that was. And Mr. and Mrs. MacLachlan, was it?"

Merrick smiled down at Madeleine, circled an arm around her waist, and drew her near. " 'Til death do us part," he said.

The man cleared his throat and flipped back and forth through a few of the pages. "The twenty-second, then?" he said. "But might it have been June? A verra popular month for weddings, June would be!"

Merrick shook his head. "Absolutely not."

Madeleine did not like the look of vague confusion which was dawning on the bald man's face. "It was the twenty-second," she said leaning forward to see that he had flipped over into August. "No, that's too far. Go back a page."

He did so, then looked up at them blankly. "There's

naught here for a MacLachlan," he said. "Not in June, July, or August."

Merrick's face fell, as did his arm. "But that is impossible," he said darkly. "Give me the book." He paged back and forth a little crossly.

Madeleine looked up at the bald man. "There must be another register," she said.

The bald man shook his head. "Not here, ma'am," he said, rubbing his palms a little nervously on his jerkin. "Mayhap you did the deed over at Gretna Hall? They cut into our business some a few years past."

Madeleine looked about the little room in stupefaction. "No, it was *here*," she insisted. "I recall it well."

The bald man lifted his hands and tried to grin. "Aye, well, if *he* remembers it, and *you* remember it, the rest of it doesna' much matter, eh?"

Merrick leaned halfway across the counter, as if he might drag the poor fellow over it. "Call me sentimental," he snarled. "But I want to *see* the bloody thing."

The man backed judiciously away. "To be sure! To be sure!" he said. "We've just made a mistake of some sort. Still, have you the marriage lines, sir? All's right and tight, legal-like, long as you've the proper papers, whether your name be in this book or not."

Madeleine had seized the register and turned it around. Merrick had withdrawn the marriage lines from his pocket case and was waving it at the bald man. As their argument grew more heated, Madeleine thumbed more anxiously through the pages.

"Well, this is very odd," she said sharply.

Both men fell silent, and looked down the counter at her.

Madeleine pointed to the book. "There were eleven marriages here between the fifth of July and the twenty-first of July," she said. "Then nothing further until the tenth of August."

The men looked at her blankly.

Madeleine lifted both brows. "Well, does that not strike you as odd?" she asked. "Or are the two of you bent on simply quarreling over it until the names just mysteriously reappear?"

Merrick snatched the book. The bald man peered at it, and scratched his head. "That doesna seem quite right," he agreed.

"Where's the fellow who signed this thing?" Merrick demanded, stabbing his finger at their marriage lines. "Living? Or dead?"

"Dead, that fellow is," he said grimly. Then he went to the door behind him, and shouted into the shop. "Ezekiel!" he shouted into the gloom. "Ezekiel, you're wanted out here!"

Merrick and Madeleine exchanged wary glances. But the man who appeared did indeed look far too young to be the man who had married them. His eyes had a heavy look about them, and he was chewing rather languidly on what was left of a green apple.

"This is Ezekiel," said the bald man, setting a kindly hand on the fellow's shoulder. "That's his father's signature you've got there. Ezekiel has a fair mind for dates and numbers. Perhaps he'll recall something about it."

Ezekiel nodded, his motions oddly exaggerated, and swallowed his mouthful of apple.

"These folk were married here back in '18," the bald man explained. "Do you remember July of '18, Ezekiel?"

The younger man blinked, then slowly nodded again. "Th-Thirty days hath September," he said in an unusual monotone. "April, J-June, and November. All the rest have thirty-one."

"We are talking about July, for God's sake!" said Merrick sharply.

Madeleine put a restraining hand on his sleeve. The young man, she realized, was a little slow, though it was not immediately obvious. "Yes, July of 1818, Ezekiel," she said calmly. "There is some sort of gap in the register."

Ezekiel nodded, and began his poem again. "Thirty days hath September," he intoned. This time, Merrick waited, albeit impatiently, until the lad was done. "Excepting February alone/ which has twenty-eight days clear/ and twenty-nine in each leap year," he finally finished.

"Quite so, Ezekiel," said Madeleine.

Ezekiel smiled vaguely, then bent his head to the page, his broad brow deeply furrowed. He began to mouth words to himself as his forefinger ran down the page.

The bald man was looking on a little wearily. He clearly did not know what difference the register made, since the fact that there was a marriage did not seem to be in dispute. Madeleine wondered, too. She *had* married Merrick here, and she assuredly did not need the register to tell her so—not after ruing the day for almost thirteen years. She was not even sure why she had wished so desperately to see it again.

"MacLachlan," said Ezekiel, jerking his head up suddenly. "Twenty-two July. Capstone, twenty-three July. Hetwell, twenty-three July. Martin, twenty-six July. Anders, twenty-nine July."

Merrick stopped him by laying his hand softly over

Ezekiel's. "What are you reading?" he asked, his tone gentler now.

Ezekiel pointed to the center binding. "P-page is gone," he said. "One page. Ten names. Vickers, thirty July. Elderwood, three August. Pickering, five August."

The bald man stopped him. "Thank you, Ezekiel," he said, then he returned his gaze to Merrick. "He could go on like that all day," he said almost apologetically. "He used to memorize these things for amusement."

"Aye, and it's a damned good thing he did," said Merrick. "Since you've been so careless as to lose a page."

Ezekiel was shaking his head violently now. "N-Not lost," he said. "Not lost. Flora took it."

"Flora?" The bald man looked at Ezekiel strangely. "Who the blazes is Flora?"

Ezekiel blinked again. "Papa's friend," he said. "She talked . . . p-p-*peculiar*. And gave money. English money. For the page. A-And she kissed him. Sixteen guineas, three pounds, f-four shillings."

Merrick turned to the bald man incredulously. "Good Lord, that's twenty pounds."

But Madeleine had bent back down to examine the register. Ezekiel joined her. "Sh!" he whispered, pointing to the gutter between the pages. "Flora had a razor. See?"

Madeleine patted him on the hand. "Thank you so much, Ezekiel," she said. "You have been of great assistance to us."

Merrick turned away from the bald man, who was clearly trying his temper, and shook Ezekiel's hand. "Yes, thank you very much," he said. "Perhaps you ought to write all those names down again someday?"

Ezekiel nodded. "All right," he said. Then he vanished into the back of the shop.

"Trouble is," said the bald man, "he can't write. Any number, citation, or sum, he can recall in an instant, and he can read a bit. But he cannot write so much as his own Christian name."

Merrick looked at the man in exasperation. "Well, damn it, *you* can write, can you not?" he snapped. "Good Lord, does the poor fellow have to do everything himself?"

Madeleine interceded, taking Merrick by the arm and propelling him from the smithy. Outside in the yard, he hesitated. "There's no getting to the bottom of this, is there?" he grumbled. "That page has just vanished on the wind."

Madeleine gave him a crooked smile. "Vanished into someone's pocket, more likely," she said. "But given the range of dates missing, it was taken at least two weeks after we were married."

Merrick looked at her darkly. "And what do you make of that?" he asked. "That your precious papa had nothing to do with it?"

"Obviously, Merrick, someone wanted to make a marriage more difficult to prove," she said coolly. "And they were willing to pay a price in order to do so. But given the nature of Gretna Green marriages, it might have been any one of ten irate fathers."

Merrick gave a dubious snort. "Oh, let's venture a guess as to whose!"

Madeleine looked down at the graveled yard. "I shan't defend him, Merrick," she said, her voice soft. "Hard as it may be for me to think he might do such a thing, I must accept that it is possible. Did you think that I would not?"

Merrick stared into the distance and dragged a hand through his hair, the sun glinting off his ever-present signet ring. "I hardly know what to think anymore."

"My father could not have done it himself, for we left in great haste," Madeleine went on. "But is it possible he could have paid someone to do it? Yes, I daresay it is."

And Madeleine had a fair idea of just who it might have been, too. But first, she needed to talk with Eliza.

Merrick was still standing in the smith's yard. "I am sorry, Maddie," he finally said. "I am sorry you are having to face the truth of what your father was."

"As am I," she said quietly. "And if you do not mind, I should really rather not talk about it."

"Aye." The word was tight. "Fine, then."

She forced a smile, and took his arm. "Come, Merrick. May we go back now?"

For an instant, he hesitated. "In a sudden rush, are you?"

"Not I," she answered coolly. "You are the one with all those pressing business letters to write."

They walked in silence back to the old inn, her hand on his arm. His steps, usually swift with impatience, were almost sedate, as if he dreaded the return. She could tell that he was deeply preoccupied with something, but she was afraid to ask what.

In the reception parlor, the innkeeper had returned to his desk and stood sorting through the post. Merrick pulled her into a smaller parlor near the taproom. Both rooms were empty, save for a red-haired potboy who was clearing away the last of someone's meal.

"You look tired," said Merrick. "I am going to send for tea."

Madeleine *was* tired—tired of the day's events, and a little tired of Merrick's imperious tone. Still, tea did sound welcome. She draped her shawl over a chair at the small table. The potboy had darted toward the kitchens with his tray, so Merrick strode off in search of help. He soon returned, drew out her chair, and with his eyes, bade her be seated.

Madeleine sat down without argument, her head still swimming with conspiracies. They managed to make relatively civil conversation about nothing of importance until the tea came. Madeleine poured two cups, then entirely forgot hers.

Merrick looked at her from beneath a sweep of dark lashes. "So, weren't you the least bit curious, Maddie, about Gretna Green?" he asked softly. "Didn't you wish to see this little village just one last time?"

She shook her head. "I should rather we'd passed on by."

"And yet, there you were at the smithy." There was a hint of a challenge in his tone.

Madeleine lifted one shoulder. "I just wanted to see . . ." She waited a moment, and tried to pick up her words again. "I just wanted to see our names, Merrick, in the register. I think . . . I think I just wanted to—to prove something to myself. Can you not understand? Can you comprehend wanting to see something, and yet not wanting the pain of looking at it?"

"Oh, aye." His vivid blue gaze caught hers, and held it. "Quite well."

Madeleine leaned over the table a little. "I shan't claim, Merrick, that I ever believed everything my father said," she whispered. "But not being able to find those annulment papers—dear heaven!—one begins to wonder what else might not be so. Things one has built one's life upon. Good God, I just never dreamt . . ."

He covered her hand which rested upon the table, and squeezed it almost violently. "And I never dreamt you would believe such a thing of me, Maddie," he rasped. "How could you think it? That I would annul our marriage—or even marry you for your money? *How*?"

She shook her head. "He showed me the papers, Merrick," she said again. "They looked real to me. But before that . . . before that, there was the letter. I keep forgetting about that." She cut her gaze away, unable to look at him.

"The letter?" he finally said.

Her free hand—the one in her lap—began to shake. "You may wonder how I can so easily believe that my father would bribe someone to cut that page out of the register," she said. "It is because I knew he had done such a thing before."

"Maddie, what are you talking about?"

She tore her eyes from his. "I know about your letter to the architect in London," she whispered. "I know because Papa brought it here to Gretna Green. He paid someone to steal it, I daresay, from Mr. Wilkerson's office."

"Wilkerson?" Merrick looked truly confused. "I must have sent him a score of letters over the years, but none worth a shilling, so far as bribes go."

"This was your first letter," she said. "The one in which you promised him payment of thirty thousand pounds for your half of a new business. You were to pay him in August, you said, as soon as you had the money."

"Holy God!" said Merrick. "And what kind of business did the devil have me buying for that great sum?"

She looked at him strangely. "An architectural firm, was it not?"

"Maddie, if an architect had thirty thousand pounds, he'd hardly need to work."

Again, Madeleine shook her head. "Papa said you had to have a lot of money," she persisted. "He said it was for—oh, God, I don't know!—something about surety bonds or insurance or some such thing, because you were to take on such magnificent projects."

"Aye, 'tis true in part," Merrick agreed, but his face was going black with rage. "A new business burns through a man's money and pays but bloody little for a long while. But what I promised Wilkerson was three thousand pounds, which I'd already arranged to borrow from my grandmother."

"*Three?*"

"Aye, and if you saw a letter that said *thirty,* then trust me, Maddie, your father's forger had been at it again."

The sick, sinking feeling had returned to the pit of her stomach, a mix of rage and crushing regret. She forced it away. Merrick's eyes were flashing with anger now. "But Papa claimed, Merrick, that that was why you married me," she insisted. "Because you had a chance to join in this new firm—a chance to have your dream—and that you needed my money to do it."

"Thirty *thousand pounds* of it, Maddie?" he answered incredulously. "And you believed that? Christ Jesus, what kind of crackbrained gudg—"

She had the cup in her hand before she scarce knew

what she was about. The warm tea hit him full in the face. Merrick said not a word, but merely glared at her, then withdrew his handkerchief and wiped off his face.

"I daresay I ought to apologize for that," she hissed. "But I shan't, for I've been waiting thirteen long years for the chance. Now call me a crackbrained gudgeon a third time, the next thing to hit you will be a good sight worse than tepid tea."

Merrick tossed his handkerchief down in disgust. "Let me rephrase that," he said tightly. "No—you know what, Maddie?—Let's just not bother." He shoved back his chair and stood. "I'm sick to death of trying to make sense of all this."

She, too, pushed her chair back. "Had enough, have you?" she challenged. "Well, just take me back to London, for God's sake! You mean nothing to me now, Merrick MacLachlan. I want to go home."

Merrick planted both hands on the little table and leaned into her. "Go where you damn well please, ye razor-tongued shrew," he growled. "And fair fa' ye! 'Tis a good riddance to a bad bargain, so far as I'm concerned!"

To her mortification, tears sprang to her eyes. "I cannot go!" she cried. "You and your vile piece of paper are holding me hostage! I daresay I'm lucky you've not forced your—your *attentions* on me as you have threatened!"

"Aye, you wish!" His blue eyes were afire now, his Scots accent growing thicker by the second. "Now, listen to me, woman, and listen well. I wouldn't have ye bare-arsed naked on a big silver platter. You're naucht to me, and the paper bedamned, so go the hell home. The lad's safe enough wi' me, and ye bloody well know it!"

"I don't know it!" she lied. "How can I? Did you take care of me? *Did* you, Merrick?"

He was literally quivering with rage. "Aye, go on, then, ye damned she-wolf," he rasped. "Rip out my guts! I'll have the boy back by All Saints', so just get on your bloody broomstick and—"

"All Saints'!" she cried. "But—but that's months from now!"

"Oh, aye, four of them!" he agreed. "But since you've been enjoying the benefit of his company for the last twelve goddamned years, I dinna think I was asking over-much."

Madeleine stood, trembling with indignation and trying to think of another insult to fling in his face when a faint giggle permeated the awful silence. Her head whipped around, and her eyes caught a flash of white apron as the red-haired potboy vanished around the corner.

Shame and embarrassment flooded over her then. Un-steadily, she sat back down.

Merrick did not seem to care. With a violent kick of his bootheel, he shoved the chair back under the table, then stalked from the room. As soon as his footsteps faded up the stairs, Madeleine let her face fall forward into her hands.

Dear God! What had she done this time?

Damn Merrick MacLachlan and his temper and his almighty pride straight to hell! And damn her, too. For the awful truth was, it was not just Merrick with whom she was angry. It was herself. She *had* been a gudgeon. And she had been weak, too. She had given up on her marriage.

Once her father had stowed her firmly away at

Sheffield, her life in London—her life with *Merrick*—had all seemed a distant fantasy. The bravado which had led her to elope with him had utterly failed her. Without him, she had collapsed, falling into a mental abyss so dark and so hopeless, it had just seemed easier to sleep and to cry than to get up and *do* something about her plight.

Why had she not simply walked away? Why had she not tried to find Merrick, and insist on hearing the truth from his lips? She could have sold . . . something. Her jewels? Her clothes? And she could have stolen a horse from the stables, she supposed, and made her way back to London. She could have written to someone, perhaps to her aunt in London, and begged for her help.

But she had done none of those things. Because somehow, she had allowed her father to convince her that Merrick had not wanted her. She had let him subtly undermine what she knew in her heart was true. She had let him make her feel like a little girl again. And she had accepted his lies—lies which she now realized were not even *good* ones—because she had been brought up to believe her father had her best interests at heart.

Merrick carried his own blame, yes. But she had failed her marriage. And thereby, her child.

Madeleine pressed the heels of her hands into her eyes. Yes, there, perhaps, was the awful truth of it. There was blame enough to go around on all sides of this mess, and the ache in her heart was growing heavier with each passing day of this miserable, ill-considered journey.

Slowly, and with a deep sigh, Madeleine rose, took her shawl from the back of the chair, and made her way up the stairs. Tomorrow would be a trying day, and she had brought much of it on herself. Nonetheless, she was not about to turn back now. Whatever fate lay ahead for her and Merrick—and for Geoff, too—she would somehow summon the strength to see it through this time. She would not give up again, though today, it seemed, Madeleine scarce knew what she was fighting for.

Chapter Seventeen

Were it no' for hope,
the heart wad break.

Madeleine went downstairs early the next morning, in the faint hope of avoiding Merrick for as long as possible. Soon enough she would be trapped with him—and with his glittering eyes and hard, black glower—in the tight confines of a carriage, a torture which would last for the rest of the day. Last night he had been absent from dinner, thank God, though no one seemed to know why or where he had gone.

In the reception parlor, the innkeeper was out again, and in his place was the stout little woman in the starched white cap whom she'd seen dusting the previous day. "Good morning to ye, ma'am," said the woman, peering at her over her spectacles. " 'Tis a fair day for traveling, if ye mean to be awa'?"

"Yes, regrettably I must," Madeleine returned, extracting her purse. "I am Lady Bessett. May I settle my accounts?"

"Aye, to be sure." The woman withdrew a ledger from beneath the desk, and totted up the amounts for bed and board, and well as the stabling.

Madeleine was counting out the money when she heard the tread of heavy boots coming down the steps. She turned to see Merrick hit the last stair and head for the front door. His expression was grim, his every muscle taut as a cat's beneath his elegantly cut coat and snug buff breeches. Though he must have seen her from the corner of his eye, he neither turned nor acknowledged her presence by so much as a curt greeting.

The woman behind the desk was watching Madeleine as she observed him leaving. She cleared her throat with a delicate little sound. " 'Tis a pity, is it not?" she said sotto voce. "And such a fine-looking gent he is, too."

Madeleine turned back to look at her. "I beg your pardon?" she said. "What is a pity?"

"Och, that wicked scar!" she said. " 'Tis no wonder, of course, that you noticed it."

It was on the tip of Madeleine's tongue to say that she had not noticed it—for indeed, she had not. She no longer saw the scar at all, for her apperception of the man as a whole had long ago overwhelmed that one small physical imperfection.

The woman at the desk clearly did not realize they had arrived together. "He gives you regular custom, I collect?" said Madeleine quietly.

"Oh, aye," she said. "Has businesses in London, he does. But passes by once or twice a year going to his family up in Argyll."

The devil must have been in her then, for it was the only explanation for what Madeleine did next. "His family, did you say?" she responded coolly, taking the change the woman offered her. "So he is married?"

The woman closed the ledger and shook her head.

"Now that, I cannae tell ye," she confessed. "He was once, and that I do know, for 'twas his purpose in first coming here, or so my brother said."

"Your brother?"

"The innkeeper," she clarified. "I've been here but a few years, myself. Came down from Perthshire after I was widowed."

Madeleine had half turned to watch Merrick through the window as he gave instructions to both the coachmen and circled about inspecting the carriages. "So his was a Gretna Green marriage?" she murmured, her tone faintly scandalized. "An inauspicious beginning, to be sure."

The woman arched one brow and nodded. "Oh, aye, that it surely was," she said. "If even half what they tell is true."

Madeleine turned back to the desk. "There was a scandal?"

The woman's gaze darted left, then right. She was clearly eager to gossip. "Aye, the wife *vanished*!" she whispered. "Just a young slip of a girl—English, like yourself, 'twas thought—though he's not, o'course. But the girl's father came after them, and took his revenge, then carried the girl off." Here the woman leaned halfway over the counter, her eyes wide. *"And she was never seen again!"*

"No?" Madeleine pressed her hand to her heart. "You cannot mean it?"

The woman pursed her lips, and shook her head. "And she's not been seen with him, ma'am, from that day to this, and you may well believe it."

"I do," said Madeleine. "I knew of a situation very like it once."

The woman narrowed one eye knowingly. "Did ye?"

she asked. "Well, 'twas like one of those novels they sell in Princes Street, I thought."

"And this father—this dreaded kidnapper—what was his name?"

Again, the woman shook her head, her starched cap bouncing. " 'Twas never known," she admitted. "And he took great pains to ensure it. Blacked the crests on both his carriages and came in and out o' the village like a whirlwind with four hulking great brutes for footmen—if you could call 'em such. Then drove awa', wi' one of them trailing blood halfway to Carlisle, or so 'tis said."

The floor felt suddenly unsteady beneath Madeleine's feet. But then she remembered . . . *something*. Whispers. Uncertainty. One of the carriages dropping off long before they arrived home. Servants she had not recognized and had never seen again.

"How dreadful!" she whispered, her eyes fixed on the ledger.

"Oh, indeed! But the lad gave almost as good as he got, for 'twas thought the other fellow would surely die, too."

"As . . . as good as he got? What do you mean?"

"Put a pitchfork through his belly, MacLachlan did," she whispered. Then she slowly shook her head. "That was it, you see. That's where he got that awful scar. One of the brutes laid his face open from temple to chin."

When Madeleine winced, the woman pounced with relish. "Och, my lady, that wasna' a fraction of it!" she went on. "And it happened, all of it, just down the lane by the stables. All but dead, the poor lad was, my brother said, when they carried him in, and he lay here for weeks festering, still as death, 'til they fetched a priest down from Glasgow, quiet-like, to give him last rites."

"Last rites?" she whispered. "But—But he is not Catholic."

The woman looked at her strangely and turned the bill around for her inspection.

"I mean—*is* he?" she went on. "He doesn't *look* Catholic."

The woman shrugged as Madeleine began to lay out the coins. "He was wearing a ring," she said. "And he wears it still, always on his wee finger. 'Tis gold, with a little builder's square cut in it, and some Latin words, and somebody took it into their heads that it was some piece of popery, so being a softhearted man, my brother sent for the priest—for by then, the poor man was barely breathing. He was sae far gone, even his servant left."

The horror was rising like bile Madeleine's throat. *"I was hurt,"* Merrick had said. *"I wrote you as soon as I was able."*

Dear God. He had meant it literally. "They . . . they beat him?"

"Nigh to death," said the woman sadly. " 'Twas terrible, to hear my brother tell it. They called out the magistrate, but och! What can ye do? The man was rich, and the laddie wasna. No one was aboot to look too hard for that one, aye?"

Through the window, Madeleine could see that one of the ostlers was holding the head of a big, prancing bay which looked fresh as the morning's dew. With a stroke down the great beast's neck, Merrick drifted away from his coachman, still shouting out the last of the morning's instruction. In a moment, he would be through the door.

Her knees unsteady, Madeleine turned back to the desk and seized the woman's hand. "There was a servant," she said abruptly. "You—you mentioned a servant. Who? Of what sort?"

The woman drew back an inch. "Well, 'twas just the young lady's maid, I believe," she said. "But my brother said she wasna' any help. Claimed she knew naught of the fellow, nor where his family might be found. I daresay they were worrit sick."

"Dear God," said Madeleine, shoving her coin purse into her reticule. She looked about in desperation. "I—I am so sorry. I must go. That was . . . that was quite horrible. I thank you. For—for your kindness. More than you will ever know."

And with that string of inanities, Madeleine bolted toward the stairs. She had scarce made the first turn when she heard Merrick jerk open the door.

Fifteen minutes later, after calming down sufficiently that her legs no longer trembled, Madeleine came back down with Geoff and Mr. Frost. The boy was chattering happily about the day's travel. Despite her near-constant preoccupation with Merrick, Madeleine had not failed to notice that the child seemed happier and far more balanced these last few days. Mr. Frost, too, looked content. His young face was not lined with worry.

Together, they went out into the sunshine of the yard to load their hand baggage. The big bay horse was still wheeling about anxiously, and tossing up the occasional stone as he did so. Merrick appeared around the corner of the carriage, and for the first time Madeleine realized that his snug buff breeches and high Hessian boots meant that he was dressed not for the carriage but for the saddle.

"Good morning, sir," said Mr. Frost. "That is quite a fine-looking beast."

"Thank you," said Merrick. His eyes looked not just grim, but weary. "He is a recent acquisition."

"He is yours, sir?" said Geoff in some surprise.

Merrick looked down at the boy, and something which looked like regret sketched across his face. "Yes, Geoff, he is mine now," he answered. "I decided it might be best if I rode on ahead to Castle Kerr, so that my grandmother might make ready for your arrival."

Madeleine's heart sank.

Merrick had decided he could not bear to share a confined space with her for another three days, more likely. She should have been glad: glad for the chance to escape his glittering, accusatory gaze and his almost overwhelming presence in the carriage. So why did she feel so disheartened? Why did she fear this was but another unbreachable chasm between them then? If it was, she hoped her little tantrum had been worth it. Just now, it did not feel so.

Madeleine opened her mouth to speak, to ask him to wait, or perhaps, even, to apologize. But so much had already gone unsaid, there seemed no purpose in it. He glanced at her, a fleeting, almost hopeful look. Confused, she closed her mouth. He turned away.

With a few last words to his coachman, Merrick led the big beast around, slid a foot into the stirrup, and swung himself smoothly into the saddle. "Phipps will look after you well," he said, to no one in particular. "He knows the best inns, and Grimes knows the roads like the back of his hand. The weather will continue fair, I believe."

"Good-bye, then, sir," Geoff's voice was very small.

"Yes, good-bye, sir," Mr. Frost chimed. He and the boy waved. Merrick touched his crop to his hat brim, then set his heels to the bay's flanks. The big horse sprang, and in an instant, he was gone.

Geoff climbed into the carriage looking almost inconsolable.

Mr. Frost followed him in. "Don't worry, Geoff," he said. "We have lots to do."

Geoff nodded, but his gaze was fixed firmly at his feet. Madeleine dipped her head in an attempt to see his eyes and tucked a wayward strand of the boy's hair back into place. "Shall you miss Mr. MacLachlan, my dear?"

Still studying the carriage floor, Geoff nodded. "He is interesting," said the boy. "And I had some things . . . some things I wished to ask him. He said I might. Ask him things, I mean. If I had questions."

"Of course you may." The child's dejection left her feeling even further downcast. "What sort of things did you wish to ask, my love?"

The child lifted both shoulders. "I don't know," he mumbled. "Just some things. I forgot them already."

Above, Grimes shouted back to Madeleine's coachman. The crack of the whip sounded. The big coach lurched, then ground forward, harnesses jingling. At the last possible instant, Madeleine turned around and watched the shabby little inn vanish in a cloud of dust. *And good riddance,* she thought.

But strangely, it did not feel like good riddance. In truth, it felt . . . well, a little tragic. As if she were leaving something important behind. But perhaps it was just this inn, this village. It was the place where the marriage of her dreams had begun with such hope and ended all too soon in a tragedy. Being here again had set her every nerve on edge. It had brought back too many things she had no wish to remember, and it had left her feeling just a little ashamed.

Had she really spent the last thirteen years trying to blame Merrick for what had been, after all, a shared failure? Whatever Merrick's sins, he had not abandoned her at the inn. Not willingly. If the past few days had not made that plain, the innkeeper's sister certainly had. The truth had first sickened her, then angered her. *Her father* had done that to him. And for what? Pride? Petulance? Madeleine was suddenly very glad that he was dead.

All of it left Madeleine wondering just what else Merrick had not bothered to tell her. And she wondered *why*. Why did he bear his scar so stoically? Was her father the cause of his limp? But more importantly, was it just his stubborn pride which kept him from telling her? Or was he, too, just looking for something to pin their failures on?

Chapter Eighteen

*None but the pitiful pine, and a weak
heart n'er won a wise wife.*

Three days after his brother's abrupt and inauspicious departure from Gretna Green, Sir Alasdair MacLachlan stood high in the southeast bartizan of his castle, staring hard into the distance across the glistening loch. His arms were crossed over his chest, his fine lawn shirt open to the throat and to the wind. No carriage had yet appeared in the distance to disturb his newfound family harmony. But one was surely coming, and Sir Alasdair was none too glad of it.

"Now, tell me again, Merrick," he said to his brother. "What made you think this trip was a good idea?"

Merrick placed both hands on the stonework and leaned into the wind, hoping it might clear his head. "I wanted the boy to see Scotland," he said vaguely. "I wanted him to meet Granny MacGregor—and you, of course."

"Of course," echoed Alasdair dryly.

There was a long silence, punctuated by nothing but the soughing wind. "Alasdair, he has the gift," said Merrick quietly. "He has it, and he does not know why."

"The devil!" his brother responded. "The gift? Are you sure, Merrick?"

"Oh, aye, I'm sure," he said grimly.

Alasdair gave a low whistle. "Damn. Does Granny know?"

"I've not told her." Merrick's knuckles had gone white from clutching the stonework. "I'll likely not need to."

"No, for she will know it anyway," Alasdair agreed. "But the lad does not yet know he is yours. Indeed, if what you say is true, and if you keep agreeing with the woman and her impossible demands, then he may *never* know. What, then, is the purpose?"

"He *will* know he is mine," gritted Merrick. "By God, eventually, he will know."

His golden-haired god of a brother turned to him, one eyebrow skeptically lifted. "This woman still has you under her thumb, brother," he said. "I cannot like it."

Merrick shoved away from the wall. "Damn it, I thought we would be made welcome here," he snapped. "I thought I might count on my family for support. Do you wish us to go, Alasdair? We can be halfway back to Glasgow by tomorrow afternoon, if that is your wish."

Alasdair watched him in silence a moment. "You know that I do not wish you to leave," he answered. "And yet I certainly have no wish to watch you suffer again. Do you think it has been easy on any of us, these many years? Watching you live half a life, eaten with bitterness? And now, knowing what that woman has done to that child— to *our* blood?"

Merrick curled his hands into fists. "She was young, Alasdair," he said quietly. "Her father tricked her and played upon her sense of duty. And we were both of us unutterably stupid."

"Her actions suggest a cunning with which you do not seem to credit her," his brother answered. "She has managed to pass off your bairn as another's these past dozen years and hidden her marriage to you as if she were ashamed to be a MacLachlan."

"Aye, play the great laird when it suits you, Alasdair," said Merrick sourly. "As if *you* have spent the last fifteen years elevating our good name to lofty and respectable heights."

Alasdair looked suitably shamed. "Well, what happens now?" he asked. "The lady arrives, is embraced by her long-discarded family, and then what? Is all forgiven?"

"Aye, perhaps it is time to do just that," Merrick answered. "For I've no more fight left in me, brother. But Madeleine does not come here as my wife."

Alasdair was silent for a long moment. "There is no hope, then, of a reconciliation?"

"No," he answered. "She does not love me. And I have grown bitter and wiser."

"Then your bitterness damns you to a life lived alone," his brother warned. "And recall if you will another of Granny's favorite adages: *A man gets wisdom at his own cost.*"

With both hands, Merrick shoved himself away from bartizan's low stone wall. "Well, what the devil would you have me do?" he snapped. "Two minutes ago, you thought I was clutching a viper to my breast. Now you would have me reconcile?"

Alasdair considered it. "Well, I would prefer she vanish from the face of the earth," he finally said. "I would prefer you to be able to marry again. But since that is not possible unless one of us gives her a shove down the well—and we'd have to look to Esmée for that; she's the only one with the mettle for it—then we must think of the child instead."

"Which is precisely what I am doing," said Merrick, turning from the wall and opening his hands plaintively. "The boy is a MacLachlan. He has a right to his heritage and to his family."

"And a right to his father," said Alasdair. "Aye, you're doing all you can. I know you are. I was just damned shocked, old boy, to see you riding across the bridge yesterday."

"Esmée did invite me," he said quietly. "The day of the wedding."

Alasdair looked vaguely surprised but not displeased.

"I hope she meant it," Merrick went on. "I hope she does not mind this intrusion. It is, after all, your wedding trip."

"This is your home, Merrick," said Alasdair, and he sounded sincere. "We are all of us happy you've come."

Merrick managed a sideways grin. "Sorcha is not," he said. "The little imp bit me yesterday when I picked her up."

Alasdair winced. "Damn!" he said. "I thought we'd broken that nasty little habit."

"Well, good luck to you with that one, old chap," he muttered. "I should account myself lucky, I suppose, that young Geoff is twelve years old."

"Sorcha will still be biting when she's twenty," Alasdair grumbled. "Well, at any rate, Granny MacGregor is over the moon with joy that you've come. You have usurped my role, I believe, as the prodigal son."

Just then, Merrick caught the sight of what looked like dust coming up the edge of the loch.

"Damn me, there they come!" Alasdair gave Merrick a heartening slap between the shoulder blades. "Buck up, old boy. I'd best go down and have everyone make ready."

Merrick barely heard the ancient wooden door scrape open behind him. He watched the dust rise in an ever-nearing semicircle around the loch, and his mind again turned to Madeleine. He was halfway surprised she had not turned back, given their last afternoon together.

Of course, the whole thing had begun innocently enough. He had been at first stunned, then oddly pleased, to see her standing so awkwardly in the smithy. She had clutched her shawl with an unexpectedly girlish charm, her cheeks flushed from the brisk walk, her eyes wide with uncertainty, and for an instant, he had been hurled back thirteen years.

But somewhere along the line, their sentimental interlude had gone all to hell, and his words to Madeleine when they parted had been hard and ugly. He had been, as usual, too blunt and heavy-handed. And Madeleine had struck back in a way which had been deliberately calculated to wound. Well, wound she had. With a few cruel words, she had brought back to him on a powerful rush the sense of loss and rejection which he had felt as a young man—and had never really shaken off.

Now, a full three days later, he could not get past the pain which kept clouding any vision he might have had of the future. For once, he was desperately glad he did not share his grandmother's gift. Were he to see the future, it might well blight the remainder of his days. He was beginning to fear his last years would go on just as this previous dozen had—which implied that at some point in these last few weeks, he had been foolish enough to allowed hope to kindle in his heart again. To have Madeleine dash it so thoroughly had brought him crashing back down to reality.

Alasdair was right. He was to have no real life, and no helpmate with whom to share it. He would have no family of his own, save whatever part of Geoff's affection he was able to wrestle away from his wife.

He was sorry now, deeply sorry that he had threatened Madeleine with the courts. And he was especially sorry about the vile remark he had made concerning his conjugal rights. The legalities of the matter aside, the moral truth was he had no rights, and he'd sooner have no woman at all until the last of his days than to have one taken to his bed by force. He had let the whisky and the anger and his rekindled lust do his talking that night, and long would he rue it.

The truth was, he was better suited to women like Bess Bromley, a woman who valued nothing but pleasure, pain, and the price of raw, dispassionate sex. Women who were so opposite what his wife had been that having them could sate his needs without making a mockery of his memories. Merrick had not the benefit of his brother's angelic beauty or glib tongue. There was a darkness about his soul which he could not explain, not even to himself, and only during those few brief weeks with Madeleine had it seemed to leave him. Fleetingly, it had lifted in Treyhern's shabby little pantry. Dear God. That feeling, that indescribable moment of pure joy was enough to cause a man make a fool of himself—again and again.

But Merrick had suffered a just punishment for that

lapse in judgment: day after day of sitting opposite Madeleine in a snug little carriage. Night after night of envisioning what she might be doing behind the tightly closed door of her bedchamber. Half a dozen trips up and down the corridors each evening, often pausing to lift his hand to knock, then thinking better of it.

So here he was, trying very hard not to think of that night at Treyhern's. It was hard. Damned hard. For so long, Madeleine had been nothing but a fantasy—but unlike most such fantasies, the reality had far exceeded the dream. He still shuddered when he thought of it.

The lead carriage—*his* carriage, the one which was bringing him his wife and child—was rounding the last of the loch. Soon it would come rumbling across the arches of the bridge, and out into the very loch itself, all the way to this rocky little spit of land which some long-ago warrior had fortified against his enemies. But Madeleine, the most dangerous thing his heart had ever known, would be allowed to roll right under the portcullis and stroll into the house unimpeded.

Suddenly, something like panic gripped him. It was said in the City that the Black MacLachlan feared no man and feared no risk. But he was unaccountably nervous at the prospect of seeing his slight, demure wife again, and being near her was the greatest risk he knew. He had been known to spend half a million pounds with scarcely a second thought and level entire city blocks at the drop of a hat. But a small female shook him.

Damn. There was naught to be done for it now. He had forced her to come here, had he not? Merrick dragged open the heavy wooden door, ducked low, and started down the twisting stairs.

He found his grandmother in the Tower Room, which she had long used as her private parlor and study. She closed the distance between them, her gait still strong.

"Och, she has come, laddie," said his grandmother, her hands going to his open shirt collar to neaten it. "Do ye no' wish a neckcloth?"

Merrick shook his head.

His grandmother set her palms against his chest and caught his gaze, holding it quizzically. "What is it that ye want, Merrick?" she asked softly.

He took one of her hands, folding the softly withered fingers around his own as he lifted to his lips. "Granny, I hardly know," he said.

"Och, I do na' believe that," she said. "But what is it ye want of *me,* laddie? I knew before ye got here that ye were coming—and wi' a purpose, too."

He watched her appraisingly for a moment. "It is the boy," he finally said. "You will know it when you see him."

She pursed her lips, and nodded. "Aye, then." She wrapped her hand around his arm. "We'd best go down."

Madeleine watched through the carriage window as they sped along the last quarter mile of their journey. The beauty which surrounded them was beyond anything she might have imagined. The loch lay before them like a sheet of blue glass suspended from the heavens, and cradled by the soaring green mountains. Her next breath was stolen by the castle itself. From a distance, the massive gray edifice seemed almost to float upon the loch, its walls, turrets, and towers shimmering silver in the water below.

The carriage was lurching slightly left, nearing the castle's approach. Even Geoff gasped when the bridge came fully into view. It was like something from a fairy tale, with its high-arching semicircles seemingly built upon nothing but rubble and water.

"Magnificent," whispered Mr. Frost.

Just then, the carriage made a sharp turn to bear onto the bridge.

"Look!" exclaimed Geoff. "We are going right out over the water!"

The carriage wheels rumbled more loudly, and the house was rapidly nearing. It was by no means a large castle, but it rose proudly from the rocky promontory beneath, its entire circumference walled in stone at least twenty feet high. The portcullis was up between the two small towers which guarded the castle's entrance, and they rolled beneath and into the close, stopping before a wide double door of rough hewn wood which was thrown open on both sides.

A wide but short flight of stone stairs came down into the forecourt. Sir Alasdair stood near the top. Madeleine recognized him at once, for the years had little altered his golden beauty. He carried a child on his hip, and a diminutive young lady stood beside him wearing an emerald green stole over one shoulder.

Just then, Merrick stepped out into the sunlight, an elderly lady on his arm. She was reed-thin and tall, her shoulders unbent by time. Her hair was bound in a silvery knot at the nape of her neck, and, like the younger woman, she wore a light wool stole across one shoulder, this one blood red.

This, doubtless, was the grandmother. Madeleine felt a shiver of unease upon seeing her bladelike nose and strong cheekbones. Could such a woman see into one's future?

Or into one's heart? That was just nonsense, was it not? On the other hand, if it were total nonsense, then it meant she had dragged Geoff off on this dreadful journey for nothing.

There were no servants in sight. Sir Alasdair came down to help them from their carriage. When he caught Madeleine's hand to help her step out, their eyes caught, too. She saw a flash of recognition and, lurking behind it, a barely veiled mistrust.

"Welcome, my lady, to Castle Kerr," he said coolly. "I hope you will make my home yours."

He did not sound as if he quite meant it.

Merrick was conferring with Phipps about the baggage. Madeleine noticed that his heavy, raven-colored hair had grown too long since they had left London. Today, dressed for the Scottish countryside, he looked very different. Beneath an unadorned waistcoat, he wore a plain shirt of a heavier, softer cloth than Madeleine was accustomed to. No cravat or stock circled his collar, and instead, it lay open at the throat. He wore his snug buff breeches and tall brown boots, and on the whole, he looked every inch a rural Scottish laird.

Just then, Phipps nodded and stepped away. Merrick came forward, speaking first to Geoff, then to the others. Introductions were made to Alasdair's wife. The young lady looked far younger than Sir Alasdair, and she appeared to be a Scot as well. Her name was Esmée, and Madeleine was surprised to learn they had been wed but a few weeks.

The surprise was forgotten when the elderly woman came forward to greet them. Lady Annis MacGregor looked even more unyielding when seen up close. With little regard for the others, her grandsons included, she went straight to Geoff as if drawn by a magnet, kneeling ever so slightly.

"Aye, this would be the one, would it no'?" she said, looking the boy straight in the eyes.

Merrick joined them. "Granny, this is Geoff," he said. "Geoffrey Archard, her ladyship's son."

The old woman set a hand to the boy's cheek, and her eyes flared wide. *"Sac trom air a' chois chaoil!"* she whispered.

Merrick gave a nervous cough. "Granny, we've little Gaelic."

Her hand still on Geoff's cheek, the old woman turned to look at her grandson. " 'Tis as you said," she answered. "And a heavy load for a slender leg."

Over the boy's head, Merrick and Madeleine exchanged glances. The old woman stood. "This one maun come w' me," she said firmly, taking Geoff's hand. "Alasdair, will ye take everyone intae the armory for tea?"

Madeleine shot a questioning glance at Merrick. He inclined his head ever so slightly. He was right, of course. There was no harm in Geoff's going away with the old woman. They had already vanished into the shadowy entrance to the castle when Alasdair's wife touched her lightly on the arm.

"Will you wish to bathe and change from your traveling clothes, my lady?" she asked politely. "I should be pleased to show you to your rooms."

Madeleine looked about. Phipps was helping Eliza take down the hand luggage. "Yes, thank you." She returned her gaze to Lady MacLachlan. "That would be most welcome."

The young woman led her up the steps and into the house. "I hope you will call me Esmée," she said, starting up a twisting staircase to their left.

"You are very kind," she answered. "And I am Madeleine."

Madeleine took in her surroundings as they turned corners and traversed small corridors. "Do you know where Lady Annis will have taken my son?"

"Up to the Tower Room, I daresay," said Esmée. "It is the castle office, and her sitting room, too."

"Is that far?" she asked, trying not to sound anxious. "Either the house is terribly large, or I am disoriented."

"You are disoriented," she said, smiling at Madeleine over her shoulder. "The castle is small by English standards, but very rambling. There is one staircase which goes nowhere, and a couple of doors with nothing but walls behind them."

They had turned into a long room hung with portraits. "My, I have never seen so much stone in one place before," Madeleine mused. Like the rest of the castle, the place looked to be made of little more than granite, including the high, vaulted ceiling.

Esmée laughed. "Medieval, is it not?" she said. "This is the old billeting hall, but it is used now as more of a drawing room. It was built in the fifteenth century, and little changed. I am afraid the MacLachlans have never believed in wasting money on decor."

The entire house had a certain charm, a Scottish charm, she supposed. Were the house an English one, it would surely have been paneled and plastered long ago, but so far, Madeleine had seen no paint, no pilasters, no pier glasses, indeed, not so much as a lick of gilding. Save for the exquisite Turkey carpets and still-brilliant tapestries, the castle appeared to have been left untouched for about four hundred years.

After passing through the billeting hall, they reached another flight of stairs. Eventually they came out in a short flagstone passageway which, even at this hour, was lit by flickering sconces. Esmée paused at a short, wide door, lifted the wrought-iron latch, and gave the door a little shove with her hip. "Old houses," she said apologetically, as the door scraped, then swung inward.

The room was not large, but it was glorious. Shaped like a half-moon, the chamber was fitted with a fine old four-poster bed with woven wool hangings and a matching counterpane. One wall was hung with tapestries, whilst the concave wall was set with a deep window fitted with an embroidered window seat. The window was clearly a recent alteration.

Madeleine went to the window, threw back the draperies, and looked out. The effect was dizzying, for the room gave the impression of being almost suspended over the loch. Esmée appeared at her elbow. "Breathtaking, is it not?"

"I have never seen the like," said Madeleine.

The loch could be seen in its entirety from this vantage point. It was shaped like a perfect oval, with a tiny, tree-filled island dotted in the center. She watched the shimmering water for a moment, then reluctantly turned from the window. Esmée was staring at her.

"Is something amiss?"

Her hostess shook her head as if to dispel a dream. "No, I am sorry," she said in her faint Highland accent. "You must excuse me. It is just . . . well, just seems so strange to have you here. I'd no notion until yesterday . . . well, that Merrick even *had* a wife."

Madeleine opened her mouth to say that she was not his wife, that their union had long ago been torn asunder. But she was no longer sure that that was truly so, not legally—and on her part, not even emotionally.

She was saved from blurting out such a foolish response by a noise at the door. A servant in woolen breeches and a long, leather vest was carrying in cans of water. Eliza followed him in with two portmanteaus.

Esmée moved to the door. "I should leave you now," she said. "I shall see you downstairs shortly. Do make yourself at home."

Dinner that evening was served at six, and for Madeleine, it was an awkward affair. Because the only other child in the house was Esmée's sister, Lady Annis decreed that Geoff was to dine with the adults. Somewhat cowed by the new faces, the child said little. Merrick, too, was quiet, but more than once Madeleine felt the heat of his gaze upon her. Between Mr. Frost and Sir Alasdair, who was in his usual charming form, the dinner conversation carried on reasonably well. Lady Annis seemed content to observe, but she watched much as a hawk might watch its prey.

Madeleine wondered what excuse Merrick had given his family for their unexpected visit. Of course, everyone save Geoff and his tutor knew that Madeleine had once been Merrick's wife. Sir Alasdair was only too well aware. Though polar opposites in both looks and temperament, the brothers had always been close, and Alasdair obviously blamed Madeleine for the ruined marriage.

After dinner, the family retired to the drawing room for cards, save for Lady Annis, who pleaded the infirmities of old age and retired to her sitting room on Merrick's arm. Mr. Frost, Esmée, Alasdair, and Geoff made up a table for whist, whilst Madeleine retired to a corner by the windows.

Across the loch, the sun was finally setting, casting a purplish shimmer across the water. Gazing at it, Madeleine was seized by the sudden urge to be out of doors. To row upon the loch, or swim in it, or merely stroll around its shore. Anything to be closer to its splendor, and to draw nearer to the amethyst mountain rising up beyond. She leaned forward, and for an instant, her hand hovered at the glass as if she might touch the beauty.

"It is called Beinn Donachain," said a quiet voice at her elbow.

Madeleine started. Merrick had returned to the room.

"Beautiful, is it not?" He was leaning over her, one hand braced on her chair arm.

She held his gaze uncertainly. Seeing no discord there, she relaxed. "And that one?" she asked, pointing further beyond.

"Beinn Eunaich." His tongue seemed to caress the words and lace them with a hint of the Highlands, which made her shiver.

"And there? What is that one?"

"Beinn Larachan."

"Beinn Larachan," she echoed. But from her lips, the word did not fall so beautifully. "Their names are lovely," she remarked. "What lies beyond?"

Merrick sat down in the adjacent chair, and propped his chin on his fist. "More mountains?" he answered, as if it were a question, and not an answer. "Loch Etive. Loch Linnhe. And on to the Isle of Mull, I suppose."

On impulse, Madeleine leaned nearer. "And this loch," she said, her voice coming out too softly. "What is it called?"

"Loch Orchy," he said. "But as lochs go, it is a mere pond."

"It seems enchanted," she said. "Indeed, this whole place seems enchanted. Your brother is most fortunate."

"Aye, he is," said Merrick with a muted smile. "And I think perhaps he is finally beginning to realize it."

Madeleine looked at him quizzically. "Did he not do so before?"

Merrick's expression grew more serious. "I think he was blinded by the pleasures of town for a time," he answered. "My grandmother has been left to steward the place—not that she has objected."

A ruffle of laughter broke out at the game table. Madeleine looked up to see Sir Alasdair tossing his cards into the air, scattering them across the carpet. Geoff fanned his hand across the table triumphantly. Inwardly, Madeleine smiled. Geoff was enjoying his new liberties. But in truth, the boy had begun long ago to seem old beyond his years.

She was recalled to the present by Merrick's light touch on her arm. "My grandmother wishes to see you," he said quietly. "May I show you to her rooms?"

Madeleine felt a flash of trepidation. "Yes, of course."

Merrick rose, and escorted her from the room. This time their path through the house was more direct. After climbing the circular stairs again, Merrick paused at another of the too-short doors and rapped softly with the back of his hand.

At her answer, he pushed the door open. Lady Annis

MacGregor sat in an ornately carved armchair by the hearth, and a low fire burned in the grate. She motioned Madeleine forward. "Come, my dear, and sit," she said. "I hope ye will no' mind the fire. This time o' night, I do feel my years."

Merrick was pulling the door shut. Her head swiveled around. "Pray do not leave us, Merrick," she said a little sharply. "I would speak with ye as well."

With a look of reluctance, he ducked beneath the lintel and came in. He did not sit, but instead took up a spot by the mantel and crossed his arms over his chest, a stance Madeleine well recognized.

Lady Annis turned her attention to Madeleine. "I welcome ye most belatedly, my dear, tae Castle Kerr," she said. "I had hoped tae see ye long ere now."

It was a subtle rebuke, cloaked in politeness. Madeleine managed to smile. "I thank you, Lady Annis," she answered. "Your home is lovely."

The old lady tapped one fingernail on her chair arm, which was carved, somewhat appropriately, in the shape of a hawk's claw. "Young Geoffrey is a fine, fair laddie," she said at last. "Alas, I fear he has oftly been an unhappy one."

"Did he tell you that?"

"Aye, near enough," she answered. "Though 'twas unnecessary. The burden—and the responsibility—which he bears is great."

"You believe in this business, then?" asked Madeleine. "This . . . clairvoyance which Merrick speaks of?"

"Oh, aye," she said quietly, her gaze turning uncharacteristically soft. "I have seen it too long and too well. 'Tis in the blood, both MacGregor and MacLachlan."

Merrick laughed. "Aye, for we're all cousins, one way or another."

The old lady inclined her head almost regally. "Aye, so we are."

Madeleine could not entirely hide her skepticism. "And so you can just . . . see into the future? Whenever you wish? Is that it?"

The old lady shook her head. "Ye mistake what it is, my dear," she said. "There are nae gypsies here polishing balls of crystal. It is, for some, as the Bible says. *Unto you is given to know the mysteries of the kingdom, but to others in parables; that seeing they might not see, and hearing they might not understand.'* And there are many, lass, who do not understand."

"I am *trying* to understand," said Madeleine a little stridently. "Are you saying that he . . . he can predict the future? That he can read people's minds?"

The old lady shook her head. "No' that, my dear," she answered. "He sometimes spaes visions of what's tae come, aye, but in flashes. And the lad is in tune to the emotions of others, to the truths of their nature, and to things which even they may no' ken. But it is no' a'tall like mind reading."

"What is it like, then?" she asked. "I truly wish know."

The old lady narrowed one eye, and leaned forward in her ornate chair. "How d' ye know, Lady Bessett, when a room is cold?" she asked. "Explain it tae me."

Madeleine opened her mouth, then closed it, lifting both eyebrows in befuddlement. "Well, I . . . I feel a chill. On my skin."

"Aye? And what is a chill?"

"Well, it—it is the sensation of coldness."

The old lady shook a finger in her direction. "Weel

enough, sae far is it goes," she said. "But what if I were a creature capable of feeling nither heat nor cold? Then your explanation would make no' a drop of sense tae me, would it? What young Geoffery feels is like that. 'Tis a knowledge which comes no' by the seeing, nor the tasting, nor the smelling, nor the hearing of it, but in another way altogether. And if ye do na' share it, then ye have nae words for it."

Already confused, Madeleine now felt a sense of dejection. She wanted to understand; she needed to be able to talk with her child about what seemed to her a terrible affliction. But she was beginning to comprehend that that might never be possible. "Do—Do you have words for it, Lady Annis?"

She settled back in her chair. "Aye, some," she said.

Madeleine looked at the old woman sorrowfully. She had spent many hours of her long trip north remembering Geoff's childhood. His outbursts. His seemingly irrational fears. The strange things he would sometimes say. She did not like Merrick's analysis, but she very much feared he might be right. And as foreign as the concept was to her, it was the only thing which fully explained the past.

"This is a painful notion to me, Lady Annis," she said. "This idea that my child . . . that my child is not like other children. But Merrick tells me that this is so. And I must begin to believe him."

The old lady reached forward and laid a gnarled hand on Madeleine's wrist. "You child is a child like any other in all other ways," she said, and for the first time there was reassurance in her voice. "Be verra sure of that, my dear."

Madeleine nodded weakly. "What happens to Geoff when he feels this . . . this thing?"

The old lady began to tap the chair arm again. " 'Tis an opening of the mind," she answered. "Sometimes deliberate, often accidental. But the manifestation of the gift can take many forms. Dreams which foreshow the future are prodigious common; more of us ha' them than no. Often, however, we do na' recall them, or the symbolism within escapes us."

Madeleine was shaking her head. "Geoff's situation is more extreme than mere dreams," she said. "And he seems to fear that his visions *cause* things to happen."

Slowly, Lady Annis nodded. "Aye, the lad's mind is strong, but he hasna control of it," she said. "For him, 'tis as if someone is drawing a curtain, then snapping it shut again, making him feel as though he has little control of his thoughts."

"But *can* one control such thoughts?"

"Oh, aye," she answered. "Most learn, and Geoff will, too. He shall remain here at Kerr for a time, will he no'?"

Madeleine looked at Merrick uncertainly. "Yes," she said. "Yes, I daresay he shall."

The old lady looked pleased. "I will help him," she said. "Ye needn't trooble yourself further o'er it, my dear."

The remark should have sounded presumptuous, but it did not. Instead, it sounded oddly reassuring. Madeleine wondered if she was losing her mind, if this mystical old place was somehow affecting her judgment. But for the first time, she felt the faintest stirrings of hope.

"May I ask, Lady Annis, how you broached this subject with Geoffrey?"

Again, the regal tilt of the head. "I asked the lad if he knew why my grandson had brought him here," she said. "He said he didna know, sae I told him, and plainly."

Madeleine felt a flash of alarm. It must have sketched across her face.

"Och, I didna tell him of his parentage," said the old woman. "That secret's no' my burden, 'tis yours"—here, she paused to nod toward Merrick—"and *yours*."

Madeleine said nothing.

Again, the old woman leaned forward in her chair, her hands clutching at the carved talons. "And I'll tell ye plainly, the both o' you, that there's aboot three too many secrets in this business tae suit me," she said warningly. "Not just Geoff's, but the secrets the two of you are keeping fra' one anither in your prideful hearts."

Madeleine dropped her gaze. "It is only Geoffrey who need concern us now," she said quietly. "I wish to do what is right for him."

"Oh, I think ye ken what's right, my dear," she said, her voice stern. "And I think ye'll do it, too."

Merrick unfolded his arms and came forward. "Enough, Granny," he said quietly. "Madeleine and I have agreed between us what's best done for the nonce."

The old woman's eyes flared with irritation. "Aye, and when did a nonce become thirteen years?" she snapped. "What's best done, laddie, is for the two o' you tae do your duty as husband and wife and neaten up this soss that's been made o' your marriage, and do wha' is right by that child. Had ye done so at the outset, he'd likely no' be in sae sair a shape."

Merrick's visage darkened. "There were intervening circumstances."

"Nay, there was overweening pride!" snapped his grandmother. "I'll say this but once, laddie—a man's wife is his property and his duty. And should anither dare tae take her fra' him, he goes after her, and he takes her back again. There's a boat goes off to Italy every day o' the week from somewhere, aye?"

Madeleine was still gaping when the old lady turned on her. "And as for you, if ye are old enough tae stand up before God and speak your vows, then ye are old enough tae keep them," she said. "Ye cleave only untae your husband, and niver mind wha' anyone else has tae say in the matter."

"Life is not so easy, Grandmother, as you would make it out," said Merrick coldly.

"Oh, aye," she said mordantly. " 'Tis a *sair fecht!*"

Madeleine looked at Merrick. "I—I don't understand," she said. "What is she saying?"

"That it is a hard life," answered Merrick. "But I believe she is being sarcastic."

"Aye, tae be sure!" grumbled his grandmother. "For I was wed at sixteen, and I knew my duty, and I did it."

Madeleine looked down to see that her hands were shaking. Swiftly, she set them against her lap. The old woman spoke harshly, but the truth was, Madeleine was no longer sure she spoke wrongly. Perhaps it really *was* just that simple. You did your duty.

Merrick apparently did not think it was simple. He pushed away from the mantel, and went to Madeleine's chair. "Lady Bessett will wish a moment with her son before he goes to bed," he said coolly. "I will show her back down to the billeting hall now."

Relief swept over Madeleine. She stood. "I realize, Lady Annis, that Merrick and I have made mistakes," she said quietly. "But life has gone on, and . . . and things have changed. Neither of us meant to do ill by our child."

Lady Annis looked up at her a little wearily. "Och, I

am sure ye dinna!" she agreed. Her eyes fell fleetingly on her grandson, and a look of resignation passed over her face. "Just send the lad tae me each forenoon," she added. "Tell anyone who asks why that I'm tae teach him the Gaelic—which I may weel do, since nither of my grandsons have deigned tae learn it."

At that, Merrick relented. His expression softened, and he leaned forward to kiss his grandmother's parchment cheek. "Good night, Granny," he said quietly. "We thank you for your willingness to help Geoff."

"There's naucht to thank me for," said Lady Annis. "He is my blood. He is my duty."

Once they had escaped the dragon's lair, Madeleine followed Merrick back down the steps. He moved down the twisting stairs with a catlike grace, his wide shoulders limned with light from the wall sconces which burned at each turn. Neither of them spoke until they reached the foot of the stairs. He turned and offered his hand to help her down the last.

For a moment, his eyes searched her face. "My grandmother is a tad tongue-betroosht," he finally said. "I hope, Maddie, that she did not offend you."

Maddie. Oh, she wished he would not call her that!

"She said little that was not true," Madeleine managed to answer.

"Aye," he said a little sadly. "Perhaps not."

The walked together to the drawing room, neither speaking. Lady Annis, it seemed, had said enough for a lifetime. Inside the drawing room, the card game was breaking up amidst much laugher. It seemed that Sir Alasdair, a once-notorious gambler, had been soundly trounced by his young wife and his new nephew.

"Ah, my salad days are well and truly over," he complained. "Thrashed by a pair of neophytes!"

With a muted smile, his wife linked her arm through his. "I fear your salad days were over a decade past, my love," she said, "had you but acknowledged it."

Sir Alasdair responded with a wince. "Oh, the cruelty of youth!" he said. "I believe it is time to put this decrepit old man to bed."

Together, Madeleine and Geoff said their good-nights, and went up to his bedchamber. Madeleine drew the draperies, then helped him unpack his nightshirt and brushes. "Did you enjoy your visit with Lady Annis?" she asked lightly.

Geoff flung himself across the bed and dragged an arm over his eyes. "Sort of," he said.

Madeleine sat down beside him and pulled his arm away. "Is my son hiding under there somewhere?" she asked lightly. "Ah, yes! There he is."

"Oh, Mamma!" he said as if embarrassed. "That is so silly."

She tweaked his chin. "Look at me, Geoff, and quit complaining," she ordered. "Did you like her?"

He nodded, his hair scrubbing on the woolen counterpane.

Madeleine was quiet for a moment. "How did it go?" she asked. "Did you . . . learn anything interesting? Did she say anything untoward?"

He shook his head. "She likes me," he said. "We talked about . . . about things."

"Do you feel better?" she asked hopefully.

"I guess so."

Madeleine squeezed his hand. "I also met with Lady

Annis tonight," she finally said. "I went upstairs whilst you played cards. She wanted to speak with me."

His eyes widened.

Madeleine smiled. "I liked her very much, too. We had a long talk. And . . . well, she told me. Everything, Geoff. About you, I mean."

At that, Geoff looked away. His eyes blinked rapidly.

Madeleine slipped her hand into his. "It is all right, Geoff," she said quietly. "You . . . you are special."

"I do not want to be special, Mamma," he whispered. "I want to be ordinary."

She tightened her grip on his hand. "No, Geoff, I don't think you do," she answered. "You are different for a reason. You have a destiny. I am sure of it. Besides, here in Scotland, with your—your—well, with these people—you are . . . not so different."

He returned his gaze to hers, and held her eyes for a moment as if trying to read her thoughts. Perhaps, in a way, he was. "I am like Lady Annis, aren't I?" he asked, his voice a little hollow. "I have . . . the gift. That's why we came here, isn't it?"

Madeleine nodded. "You have the gift," she agreed. "And you need not hide it from me, Geoff, ever again, all right? I will always love you, and I will always be your mamma. You can talk to me when you are worried. Or you can talk to Lady Annis. Or . . . or to Mr. MacLachlan, of course."

The boy said nothing but watched her a little warily.

"Geoff," she began. But then her voice faltered. "Geoff, I . . . I have a secret, too."

"I know," he said quietly.

For a moment, she wondered if the old lady had lied to her. "Did Lady Annis tell you, Geoff?"

He looked at her a little scornfully. "I do not know, Mamma, what your secret *is*," he said. "Only that you are keeping one: And that it is something to do with me. Lady Annis didn't have to tell me that. I have known it for a long time. Is it . . . is it something bad about me, Mamma?"

She gave a sharp, almost hysterical laugh. She was still clutching his hand. "Oh, dear," she said. "Is that one of the things that has been troubling you?"

He nodded slowly, then said, "Yes, and now you are cutting my blood off, Mamma. Perhaps you should just let go of my hand, and tell me your secret?"

Madeleine was shocked to realize that a tear had rolled down her cheek. "Should I?" she asked, dashing it away with the back of her hand. "Yes, I daresay I ought."

Geoff looked at her solemnly. "I will be thirteen next year, Mamma," he said quietly. "There are things a boy should know. That's what Mr. Frost says."

"And he is eminently wise," Madeleine agreed. "But this is something you should have known from the moment you were born, and yet you did not, and it is my fault. Because the truth is, Geoff, that my secret is about your father."

"About Bessett?" he asked softly.

She shook her head. "No, my love," she answered. "No, Bessett was a very kind man in his way, and he loved you very much, though perhaps he did not always show it. But . . . well, Bessett was not your father."

"Not . . . my father?" Clearly, this had not crossed his mind.

"No, Geoff, he is not." Madeleine steeled herself for the rest of the story. "You see, I was married to someone else before. I was married to—well, to Mr. MacLachlan. He was once my husband. And he is your father."

The child's eyes had grown round. He said nothing, which made it all the worse.

Madeleine snuffled back tears. "Oh, Geoff, you cannot know how this makes me feel!" she cried. "I have both wanted to tell you, and dreaded telling you. And even now . . . oh, even now, my love, this must be our secret. Can you ever forgive me?"

At last, a look of relief passed over Geoff's face. "Mr. MacLachlan," he mused. "And—And he knows, does he not? That is also why we've come here. To Castle Kerr."

Madeleine leaned forward to kiss his cheek. "Yes, darling, that is why," she said. "Because Lady Annis is your great-grandmother. You share a special bond with her, and you needed to know that. She will be helping you in ways which I cannot, and even Mr.—well, your father cannot. That is why we will be staying here for a while."

Geoff had grown very quiet. "Mamma, I don't think you did anything that needs forgiveness," he said. "But . . . but is Alvin not my brother anymore?"

Madeleine stroked the dark hair back from his forehead. "You are Alvin's brother of the heart," she said. "And that is what matters most of all."

Geoff's face wrinkled up as if he were thinking.

Dear God, she silent prayed. *Help me answer the hard question.*

"I do not understand, Mamma," he said. "If Mr. MacLachlan was your husband, how come he isn't anymore?"

Madeleine stopped sniffling, and set her shoulders firmly back. "I think, Geoff, that it is because I made a terrible mistake," she confessed. "A long time ago, before you were born, I . . . I let other people persuade me wrongly."

"What other people?"

Fleetingly, Madeleine closed her eyes. Even now, it was difficult to speak ill of her father. "Other people in my family," she said vaguely. "I was young, and weak-willed, and so I let them convince me that he—that your father— did not love me, and that I would be better off apart from him. May we leave it at that for now? I promise we will talk about it again when you are older."

"All right," said Geoff. He pulled himself up into a seated position. "Mamma, does Mr. MacLachlan think that I am peculiar? Will he wish that I was . . . well, normal?"

"Oh, Geoff!" On impulse, she bent forward, and gave him a smacking kiss on the cheek. "To him, you are perfectly normal. And he is very proud of you. Both of us are very proud of you."

Geoff seemed to consider it. "I like Mr. MacLachlan very much," he said. "He knows a lot of interesting things. Do you think he will mind being my father?"

"Oh, Geoff, no," she said, swiftly covering his hand with hers. "Indeed, if anything, he thinks that I am to blame—"

A sharp knock at the door made Madeleine almost leap from her skin.

Merrick stuck his head into the room. A look of acute discomfort passed over his face. "I beg your pardon," he said. "I wished to say good night to Geoff."

"Yes. Yes, of course." After another swift kiss to Geoffrey's cheek, Madeleine leapt from the bed. "I shall leave you to it. Good night, my dear. Remember to clean your teeth, please."

Merrick came in reluctantly, then hesitated, seizing her

wrist as she passed. "You have been crying." It was not a question.

Madeleine gave another pathetic laugh, and dabbed beneath her eyes with the back of one hand. "Only a little." Her face fell yet again. "Merrick, I . . . I have done as you wished. I have told him."

Shock flitted across his face. Madeleine jerked her wrist from his grasp and hastened across the room. She could feel Merrick's eyes boring into her back, but she dared not turn around for fear of what she might say or do.

Chapter Nineteen

A pennywecht o' love
is worth a pound o' law.

S he made her way through the old castle and to her bedchamber in haste. Eliza was still at work when she entered. Madeleine's night things had already been laid out on the bed, and the maid was now organizing the contents of her dressing case on the dainty toilet table.

"Good evening, ma'am." Then she looked up, and her smile faded. "Oh, my lady. What has happened?"

Madeleine looked at the nightclothes, then looked longingly at the wardrobe, which stood open. Her cloak was hanging from a peg on the door. "Well, I have done it, Eliza," she said, going to the wardrobe for the cloak. "I have told Geoff the truth."

Eliza cut a strange, sidelong look at her. "Told him what truth, ma'am, exactly?"

Madeleine exhaled a deep breath. "That Mr. MacLachlan is his real father," she answered.

In all the years they had been together, she and Eliza had never really spoken of it. It had not been necessary; a healthy, eight-pound babe delivered far from home scarcely six months after one's wedding day could mean but one thing.

"I realize, Eliza, that you have long known the truth," said Madeleine, folding the cloak over her arm. "And now Geoff knows it. He has the right, do you not think, to know his father?"

At last, Eliza looked up. "Aye, perhaps," she said, "but does Mr. MacLachlan deserve the child?"

Lamely, Madeleine lifted her shoulders. "I think, Eliza, that he truly does," she said quietly. "And I think it was wrong of me to leave him all those years ago."

Eliza bristled. "With all respect, my lady, it's not like you went willingly," she answered. "No one remembers so well as I those weeks you lay ill, half-hysterical with grief, unable to eat nor sleep. 'Tis a wonder you carried the child at all. And why did he not come for you if he truly wished to be your husband?"

Eliza's words brought back some horrible memories. "Apparently, he was not able to come for me," Madeleine whispered. "He . . . he was injured. My father's doing, I collect."

"Injured?" said the maid skeptically.

"Yes, very badly, I collect," Madeleine said. "I begin to wonder . . . yes, I begin to wonder if that was not my father's intent. To leave me a young widow. I have not learnt the details, but I mean to have them soon enough. In any case, when he was well again, he—well, he chose not to pursue me. It was his pride, I daresay."

Eliza's gaze fell to the open dressing case in the chair. "Well, I have never liked him, ma'am," she admitted quietly. "In the village, they say he *is* prideful, and that he bankrupts men for sport—or so Mrs. Drexel heard. And that he's rich as Croesus, too, and owed money by half the *ton,* who live in fear he'll come to collect it, for most of 'em haven't a pot to piss in—begging your pardon, ma'am."

"Well, they haven't," Madeleine agreed with a muted smile. "So perhaps they are merely envious?"

Eliza looked a little ashamed. "Well, I wondered at that, too," she admitted. "For Mr. Phipps speaks ever so highly of him."

"Does he indeed?"

Eliza nodded. "Oh, he admits Mr. MacLachlan is a hard man, and a bitter one, too. But honest, he says. Very honest, and fair to the people who work for him. But ruthless with anyone who crosses him." She lifted her head and caught Madeleine's eyes. "Still, I suppose that is all one can ask, don't you think, ma'am? That he be honest? I suppose he would make a good father for a boy who had none?"

Madeleine managed to nod. "I am sure of it, Eliza," she said. "I would never risk Geoff's happiness. Do not worry about what other people say. Now I am going out for a walk around that lovely loch. Otherwise, I think I shall go mad. I want you to go upstairs to bed, all right?"

"Yes, ma'am," she said, bobbing a curtsy. "You will be careful, my lady, will you not?"

"Yes, thank you." Madeleine nodded. "But the moon is bright. I shall be perfectly safe."

The maid was halfway to the door when Madeleine stopped her. "Eliza, one last question, if I may?"

"Yes, ma'am?" She turned.

"You spoke some weeks back about Florette," Madeleine began. "Did you—did you know anything, Eliza, that you did not tell me?"

Eliza's eyes flared with alarm. "No, ma'am," she said. "I told all I knew—for a fact, I mean."

Madeleine narrowed her gaze. "What does that mean, 'for a fact'?"

Eliza shrugged innocently. "Well, 'twas said she wrote to the master, ma'am," said the maid. "And Aunt Esther said that after a time, the master became quite put out over it."

"How many times, Eliza?" Madeleine demanded. "How often? And where?"

She shook her head. "I'm sure I don't know, ma'am," she confessed. "Well—to London, I reckon? Aunt Esther said that Mr. Trout—that was the London butler, you'll recall—anyways, Trout used to say that the master would turn dark as a thunderhead when her letters came and go about in an ill mood for days after."

"I see."

Eliza looked a little sheepish. "And Aunt Esther took it into her head, ma'am, that the master was sending the girl money," she admitted. "Why she thought that, I cannot say, but she was never one to make things up."

Madeleine frowned. "I think I know why. I think . . . I think Florette was helping Father. And later, possibly blackmailing him."

"Blackmail, ma'am?" But Eliza did not seem surprised.

Madeleine considered it. She had barely known Florette. The girl had been hired by her aunt after Madeleine's arrival in London, for her father had insisted that a French maid would lend Madeleine a sense of style.

Madeleine did not think Florette had started out as a spy. She had been far too complicit in Madeleine's romance with Merrick for that to have been the case. But faced with the possibility of being turned off without a reference, no doubt it had been all too easy for the girl to become a turncoat.

"Eliza, did you ever hear anyone call Florette 'Flora'?"

The maid shook her head. "No, ma'am. But they're the same, aren't they? One French, the other English?"

Slowly, Madeleine nodded. "More or less," she agreed. "I think Florette stayed behind in Gretna Green. When I asked for her, my father told me he had turned her off. But I think he lied. I think he left her there to spy on Mr. MacLachlan, and . . . and to do other wickedness, too."

"Oh, that I do not doubt," grumbled Eliza. "Always looking out for herself, that one was."

"And yet I found nothing from Florette in Papa's correspondence," Madeleine mused. "Indeed, I found nothing at all about me, or my . . . well, my strange situation."

"Well, begging your pardon, ma'am," said Eliza. "But if you didn't find those things in his files—things you *know* existed—then perhaps they weren't there for a reason."

Madeleine managed a weak smile. "Yes, I fear you are right," she murmured. "Thank you, Eliza, for your candor."

With her cloak still over her arm, Madeleine made her way back through the twisting corridors and down to the castle's forecourt. The front door was unlocked, the stone courtyard awash in moonlight. Soon Madeleine was standing a good distance along the shore, and looking up at the back of the castle.

Lady Annis's rooms in the tower were easily identified; lamplight still shone from the high, narrow windows. Her own room she could see, and Geoff's—well, that was less certain, for all the lights were out on that side. Fleetingly, she wondered which bedchamber was Merrick's. But that was really none of her business, was it? She had long ago forfeited her rights to his life's details.

Madeleine tossed the light cloak about her shoulders and set off along the loch's even shoreline. Give her odd, restless mood tonight, sleep was unlikely. Far better to take in the cool evening air and hope that it would soothe her. She realized that her relationship with Merrick was damaged, perhaps irreparably. She hoped she had not just done a similar damage to Geoff. It occurred to her belatedly that it might have been unwise for her to leave the boy alone with his father so soon. She had lobbed an emotional mortar shell into a twelve-year-old child's life, then left him to deal with the aftermath.

No. No, it was not so dire as all that. Merrick would know what to say to Geoff. Whatever his failings as a husband, he was going to be a good father. She knew it with a mother's instinct. Perhaps he did not yet love Geoff as she did, but he valued the boy on a level so deep she could not but respect it. He had set aside the most important thing in his life—his beloved business—to bring the child on this long journey. No man did that lightly, and she had a feeling Merrick had done it far less lightly than most.

She stood almost directly opposite the little island now; it was easy to make it out in the shimmering moonlight. On the path up ahead there was something like a little boathouse—just a shed, really, with a planked pier which ran out into the water for a few feet on tall, rickety pilings. Madeleine made her way to it, and stepped lightly onto the planking. It felt perfectly sound. Gingerly, she walked its length, and feeling not so much as a quiver, sat down in the pool of moonlight at the very end. Then she set her forehead to her knees and bawled like a newborn calf.

Between those great, gasping sobs, Madeleine tried to figure out just what it was she cried for. For the first time in years, she had begun to feel there was a hope for Geoff's happiness. No one here had treated her with true unkindness, not even Sir Alasdair. Merrick had been civil, even a little protective whilst they had been with his grandmother. Life could have been—indeed, often *had* been—so much worse.

But the truth was, Madeleine was beginning to understand that a place in Geoff's life must be carved out for Merrick. She would be faced with seeing the man on a regular, if not frequent, basis. Suddenly, the loneliness and the aching sense of grief all washed over her again, drowning her in sorrow. Dear God, what had she done? And was there any possible way of undoing it?

She gave in to the tears for a good ten minutes, then forced herself to stop. It was a little survival mechanism which she had learned long ago: have a good, long cry, then get up and get on about the business of life. No one ever died from unrequited love. She had lived better than a dozen years in just such a state. She withdrew her handkerchief and summarily dried her tears, then knelt to dip it into the loch so that she might bathe her face. The water was shockingly cold but wonderfully refreshing to her hot, tear-stained cheeks.

Suddenly, a little bump beneath her recalled Madeleine to the present. She looked down to see that a boat—well, something remotely like a boat—was moored to the little pier below, and it was this which had bumped against the front piling. She set her head to one side and studied it. It was a raft, she thought. Or some sort of large, flat punt? Two impossibly long poles lay tied along one side. But where would one go in such a thing? She looked up, and straight ahead.

To the island.

The island was just large enough for a picnic on a leisurely afternoon. Fleetingly, she considered it, then cast the thought away at once. She really did not know how to use such a contraption. Most likely she would drift about in the loch all night, or drown herself trying to get out. And then where would Geoff be? He would have a new father and no mother. She gave a hysterical little laugh and pressed the back of her hand to her mouth.

It was then that she saw the light. Not some eerie specter across the water, but a yellow shimmer approaching from behind the boathouse.

"Madeleine?" Merrick's whisper came out of gloom. "Madeleine! What are you doing out here?"

She turned, deftly moving her skirts. "I might ask the same of you," she said, as he strode the length of the little pier.

He hung his lantern from one of the pilings. "Geoff and I saw you go out," he explained. "I was concerned. The loch can be more treacherous than it looks."

"Have I a pair of spies on my heels, then?"

He gave a muted smile but did not look her in the eyes. "We were at the window with the lamp out," he said quietly. "We were studying the night sky."

Madeleine smiled up at him. "Geoff has an insatiable interest in astronomy," she warned. "If you know anything at all of the constellations, he will pepper you with questions."

He knelt beside her and set one knee to the planking. "I could show him little tonight," he confessed. "The moonlight makes it impossible."

Madeleine looked up at it. "It will soon be full, will it not?"

He shrugged and set one hand on his thigh—a thigh which was encased in the elegant, well-cut trousers he had worn to dinner. "A day or two past, I think."

He studied the moon quietly for a moment, his eyes narrowed as if he watched instead the sun.

"How did you find Geoff?" She blurted out the words too fast, anxious to fill the silence.

"Well enough. A little confused, perhaps. And tired from all the travel."

"He is not . . . oh, I don't know! Angry with me?"

Merrick shook his head. "He accepts life's vagaries much as my grandmother does," he said. "Nothing ever really surprises them, you know. It is a part of . . . of how they are."

Madeleine sighed. "He said he knew I'd been keeping something from him," she admitted. "And that it was about him. But he wondered if it was 'something bad,' whatever that means."

"They can sense dishonesty, you know," he said. "No— I'm sorry—that was a poor choice of words. They can sense *dissemblance*. And half-truths. They . . . they *know* things. I tell you, Madeleine, it can be uncanny."

" 'They,' meaning people like Lady Annis and Geoff?" she suggested. "Two months past, you could not have convinced me of that."

"And now?

In the moonlight, she watched him. His eyes still had not met hers. "I . . . I believe it," she whispered. "I believe in many things now that I'd once thought impossible."

At last he turned to fully face her. "Was my grandmother right, Maddie?" he rasped, his voice suddenly thick with emotion. "Tell me. Should I . . . should I have come for you?"

Her eyes widened. "To Italy?"

"To the ends of the bloody earth," he said. "Were that where you had gone."

Madeleine just shook her head. "Merrick, we can none of us look back," she said. "What's done is done. Life goes on."

"Maddie, those are such clichés," he said. "*Should* I have come for you? Should I have taken you from Bessett? *Would you have come home with me?* Tell me, damn it. I need to know."

Madeleine twisted her hands in her lap, feeling like a seventeen-year-old girl again. "Oh, Merrick!" she whispered. "I just don't know! By then I was so confused."

The truth was, however, she likely *would* have gone with him. Yes, to the ends of the earth. But what good would such truths do now? She was beyond bitterness and hate. She had no wish to see Merrick rip himself apart with guilt over an old woman's harsh words.

He looked squarely at her then, his eyes tinged with grief and not a little remorse. "It is so much easier, Maddie, when I can lay all the blame at your doorstep."

She shook her head. "And what of me, Merrick?" she asked. "Your grandmother does not mince words. Did I dishonor my vows? I . . . I thought not. I thought I'd no other choice but to marry Lord Bessett and go away."

"But why, Maddie?" This time, there was no anger in his words. "Why? Was there . . . no other choice?"

"None that I could see," she whispered. "Merrick, I do not ask that you forgive me. If you wish to wrap your anger around you like a shroud—which is what I fear you have been doing—then it is none of my business. But now you want a part in Geoff's life, and I . . . well, I believe that would be best for Geoff, too. I will sacrifice anything, Merrick, for my child's welfare, even my peace of mind."

He looked at her beseechingly. "What are you saying, Maddie?"

"Merrick, I was just seventeen," she whispered. "I had no knowledge, really, of the world. And I was—or believed I was—a prisoner in my father's home. He had carried me back from Scotland by force with every intention of finding some way to marry me off to serve his political purposes."

"Oh, Maddie!"

She reached out and took hold of his wrist. "And then I learnt that I was with child, Merrick," she went on. "Can you comprehend my fear for the babe I carried? I had not heard from you in two months. My letters to you in London went unanswered—assuming they got out of Father's house, which I now doubt."

"Christ Jesus."

"Bessett offered me a way out, and a name for my child. What else was I to do? I was not so brave as your grandmother would have wished. Some might say I behaved quite spinelessly. But I meant it then as I mean it now: no sacrifice was or is too great if it serves my child. And that marriage was my sacrifice."

"As I am now your sacrifice?" he asked, his voice hoarse. "Do you hate me so much, Maddie, that you wish never to have to see me again? Will it pain you to have to see me on your doorstep?"

She shook her head. "We must find a way to go on."

"All right," he said softly. "So what is it, then? Am I a long-lost cousin? The boy's godfather? What lie are we going to tell society, Maddie?"

"Society can go to hell," she said. "Merrick, why did you never tell me what my father did to you?"

He looked at her blankly.

"That scar," she said, her voice firm. "He did that, and worse. I know, because that woman at the inn told me."

He cursed beneath his breath and sat silent and stoic for what seemed an eternity.

Well, damn him, Madeleine thought. She would sit out here until dawn, if that was what it took to get an answer from the man.

"Maddie, I don't know," he finally said. "And what difference does it make now? I told myself that you had sided with your father over me. That you didn't wish to hear ill spoken of him. But perhaps that was just a part of my—what did Granny call it?—yes, my overweening pride. Or perhaps it was a part of that shroud of anger you just accused me of having."

"Perhaps it was," she murmured. "And I did love my father, Merrick. Even until the last, I believed he had my best interests at heart. But . . . but he did not, did he?"

Merrick cleared his throat a little roughly. "I was not much of a catch, Maddie," he admitted. "I am sure he felt that you could have chosen from amongst a hundred better, richer men."

"How frightfully broad-minded of you," she said dryly. "But I do not think that gave him leave to have you beaten half to death. And I think we both know now that he would have married me to the devil himself had it better served his needs."

Merrick's hands clenched into fists. "Damn it, Maddie, do you realize that all this—or the worst of it—could have been avoided had I done one simple thing?"

"What?"

"If I had just told Alasdair what we were about," he answered grimly. "I should have asked for his carriage and told him we meant to marry. But for once in my accursed life, I wanted to be the dashing rogue. I wanted to be . . . I don't know—I wanted to be Alasdair, I suppose. And so I pinched his carriage and thought it a great romantic adventure."

"Oh, Merrick!"

He looked at her almost shamefacedly. "Had I told him, Maddie, he would have come looking for me when I didn't return home. He would have come to Gretna Green, and he would have been sharp enough to see which way the wind blew and put a stop to your father's tricks. But I told no one. Aye, perhaps Granny was right about that overweening pride after all."

"They left you badly hurt," she said.

"They left me half-dead," he said grimly. "And they meant to. But I remember nothing of those weeks, Maddie. The only clear memory I have is of hiking up that long carriage drive to your father's house, half-drunk on laudanum to stanch the pain."

"Hiking?" If ever he'd come to Sheffield, this was the first she had heard of it.

"Actually, I think I was on horseback," he admitted. "The bone in my leg had not fully healed, and my hip was—well, a damned mess. But in my mind, I walked. In my dreams, that is how I remember it."

"I never knew."

He shrugged as if it did not matter. "Well, it did no good, for your father was gone, and you had remarried, they claimed. Two weeks earlier."

"Dear God." It was all sinking in on her now. *Two weeks?* "Merrick, do you remember my maid?"

"Florette?" he said, his tone curious. "Oh, aye. Painfully well."

"I think she was Papa's spy. He left her behind in Gretna Green."

"Aye, to wait for my funeral, no doubt," he said darkly. "She swore to me, Maddie, that you had changed your mind. She brought your father down to the stables, and . . . and she told me you had had a change of heart."

"Dear God," she said again. "And she is the one who cut that page from the register. I am sure of it now. The names are too similar. Flora. Florette. Papa must have paid her."

They sat in silence for a moment, Madeleine turning all the ugly truths around in her mind. Yes, many people had conspired against them. But there was a part of Madeleine which believed that true love would always prevail—and that if it did not, then it was not true enough. Or that you were not brave enough or strong enough to deserve it.

"Well, this is old history now, is it not?" she said quietly. "A lifetime has passed since then."

He turned to look at her. "Aye," he finally said. "A lifetime."

Madeleine shifted her skirts, half-meaning to rise and walk back to the castle. "Well, I am glad, I suppose, that we have had this talk," she said. "Perhaps it is no less tragic, but I am glad that we have laid some old ghosts to rest."

"I am glad, too," he said, but his voice was hollow.

It was time to change the subject. Time to begin as she meant to go on—as Geoff's mother, and, were it to prove remotely possible, as Merrick's friend. She forced a more conversational tone. "Tell me, what is that little island there?" She lifted her hand and pointed into the gloom.

"It is a little island," he answered.

Madeleine forced herself to laugh. "Wretch!" she said. "Can one go there? Is that what the little barge is for?"

Merrick peered over the edge of the pier. "I would hardly call that a barge," he answered. "It is naught but a sort of raft which is kept for summer entertainments. But yes, it can be punted out to the island or simply set adrift on the water."

She leapt to her feet. "Take me out there," she said impulsively.

"Now?" He looked up at her as if she'd lost her mind. "In the dark?"

She reached a hand down to him. "It is not dark," she said. "The moon is so bright one cannot see the stars. You said as much yourself."

With a look of grave reluctance, he let her draw him to his feet. He looked down at the raft, and shrugged. "Can you swim?"

"Reasonably well," she said. "Certainly I can thrash about and scream for help most efficiently."

"Aye? Good enough, then."

He was actually going to do it? Madeleine was inexplicably elated.

Merrick grabbed of the piling above the raft, and stepped down with his lithe grace. It dipped beneath his weight, but he balanced neatly on his stronger leg, turned, and offered a hand to Madeleine.

It was a little awkward, and a little frightening, too, to step so far down onto what was surely an unsteady surface. But she had asked, so she gathered her skirts in one hand, hiked them up, and stepped. Somewhere in mid-step, however, Merrick caught her around the waist with an impossibly strong arm and lifted her neatly into the center. She landed with a loud shriek, then quickly clamped a hand across her mouth.

By the flickering lamplight, she could see his eyes dance with humor. "You'll have them all rushing out here to rescue us, Maddie," he said. "I am not perfectly sure how I would explain the fact that two rational, responsible adults are about to do such an impulsive, foolhardy thing."

She held his gaze a moment. "But one cannot truly savor life without having at least a little danger in it," she murmured. "How long has it been, Merrick, since you did anything reckless?"

"Well, that would be—" He pondered it for a moment, "—about twelve years, eleven months, and . . . oh, two days?"

"Ah," she said quietly. "You are speaking of the day we left London for Gretna Green."

Her heart sank a little at the thought. But he probably spoke the truth. It probably was the last impulsive, irresponsible thing he had done. Or at least it must seem so to him. She cleared her throat sharply. "This rides frightfully high in the water," she said. "Do you think it will turn over?"

"Impossible," he said, taking her hand again. "Look here, sit down in the center, and you'll not feel so much as a list."

She sat. "What about you?"

"Oh, I'll manage well enough," he said, kneeling to unfasten the mooring. "I've been doing this since I was a lad. Now, what does my lady command? To the island?"

She considered it. "I wish to see it, yes."

"Your wish is my command."

Soon Merrick had a pole in hand and was pushing them away from shore.

"Will that thing really touch the bottom?" she asked uneasily.

He laughed. "In a few spots, I pray," he said. "We are on the shallow end of the loch, and it is not especially deep this time of year."

Thus reassured, Madeleine set her hands behind her, leaned back, and looked up into the moonlit evening. With the night sky drifting above her, and the rhythmic *slosh, slosh* of Merrick's exertions, the raft did indeed feel perfectly steady—and delightfully relaxing.

"The current tends always to pull toward shore," he said. "I'll punt into deeper water, then we'll just drift round the loch—I hope."

They slid across the water in silence for a time. What little current there was could be clearly seen in the moonlight. On deep, smooth strokes, Merrick drove the raft forward until, eventually, the exertion wore down his sense of propriety. With the island but a few yards away, he laid down the pole, and stripped off his coats, tossing them down beside her. A cloud of musky male scent tinged with something soapy and spicy settled over her for an instant.

"You have changed your cologne," she said on impulse.

He hesitated for a moment, and half turned to look at her. "Have I?"

She reclined onto her forearms, and looked up at him. "Yes, I noticed it that night at—" Embarrassed at the recollection of what they had done at Lord Treyhern's, she faltered.

"Yes, I comprehend," he said dryly, taking up his pole again. "I lied to you earlier, did I not?"

"Lied?"

He would not look at her now. "When you asked me what was the last reckless thing I had done."

Madeleine pondered it for a moment. She rolled onto one elbow and looked at him quite directly. "Merrick, did you never do anything reckless unless . . . well, unless *I* was involved?"

"No," he said pensively. "No, Madeleine, I think not." He did not miss a beat, however, the strong muscles of his back working rhythmically with his arms to punt the raft smoothly along the water.

She watched his muscles work, the moonlight white on his linen shirt. "Well in any case," she finally went on, "your old cologne smelled more of lime. But this one—" She sniffed the air almost indelicately. "Yes, it is a woodsy-nutmeg sort of scent."

He laughed. "It is whatever Phipps bought," he said. "I can assure you no thought went into the matter."

Merrick's every sense was acutely aware of Madeleine's

presence. He was a little astounded by the fact that she still remembered his old cologne. He could feel her eyes upon him, and he wondered what was on her mind. Was she thinking, as he most certainly was, of their intense, almost desperate lovemaking in Treyhern's pantry? The memory of it should have been laughable, yet it was anything but.

He shook off the thought, and drove the pole deep. He was still striking the bottom, but barely. Madeleine had surprised him tonight with her sudden revelation to Geoffrey. He had almost looked forward to more of a skirmish on the issue. He was not a quarrelsome man by nature, but where Madeleine was concerned—well, any sort of dialogue, any kind of emotion, no matter how vitriolic or passionate, seemed better than nothing.

But this time, it was over. She would sacrifice anything, she had said, even her own peace of mind, for her child's happiness. Well, he had no wish to strip away that last vestige of comfort from her. So far as he could see, she'd known damned little of it. What he wanted to do was . . . well, to salvage something of this mess they had made. What he wanted was . . . *her*.

Was there a prayer? Any hope at all?

He was sorely regretting his cruel words to her that afternoon in the inn. He had called her a shrew and a she-wolf, and possibly worse. He had been out of his mind with anger toward her father and his machinations, and he had been angry with Maddie for doubting his motivations for marrying her. His audacity that afternoon was trumped only by his earlier threats, holding their marriage lines over her head, and then threatening to exercise his conjugal rights.

"We are in deep water now, are we not?" Her soft voice cut into his consciousness.

Oh, she did not know the half of it. "Aye, very deep."

"I do not think the pole is touching the bottom."

He stood, he realized, on the edge of the raft, the pole still clutched tightly in his hands. "No, but it quickly becomes shallow again as we approach the island."

"Merrick, why do you not put that down and come sit beside me for a while?"

He looked down at her. "Do you not wish me to push us forward?"

She shook her head. "No, I think you should sit down," she said. "Let's just see where we go from here."

Merrick almost laughed aloud. He believed a man went only where he pushed to go; Maddie thought they should just drift a while. There was a hidden meaning there, he feared, could he but figure it out. He laid the pole down, bound it tightly, then sat down beside her. A strange silence fell over them, and for what seemed on eternity, neither spoke.

Eventually, Maddie reclined on her forearms again. The trim, perfect ankles which peeped from beneath her skirts were crossed casually, as if she relaxed in the grass at a family picnic. He followed suit, pushing his coat against the low gunwale, and moving as if to stretch out on one elbow. But had not quite gained his balance when the raft jerked hard, throwing him half on top of her.

Madeleine shrieked, and grabbed him around the waist.

"Bloody hell!" said Merrick. He looked up through a shock of disordered hair at the tree branch hanging out over them. "Well, we have drifted into your little island, Maddie."

Pinned beneath him, she gurgled with laughter. Merrick shifted his weight to lift himself away, then made the mistake of looking down at her. And just like that, it happened. Her smile faded to something entirely different. He was suddenly and very acutely aware of her body beneath his, of the curve of her hip, and the rise and fall of her chest, much of which was bared by the dinner gown she still wore.

Madeleine made no move to disentangle herself. And she had stopped laughing. Instead, her eyes were searching his face. Against his better judgment, he drew the back of his hand down her cheek. "Oh, Lord," he whispered. Her eyes went soft, and the muscles of her long, elegant throat worked up and down. He lowered his head, and tentatively kissed her.

"Maddie," he whispered against the corner of her mouth.

Beneath him, she exhaled on a sigh, and let one hand slide from his waist to his back, gently binding them together. Almost of its own volition, his arm circled around her, until his hand cradled the back of her head. He bent his head to hers, and kissed her again. Her lips were warm and pliant. Expectant. Eager. He molded his mouth over hers with a gentleness he had not known in thirteen long years, and Maddie melted against him, her head going back as she opened to him.

He thrust his tongue deep, and was lost. Lost in the velvety sweetness of her mouth. His eyes closed, and the world spun away. Everything moved with exquisite lethargy then. They kissed for what could have been hours. But eventually, her hands found his cravat, and drew it from his neck.

His hands cradled her face. Her slender fingers slid beneath the waist of his trousers, and slowly drew out his shirttails. But all the while she kissed him, lifting her head from the boat with a sweet eagerness. Their mouths met, again and again, until her lips were softly swollen, and her eyes were needy.

He lifted himself a little away. "Maddie, we—"

"Sh!" She lifted her head to follow him, brushing her lips lightly over his. "Don't speak. Don't stop. Just . . ."

"Drift?" he suggested. "And see where we go?"

"I know where I am going," she whispered. "At least for tonight, if you will take me."

He kissed her again, hot and open-mouthed, and this time, it was not slow. Beneath them, the raft gently rolled with the water's motion. They came apart panting, and holding one another's gaze as if they both feared the moment might vanish and bring them back down to earth.

"Undress me," she whispered.

He looked at her incredulously, but hope already burned in his heart. "Now?" he asked, his voice quiet, and surprisingly steady. "Here in broad—"

"—broad moonlight, yes." Her eyes were certain. "Take off every stitch, Merrick, slowly, just as you used to do. I want to feel your hands on me again. And I want to know . . . I want to know if I have changed in your eyes."

He drew one finger lightly down her cheek. "You have not changed, Maddie," he rasped. "You never will."

Her gaze broke from his. "I am older," she said. "I have borne a child. And gained a few pounds. But I am hoping that the moonlight will cast it all in a romantic light."

"You have ripened from a girl into a woman," he said, his hand going to the fastening of her cloak.

He was going to do it, he realized. He was going to do

just as she asked. He was going to undress her in the moonlight. It was madness. And would he regret it? Perhaps. But given even half an opportunity, he was going to kiss and suckle her every inch, and make love to her with his hands and his mouth and his cock until she cried out with pleasure. If half the castle came running at the racket, so be it.

When the cloak was unfastened, he spread it to the sides. With one finger, he drew down the sleeve of her gown, kissing down her neck and around the turn of her shoulder as each precious inch was unveiled. Beneath him, she shivered with delight, and skimmed her hands beneath his shirt, and up the damp, rough flesh of his back. If she felt the scars, she gave no signal.

"Take this off," she begged, urging the shirt higher.

He lifted up, and obliged her, drawing it over his head and off his arms, barely breaking his gaze. She gave a soft gasp, and slid her palms up either side of his chest. "You are . . . glorious," she whispered. "And you—well, you are *not* the young man I married."

"No?"

"Most definitely not." She sat up, and with her hands on his shoulders, bent her head to nuzzle his neck, and lower. "No," she said between kissed. "He was a beautiful Highland laddie. But you—ah, you are a magnificent man."

He crooked his neck to look down at her. "Seen a great many of them, have you?"

"Hundreds," she said, still kissing his chest, his shoulders, even down his arms. "Have you any idea how many naked statues there are in Rome? Or Naples? Or Paris?"

"Aye, probably . . . hundreds."

"And none to hold a candle to you," she said, her tongue coming out to tease lightly at his nipple.

"Could they not?"

She laughed, and shook her head. "My father once warned me that your shocking propensity for manual labor would roughen your hands and coarsen your skin," she whispered. "But he forgot to mention . . . the benefits."

Her hands were caressing the muscles which layered his ribs. He looked well enough; he was a big, physically strong man in the prime of life. But he had never thought of his body as beautiful. And she mightn't either, should she get a glimpse of his back in good light.

"Maddie," he whispered, his voice a little urgent. "Maddie, love. Some of me is no' so beautiful."

She stopped what she was doing. "You are dropping your t's."

"What?"

"Your t's," she said again. "I can always tell when you are upset. You start to sound like a Scotsman."

He grinned. "Aye, well, that's wha' I am."

She looked at him with eyes which were soft with desire, yet alight with good humor. He had always loved that; he loved that she could feel and show half a dozen emotions at once. "What part of you is not beautiful?" she asked, dropping her gaze to his nether region. "And I surely know which part it's *not*."

"Aye, that part's the same," he admitted. "But my back—well, it looks a good deal worse than my face."

"Turn around."

God, he was a damned fool. But he had started it, and so he did as she insisted, sitting up, and half–turning away from her. There was a long, dead silence which seemed to stretch into infinity. Then Maddie set her lips to the turn of his neck. "Ah, Merrick," she whispered from behind him. "I am . . . sorry beyond words."

He gave a grunt of sarcastic laughter, but she said no more. Instead, she sat up and snuggled her breasts against his back. "Still beautiful," she murmured, setting her lips to the turn of his neck, then to his shoulder, and down the turn of his scarred back. Little butterfly kisses touched him everywhere as her arms came around him, and her hands slid up the curving muscles of his chest.

She rose onto her knees behind him, kissing and nuzzling until her clever fingers found his nipples and her mouth found his earlobe. She nibbled gently at first, then drew it into the warmth of her mouth, slowly suckling him in a seductive, shocking erotic imitation of . . . well, of something one did not use one's ears for.

He withdrew from her embrace and turned. "Maddie," he said. His shaking hands went to the buttons of her dress, methodically slipping them free. When it sagged loose, he pushed the fabric away with quick, desperate motions. *Slow,* he warned himself. *This time, go slow.*

He could see her breasts, her small erect nipples, through the fine lawn of her shift. His mouth sought them out, suckling until the fabric clung damply. He lifted his head, and the sight was enough to undo him. On his knees now, he undressed her a little less slowly, and a good deal less gracefully, than he might have wished. And when she was naked, he urged her back into the pile of clothing.

"Lord, Maddie," he said. "You are a vision of heaven."

In the moonlight, she closed her eyes almost shyly. He looked down to see that his trousers were drawn tight over his groin, his erection straining hard against the fine fabric. Maddie's intent was clear. He toed off his shoes and began to hitch loose his buttons.

When he looked up again, Maddie was watching him, and there was an unmistakable heat kindling in her eyes. She sat up abruptly, her hands going to the close of his trousers. Wordlessly, she unfastened the last button, then eased one hand down his belly, down to touch him. It was a small gesture, tame compared to the greediness of the women he was used to. But inexplicably, his breath seized.

With one slender hand, she tormented him, whilst the other pushed away at the wool and linen until the strength of his erection jutted free. His trousers bagging to his knees now, he bowed back, and let her touch him, reveling in the slightest brush of her fingers. The brushes became more intense. Soon she was stroking the heated length of his cock, and the other hand had slipped even lower.

On a groan, he seized her wrist. "Maddie love, you need to stop," he said between gritted teeth.

She said nothing, but her hand stilled. Then he felt her lips on his collarbone, and realized she was fully on her knees, cleverly balancing with the raft's faint motions. He shuddered when she took his nipple between her small, white teeth. And then she moved lower, kissing the dusting of hair on his belly, bent deeper, and kissed his taut, hot flesh. His whole body trembled with delight.

She had touched him this way but once, long ago, and he had been both ashamed and grateful. Some ten days out of London, they had passed the night in a charming little wayside inn near Penrith, and had dinner brought up to their rooms. With it had come perhaps a little more wine than was wise. Afterward she had begged him to tutor her in the ways of less conventional lovemaking. Perhaps selfishly, he had obliged her. He had allowed her to do things that—well, that no lady should ever be expected to do.

But Madeleine had been an eager student, almost as eager as she was now. Her tongue came out and stroked lightly down his length. "Merrick?" she murmured, her lips pressed to the tender flesh at the joining of his thigh. "Do you remember . . . this? May I do it?"

He caught her wrist again. "I remember," he said.

She looked up at him, all wide, moonlit eyes and soft innocence. He couldn't say yes. But God help him, he couldn't say no. Madeleine smiled and bent her head. Her lips came over his crimson head, making his knees shake. With one hand at the base of his cock, she bent so far forward he could see her dainty little toes peeking out from beneath her bare buttocks, then she swallowed his flesh, inch by searing inch as they floated upon the loch. Bending lower and lower. Pushing him nearer and nearer to madness.

One of his hands went back to clutch at the low gunwale. She moved over him, tasting and sucking. Running the delightful tip of her tongue down his length, and sending a shudder through his body. When he gave an inhuman groan, Madeleine's hand slipped between his legs to cradle his ballocks as she intensified the motions of her mouth. Her other hand worked his shaft mercilessly, stroking down the slick wetness, over and over.

Merrick tipped back his head, and gasped through his teeth. "Maddie, oh!"

Fleetingly, she hesitated. "Should I sto—"

"No," he uttered. "Not . . . not *yet.*" His hands seized her shoulders as if to steady her, his arms corded by his efforts at restraint.

She pushed him gently away and returned to her erotic ministrations, every stroke a pleasure he had never known. There was pure beauty in her efforts and an element of sincere feminine pleasure. Raw, primitive lust throbbed in his veins and in his head. He opened his eyes, watching with awe as her lush, full mouth sliding over the head of his cock, devouring him with pleasure.

Her hand tightened, and she repeated the efforts. Merrick thrust his fingers into her hair, but whether to still her motions or urge her onward, he could not say. He had to fight the urge to thrust himself deeper. Somehow, he gritted his teeth and spoke.

"Enough, love," he choked. "Stop. *Truly.*"

She stopped, and rose up, never taking her hand away.

He pulled her to him, and kissed her passionately. "Lie down, Maddie, on the cloak," he whispered. "Let me love you."

Let him love her? What an absurd question. He had loved her always. He would never stop loving her.

Madeleine's eyes were warm, but a little uncertain. She rolled back onto her elbows, and he followed her down, reaching out to snag a fistful of clothes to pillow her head. The moonlight washed over her, lovely and pure. She was perfection, this woman. His wife. Her breasts were full, but not large, her nipples dusky pink circles against alabaster flesh. He kicked off what was left of his clothing and crawled almost predatorily over her.

He took her mouth, thrusting languidly inside with firm, sure strokes, offering a promise of pleasure to come.

He suckled her breasts, biting just hard enough to make her arch and cry out. Her fingers went to his buttocks, digging into the muscles as her breathing ratcheted up and up.

Merrick slid from her grasp, and set his hands flat against her ribs, then slid them up to capture her breasts as his mouth worked its way lower, all the way down, feasting on her delicate skin as he went. At the soft thatch of curls, he probed gently with his tongue, then slid deeper, seeking the treasure beneath. Her nipples were hard beneath his thumbs, her little nub erect and waiting. He stroked it ever so slightly, again and again, until Madeleine's breathing began to catch.

"Oh!" she whispered, when he set his hands firmly against her inner thighs.

He bent forward, urging her wider. "Madeleine," he murmured. "You are perfection."

She said nothing, but from the corner of his eye, he saw her hand fist hard in the fabric of the cloak. He slid his thumbs up the delightful creases of her thighs and opened her flesh to his hungry mouth. She made a soft sound of pleasure, and, gently, he slipped a finger into her snug sheath, taking great satisfaction when she rode down on his hand.

Lightly, he licked her clitoris again, and this time she did cry out, a breathy sound of agony and pleasure. Soon, she was shuddering. He worked her slowly with his tongue and his fingers until her cries were soft, and sweetly rhythmic in the darkness. Then one last stroke, and Madeleine called out his name. Once. Twice. And then she cried out and rocked beneath him for what seemed an eternity. When it was over, he rested his head against the softness of her thigh, and, strangely, he wanted to cry.

He did not. Instead, he mounted her, squeezed his eyes shut, and thrust inside on one perfect stroke. Madeleine's flesh was still contracting with pleasure all around him. And later, it was not perfectly clear to him where one orgasm had ended and another had begun. He knew only that he rode her furiously, his every muscle taut, his hips thrusting and thrusting, driving toward that perfect union, that moment of oneness he had missed for so long.

Her fingers dug into his flesh, spurring him on. His name was on her lips again, a soft sound of pleading in each breathless cry. Her body arched like a bowstring, her hips coming up to meet his, stroke for stroke. And then there was a splintering in his head, an infinite moment of pure pleasure and Maddie's beauty like a white light all around him. His head was thrown back, his mouth soundlessly open, aware of nothing save his own pleasure, and Madeleine almost sobbing beneath him.

Long moments later, they lay wrapped in each other's limbs, sated and weary. He reached over his head, found his coat, and tucked it around her body. She smiled, stuck her nose into the folds, and deliberately drew in his scent.

"I have always loved the way you smell," she whispered, her eyes closed. "It was the first thing, I think, that I noticed about you."

He crooked his head to look down at her. "The devil?" he murmured. "Not my wit and my charm?"

She laughed and opened her eyes. "You have wit and charm," she said quietly. "Why must you always poke fun at yourself, Merrick? Not everyone finds Alasdair so enchanting, you know."

He smiled and tucked her head beneath his chin.

Perhaps Madeleine was right. But for years, he had been unable to escape the belief that Alasdair would never have been fool enough to lose her. Women never left Alasdair. No, they flocked to him. Alasdair would have found a way to charm her, and her father, and all her distant kin, too, most likely.

Ah, but this was a moment of happiness, however fleeting. He wanted to savor it. Beside him, Madeleine tucked herself closer and laid her cheek against his chest. It was utter bliss, almost better than the lovemaking itself. They had drifted around to the back side of the island, which was steeped in shadows from the trees. Merrick tipped his head back, and looked up at the night sky. The moon was beautiful, a sharp and shining sphere on the wane. The air was cool, the gentle swell of the water infinitely soothing. He closed his eyes and was at peace.

Until Alasdair's voice came bellowing across the loch. "Lady Bessett?" he cried. "Hello! Hello!"

"Oh, God!" Madeleine jerked to her knees in a flash, looking like a schoolgirl caught in a prank, and tipping the raft precariously. Swiftly, she snagged her shift, and jerked it on. Merrick started to caution her to silence, but Alasdair's voice sounded worried.

"Lady Bessett!" he called. "Madeleine? Are you there? Are you all right?"

She looked like a startled deer. "I am fine," she called, frantically snatching her stays. "We—we are fine."

Merrick had his trousers on now. "We are fine, Alasdair. Just . . . punting about."

"Ah." Though the voice was quiet, the word still carried across the water.

Madeleine was pawing like a rabbit through the pile of clothing, extracting shoes and her gown and God only knew what else. Swiftly, Merrick snatched up their drawers, stockings, his neckcloth—anything not essentially obvious—and stuffed the wad down the back of his trousers. Then he yanked on his shirt and coats, cuffed up his trousers, and untied the pole.

In moments, Madeleine had made herself outwardly presentable, though Merrick feared Alasdair would have little doubt as to what they had been up to. He punted slowly to shore as Madeleine repinned her hair. But as they approached the pier, he could see Alasdair in the puddle of yellow lamplight, still staring out across the water, his expression stricken. Something white dangled from his hand.

"Good heavens, Sir Alasdair," said Madeleine brightly as the raft gently bumped the piling. "You gave us quite a start."

Alasdair reached his empty hand down to help her onto the pier. Merrick began to tie up the raft while glowering up at his brother. What a damned intrusion this had been.

But Alasdair had eyes only for Madeleine. "I heard a noise on the loch," he said, his voice fretful. "A—A sort of human cry. And so I came out, and made my way along the shore. When I got here, I found this lying on the planking."

He was holding a lady's handkerchief in his hand. It was sodden and rather disheveled, but even in the lamplight, Merrick could see the dainty M embroidered on its corner.

Madeleine snatched it. "Oh, thank you, Sir Alasdair," she said. "I certainly did not mean to worry you."

Merrick shoved his feet into his shoes. That done, he stepped up onto the wooden planking. Alasdair grinned down at his cuffed trousers. "You look fourteen again, old boy," he said. "Still playing the Pirate King?"

Merrick looked up at him grimly. "Aye, something like that."

Finally, his brother blanched. "Ah," he said. "I collect I have intruded."

"Not at all," said Madeleine hastily. "We were just on our way in. We were laughing. A little raucously. We apologize."

"Laughing. Yes, of course." Alasdair was nodding like an idiot and trying to keep his mouth from twitching into a grin. "The loch is lovely by moonlight, is it not, Lady Bessett?"

"Very lovely indeed," said Madeleine briskly. "Thank you, Merrick, for that delightful excursion."

"It was my pleasure."

She yawned almost theatrically. "I believe that I am for bed now," she said. "Merrick?"

"I am not yet tired," he said. "Go, by all means. Take my lantern."

A look of uncertainty flitted across her face. He could see her desire to linger, and Merrick was beyond giving a damn what Alasdair thought. But for Madeleine, propriety won out.

"I know my way like a cat in the dark, Lady Bessett, if you trust me?" Alasdair offered his arm, and, together, they strolled sedately down the pier.

Grimly, Merrick set one shoulder against the piling and watched them until they had vanished from the flood of lamplight. Damn Alasdair to hell for interrupting!

Though admittedly, his concern had not been misplaced. The loch could be dangerous to those unfamiliar with its secrets. But it had felt to Merrick as though he and Madeleine were so close to . . . well, to *something*. An understanding? A compromise? He was not sure. But he was sure she still desired him as much as he still desired her. And damn it, they were husband and wife. He had a right to . . .

No. He had a right to nothing. His grandmother had been correct. He had let his pride, not Maddie, play him false all those years ago. Whatever Maddie's mistakes, he had to remember her youth and inexperience. He thought again of Lady Ariane Rutledge, a mere child at seventeen—and she was a sophisticate compared to Madeleine at that age. Was he to punish Madeleine forever for her choices? Was there anything left of their marriage save for that damned piece of paper he kept threatening her with?

Suddenly, in those few short moments, Merrick was forced to weigh the options for the rest of his life. Was it to be the Bess Bromleys of this world? Was it to be heat and darkness? Or sweetness and light? Pleasure? Pain? Could a man so jaded have a love that was pure?

With Madeleine, he could. He was sure of it now. But he recalled an old saying of his grandmother's; one which he'd always thought trite. *If a man loves a thing, he maun sometimes let it go.* It no longer seemed so trite. He took down his lamp and returned to the castle.

Fifteen minutes later, he stood at Madeleine's door. Rapping softly with the back of his hand, he waited impatiently. She opened the door in her nightdress, her blond hair down about her shoulders.

Her green eyes widened, joyously, he thought. "Merrick."

He managed a smile and handed her the lace-trimmed drawers and neatly folded stockings. "I thought I'd best not let Phipps find these on the morrow."

Blushing, she took them.

"Madeleine, may I come in?" he said. "I have something else, which I should like to give you. Or *show* you, perhaps, is the better word?"

Her eyebrows lightly lifted. "Yes," she said, pulling the door wide. "Yes, of course."

It seemed strange to see her in her nightclothes again. Her hair swung nearly to her waist, and her bare toes peeped from beneath the white lace hem of her gown.

He turned his attention away. There would be other times to admire her hair and her toes—if he were a very, very lucky man. And there was only one way to find out. He felt like Alasdair betting the whole of his fortune on one turn of the cards—except that this was so much more than his fortune. This was his life.

A lamp burned on her dressing table. He extracted his pocket case and withdrew the precious paper within. She followed him to the dressing table. "Merrick?" she said sharply. "What . . . what are you doing?"

Merrick sent up one last prayer, curled the document around his finger, and dropped it down the glass chimney. Her hand darted for the lamp. "Merrick! My God!"

He seized her hand and jerked it back, lest she burn herself in some foolish act of gallantry.

They watched wordlessly as the corners of their marriage lines curled into hot, glittering cinders, then burst into full flame. In moments, it was over. A pile of gray ash lay around the wick, and the walls of the chimney were black with soot.

Madeleine had set her fingertips over her mouth, her eyes wide. "Merrick," she whispered. "Dear heaven, why did you do such a thing? And why do it now, after keeping it all these years?"

Merrick stared at what was left of his marriage. A teaspoon of ash. Ah, well. Perhaps that was all it had ever been—or ever would be. However his gamble played out, he must live with the consequences; he no longer had an ace to stick up his sleeve.

He looked up from the lamp and caught the eyes of the woman who had once been his wife. "I kept it not because it was some sort of evidence, Maddie," he said, "but because it was all I had to cling to. Now it is gone. Our names in the marriage register are gone. Mr. and Mrs. MacLachlan are no more."

She had gone pale as if with fear. "Wh-What are you saying?"

"That I have no hold on you," he said quietly, "nor you on me."

"But I thought—I thought . . . "

He pinned her with his ice-blue gaze. "Aye what did you think, Maddie?" he whispered. "When I spoke my vows thirteen years ago, I meant them, and for all my life. I thought we would be together always, in the good times and bad."

She shook her head a little desperately. "I believed that, too."

He set his hands on her shoulders. "But you were young—too young—and you knew nothing of adversity. I *did* know it, Maddie. I knew it well, for I'd never been sheltered. But I had pride, and the sin of my temper to weigh me down. And now the whole damned mess is naught but cold ash, to be swabbed out tomorrow by one of Alasdair's footmen. It is over, Maddie. All we have between us now is what we choose."

She looked a little sick. "Merrick, I do not know . . . I hardly know . . . what to say."

He nodded. "Aye, so think on it, Maddie," he answered. "And for God's sake, do not let what we did tonight cloud your thinking. This is your second chance. You are a free woman. You may marry where you please, go where you please, and live as you please. I can force you to do nothing."

"But—But what about Geoff?"

Merrick shook his head. "The paper's burnt, Maddie," he said. "Whatever Geoff and I build now will be up to us."

He left her still standing by the dressing table, one hand pressed to her heart. He moved quickly, too, and shut the door behind, lest he do something unutterably foolish—like beg.

Chapter Twenty

There's nae fools like auld anes.

The following morning, Madeleine went down to breakfast to find the dining room empty, save for Sir Alasdair and his wife, who greeted her cheerfully. She did not miss, however, the odd, surreptitious looks Merrick's brother kept cutting in her direction when he thought she was not looking. He was quite likely regretting his late-night walk up the loch.

Perhaps it would have been better for all of them, Madeleine considered, had she and Merrick been left alone to finish what they had started. But finish it how? To what end? Madeleine did not know. Nonetheless, something about Sir Alasdair's interruption last night had turned Merrick's mood. She was still heartsick at the loss of their marriage lines. What on earth had he meant to prove?

Of course she should have been relieved. Without that little piece of paper, Merrick had no hold over her whatsoever. So why did she feel unutterable sadness instead of the total relief she should be experiencing?

Esmée came around to refill everyone's coffee, and somehow, Madeleine forced her attention to the meal. The three of them chatted amiably enough about the weather, a village festival which was just a fortnight distant, and about the ceaseless demands of keeping up an estate as old as Castle Kerr.

"Is that what's become of Merrick again?" asked Esmée. "Is he still off attending to that dyking?"

"Aye." Sir Alasdair set his coffee aside and dabbed at his mouth with his napkin. "Whoever said 'idle hands do the devil's work' was not speaking of my brother. We'll not likely see him again before dinner."

When she had finished breakfast, Madeleine excused herself and went to find Geoff so that she might take him up to Lady Annis's rooms. A maid was clearing away the last of their breakfast in the makeshift schoolroom. Mr. Frost, who had been given the morning off, declared his intention of walking to the village, some three miles distant.

Geoff was in a strange mood, almost elated. "Are you pleased to be spending some time this morning with Lady Annis?" asked Madeleine as they set off.

"Mamma, I am so excited," said the boy. "I have a hundred questions. Do you think Lady Annis will mind answering them?"

"Well, perhaps not more than a dozen or so today, my dear," said Madeleine with a laugh. "But I believe the purpose of our visit is so that you might ask your questions— all of them, eventually."

At the door, Madeleine bent down to neaten the boy's coat. "Well, Geoff, you look a very presentable pupil."

He surprised her then by darting forward and hugging her neck quite tightly in a way he had not done since he was a little boy. "Oh, it is going to be a wonderful day,

Mamma!" he said, his face aglow with happiness. "I just know it is. My life is about to change, forever and ever, and soon it will be perfect!"

Madeleine felt a sudden swell of joy. Could it be she had not fully comprehended just how much these visits with his great-grandmother meant to him? Yesterday he had seemed pleased, but not euphoric. But this morning, euphoric really was not too strong a word. Geoff really did seem a different child. Sending up a little prayer of thanks for Merrick's wisdom in bringing them here, she kissed the boy, then knocked upon the door.

After leaving Geoff with his great-grandmother, Madeleine felt at loose ends. Her happiness about Geoff dimmed just a little once the boy was gone. Feeling vaguely dejected, she decided to walk around the loch. A part of her wished to see it in the light of day, as if doing so might give her a certain clarity on all that had happened last night.

At the old boathouse, she lingered. The strange punt was still moored there, and the sight of it made Madeleine's heart lurch. They had shared so much there, she and Merrick. One night of honesty had seemed to undo so many years of doubt. And one night of lovemaking—well, it had merely fanned the flames of a fire that would never die. She was sure of it now.

To her mortification, the tears were pressing in on her again. Good Lord, what a watering pot she'd become! Hastily, she wiped them away and set off at a more energetic pace.

Her mood had little improved, however, by the time she circled around the bottom of the loch and across the little stone bridge to the other side. Halfway down the far shore, her spate of self-pity was cut short when she met Sir

Alasdair coming in the opposite direction. He did not look as though he was out for a casual stroll.

"Good morning, Lady Bessett," he said. "You are taking the fine Highland air, I see."

Madeleine sniffed discreetly. "Yes, your home is lovely, Sir Alasdair."

He turned and offered her his arm. "May I join you?" he asked. "I confess, you see, that I have deliberately waylaid you."

Madeleine had little choice but to take the proffered arm.

Sir Alasdair set off at a sedate pace, pausing from time to time to point out bits of flora or fauna he thought might interest his guest. There was an abundance of wildflowers along the meadow. Butterflies and hawkmoths flitted here and there. In the distance, the gorse and heather were about to burst into bloom. Alasdair rattled on, and Madeleine attended with half an ear.

Eventually, her disinterest seemed to dawn on him. "I perceive, Lady Bessett, that I owe you an apology," he finally said. "My intrusion last night was not welcomed."

Madeleine cut a sidelong glance at him. "It was not unwelcome, by any means," she said. "Besides, it hardly matters now."

He looked at her strangely. "My brother thought it mattered," he said. "Of that, you may be sure."

"Did he say as much?"

"Oh, he did not need to," said Alasdair. "The Black MacLachlan can speak volumes with his glower."

She gave him an odd half smile. "He is the Black, and you are what? The Fair?"

He laughed. "Aye, something like that."

They continued along the loch in silence for a time.

"You do not like me very much, do you, Sir Alasdair?" she finally said. "I am very sorry to have come here, and cut up your peace—and during your wedding trip, of all times. In my defense, I can only say that your brother insisted."

"Yes, I have been wondering about that," he said musingly. "And I do not in any way dislike you, my dear. But I dislike immensely the life my brother has been consigned to these many years."

"And you think it my fault," Madeleine finished.

He surprised her then by covering her hand with his where it lay upon his coat sleeve. "I think there is blame enough to go around," said Alasdair. "You and Merrick made some bad choices, aye. But I look back now, and think that perhaps we, his family, stood idly by, too. It is possible we could have brought pressure to bear on your father, had we but tried."

Madeleine gave a bitter laugh. "Oh, what is that wonderful Scots' expression?" she asked. "'Save your breath to cool your porridge?' Yes, that's the one wanted here—for you surely would have wasted it on my father."

Sir Alasdair shrugged. "Aye, most likely."

"In any case," Madeleine went on, "you may set your mind at ease. Merrick has found a way to put an end to our marriage once and for all."

Sir Alasdair cocked one of his beautiful eyebrows. "The devil?" said. "I should like to know how."

"I don't know if he has told you that the record of our marriage was destroyed at Gretna Green," she began. "It was done within days of the wedding—my father's work, I gather. And then, last night, Merrick . . ." She could not find the words.

"Yes? Go on." Sir Alasdair squeezed her hand.

"Last night, after . . . after you brought me home, he

came to my bedchamber, and he—well, he b-b-burnt our marriage lines."

"The devil!" said Alasdair again. "He *burnt* them?"

Madeleine was crying in earnest now. "He—he dropped the paper down my lamp," she said. "And-and he w-would not let me get it out again!"

Sir Alasdair drew her near and set an arm about her shoulders. "Now, now, my dear!" he said, extracting a handkerchief with something of a flourish. "Dry your eyes, please. Now tell me again—and leave nothing out."

She repeated the story, and added in much of what Merrick had said, too.

Mortified, Madeleine finished her snuffling. Sir Alasdair resumed his sedate pace, which felt a little soothing now. "So you are free now to marry whom you please," he said. "As is my brother. After all these years. How truly remarkable!"

Madeleine nodded. "There is no evidence that our first marriage ever took place," she said a little sadly. "Everyone who knew anything is dead or has disappeared. All the records are gone. So . . . so any risk of embarrassment to your family is now over. I hope you are relieved."

"Indeed, I am." But strangely, he was grinning. "Maintaining my family's good name has always been my foremost concern. Ask any of those rogues and roués I used to run with."

"Kindly do not make fun of me, Sir Alasdair," she said. "I am quite serious."

Again, he crooked his head, and looked at her strangely. "You would not try to hold the old boy's feet to the fire, my dear?" he suggested. "You might get away with it, you know."

Madeleine blanched. "After all that Merrick has been put through?" she said, horrified. "I certainly would not."

Sir Alasdair nodded. "So all's well that ends well, eh?" he said. "Unless, that is . . ." His words fell away, and the eyebrow went up again.

"Unless what?"

He stopped, and shrugged. "Unless one of you still *wished* to be married."

Wordlessly, Madeleine looked at him.

"Or both of you," he went on. "But now you would be in a dashed awkward position, would you not? You would have to stop spitting at one another like cats, and one of you would have to . . . well, to court the other properly, would you not? Indeed, one of you would have to *propose* to the other."

Madeleine blinked, trying to clear her head. "Propose—?"

He nodded as if it were the simplest thing in the world. "Propose marriage," he said. "One of you would have to admit that you very much wish to be married to the other. Personally, I can highly recommend the married state. And after all, you are very young to be a widow, my dear."

"But-but I am not a widow," she said. "*Am* I?"

Alasdair lifted one shoulder. "Well, it would certainly seem so to me," he countered. "And now, you get to decide what you will do with the rest of your life. I caution you to choose wisely. Marriage is forever, you know."

His gentle irony escaped her. Madeleine felt suddenly as if she could not get her breath. All of life's possibilities— her hopes and her dreams—all of them flooded forth. And all of them included Merrick. They always had.

Sir Alasdair cleared his throat a little roughly. "In any

case, my dear," he said, "it would be the most natural thing in the world for my brother to bring his chosen bride home to be married in the village church on such a special occasion, would it not? After all, Esmée and I cheated everyone of that pleasure. The wedding bells would likely ring for two or three days."

Madeleine was still on the verge of hyperventilating. "Sir Alasdair, this is quite an incredible notion."

"Well, it is merely an option to consider," he remarked. "But you might wish to move in haste. Fortune favors the bold, and the twenty-second of July is a lucky day, I am told, for weddings. If you rush that courtship along and pop the question pretty promptly—why, I daresay you just might make it."

Madeleine sucked in a deep breath. "Sir Alasdair, whe—"

"Across the main road," he interjected, pointing at the wood opposite the castle's forecourt. "There is a little lane—a cart track, really—which leads to an old barn, and in the glen below, we are putting in a dry-stane dyke—a sort of fence."

"Yes. Thank you. Thank you so much." Impulsively, she popped onto her toes and kissed his immaculately shaved cheek. "I should just go then, do you not think?"

"Oh, it is not my job to think, my dear," said Sir Alasdair. "I am just a pretty face. Ask anyone who knows me."

But Madeleine barely heard the last. She was off at a most unladylike pace, her heart in her throat. *Was she to be given a second chance?* There was no way to be sure—not unless she was willing to dredge up her courage and ask for it.

Perhaps it really was not too late. She would risk anything, anything save her child, on even the slenderest chance at the happiness and the marriage she had so foolishly deferred. This time, she knew too well what was at stake. This time she would neither waver in her certainty, nor doubt her husband's affection. She would be strong, for better or for worse.

She remembered then something he had once said to her. *"Only the heart can bind a person, Maddie,"* he had said, *"To a home. Or to anything else that truly matters. A piece of paper is otherwise meaningless."*

He had been right. The paper meant nothing. But Merrick—oh, he meant everything!

It took no more than five minutes to make her way down to the glen, which rolled out like a carpet of green and was dotted with sheep. At the foot of the pasture, she could see half a wall and a straggle of stones along its future course. And beyond them, a lone figure, dark and broad-shouldered, stripped to the waist, swinging a sledgehammer high and bringing it down strong.

She went down the glen at a run.

Merrick was half–turned away from her, shaping stone as neatly as another man might cleave a piece of wood. His back looked broad and powerful in the morning light. As he turned to position one-half of the stone into the wall, he must have noticed her. Madeleine slowed her steps from a run to a girlish trot, and approached the wall, breathless.

He stood looking at her for a moment, his forehead already sheened with sweat, and tossed down his sledgehammer. "Good morning, Madeleine," he said, dragging an arm across his forehead. "You're coming in a great haste. Naught's amiss, I hope?"

She shook her head, then tried to catch her breath. "No, I just I wanted to ask—" she began awkwardly. "I wanted to know, Merrick, if . . . if I might . . . or if you would like to—no, that's not quite right."

With a smile, he propped one elbow on the wall and leaned his taut, rangy body halfway across it. "Why, I've never known you to be tongue-tied, Maddie."

She smiled back, suddenly shy, and feeling very much as she had felt that day at the picnic, when Merrick had plucked her from the midst of her quarrelsome cousins and stolen her heart away. "I want to know, Merrick, if I might . . . if I might pay court to you? Now that you are . . . unattached?"

He laughed, straightened up, and came around to her side of the wall. "Well, I don't know, lass," he said, crossing his arms over his chest, and setting one bootheel back against the wall. "Would your intentions be honorable?"

Madeleine caught her hands behind her back. "Not . . . not especially, no," she admitted. "They would be more or less like last night's."

Merrick's smile widened to a grin. He looked quite breathtakingly handsome with his braces slipped off his shoulders, and his muscles aglow with the force of his exertions. His shirt hung from a tree limb in a little copse nearby, and the dusting of dark hair across his chest dwindled down his taut belly to vanish beneath the waist of his homespun trousers. He narrowed his silvery gaze and looked at her.

"Well, I'm a working man, Maddie," he said, as if warning her off. "There's no' much pretty about me. I'll have rough hands and sunburnt skin all the days of my life."

"I . . . I was rather counting on it," she said. "Besides, if it was pretty I wanted, I could always have courted your brother."

At that, he bellowed with laughter. Then a moment of seriousness settled over them.

Madeleine began to wring her hands. "Oh, Merrick!" she said. "I wish—oh, I wish you had not burnt that paper!"

He shook his head a little sadly. "It was not a marriage we had, Maddie," he said. "There was no use hanging on to something that never really was."

She snagged her lip in her teeth. "Merrick, I lied," she said. "I do not want to court you."

His face fell. "Do you not?"

She shook her head. "No, though I will if that's what it takes for me to prove myself to you."

Again the narrowed eyes, the long, assessing look. "What is it, then, that you want, Maddie?"

"I want—I want to marry you," she whispered. "I—I am asking you, Merrick, to marry me. To be my husband. To be Geoff's father; to adopt him and give him the name he was meant to have. I am asking you to live with us, and to share our lives and our home forever. And if you will do it, I will be a good wife always. I will never falter. I . . . I will never let you down."

He opened his arms, and she ran into them, hurling herself against the strong wall of his chest. "Be sure, Maddie," he said into her hair. "Don't throw yourself away on a stubborn, prideful man like me. You're too fine a woman. Take your time, and be sure of what you want. Whatever it is, I'll see you get it."

"I *am* sure," she cried. "I have been sure for thirteen years. I have never loved anyone but you, Merrick, and I never will. I—I need you. And Geoffrey needs you, too. If you want to wait, I will. I will wait another thirteen years."

"Shush, Maddie." And then he was kissing her, a long, languid kiss, infinite in its sweetness. Infinite in its promise. "And I have loved none but you," he said when at last he lifted his lips from hers. "Aye, I'll marry you, Maddie. You have only to name the day. Tomorrow would not be soon enough."

"The twenty-second of July," she said swiftly. "In the village church."

He lifted both brows and looked down at her, his ice-blue eyes alight. "The twenty-second, eh?"

She looked up at him ruefully. "If we choose another day, Merrick, I'll never get my mind round it," she said. "For that's the day I've always accounted my wedding day—and burnt paper or no, I'll still be adding thirteen years to that anniversary every time we celebrate it."

He kissed her again, swift and hard. "The twenty-second it is, lass," he said. "But that's almost a fortnight away. What'll we do with ourselves 'til then?"

Madeleine drew back, let her eyes run down his half-naked body, then glanced at the little copse of trees. "What is that wonderful old Scots' saying, Merrick? 'Be happy whilst yer living, for ye'll be a lang time dead?' "

"Aye, and well said," Merrick agreed. "It's one of Granny's favorites."

Madeleine looked him in the eyes, and smiled. "Well, I feel as if I have already been a long time dead," she said without grief or despair. "And now, Merrick, I should like you to take me over there beneath that shady copse of trees, and make me very, very happy."

Love is timeless...

Bestselling historical romance from Pocket Books

One Little Sin
Liz Carlyle
One sin leads to another...

First in an exciting new series!

Two Little Lies
Liz Carlyle
Because just once is never enough!

His Dark Desires
Jennifer St. Giles
Can she resist the passion in his eyes—or the danger in his kiss?

Outlaw
Lisa Jackson
The only woman who can tempt him is the one woman he swore to destroy...

The Lawman Said "I Do"
Ana Leigh
All he wanted was a night of pleasure. But she wanted so much more...

13445